TENDER LONGING

He bent to kiss her and felt the softness of her lips on his, the thudding of her heart against his chest. He swung her up in his arms and gently lay her on the bed, engulfed with the all-consuming tide of love he had felt for her that night in London when their daughter had been conceived, before his battalion had sailed for France.

And this, Charlotte thought dreamily as she lay there feeling Rowan's warm, gentle hands caressing her body, was what she had waited and hoped for, the moment when they would relive their first, passionate mating, when she would experience the utter joy and peace she had known so long ago.

When their lovemaking was over and they lay together warm and secure in each other's arms, it seemed that here in this attic room, the words of love spoken by its former occupants hovered like bright, warm ghosts; that if only they could stay locked in each other's arms, they could shut out the rest of the world forever. . . .

LOUISE BRINDLEY
FOREVER ROSES

PINNACLE BOOKS
WINDSOR PUBLISHING CORP.

Published in Great Britain as OUR SUMMER FACES

PINNACLE BOOKS

are published by

Windsor Publishing Corp.
475 Park Avenue South
New York, NY 10016

First Pinnacle Books printing: February, 1989

ted in the United States of America

Part One

Chapter One

The keen November wind driving in from the sea brought with it a scattering of raindrops, and moaned its curious plainsong among the chimneypots of the fishermen's cottages nestling in the lee of the Castle hill.

Normally the children would have been at school, the women busy about their washing, for this was a Monday, and the rain would have made no difference to their boiling and starching.

But there would be no school on this particular November Monday. The playground gates were securely locked, the hopscotch squares innocent of tossed pebbles, nor had the women given a thought to washday.

They stood, in huddled groups on the pavement, holding the smaller children by the hand, their heads covered with shawls, conversing in shrill, excited voices, glancing up to see the time by the parish church clock on the hill.

Then suddenly, as the hands of the clock slipped inexorably toward eleven, their chatter died away. The silence was intense, as if mankind held its breath. They simply stood there—waiting. Some wept.

In a terrace house in Friar's Way, near Scarborough's red brick hospital, the fire in Annie Grayler's kitchen burned brightly. It was a neat, clean little room with polished brass ornaments on the high mantelpiece with its edging of bobbled green chenille. The big marble clock between a pair of Staffordshire dogs stood at one minute to eleven.

Annie twisted her hands together nervously, and jumped when a lump of coal fell off the banked-up fire into the hearth. Joe looked up from his chair near the fire as the clock began to strike.

Charlotte entered the room at that moment, holding the children by the hand, her head, with its crown of shining, copper-colored hair, held a little to one side in a listening attitude.

"It's over at last!" Annie said in a low voice. "Do you understand, Joe darling? The war is over!" She cradled her husband's head tenderly in her arms. Joe, who seemed like a child to her now.

Joe smiled, but he experienced no deep feelings of happiness or relief, despite the slight upcurving of his lips. They still moved swiftly and silently against a great overhanging pall of gunsmoke, those khaki-clad figures trapped in the dark well of his memory, running and stumbling, with fixed bayonets, across the churned-up mud between the trenches.

The children, Kathy and Laurie, too young to understand why this day was different from any other, clamored to play with their toys; the alphabet bricks Joe had painstakingly fashioned from driftwood washed up by the tide on Scarborough's south beach, patiently paring the wood with a penknife held in his shaking fingers; the rag dolls Annie and Charlotte had made for them from odd colorful scraps of dress material and worn-out stockings.

When Charlotte opened their toy box, they seized their treasures as a miser seizes gold, and squatted on the mat at Joe's feet, their brown wool dresses and scalloped flannel petticoats bunched up beneath their short, sturdy legs.

Four years of war had left their mark. Four years of deprivation and struggling to make ends meet. The children, in common with many another in the poorer quarter of town, had never known the pleasure of owning brand

8

new toys or wearing anything besides homemade clothes. It was not unusual to see growing lads wearing cut-down suits and shirts, their feet encased in boots several sizes too big for them.

There was no shame in "making do," Charlotte thought, as long as they were happy and had enough to eat, although it worried her to see scraps of humanity sitting on doorsteps eating bread and dripping, their faces pinched with the cold.

Holding back the curtain, she saw that the neighbors were busy decorating their houses with bunting, and children were dancing into the street, muffled in scarves safety-pinned at the back for warmth. Annie hurried through from the scullery, cheeks flushed with excitement, carrying the Union Jack she had washed and ironed in readiness to hang out of the front bedroom window.

Charlotte scooped up Laurie, whose legs were too short to climb the stairs, while the three-year-old Kathy plodded doggedly, step by step, after them, disdainful of a helping hand from her mother or her Aunt Annie. Up she went, face puckered with concentration, her auburn curls, so like Charlotte's hair in color and texture, bobbing about her shoulders.

The bedroom felt like an ice-box after the warmth of the kitchen, a neat, shining little room with brown oilcloth and a scattering of mats on the floor. The furniture, brass bedstead, wardrobe and chest-of-drawers, had belonged to Annie's mother, Mrs. Crystal. The room smelt faintly of the lavender sachets Annie kept in the blanket-chest at the end of the bed with its crisply starched valances and brightly colored patchwork quilt.

Sometimes, Annie lit a fire for Joe in the narrow, black-leaded grate, on his bad days when the shaking of his limbs made it impossible for him to go downstairs. Then Charlotte and Annie would make do with a paraffin stove, and take it in turns to carry the coal for Joe's fire. The children would play upstairs where it was warm, while

9

Charlotte got on with her dressmaking, and Annie saw to the cooking, washing and ironing. Thankfully, Joe's bad days occurred less frequently now than they used to when he was first discharged from the Army because of poor health. Constant care and nursing, and the children's company were drawing him back from the shadows to a new awareness of life.

Charlotte opened the window and held back the starched lace curtains while Annie struggled to drape the flag out of the window, laughing as the wind caught and lifted it into a kind of billowing dance, her thin face radiant with pride. "There," she said triumphantly, "that's for our menfolk. For Joe and Harry, and Rowan."

Annie's warm sensitivity brought a lump to Charlotte's throat. She supposed that she would have managed to survive these past three years without her sister-in-law's help and support, but not as painlessly.

Annie had made it clear, when she took Charlotte to live under her roof, that she held none of the moralistic attitudes prevalent among the older generation who threw up their hands in horror when girls "got themselves into trouble," as they euphemistically termed it. Her sympathy lay with those who had erred and strayed from the way like lost sheep. Her own creed was both simple and direct—"There, but for the grace of God . . ."

Glancing sideways at Charlotte, understanding her silence, apparently reading her thoughts, Annie asked, "Have you thought what you'll do when Rowan comes home?"

Charlotte, who had spent sleepless nights asking herself the same question, hunched her shoulders suddenly against the chill of the bedroom. "I'm not sure. Three years is a long time. He may have changed. I know I have."

"Not Rowan," Annie said confidently, "and neither have you. Not all that much anyway. You still love him, don't you?"

"Of course I do." Charlotte gripped her arms to keep

10

herself from shaking with the cold and nervous tension combined. Her feelings were so hard to explain, even to Annie, which was odd on the face of it, since Annie seemed to understand her feelings better than she did herself, at times.

"I know what's bothering you," Annie said, watching the flag flapping and billowing in the wind. "But those letters he sent you from prison camp were sure to be censored. He wouldn't have wanted to write anything too personal for other eyes to read."

"But they were so cold, so—formal!" Charlotte's teeth began to chatter.

"I'm glad the war's over," Annie said. "We couldn't have gone on much longer—worrying, not knowing what the outcome would be. It wasn't just the food rationing, the queuing up; trying to make ends meet. We could have gone on queuing . . ." She smiled, and the smile seemed to eat up her pale, thin little face with its enormous blue eyes. "It was not knowing—about the men; reading the casualty lists in the evening paper. I'll never forget how I felt when I knew young Georgie, who used to deliver my mother's groceries, had been killed. He was just a boy. Funny, I still think of him wobbling up the street on that old bicycle of his; the cycle-clips he wore to keep his trousers from catching in the pedals . . ."

She smoothed the edges of the starched lace curtains gently with her fingers. "The old world we loved and knew has gone forever. What worries me now is, what will it be like for the children, growing up?"

Sound erupted suddenly in the street below; running footsteps; laughter; the far-off noise of bugles, the rat-a-tat of drums, the steady tramp of marching feet, coming closer and closer.

"It's the parade!" Annie cried, craning her neck to look out of the window. "Let's go down and watch!" She swept Laurie into her arms and hurried downstairs; eyes shining, feet fairly dancing to the beat of the music. "Listen, Joe, they're playing 'Tipperary'!"

No matter what the future held for all of them, this was a day to enjoy, to hold onto, for the realization of what it meant, not just to Annie herself, but her friends and neighbors: this first day of peace, the culmination of earnest prayers. Things had taken a turn for the better when the Kaiser had abdicated. There had been a new feeling of optimism in the air, then. Now peace had come at last, she felt that her heart would burst with joy as she stood on the doorstep, one hand clenched to her breast, and watched the parade swing into view.

The pavement edges were lined with people whose faces reflected the pride they felt in the column of marching men in their khaki uniforms. Men of Yorkshire's own regiment, The Green Howards.

Wherever there were soldiers, there were bound to be girls, too, eager, laughing young girls drawn to the magic of the uniforms, the glamor of a parade. This parade had drawn them, irresistibly, from their shop counters and offices. Most of them were pale-cheeked, undernourished, and yet they had put on their best dresses, coats and hats for the occasion, and spent their hard-earned wages on sweets and cigarettes to give to the soldiers as they marched along beside them, their skirts and petticoats frothing about their ankles.

Annie pressed her fingers to her ears as the neighbors' children flocked out into the street, beating toy drums and blowing penny whistles. "Talk about peace," she cried, "it's more like bedlam!"

Cheeks pink with excitement at the unaccustomed noise, Kathy and Laurie clung to their mother's skirts, clamoring to be picked up.

"Why don't you take them into town?" Annie suggested to Charlotte. "The fresh air will do them good!"

What Annie really meant was that the fresh air would do Charlotte good. She had worried a great deal lately about her sister-in-law's lack of color, the brown smudges beneath her eyes which betrayed the long hours she spent at her sewing machine to earn money toward the household expenses. And whatever extra money Charlotte earned was quickly spent in the corner shop on "treats"; extra milk for Joe, licorice sticks for the kids, a tin of fruit, or salmon, for the household, if the grocer had any in stock. If he had not, Charlotte would be sure to come home with a couple of bundles of sticks, bound with wire, or a cake of Monkey Brand soap. But she never came home empty-handed.

Annie quickly dressed the children in their outdoor things, and seated them at either end of the second-hand baby carriage she had purchased from a neighbor for five shillings, just after Laurie was born, because she couldn't afford a new one. The thought rankled, as much as anything ever rankled with the forgiving Annie, that the woman had at first accepted the offer of five shillings, and then started to whine that five bob wasn't much for a pram worth double.

"Oh, very well," Annie had said patiently, knowing how much she needed that pram, "I'll give you five shillings cash, and do a month's washing for you to make up the amount."

"Huh, all right, then," the woman agreed reluctantly. But she knew that Annie Grayler had gained a good reputation as a laundress, and she would pile as much washing as possible onto her shoulders to make sure she got her money's worth. "Even so," she'd said sourly, "I'd rather have had a ten-bob note!"

Now, Charlotte pushed the pram into the street, laughing and screwing up her face at the noise; the blare of the bugles, the beat, beat, beat of the drums, and the raucous sound of handbells rung by the drivers of the milk wagons and coal carts which had joined the rear of the procession.

Kathy and Laurie would not remember this day, but

they had a right to it, and to the peace their fathers had fought and suffered for.

It was impossible, she found, not to enter the spirit of this Armistice Day; the joyful release of emotion, the explosion of goodwill after all the dark, joyless days of the past four years.

People were hurrying along on feet made light with excitement, singing to the music of the band, not bothering about what tune it happened to be playing; breaking into "Mademoiselle from Armentiéres," the National Anthem, or "Land of Hope and Glory," as their spirits and voices dictated, throwing their arms about each other in a wild abandonment of joy.

And yet there were tears, too, born of the same overwhelming sense of release, and memories of the men who would never come marching home again.

Charlotte could not help noticing that many of the older men and women were crying for their lost sons and grandsons. She knew exactly how they felt. She felt like crying, too, for her brother Frank, who had answered the call to arms with a kind of devil-may-care belief in his own survival. But Frank had not died a hero's death. He had simply been shot through the heart by a sniper's bullet. His going to war had not made the slightest difference one way or the other to the final victory, so far as she could see.

It was then the realization that she and Rowan were still alive in the same world, overwhelmed her. She had not dared to even think about it until now; the miracle of seeing him again, being able to touch him, to hear the sound of his voice, that wonderful voice of his which she had heard so often in her dreams. Miraculously, he would soon be coming home again.

All the doubts and fears which had tied a hard knot of resistance about her foolish, vulnerable heart, were suddenly dispelled, leaving her breathless.

She had worried that time might have changed him.

14

The three years of his imprisonment had seemed like a void to her; watching their child growing up, the child Rowan had never seen; realizing the changes in herself, brought about by hunger and fear and hard work; seeing her own face in the mirror, no longer the face of the young Charlotte Grayler, with a head full of dreams and poetry, but that of a much older woman, the widowed Charlotte Oakleigh, with a love-child to bring up and care for.

Now she thought that although time might change people physically, the human spirit would emerge triumphant, as long as there was love. Love and hope. And nothing could ever change her love for Rowan Tanquillan.

Strung between laughter and tears, she heard faintly, on the rustling November wind, the soft, insistent pealing of bells from the parish church on the hill; unheard since the outbreak of war; silent even on Joe and Annie's wedding day, three years ago.

She stopped to listen, letting the parade drift away from her, pictures from the past, as fleeting as the colored pieces in a kaleidoscope, flooding her mind: her beloved Dadda opening his shop for the day, handing herself and her sister, Maggie, a shining new penny each across the wide mahogany counter of his grocer's shop with its gleaming brass scales and rows of tilted biscuit tins; her mother, Filly Grayler, as neat as a robin, bustling about the old house in St. Martin's Square, the reins of the household held firmly in her capable fingers.

Whenever Charlotte thought about her mother, she seemed to see her, polishing cloth and Brasso in hand, her skirts all a-flurry, rubbing away at the letter-box and bell-pull as if her life depended on getting them clean enough to reflect her own anxious face; either that or sitting atop a ladder to knock down cobwebs, or washing clothes in the stone sink in the kitchen, her hands puckered with the scalding hot water, her hair tied up, gypsy fashion, with a cotton scarf.

But the old days were all over now—gone like a dream.

A thin, light rain began to fall. Turning up her coat collar, Charlotte lifted Kathy next to Laurie under the hood of the pram. Turning away from the past, she walked resolutely on towards the town center, just one of a jostling throng of people going the same way. They converged on the railway station where a tram-car, clumsily camouflaged as a tank, was drawn up on the station forecourt, from which curious platform the Mayor of Scarborough, in his official robes and dangling chain of office, had just declared the armistice.

How odd, she thought, that this was to have been "Feed the Guns" week, that posters appealing for money to keep the war going were still in evidence.

Staring at the posters, Charlotte could not help wondering how the people of France and Belgium, who had lived so long to the sound of gunfire, would react to the silence.

Perhaps they, like herself, would not be immediately able to dispel the sense of foreboding engendered by four years of bloody warfare.

Even now, as people danced merrily in the streets, oblivious of the falling rain, and long lines of lads and lasses, arms linked, formed high-spirited, human barriers on the pavements, kissing each other, kicking up their heels, and singing at the top of their voices, Charlotte could not believe that the fighting was over.

Suddenly, a carriage full of young Army officers from the convalescent home on the seafront appeared, clad in hospital blue uniforms, scattering pennies for the children to catch. Watching them, she thought of Joe, her brother Joe for whom the war would never really be over, who would carry the scars for the rest of his life.

She had woken up in the still hours of many an early morning to the sound of his distress; had tiptoed onto the landing to listen to his ravings, wondering if she dared offer help to Annie, who bore the brunt of his suffering.

But Annie was so good with Joe; she knew exactly what

16

to do for him when those nightmare visions rose up to haunt him, when he believed that he was back in the trenches again, hearing the thunder of the guns, the stutter of machine-gun fire.

Memories. There were so many memories. Annie, in childbirth, her thin hands gripping the headboard in a crucifixion of pain, her silvery fair hair darkened with sweat, her eyes enormous in the drained oval of her face; the sudden double rat-a-tat at the front door when the telegram arrived saying Joe had been wounded; keeping the news from Annie until after her baby was born.

Charlotte had fumed then against the poverty which denied her frail sister-in-law proper medical attention. But doctors charged half-a-crown a visit, and there just wasn't enough money.

"But there will be one day!" Charlotte had vowed before God, standing alone in the kitchen, anxiously waiting for the kettle to boil, staring at the colored paper stuck on the scullery window; counting the blue and white squares. "I don't know how, but one day I'll earn enough money to put an end to all this! You see if I don't!"

How she had hated that blue and white paper; the sticky fly-catcher hanging from the stovepipe, the shelf full of shabby pots and pans above the cracked kitchen sink; the dripping cold water tap which Annie had made almost beautiful with liberal applications of Brasso.

Listening to Annie's groans from the front bedroom, wondering where the midwife had got to, Charlotte had thrown down the gauntlet to a God she scarcely believed in any longer, with anger, not humility.

No woman should have to work, as Annie had worked, all through her pregnancy, taking in washing to make ends meet; scrubbing in a steam-filled scullery with blue and white paper stuck on the windows. But Annie wouldn't give in, not until she had forced her to, wrenching the brush from her hands, venting her own anger on the clothes in the sink.

"But you have your own work to see to," Annie said anxiously. "Mrs. Baxter will be coming for her dress this afternoon, and you know what she's like."

"You leave Mrs. Baxter to me," Charlotte said grimly, plunging the wash up and down, working up a fine old lather. "And you sit down before you collapse."

When the baby was born, Charlotte put her to sleep in a cot fashioned from the bottom drawer of Annie's dressing-table which she had padded out with blanket, and lined with scraps of left-over wedding dress material to make it pretty and soft enough for the tiny infant. And all the time the telegram from the War Office had been burning a hole in her apron pocket.

But Annie had guessed about the telegram the minute she heard the double rap at the door. "Only telegraph boys knock in that particular way," she said weakly, sitting up in bed, her fair hair neatly braided after her ordeal.

"And yet you never said a word." Annie's quiet fortitude had stunned Charlotte.

"I knew you would tell me in your own good time." Tears filled Annie's eyes as she looked down at her child in the makeshift cradle. "We'll christen her Laurie. Joe and I decided on our honeymoon that if we had a little girl we would call her that—after Annie Laurie."

"It's a lovely name," Charlotte said, holding Annie's thin hand tightly in hers.

"If only I could reach out to Joe this minute: tell him how lovely she is, it might help him. Oh *Joe*. Joey!"

Joe had been wounded in a daylight bombing raid near Pont-de-Nieppe, three-quarters of a mile west of Armentiéres. His battalion, the 5th Yorkshires, en route to billets behind the lines for a much needed rest after heavy trench fighting, had been harried by constant shelling and air attack.

The Battalion Commander sent a letter describing how Joe had crawled forward during an air-raid to bring in a wounded comrade; had managed to drag the man into a bomb crater near the British lines.

When, several hours later, after darkness had fallen, a stretcher party was able to scramble across the scarred and pitted earth beyond the barbed-wire entanglements, they had found Joe, severely wounded, lying across the body of his dead comrade.

The Commander commended Joe's bravery, and deeply regretted the loss of such a fine soldier from his battalion.

They knew then of Joe's physical injuries, but nothing of the mental damage he had suffered, lying for hours in a foxhole, his nervous system shattered by the sound of continuous gunfire; the whine of shells and exploding bombs all about him; the horror of a stiffening corpse beneath him, a man he had known and liked, who, a few short hours ago had marched beside him, laughing, and smoking a cigarette.

Turning the pram homeward, Charlotte remembered Annie's pale, resolute face when they knew Joe had been sent, by hospital ship, to Southampton.

"I must go to him," she said.

"But you are not strong enough!"

"I must be strong enough, for Joe's sake!"

"Let me go instead," Charlotte had begged her, but Annie wouldn't hear of it. "No," she said firmly, "Don't you see, dearest, if I didn't go, Joe would think the worst, that I was too ill; maybe that I didn't love him anymore?" Her mouth had worked pitiably. "I *must* go to him. I'm his wife."

"Oh, God," Charlotte said bitterly, "why is everything so totally *unfair?*" She'd relented, then, not wanting Annie to think that she resented her going to Joey. After all, only two women as close as she and Annie were to each other could view, dispassionately, their different relationship to the man they both loved.

"One thing's for sure," she had said, marching resolutely into the front room where her sewing machine was set up, "at least you'll go with all flags flying!"

She had bought a length of gray wool, in the market, only yesterday, more than enough material to make Annie a new coat; had stitched, night long, until her eyes ached, to finish that coat.

Next morning, she had pressed some money she had managed to save from her sewing into Annie's hand, towards her train fare, and walked with her to the station to see her off, pushing the baby in its five-shilling pram, with Kathy clinging to the handle.

"Give Joey my love," she said huskily, as the train moved away from the platform.

"I will!" Annie had stared, with tear-filled eyes, from the carriage window. "Look after Laurie for me!"

"Of course I will!" Looking down into the pram, Charlotte had known that she loved Laurie as much as she loved Kathy.

The rain was falling faster now; the gray light of a November day was quickly fading to a monotone of gray: gray skies; gray pavements; gray houses. Everything seemed the same color, except the ridiculously bright Robin's Starch advert in a cornershop window, and the sudden, flaring, somehow comforting light of a gas-jet in a room above the shop; a room where an ordinary housewife was setting the table for tea, not bothering to draw the blinds because, this, after all, was Armistice Day.

Turning the corner near the hospital, Charlotte saw that a lamplighter was busy making sure that all was in order for the coming darkness when the town would be lit up again, after the blackout.

The man, wearing a ragged coat, grinned down at her from his ladder.

"Those children of yours are in for a surprise when it

it gets dark," he said, tossing away the tab end of a Woodbine cigarette. "They won't have seen street lights before." He chuckled hoarsely. "It'll be like old times!"

Like old times, Charlotte thought. Ah yes, little gleaming fireflies of light trapped in the puddles; soft, effulgent lamplight blossoming against the dusk of a winter evening; a necklace of lights strung along the bay, against the darkness of the sea washing in on the shore.

A feeling of pure happiness swept through her, despite the rain.

Until this moment, she had not realized how much she had missed street lamps, those misty chrysanthemums of light reflected in wet pavements.

Pushing the pram homeward, Charlotte knew that seeing the lamplighter at work had done more to make her realize that the war was over than all the bands and the fluttering Union Jacks had done; the lamplighter and the sound of bells from the church on the hill.

When all the parades were over and done with, and this strange, euphoric day had slipped into the pages of history, what she would remember most clearly would be that beacon of light in an upstairs window; a cheeky Robin's Starch advertisement; the sweet, clean touch of the rain on her face; the feeling that her life was about to begin all over again.

Chapter Two

When Charlotte received the telegram saying that Rowan had arrived in Southampton, that his train was due at Waterloo on November 21st, she knew she had no choice other than to tell her mother and Maggie that she was going to London to meet him.

"There'll be a row about it," Annie said, pulling a face, "why don't you simply go—and tell them about it afterward?" Charlotte looked pale and tired, as if she hadn't slept properly since the telegram arrived, and she knew only too well the kind of reception Charlotte would be given at her sister Maggie's house.

"There'd be an even worse row if I did that." Charlotte settled her hat firmly on her head. "Best go and get it over with."

"Good luck!" Annie watched anxiously, from the front room window, her sister-in-law's trim figure hurrying along the frost-filmed pavement, saw her turn at the street corner to raise her hand. Poor Charlotte. Annie thought briefly of Daniel and the lion's den.

Charlotte's mother, Filly Grayler, had lived at her elder daughter Maggie's squeezed, inhospitable house in Garibaldi Street, ever since her husband had died, and although she and Maggie did not see eye-to-eye at times, they were at least united in their condemnation of Charlotte's affair with Rowan Tanquillan, which they felt had brought shame on their hitherto decent, respectable family. Only wanton women, in their view, got themselves pregnant by married men. Feelings—love—didn't enter their reckoning. Charlotte had done wrong, and she must suffer the consequences.

Charlotte knocked at Maggie's front door, and waited, shivering with cold and nervous apprehension, dreading the moment of the door opening to reveal her sister's hostile face. She knew exactly what she was in for, and silently shored up her defenses for the battle to come.

"Oh, it's you! What do you want?" Maggie's lips tightened.

"I'd like to speak to Mother. Alone, if you don't mind."

"And suppose I do mind?" Maggie wore a flowered pinafore, and her hair was still in Dinkie curlers. She crossed her arms belligerently, exposing the soft mottled flesh beneath the rolled-back sleeves of her black pullover. "Oh, very well then. It's too cold to stand gabbing out here. Wait in the front room. But don't you go upsetting her. I have enough trouble with her as it is."

Maggie's front room was cold and formal, like a doctor's waiting room. The fire was never lit there except on Christmas Day. On every other day of the year, the grate was embellished with crossed paper fans. Never, at any time since her fall from grace, had Charlotte been summoned into the back room where a bright fire burned from morning to night, even at the height of summer.

As Charlotte had expected, her mother was outraged, incensed, when she knew that Rowan was back in England, that Charlotte was going to meet him, taking Kathy with her.

"You have no right," Filly cried indignantly. She spoke with one trembling hand to her face, conscious of having had some of her back teeth out recently, of looking much older as a result. Her teeth had started bothering her a great deal lately, plus the fact that her once abundant brown hair seemed much thinner now; that the temples

23

were flecked with gray. She blamed Charlotte for that: all the worry of the past four years.

"Kathy has a right to see her father," Charlotte said defensively.

"Oh yes," Filly cried scornfully, "and I daresay his wife thinks that her child has the same right! My God, Charlotte, have you no shame?"

"You know that Rowan and his wife separated some time ago . . ."

She was not allowed to finish the sentence. "And whose fault was that, my girl? Coming between a man and his wife!"

Charlotte endured the outburst until Filly said, "As for Annie Crystal, she should have known better than to give you a place to stay!"

Charlotte turned angrily then, tall and proud, seeming to fill Maggie's poky front room with her towering presence.

"You can say what you like about me, Mother, but don't dare say anything against Annie! There is more charity in her little finger than there is in the whole of your body!"

Once the words were out, she would have given anything to retract them. "I'm sorry, I didn't mean to say that. If only you would try to understand how much I love Rowan . . ."

She stood helplessly as Filly crumpled into a chair. "Mother, please . . ." She took a step forward to comfort her.

Things might have been different between them if Maggie had not swept into the room at that moment, bursting with self-righteous indignation, holding her dark-haired little girl, Peggy, in her arms.

"Now look what you've done! I told you not to go upsetting her!" Maggie had taken out her curlers and her hair stood in an unbecoming frizz about her fat red face. "Take no notice of her, Ma! Let her go to that fancy man

24

of hers! Let her live in sin with him if she wants to! It's a case of good riddance to bad rubbish, if you ask me!"

"Nobody did ask you!" Maggie's holier-than-thou arrogance irritated Charlotte past bearing. "And I don't think you should have brought Peggy in here." She glanced anxiously at the child whose face was beginning to pucker at the sound of raised voices.

"She's my kid! This is my house! I'll do as I damn well please," Maggie burst forth, resting Peggy on one of her broad hips as the child struggled to be put down. "Oh, be quiet, now," she admonished her, slapping her daughter, who started to cry. "Now look what you've done! It's all your fault!"

Maggie's eyes were as cold as ice although her ample bosom heaved with the heat of her emotion, and her red-veined cheeks were flushed with anger. "You make me sick, Charlotte! Coming here with all your airs and graces—after what you've done! Why, you're nothing but a common little—tart!"

"Maggie!"

"It's the truth! I suppose you think that marrying that poor fool, Will Oakleigh, after you'd got yourself pregnant by Tanquillan, made a decent, honest woman of you? Ha!" she snorted. "What a laugh! And you carrying on behind Will's back all the time with that fancy man of yours!"

Charlotte's lips trembled. "That is simply not true . . ."

"Oh, isn't it?" Maggie's tongue was running way with her now. "Well, I'd say it came as a relief when Will got himself killed saving the life of that crazy Alice Tanquillan! Pity she wasn't killed too! Seems to me the Tanquillans are all rotten to the core!"

This battle had been in the air for a long time. Peggy began to scream at the top of her voice, frightened by her mother's hysterical anger. Filly half rose from her chair to intervene, but the incensed Maggie turned on her aggressively.

"Sit down and shut up, Mother! This is between Charlotte and me! It's time someone told her what's the truth!"

Charlotte said, in a low voice, "Take care, Maggie! Don't forget that my Kathy is a Tanquillan, too!"

Maggie turned on her sister with renewed fury, goaded to further anger by her quiet dignity and beauty. Charlotte had always been slim and beautiful, herself the fat, ugly one of the family. She could never forgive Charlotte for that. "Oh, yes," she scoffed, "then why have you sailed under false colors all this time? Why have you led everyone to believe that Kathy's name is Oakleigh?"

"To satisfy self-righteous prigs like yourself, for one thing. Because the world is full of people like you, Maggie; smug, narrow-minded people all too anxious to condemn what they cannot understand. But never dare to say again in my hearing that I was relieved when Will Oakleigh was killed. Will was a decent man who did his best to help me. He knew I was pregnant when he married me! I thought that we could build up a worthwhile life together. But never, *never* either you or Mother dare to blame Annie. She is more of a sister to me than you have ever been!"

"Get out! Get out of my house!" Maggie screamed at her. "And you—shut up!" She lashed out angrily at the weeping child clinging to her skirts for comfort.

"Yes, that's right, Maggie," Charlotte said coldly, aware of the trembling of her legs beneath her skirts, "vent your spite on an innocent child! It's a hard lesson to learn that the innocent often have to suffer for the crimes of the guilty!"

Outside in the street, Charlotte's held-back tears flooded down her cheeks as she remembered how close she and Maggie had once been, as children. The whole family had been close then, Mother and Dadda, Frank, Harry, Joe, herself and Maggie. Now everything was changed. Frank and Dadda were dead, Joe lived in a world of shadows, she and Maggie were enemies, and she had forfeited her mother's love and respect.

And yet she must go to Rowan. Nothing would ever change the love she bore him. Nothing could erase the memory of the night Kathy was conceived, the night before his regiment sailed for France in that terrible winter of 1914. She remembered Rowan's gentleness and sensitivity, the feel of his arms about her as they lay together in that London hotel room; the passion of their loving, the inexplicable joy of giving all that she was, or could ever hope to be, into his care and keeping.

Annie was in the kitchen doing the ironing when she returned. "I told you you shouldn't have gone," she said, as Charlotte sank, sobbing, into the chair near the fire.

She spat on the iron to test its heat, and thumped it down impotently, on a linen towel. "I knew they'd upset you, and you had enough to worry about without that!"

"Never mind about me. What about you, Annie? You'll have more than enough to worry about too, when I go away. How will you manage without my money?"

"You leave that to me," Annie said cheerfully. "Joe's getting better every day, and now we've got that bit of extra pension from the government, we'll be as right as rain."

Charlotte watched Annie thumping away with her iron. Not a movement was wasted. No detail of the difficult future facing her sister-in-law had been overlooked in that tidy, honest mind of hers. She set about pressing a man's flannelette shirt, for which she would receive a penny payment.

"You'll feel differently when you get to London," Annie said, switching irons. "Your friend Mrs. McKenna will put you up until you and Rowan decide what to do. You mustn't look on the black side."

"Laurie will miss Kathy to play with," Charlotte said, drying her eyes.

"Oh, don't worry about Laurie," Annie said airily. "She'll be all right. I'll take her to Peasholm Park to feed the ducks. She'll love that. I might even take her round to Maggie's house to play with Peggy."

"I—I don't think that would be a very good idea," Charlotte said bleakly. "We had a terrible row . . ."

"It's not Maggie I'm worried about," Annie said, folding the shirt, "it's Peggy! I feel sorry for that poor little kid. She seems so—lonely."

"I've never known anyone like you before," Charlotte said, amazed by the quiet Annie's inner strength and flexibility.

"And you'd best wear the coat you made for me when I went to Southampton to see Joe," Annie continued. "It's much smarter than that old black one you're wearing now. And you can take my fur necklet, too, if you like."

She scuttled suddenly towards the kitchen dresser, lifted down a fancy teapot, and emptied the contents onto the table.

"And here, you'll need some money."

"Three pounds? I can't take that. Where did it come from?"

Annie's face crinkled with laughter. "I didn't steal it, if that's what you mean. I pawned my locket!"

"Your mother's gold locket? Annie! You shouldn't have done that!"

"Why not, if I wanted to? The man who owns the pawn shop was ever so nice to me. He promised faithfully not to let it go. I've thought it all out very carefully. I can save a shilling a week from Joe's money, and . . ." She stopped suddenly, a guilty flush suffusing her face.

"And—what?"

"Oh, nothing."

"Annie Grayler, what have you done?"

Annie wrinkled her nose appealingly. "Well, if you must know, the same as I did with the pram. I'm going to do his wife's washing for a few weeks until the debt's paid

28

off. No, don't start lecturing, Charlotte. It's all arranged."

Charlotte arrived at Bridie McKenna's house, in Bloomsbury, late the following afternoon, feeling weary and dispirited. It had been a long, tiring journey; having to change trains at York; struggling with a heavy case, a holdall, a string bag containing a few of Kathy's toys, and Kathy herself, fretful at leaving Laurie and her Aunt Annie.

Now as she stood on the pavement, fiddling in her purse to find enough money to pay the taxi driver, she wondered what the house would be like without Jenny's shining presence; how she would feel when the realization that Jenny was gone really came home to her. She had loved Jenny so much.

Suddenly, the front door of No. 12 Walbrook Terrace opened, and there was Bridie McKenna, as thin and brisk as ever, her graying hair swept back untidily from her quizzical face with its piercing blue eyes, holding out her arms to her. Charlotte hurried up the steps to hug the woman who had given her shelter before Kathy was born, who had seen her through the traumatic events leading up to the birth of her child.

"Come indoors," Bridie said, in her lilting Scottish voice, "you must be worn out. And is this really Kathy? How she's grown. She was just a babe in arms when I last saw her."

Charlotte thought, as she crossed the threshold, that the house had not changed; Bridie had not changed, except that she looked slightly older; more careworn. Only she had changed.

It seemed to Charlotte, as she stared about her, that nothing could be counted as sure and certain any longer, that life moved inexorably forward, changing and altering

29

by the minute, as transient as sunlight on a summer stream.

If only Jenny were here to greet her. But Jenny had died giving birth to her brother Harry's stillborn child, after a fall.

"I know what you are thinking," Bridie said gently. "People like Jenny happen rarely in a lifetime. I still miss her, too, more than I can possibly say."

"Yes," Charlotte said quietly, "I know."

As long as she lived, she would never forget Jenny, whom she had loved as a sister, the way she loved Annie. Dear, unpredictable Jenny, the eternal, laughing rebel, who had sharpened her own intellect to a new awareness of life, who had once waved a suffragette banner high in the air in Trafalgar Square; refusing to be beaten down or overwhelmed by officialdom.

If only her child had lived, they—she and Harry—would have called her Rose Picardy. Charlotte knew why, because of that old wartime song:

Roses are blooming in Picardy,
In the hush of the silver dew,
Roses are flowering in Picardy,
But there's never a rose like you.

Charlotte's eyes misted over with tears. It was simply another result of that great, gobbling monster of war that Jenny had died, leaving Harry inconsolable at her loss.

It had happened during an air-raid, when the zeppelins were overhead, bombing London. Jenny, heavily pregnant, had missed her footing on the cellar steps on her way to take shelter.

Bridie had hurried down to find her lying in a crumpled heap on the cellar floor, bleeding badly; had rushed blindly from the house to seek a doctor, but there was no doctor to be found anywhere.

30

Jenny had died, early next morning, in Bridie's comforting arms.

Afterward, Harry, released from the Army, had embarked on a government farming scheme, wanting, needing, somehow, to come closer to the land he had fought and suffered for.

"GREAT BRITAIN WELCOMES HER BRAVE PRISONERS OF WAR"

The banner, snapping and billowing in the wind chasing through the arches of Waterloo station, was printed in bold black letters on a grayish-white background. Soon they would come in by train from Southampton, those remnants of the great battles of the Somme: men captured at Ypres, Mons, Loos, Armentiéres—places few English people had heard of before grim newspaper reports from the front had made household names of them.

The inevitable military band was grouped in the forecourt, half frozen by the keen November wind whistling about their ears; blaring forth the old familiar war tunes.

Charlotte gripped the railings, her knuckles showing white with tension. She was sick and tired of "Pack up Your Troubles." It seemed incongruous to turn this somber occasion into some kind of parade. There was enough noise as it was, the shunting of engines, the ear-splitting noise of steam-letting, the clanking of hand-barrows.

Anticipation, anxiety, and hunger twisted into a hard knot of resistance deep inside her. She felt edgy and afraid, waiting for a train that was already half an hour overdue.

Trembling with the cold, she paced a few steps up and down, up and down, then crossed to a sweets and cigarette kiosk and asked the woman behind the counter for a bar of chocolate to ease her hunger pains, wishing she had eaten at least a slice of toast before leaving Bridie's house.

"Sorry, dear," the woman said, "ain't got any left.

31

Chocolate, that is! Why not take a packet of Woodbines?"

"No. I mean, yes. Thanks!" Charlotte shoved the money across the counter.

"Got any matches, have yer?" the woman asked cheerily.

"No, I haven't."

"Wotcher gonna do then, ducks, chew 'em?" She sighed impatiently.

"Well, I don't know. That is, I hadn't really thought. I don't smoke myself, you see." Charlotte said desperately, "I'm just waiting for the Southampton train to come in. I thought my—my young man might like them."

"Oh yes, the bloody heartbreak train," the woman said sympathetically. "Here, take the matches! Give 'em yer feller. That's the least I can do for the poor devil.'

Rowan stared out of the carriage window. England. He was home again in England, and yet he felt no real sense of freedom, no loosening of the shackles of his mind.

Even the clothes he wore stank of imprisonment. He had grown unaccustomed to the speed of trains and traffic; unused to conversation, to music, good food—and compassion.

He had not realized, until he stepped onto English soil again, how slowly he moved, like an old man with stooped shoulders. The sight of a Salvation Army band on the docks at Southampton had unmanned him. Tears had run down his cheeks at the sound of "All Things Bright and Beautiful." The same thing had happened when a smiling young nurse had taken his arm to help him down the gangplank.

The stamp of weariness on the faces of his fellow prisoners reflected his own lethargy. Their fingers had shaken on cigarettes lit for them by the Red Cross helpers. Their smiles were a mere upturning of the lips in gratitude for the kindness of strangers. They had forgotten how to smile with their eyes. Laughter was a lesson to be re-learned in time, as they would have to re-learn how to drink from cups, how to eat without wolfing their food.

His old way of life, along with the man he used to be, seemed alien to him now. Was this the way amnesia victims felt—as if reality were blanketed by a kind of fog? He would never again drink water without wondering if it had been spat in.

He thought vaguely of how his first hot bath would feel to him, and a clean shirt against his skin; the texture of a leatherbound book in his hands; the softness of a feather pillow beneath his head.

His mouth trembled as he thought of Charlotte. Throughout the long years of his imprisonment, the memory of her had been his lodestar. Now the thought of seeing her again filled him with a sick, nervous apprehension. God, what a fool he had been to send her that telegram. Better by far to have waited until after officialdom had done with him.

Familiar landmarks were coming into view: the sprawling tenements of London. How shabby and scarred the houses looked. He wished the train would not stop but speed on and on into a kind of limbo. He had no desire to face the business of returning to his battalion headquarters to undergo examination and questioning. Above all, he would never go into the hospital.

When they had done to him all the things that were necessary to return a prisoner of war to normal civilian life, then, and only then would he decide what to do about the woman he loved.

Ghosts, he thought. Charlotte had once told him that she believed in ghosts trapped in some kind of eternal time-bubble. That day they had spent together, wandering hand in hand along the Embankment, watching the oily river flowing towards the sea, returned to haunt him as the train came to a halt.

But he loved Charlotte too deeply to tie her to the ghost of the man he used to be.

Charlotte watched the men dismounting stiffly and silently from the train. The band struck up "Land of Hope and Glory" as they filed along the platform.

Hands clenched on the railings, her eyes swept their faces for her first glimpse of Rowan. Her heart missed a beat. He was not among them. As they came closer to the barrier, she realized that she had looked at him twice without recognition.

Stifling a cry of horror, she stepped back to regain her composure, shocked by the changes in him, her eyes blinded with tears. Then, she choked back her sobs resolutely. Rowan would not want her pity.

Crowds of people, there to meet their menfolk, surged about her, almost sweeping her off her feet. Some of the men were weeping unashamedly in the arms of their families. Others smiled briefly at proffered chocolate and cigarettes, stunned and bewildered by their reception.

Standing in the cold, Charlotte knew that her fears concerning Rowan had been well founded. The horrors he had endured were clearly written in the deeply-etched lines of suffering about his eyes and mouth; in the thinness of his body, the way he moved, like a tired old man.

Pity gave way to anger, deep, burning anger against those who had sapped men's pride and vitality in such a brutal fashion. Whatever she had felt for him before was deepened and strengthened now. Pity and anger were washed away in an overwhelming tide of love as she stepped forward to meet him.

"Rowan!" She spoke his name in a voice vibrant with emotion.

He lifted his head, staring at her with a dawning awareness that she was really there; not a ghost or a figment of his imagination, but his flesh and blood Charlotte, her hands outstretched in welcome. Her lips trembled in the pale oval of her face, the glowing wings of her bright red hair were bouffant beneath the wide-brimmed hat she wore, a little fur necklet was clasped beneath her proudly uplifted chin, a bunch of violets pinned to the fur.

Violets! He remembered that he had once given her violets in another place, another time, on some other station platform, long ago. The scent of them reminded him of springtime in England, of pale, rainwashed skies and catkins growing in hedgerows, of so many things he had thought never to see again.

He had half-forgotten how sweet and fragrant she was until he held her in his arms once more, how slender, yet how strong. He marvelled at the way her back curved down to her waist; how firm her breasts were; how long and dark her lashes.

Burying his head against her throat, he inhaled the fragrance of her; the scent of violets intermingled with oatmeal soap and papier-poudre tissues.

He felt her long, supple fingers caressing his hair; heard the irregular sound of her breathing; sensed the quick beating of her heart against his; the gentleness of her lips on his mouth.

Nothing had changed between them, he knew that. He loved her now more than ever before. And yet everything had changed. This moment could not last forever. Time could not last forever. There was so little of it left now. He could not trust himself to speak. All he could do was murmur her name, over and over again.

"Charlotte! Charlotte! Oh, *Charlotte!*"

She touched his cheek with her fingertips, knowing that the essential Rowan had not been lost to her. Time and caring would soon put back the flesh on his bones. Sleep would erase the dark shadows beneath his eyes. She wanted to hold him and care for him always; bring back the laughter to his lips.

"Can you come home with me now?" she asked shyly. "There's a room for you at Bridie's."

"Not just yet, darling." He forced himself to speak naturally. "I have to go to headquarters with the others. It's a matter of routine; medical checks; demobilization. I'm sorry."

"Yes, of course, I should have known. But you will come to Bridie's as soon as possible?"

Now that she had found him again, she could not bear the thought of losing him for even the shortest space of time. "There's so much to talk about; so many things I want to tell you. I—I've brought Kathy with me . . ." She clasped his cold fingers in hers. "But I mustn't be too impatient. Now there's all the time in the world."

A shadow crossed his face. "I must go now, the transport's waiting."

As he moved slowly away from her, a sudden tremor ran through Charlotte's body. She stood by the railings, watching him out of sight, gripped by a sudden, nameless fear, remembering the frozen expression on his face when she said, "Now there's all the time in the world."

Chapter Three

On the way back to Walbrook Terrace, Charlotte found herself curiously detached from the rest of the passengers on the swaying bus.

She saw, but did not notice, the piles of fruit and vegetables in the greengrocers' shops, the placards outside the newsagents, covered with crisscrossed wire to keep them from blowing away; the advertisements for St. Bruno and Swan Vestas; the gaslit windows of the grocers'; the dark gray clouds, the lowering sky which threatened snow.

Walbrook Terrace consisted of a seam-straight row of three-story houses with steps to the front doors, and basement areas with steps leading down, fronted with railings, separated from the almost identical row of bay-windowed houses opposite by a central garden known to the residents of both Walbrook Terrace and Walbrook Gardens, across the way, as "The Park."

Charlotte had often wheeled Kathy there as a baby in the autumn of 1915. She remembered the feelings of weakness and leathargy she had experienced then, watching the pearly October sunlight dappling the paths beneath the trees, wondering if Rowan were alive or dead. Her heart had been seared by the sight of the scarlet-berried rowans in bloom, her mind numbed and stultified with anxiety, her body drained of energy and purpose after the birth of her child, as if she were filled with insipid, lukewarm water, very much the way she felt now.

The wind bit deeply into her as she hurried along beside the precise march of black railings fronting the houses. As she struggled up the steps of No. 12, clinging onto her hat, head bent against the cavalry charge of the wind, the first snow of the year began to fall, driven in flurries along the icy pavements.

Bridie was coming downstairs, her hand resting lightly on the banister. She had been up to put the finishing touches to Rowan's room, supposing that he would return with Charlotte, and stood there gazing expectantly at the front door, eyes bright, a smile of welcome on her lips.

The minute Charlotte stepped into the hall, Bridie could see that something was wrong. "My dear," she said, "you look half frozen. I'll make you some tea."

The war years had not dealt kindly with Charlotte, she thought as she bustled through to the kitchen to put the kettle on. Her cheeks had lost the glow which had reminded her of the apricot bloom of tea-roses. There were pale brown smudges beneath her eyes, and she was far too thin. And yet, strangely, the new air of maturity about her added to rather than detracted from her beauty.

Life could not have been easy for her, bringing up her child without the help and support of the father, with a sick brother to help take care of, and a sententious mother to contend with. Bridie had kept a tight rein on her tongue when Charlotte told her what had transpired between her mother and herself. As for that sister of hers . . . Bridie slammed the lid of the tea-caddy abruptly. She would like to take that self-righteous young madam firmly by the shoulders and shake her till her teeth rattled.

She tapped her foot impatiently, waiting for the kettle to boil. Families! Tucking back a strand of graying hair behind her ear, Bridie angrily pursed her lips. What Charlotte needed was supportive action to help her through the difficult days ahead, not a lecture on morality. She sighed deeply, unpursing her lips, allowing a little whistling breath to escape. Bottled-up anger was a destructive

38

emotion at best, and she seldom wasted her time thinking destructive, negative thoughts, or doing negative things.

During Charlotte's absence, she had trotted down to the shops with Kathy, to wangle as much food as possible. She hadn't done too badly, either, considering that goods were still in short supply, coming back with a tin of salmon, a pound of butter, a packet of Mazawattee tea, and enough cod for a fish pie.

She was pouring boiling water into the teapot when Charlotte came in with Kathy. Bridie was dying to know what had happened at Waterloo Station, but one glance at Charlotte's pale, set face made her hold her tongue. What could have gone wrong? She could almost sense the struggle Charlotte was having to gain control over some overwhelming emotion. She looked grief-stricken. Bridie had known Charlotte a long time, but she had never seen her look like this before.

"Well, the tea's ready. Shall we go into the other room to drink it?"

Charlotte drew in a shuddering breath. The rising tension inside her became suddenly unbearable. Hands clenched, fighting against rising tears, she said in a low voice, "I didn't recognize Rowan at first. That was the worst moment of my life: actually not knowing him. Oh God, Bridie, he looks so ill!"

"Ahhhh!" Bridie held Charlotte tightly, comfortingly, in her arms. "But that's only natural after what he must have been through. I read somewhere how bad things were for some prisoners of war. Not the officers so much as the rank and file. I daresay he hasn't had all that much to eat recently, the poor lad! But you mustn't worry, we'll soon have him well and strong again."

"I can't explain, but it's more than that; more than hunger. It's as if the light that shone inside him has gone out."

"Come through to the other room, it's warmer there. You'll feel better when you've drunk your tea."

Kathy was beginning to whimper, wanting to be taken

39

notice of. She stood on tiptoe, puckering her face, pointing at the milk jug. "Yes, you shall have some milk, my baby," Bridie said. "Away to the other room with you, then you can show me your picture books." She picked up the tray with the tea and milk and plate of biscuits, but Charlotte made no move to follow her. She had turned to stare unseeingly out of the kitchen window, her hands gripping the edge of the sink.

Bridie hesitated in the doorway, sensing that now the child had gone, Charlotte was crying, betrayed by the slight movement of her shoulders; letting her tears run down her cheeks, unchecked.

"Oh, my dear!" Bridie set down the tray and hurried across to her, laying a sympathetic hand on her arm, knowing that something deeper than tension, cold, disappointment, hunger and sleeplessness affected her, something that had broken her spirit. "There's something you haven't told me. What is it? You know you can trust me."

Charlotte turned slowly, her cheeks wet with tears. "It was the way he looked at me when I said something about there being all the time in the world. I said it to comfort him, but it didn't. I can't explain but I *know* what he was thinking—that there wasn't all the time in the world; hardly any time at all left. I may be wrong. I hope to God I *am* wrong, but I just had the strangest, most terrible feeling that Rowan is—dying . . ." She covered her face with her hands.

"Surely not! Oh, dear God!" A sudden vision of Rowan, as she had first seen him, sprang to Bridie's mind, the day he came to the house to tell Charlotte that Will Oakleigh had been killed. She had thought then that Rowan and Charlotte were born for each other, molded by Nature, in her kindest mood, to a rare pattern of loveliness and personal integrity.

She could see him now, standing there in the hall, waiting for Charlotte to come downstairs; strong and handsome in his Ranger's uniform, the sun behind the stained-glass panel splintering in radiance about him, dappling his warm, tanned skin with the colors of a rainbow, shining on his dark hair like a halo. She remembered the expression of joy on his face when he saw Charlotte, the way he held out his hands to her in a warm, compassionate gesture.

Bridie remembered then her own philosophy which had carried her through the often difficult years of her life, that it was no use meeting trouble halfway. Straightening her shoulders, she said, "You're just tired out, my girl; letting your imagination run away with you. Now come and drink your tea."

The medical officer had heard similar stories a hundred times before. He had, at first, refused to believe these accounts of German prison camps where men were tortured.

This had not happened everywhere, of course, certainly not in the camps where the Red Cross workers were allowed in to inspect the conditions of the officers and men. But eventually he had come to realize that most of the stories he heard were true.

Now, having examined Tanquillan, he seated himself on the edge of his desk, swinging his stethoscope, liking the man's spirit and bearing, those fine intelligent eyes in a face, honed by suffering, to the essentials of bone structure; skin and muscles sculpted to a kind of classical asceticism, like those of a saint or holy man, John the Baptist, or Francis of Assisi. The M.O. was filled with a deep, burning anger against those brutal German guards who had tortured their captives to break their willpower, their inborn sense of survival.

Listening to Tanquillan, he had cursed the whole dreary waste of the war. The story had been told haltingly. He had almost had to drag it out of him as a confession rather than a statement of fact. His cheek muscles had worked in sympathy and disgust when Rowan told him about that night in the German prisoner-of-war compound when, as a punishment for refusing to eat the maggoty bread and

41

moldy sausage they had been given for supper, he and his comrades had been strung up by their wrists, their feet not quite touching the ground.

He'd covered his face with his hands when he spoke of it. "They tried to sing," he said brokenly, "they sang, 'Keep the Home Fires Burning.'"

"And what about you? Weren't you strung up, too?" the M.O. asked, almost casually.

"No."

"Why not?"

"I'd rather not say." The pain of that memory seared into Rowan's mind like a branding iron. As the leader of that pathetic revolt, he had been dragged out into the compound, lashed to a post, and beaten almost senseless with rifle butts. Never as long as he lived would he forget that muddy compound with the rain beating down on the square of rotting wooden huts with barred windows, the row of gallows with their grotesque, dangling figures; the glaring searchlights which lit up the scene, the way the rain had glanced down, like spears, on the floodlit arena. And yet there had been something sweet and clean and wholesome about that falling rain which soaked him to the skin and washed away the blood at his feet.

Nothing the medical officer could say would induce Rowan to go on from there. But the M.O. knew, from bitter experience, that the scars of Tanquillan's mind would remain as deep-seated and dangerous as those affecting his lungs, unless he confided in someone. The man needed absolution from his memories as surely as a sinner needs absolution from a priest.

Rowan walked slowly in the direction of Walbrook Terrace, head bent, strangely ill at ease in his civilian clothing, carrying a small case containing his worldly goods: socks, shirts, underwear, shaving gear and a bundle of Charlotte's letters,

42

the ones the guards had not destroyed. He turned up his coat collar against the piercing coldness of the wind.

It had stopped snowing an hour since, and shopkeepers were desperately wielding brushes to clear the pavements, waging the battle of the snow with a kind of fatalistic London cheerfulness.

"Ah well, it's better clearing this bloody stuff than rubble after those zeppelin raids," called one man to his neighbor, glancing up sharply at Rowan as he did so. "Hey, mind your feet, guv! Say, are you all right, mate?"

"Fine, thanks." Rowan conjured up a smile to hide the brief terror which assailed him as he stared at the pile of brown, adulterated slush in the gutter, and shook his head to clear his mind of himself and his fellow prisoners scooping up handfuls of dirty slush to slake their thirst.

Seized by a sudden fit of coughing, he leaned momentarily against a lamp post until the spasm passed. His body was soaked in cold sweat, his legs shaking so badly that he could hardly stand up straight.

"Here, mate, come inside the shop a minute and sit down. The missis'll make you a nice hot cup of tea." The man with the brush was at his side, tugging anxiously at his sleeve, his Cockney voice betraying a rough but genuine concern for a fellow human being in trouble.

"Thanks. That's good of you, but I haven't far to go now. Walbrook Terrace."

"Oh, that's the next turning on the left, guv. Take it easy now."

"Yes, I will. Thanks again for your kindness." He walked on, desperately short of breath, his clothes clinging damply to his body. The case he was carrying felt like a ton weight, but he walked on as uprightly as possible, knowing that the Cockney's eyes were upon him, following his progress down the street.

The speed and density of the traffic almost overwhelmed him, the swaying buses, and the clanging trams rattling past on gleaming rails, their antennae sparking

43

the bewildering mass of overhead wires. He could scarcely bear the thought of being watched, and stood for a minute, pretending to read one of the placards outside a newsagent's shop, striving hard towards normality.

Glancing over his shoulder, he saw that the Cockney had lost interest in him.

They were over at last, the stringent medical examinations, the demobilisation rituals. Rowan walked on, lifting his face to the wind, assailed by the realization that he was a free man once more. He smiled grimly, remembering the medical officer's condemnation of him as a "bloody fool" for refusing to go into the hospital. "You know what this means, Tanquillan? The Army washes its hands of you! But think, man, you've earned your right to proper medical treatment. With rest, and care, who knows . . . ?"

"You mean that I might live for a year? Two years?"

"Perhaps. Who knows?"

"But doesn't that rather depend on what one thinks of as living? I would rather die on my feet that flat on my back in an Army sanatorium."

"You may think so now, but will you when the time comes?"

"I don't honestly know. But, given the choice, I would rather die in my own way, with the wind in my face, as a free man. You see, it's not dying I'm afraid of. I've faced death a hundred times before, I just want to face it on my own terms. You understand?"

"Oh yes, I understand. In your shoes, I'd probably feel the same way," the medical officer admitted.

Turning the corner into Walbrook Terrace, Rowan saw that the trees in the park were covered with snow, that the grass was as white and crisp as freshly laundered linen.

Tears for all he had known and loved, and might never know again in this life, sprang to his eyes as he unlatched the gate to walk in the unsullied snow. Memories of boyhood returned to him, hearing the bite of his shoes in the crisp mantle of white.

He turned then to look behind him at the deep imprints his footsteps had made in the snow, on this day that would never come again, and remembered Omar Khayyam's "The Moving Finger writes; and having writ moves on. . . ." When the snow melted, no trace would remain on his ever having walked in a London garden on a white November morning.

Leaning against the rough, friendly trunk of a silver-baubled plane tree, he looked up at the delicate tracery of branches above him. The weight of his body dislodged a scattering of snow, as light as thistledown, which briefly caressed his upturned face before the wind carried it away.

He wished he could have died then, at that moment, before his footprints in the snow dissolved, feeling the rough bark of the tree against his back, the weightless kiss of the snow falling on his cheeks.

He could see the door of Bridie's house from where he stood; the lace-curtained bay windows, sandstone-edged steps, the brightly polished letter-box and bell-pull. All he had to do, to gain admission to the safe, warm world that awaited him, was walk across the road, ring the bell, and step over the threshold. But he could not do it.

He clenched his hands in an agony of despair and longing, torn between his need of Charlotte and the sheer impossibility of having her. The gate leading to Walbrook Terrace was behind him. He turned blindly towards it, feeling for the latch with frozen, nerveless fingers.

Suddenly, borne on the bitter wind, came the sound of a child's laughter. A shrill, little girl's voice called out, "Look, Mama, I'm making a snowball!" Then he saw Charlotte walking down the steps of No. 12, smiling at a child with an abundance of red, shining curls spilling about her shoulders, wearing a green tam-o'-shanter perched jauntily above her heart-shaped face.

Kathy! He would have known his child anywhere, this

miniature Charlotte with her piquant, wild-rose face and quick, light, graceful movements. Even the green tam-o'-shanter worn atop her tumbling curls reminded him of Charlotte that first day they met near the slopes of Scarborough's Oliver's Mount. He had known then that hers was a face he would never forget. The words that crossed his mind that day—"Sir Lancelot mused a little space . . ." came back to him with a startling clarity.

Hidden from their view by the plane tree, Rowan saw that his child wore a thick, knitted scarf, that her feet were encased in stout little boots laced up to the ankles to keep her warm and dry.

His heart jumped when he saw the troubled look on Charlotte's face; how readily she smiled whenever Kathy looked her way, how quickly the smile faded when the child turned way from her. He feasted his eyes on her, taking in the whole of her shining presence, her tall, slim figure, the thick coil of auburn hair beneath the brim of her upturned hat, the bruised shadows beneath her eyes as she watched their child at play.

Suddenly, he was filled with a desperate longing to be whole and clean again. He had faced death fearlessly on the field of battle. It was not the sudden snuffing out of the flame of his life by a bullet that he cared about; death for a cause, an ideal, a purpose. What he could not come to terms with was the slow deterioration of his body, the rottenness of his lungs; he could not endure to inflict his own anger, despair, and suffering on the woman he loved. If he left her now, silently, without explanation, she would never know how close he had come to ruining her life.

He moved back quietly towards the gate.

Glancing down, Charlotte noticed a solitary line of footprints in the snow. Startled, filled with a dawning awareness and certainty, she looked up to see the dark outline of a man near the gate at the other side of the park. With fast beating heart, she hurried towards him, calling his name. "Rowan! Rowan! Wait! *Please* wait!"

He turned slowly to face her. She was looking up at him disbelievingly, eyes dark with apprehension. "Why were you leaving us?" she asked in a low, accusing voice.

"Not because I wanted to." What else could he possibly say to ease her pain? "You don't understand . . ."

She laid her hand on his sleeve. "Yes, I do," she said wearily. "I think I knew the moment I saw you again, but I didn't want to believe it." She drew in a shuddering breath of despair. "I have been so afraid of this, that you would leave us without a word. But didn't you know—couldn't you guess that I couldn't have borne that? Not knowing what had become of you! Oh, *Rowan!*"

"I believed that it would be the best thing to do," he said simply. A sudden, dull relief pervaded him that he had been spared the necessity of telling her that he hadn't long to live. He felt suddenly drained, empty and exhausted.

"Mama!" They had not noticed the child coming towards them. Now Kathy tugged impatiently at her mother's skirts, urging her to play at building a snowman. The child stared up at Rowan suspiciously, one foot crossed behind the other. "Come on, Mama!"

The child had sensed her mother's interest in a stranger, and wished to draw her attention back to herself.

"Come and help us," Charlotte said, slipping her hand into Rowan's. "Give us at least a little time!"

She had worried about the child's introduction to her father. Now everything seemed somehow right and natural. Charlotte understood her daughter so well; knew that Kathy would not remain at odds for very long with someone to play games with.

Other children had come into the park now, with their mothers. The crisply starched snow was no longer as smooth and white as a sheet, but churned up and dotted with footprints. Their voices, high and shrill with excitement, vibrated in the cold air like humming-tops, their blue, red, green and yellow pompoms and flying scarves daubed brilliant splashes of color against the snow.

Kathy was now laughing and chattering like a magpie, and clapping her hands gleefully as Rowan built up a pyramid of snow, her initial jealousy dissipated by her enjoyment, the feeling she had that she could bully this obliging stranger into granting her slightest wish.

Charlotte caught Rowan's eye, and knew what he was thinking. Their child had inherited certain traits of character from both of them. He smiled, eyes questioning, wondering if she had told Kathy of his existence.

"It's getting cold!" Charlotte shivered suddenly. "It's almost lunch time. We'd better be going indoors."

"No! We haven't finished the snowman yet!" Kathy's voice was shrill with disappointment. "He hasn't got any eyes!"

"No, he hasn't," Rowan agreed, holding onto his child's hand. "Will pebbles do?"

Kathy shook her red curls decisively. "No! Coal!"

"I had better go and raid Aunt Bridie's coal bin then," Charlotte said, taking a chance, a calculated risk. "Kathy, you stay here with—Dadda!"

The name she had called her own father sprang easily to her lips. Seeing the look of gratitude in Rowan's eyes, she turned and ran lightly across the road, up the steps of No. 12.

Heart hammering against her ribs, she closed the door and stood with her back to it, hands clasped, lips trembling, tears running down her cheeks, thanking God for the simple gift of snow, for that line of footprints which had led her to Rowan.

If only she could keep him with her now! But she would, she *would!* She *must*.

Chapter Four

The few weeks Rowan spent at Bridie's went some way towards loosening his mental shackles, and yet Charlotte could not help noticing how restless he was. In bed, listening, she could hear him pacing the floor of his room, up and down, up and down, night after night. Then she would long to go to him, try to comfort him, but she knew she must not, understanding that he must face life on his own terms.

And yet, in the morning, he would say nothing about having slept badly. That was the trouble, he scarcely spoke about his real feelings, and so a barrier began to grow between them which neither knew how to cross. Kathy seemed the only one capable of bridging that indefinable gap, when she scrambled up on his lap demanding to be read to from the penny comics he bought her.

It seemed, at times, that he was almost as childlike as Kathy, on a voyage of discovery of life. The way he handled a cup, with clumsy ineptness, touched her to the heart. Sometimes she would discover him alone in the front room, staring between the starched lace curtains at the park opposite. Nothing about their future had been solved or settled. In any case, it was too near Christmas to make plans other than the buying in of food, and decorating the house with holly and gummed paper chains, for Kathy's sake. Sometimes she would think, this could be our last Christmas together, and she would feel hot, useless tears welling up, almost blinding her. She dreaded the thought of Christmas Day, the stillness of Christmas afternoon after the rush and bustle of the preceding days, after the morning spent helping Bridie in the kitchen. Yet it passed off better than she had dared hope because of Kathy's delight in her new toys, the set of farm animals her Uncle Joe had carved for her; the coloring book and crayons from Annie; the doll from Bridie, the first real doll she had ever owned, with eyes that opened and closed; the clothes her mother had made for the doll; a brightly colored humming top from Rowan.

Just after New Year's Day, Rowan broke his silence to admit that he wanted to get away from London, which he disliked intensely for its memories of his past life there, his servitude to the Tanquillan Import Export Company, his parents' great house in Eaton Square, the church close by where he had married Romilly Beresford; had married her not loving her.

"I'd like to go to Wiltshire," he said, "to Aunt Kitty's. Will you come with me, darling?"

Relief washed over her. "You know I will." She rested her head against his shoulder.

"I can't explain, but I feel I can't breathe properly here. I feel trapped."

How ironic, she thought, that a man who had fought so hard to achieve freedom, remained shackled.

"A telegram has just arrived, madam."

Rivers, Kitty Tanquillan's aged butler, held the salver on which the buff-colored envelope sat as if he were holding a dead mouse, regarding all such missives as harbingers of bad news. His wrinkled face assumed an expression of doleful resignation as his mistress tore open the telegram.

"It's all right, Thomas, you can stop looking so worried. We're to have visitors. Mr. Rowan, Miss Charlotte,

50

and her little girl are coming tomorrow. Ask Mrs. Thompson to make their rooms ready, and tell the boy there's no reply."

When the old chap had finally gone, Kitty turned away from her sitting-room window, drawing in a deep breath of relief that her great-nephew was coming home at last.

So, he was bringing Charlotte and their child with him? She crossed the room stiffly, leaning heavily on her silver-knobbed walking cane, and sat down near the fire to study the telegram again, trying to read between the lines.

She had known that Rowan was back in England, and wondered if his parents also knew, but she doubted it. Rowan would not have contacted them. Thank God Alice would not be here when they arrived.

Kitty had once believed that growing old would bring a peaceful conclusion to a long and busy life. Now she thought differently. Aging had brought no easing of the often painful business of living, especially with Alice under the same roof. She felt suddenly intensely cold, and rang for Rivers to draw the curtains and light the lamps.

She had, so far, refused to succumb to the newfangled craze for electricity, nor did she care for gaslight. Grey Wethers would not lend itself to modernization. She preferred her home as she had always known it, lit by log fires, paraffin lamps, and glimmering candles, with shadows trapped in corners; the ancient beams and ceilings unsullied by electric or gas chandeliers.

Possibly she was too old-fashioned, but dusk and dimness suited her best. In all probability, Alice would make sweeping changes when she became the mistress of Grey Wethers. Kitty wondered if she had acted wisely in placing so much wealth in the hands of a mentally sick young woman, but the deed was done. Too late now to alter her will. She had certainly made a mistake in telling Alice of her inheritance, for now she had grown careless with money, casual with the servants, rude and imperious with the farm workers, dictatorial at times with Kitty herself.

Never at any time had the old lady allowed her great-niece to ride roughshod over her, but the constant battle to keep control of her escalating moods had proved exhausting.

Rivers entered the room on silent feet. "You look tired," he said reproachfully. "You've been doing too much, as usual."

"Oh heavens, man! the farm accounts—which I have always done. I must keep my mind active at least." She smiled. She and Thomas Rivers had known each other too long to stand on ceremony. "But you are quite right, I *am* tired; worried, too. If Sir Gervaise finds out that Rowan is here—and he will—I'll be in for more trouble." She paused. "They still blame me for Rowan's defection from the Company."

Rivers threw another log on the fire, venting the anger he felt towards Sir Gervaise Tanquillan and that formidable wife of his, by pressing it hard into the flames with his foot.

"They will never forgive me for leaving all this," Kitty waved a veined hand to indicate the house, "to my great-niece. Gervaise bitterly resents that, just as he resented Rowan's decision to make his own way in the world. I gloried in Rowan's courage in doing that. But I know Gervaise. Once he discovers Rowan's whereabouts, he'll do his damnedest to get him back into that wretched Company of his . . ."

"You mustn't upset yourself, it's bad for you." Thomas gently patted her shoulder, a gesture of comfort from one friend to another.

Kitty smiled ruefully. "I feel afraid at times," she admitted, "afraid of letting go the reins. But I must keep at it, I *must*, for Rowan's sake, and Alice's. I will not stand by to watch Rowan sucked back into a life he hated, nor shall Gervaise ever lay a finger on my home, not if I can help it!"

She sent the carriage to Devizes station to meet them. Drifts of snow were piled against the railings where, in summertime, the station master's geraniums and lobelia grew in neat geometric designs. The station looked different now from the way Charlotte had last seen it, and Kathy was hopping up and down with pleasure and excitement, wanting to be everywhere at once, restlessly tugging at Rowan's hand, anxious to see the horses, sheep, and pigs he had told her about.

As the carriage made its way down the road, and Kathy squealed with joy at this novel mode of transport, Charlotte thought of the times she had driven along this way with Will Oakleigh beside her, the reins held firmly in his strong countryman's hands. She could almost see him now, his legs encased in corduroy breeches, wearing a tweed coat with leather-patched elbows, eyes crinkled against the glare of the road—a silent, taciturn man.

Glancing at Rowan, she noticed with relief that he looked happier than she had seen him since his return to England. His face was lifted to the wind, lips curving upward in a smile of anticipation.

His great-aunt came out of the house to meet them, standing proudly upright, holding onto her walking cane. Charlotte hung back a little as Rowan hurried to cradle Kitty in his arms, not wishing to intrude on their precious moment of reunion.

The house was just as she remembered it. Time could never change the beauty of those gray stone walls; the long terrace with its rose-embellished balustrade. The roses were all dead now; stems brown and brittle beneath a sugar-icing film of frost, flower and fragrance dissipated by winter, and yet they would bloom again when the light warm winds of summer blew down into the sheltered hollow where Grey Wethers nestled like a jewel in the palm of a green-gloved hand.

Lamps had been lit against the gloom of a January afternoon, and shone out into the dusk with a warm, welcoming glow. In the hall, lamplight glinted on the shining copper jugs in the window embrasures; gleamed on softly patinaed rosewood chests delicately inlaid with ivory; on panelled walls and raftered ceilings.

Laying her hand, with a caressing movement, on the oak post at the foot of the wide, branching staircase, Charlotte breathed in the atmosphere of the house, aware of the indefinable scent of beeswax polish immutably blended with that of fragrant woodsmoke, wine and cooking, remembering that Rowan once told her that his great-aunt's house reminded him of French bistros with their richly intermingled perfumes. Kitty, he said, had always possessed a huge capacity for enjoyment, had loved travel, good food and wine; she had even been known to relish the occasional Gauloise cigarette or fine Havana cigar.

Charlotte had been given her old room with a four-poster bed and moss-green brocade curtains. Firelight glowed softly on the polished mahogany furniture. A smaller bed had been brought in for Kathy, whose bedtime was long since past, but the child had begged so hard to look at the farmyard animals that Rowan had succumbed to her blandishments.

Charlotte was just about to change for dinner, when Kitty came into the room. "I must talk to you," she said.

"I've been expecting you."

Kitty's hands knotted together, her eyes filled with tears. "How I managed to hide my feelings when I saw Rowan . . . Oh, God!" She drew in a deep, shuddering breath of despair. "On his last leave, I could not help marvelling at his sheer strength and vitality. He reminded me of Michelangelo's statue of David in the Piazza at Florence. But now . . ." Her voice shook. She covered her face with her hands.

"Sit down," Charlotte said gently.

"No, I don't want to sit down! I want the truth. He's dying, isn't he?"

"I don't know. I don't know . . . ! I don't want to

54

believe that. I—*can't* believe it!" Charlotte clenched her hands in an agony of despair. Tears rained down her cheeks.

" 'Tout est perdu pour l'honneur,' " Kitty murmured brokenly. "Tell me, has he spoken of it?" Her face resembled that of a Belgian peasant woman watching the destruction of her village by German guns. "Come now, the truth!" Kitty uncovered her face. Her eyes, sunk deeply in their sockets, burned with a proud, fierce light. "I want to know. I *must* know!"

"There was no need to speak of it. I think I knew from the moment I saw him!" Charlotte shrugged her shoulders helplessly. "The truth is, we haven't really talked about anything at all. It's as though an invisible barrier exists between us now. I don't know what to say or do to help him."

"Let me talk to him," Kitty suggested. "Come, it's almost time for dinner. He'll be back soon." Turning at the door, she said in that indomitable way of hers, "Trust me, my dear."

"It's no use, Aunt Kitty, I have no right to saddle Charlotte with the wreck I have become." Rowan slowly paced his bedroom, head bent, staring down at the rose-patterned carpet. "Surely you, above all people must see that? I have no money, no prospects—no future . . ."

He stopped pacing and sat down beside his great-aunt, speaking in a low, emphatic voice, gripping her hands as if to strengthen his own wavering resolve. "I have a short time to live. Do you imagine for one moment that I could condemn Charlotte to months of torment, the misery of watching me die day by day? No, I will not do it! I will not ruin her life!"

"I take it then, that you would rather condemn her to a lifetime's unhappiness thinking she had failed you, that

55

you did not love her enough to share the most precious days of your life with her?"

"*Life*," Rowan said bitterly, releasing her hands, "it's not life we are talking about! And it is not Charlotte who has failed me, quite the reverse!"

Kitty had never come up against this Rowan before, this gaunt stranger with dark, burning eyes and a suppressed passion which his lean, attenuated body seemed powerless to contain.

Kitty said softly, "Forgive me, dearest, you have drunk the sweet wine of youth, but it is the vintage wine, the longest stored, the September wine which possesses the most flavor. You must remember that Charlotte has been maimed, too, by life and circumstances." She laid a comforting arm about his shoulders. "She has borne your child, lived with the disgrace of that among her own people. Oh, don't think for one moment that I share the views of her mother and sister, but it can't have been easy for her standing up to their narrow-minded condemnation. Now she loves and needs you more than ever, as you need her. I'm an old woman. My course is nearly run, but this I beg of you, take whatever life is left to you and live it to the full."

At dinner Kitty wore an elegant black silk dress trimmed with shiny bugle beads, and a brightly colored shawl. Her white hair, fluffed out about her thin brown face, imparted a judicial air to her appearance. Her sharp old eyes were bright by candlelight. She was very much the grande dame, the mistress of Grey Wethers.

After dessert, she raised her glass in a toast. "I wish to drink to the future happiness of the two people I love most in the world," she said, catching Rowan's surprised glance across the table, "and I make no apology for speaking of the future. Come into the drawing-room, I have something to say to both of you."

When they were settled, over coffee, "I once had a lover," she said imperiously. "Oh, don't look so shocked. I was quite beautiful then." She chuckled deeply, and Charlotte knew that she was acting a little for their benefit; keeping the moment light for their sake. "His name was Gilbert Stapleford. He was my estate manager. I knew he was married, of course—the attractive men usually are . . ."

"Please, Aunt Kitty," Rowan interrupted gently, "your secrets are yours to keep. They always have been."

"I have my reasons for telling them to you now," Kitty said. "Hear me out, and you will understand why. His was not a happy marriage, I knew that all along. He had married a woman who seemed to enjoy ill health. I made that an excuse, I suppose. In any event, we became lovers. We were young and strong, deeply and passionately in love with each other. But times were much harder then than they are now, from a woman's viewpoint. When it became clear that Gilbert's children might suffer because of our relationship, I ended the affair. But I never stopped loving him."

The room was very quiet, redolent with the intermingled fragrances of coffee, burning apple logs, and the faint, wintry scent of the bronze chrysanthemums massed in great white jardiniéres on the polished side tables.

Kitty continued, "About that time, a young brother and sister, Thomas and Lucy Rivers, came to work for us. To make a long story short, Lucy married a Cornishman, Jonathan Tregaran, who ran a fishing coble from Polperro. When Jonathan was drowned, I went to Cornwall to see Lucy. I found her in a sad state, living in a fisherman's hovel with her three little children, with scarcely two ha'pennies to rub together.

"In any event, I bought a cottage for her, near Talland Bay. I'm telling you all this because Lucy still lives there, alone now since her children grew up and made their own lives."

57

Kitty's eyes kindled suddenly, with remembrance. "Later, as chance would have it, I met Gilbert again, in London. Nothing had changed between us; we were still deeply in love with each other; had so much to say that could not be said during our few meetings in Hyde Park. Then came a golden opportunity. His wife decided to spend a few weeks abroad for the sake of her health. That is when I spoke to Lucy Tregaran; threw myself on her mercy; told her the truth; asked her if she would be willing to lend me the cottage while she came here to visit her brother."

Eyes shining, Kitty continued, "I shall remember those few weeks Gilbert and I spent together as the happiest of my entire life. I think it is true to say that we found each other again in the brief time we had together. We both knew that it would never come again, that brief return to a springtime of the heart. But those days were ours for all time. No one could take them away from us. No one ever has. Gilbert died, shortly afterward."

She lay back in her chair, the winking firelight catching the shimmer of her beaded silk dress. "That is why I want you to go there, to my cottage in Cornwall. This is my gift to you. Please take it."

Glancing at Charlotte's vivid, hopeful face, Rowan knew how much she wanted to accept. But he must be realistic. He tried to keep his voice steady and unemotional. "It's generous of you, Aunt Kitty," he said, "but facts alter cases. You could not have known that Gilbert would die." His voice roughed. "It would be a very different matter for you, Charlotte. Doesn't that frighten you?"

"If I had died giving birth to Kathy, or if you had died silencing that enemy machine gun," she said softly, staring into the heart of the fire, "we would have had no future at all."

She looked up then, unsmiling, unpleading. "But it is

up to you. The decision is yours. I want to be with you always, but I'll not beg you, not if you don't want me."

A log fell into the hearth, sending up a shower of sparks. Rowan bent down to retrieve it, and knelt there, by the fire, for a while, the flames casting flickering shadows over his face, his eyes dark with longing.

Suddenly, he rose to his feet, and Kitty knew that he had reached his decision. Turning, he smiled at Charlotte, that charming, quizzical smile which reminded Kitty of the old, unconquerable Rowan she knew so well.

"We will go to Cornwall together," he said quietly. "But you do see, my love, what an impossible situation I'm in? I cannot live for very long with you, but I am very sure that I could never live at all without you."

Chapter Five

The journey proved much longer and infinitely more exhausting than Charlotte had imagined. It had scarcely seemed any distance at all from Wiltshire to Cornwall when she and Kathy had looked at the map in Bridie's book. At first the child was elated, kneeling up on the seat, looking out of the window, her nose flattened to the glass as she stared at the long ribbons of gray smoke from the engine, then she grew drowsy as the journey progressed, and fell fast asleep with her head in Charlotte's lap, rousing later to complain that she was hungry. Once fed with cake and milk, she resumed her vigil at the carriage window. Then she wanted to go to the lavatory.

They were met at Polperro by a puckish old fellow wearing a battered bowler hat and carrying a long whip to tickle his horse's rump if it turned idle. He obviously knew the occupants of every house, farm and cottage in the area, and had been forewarned of their arrival.

"It's Lucy Tregaran's place you'll be wanting then?" He spoke in a thick Cornish accent which tickled Kathy's funny bone as deliciously as the prospect of riding on the back of his cart with their legs dangling.

He took his time hoisting their luggage onto the cart, along with several other boxes and bundles containing household goods and groceries for delivery to various houses along the way, explaining that he ran his carter and carrier's business as a sideline to his main occupation as a hardware merchant.

"I hope there are not too many bumps in the road," Charlotte said uneasily from her perch on the back of the cart.

"Don't worry about that, ma'am." Godolphin climbed aboard his vehicle. "Old Foxy knows the road to Talland Bay like the back of my hand. He ain't never been known to lose a passenger yet, at least none that sat still and behaved themselves." He fixed Kathy with a piercing stare as he spoke, then grinned at her, displaying a row of broken, tobacco-stained teeth, which made her giggle more than ever. He then unearthed his pipe and tobacco pouch from his overcoat pocket, tamped down the contents of the bowl with a grimy forefinger, applied a match, and made sure that the tobacco was burning satisfactorily before flicking Foxy's rear end with his whip. "Giddap," he snorted, through a haze of blue smoke.

As the journey progressed, Godolphin betrayed a Cornishman's natural curiosity about newcomers to the district, extracting information indirectly, like jigsaw pieces to slot together later over a warm fire and a jug of ale.

"Name of Tanquillan?" he asked. "You a Cornishman then?"

"No." Rowan answered the question politely but noncommittally.

"Been in the war, have you?" Godolphin sucked placidly at his pipe.

"Yes, the Army."

"Mmm. Thought so." A pause. "You'll be glad of a bit of peace and quiet then. Nice for your missis and the little 'un. Takes after her ma, don't she, with that copper hair of hers?"

"Yes. Kathy is very like her mother."

"It'll be nice for Lucy Tregaran, getting away, I mean. Gone to visit her brother, I understand, somewhere in Wiltshire." Godolphin eased the rim of his bowler hat.

"Can't say I blame her. It's lonely down yonder, near the sea, with no close neighbors to pass the time of day with."

Charlotte shivered suddenly. It was cold perched there on the back of the cart, but her reflex action was born of more than the keen wind which lifted her hat brim and whipped tendrils of hair across her face. She was filled with an acute nervous apprehension as the unfamiliar scenery rolled by.

And yet Polperro, with its steeply descending streets, quaint harbor, the bobbing craft tied up alongside the dock, the weatherbeaten old fishermen hunched on the wharf watching the younger men at work, and the white-winged gulls with their yellow hooked beaks and cold gray eyes, awaiting the tipping of fish-gut, wheeling and diving with their unearthly, clamorous cries over a gray waste of heaving sea, had reminded her of Scarborough.

Perhaps fishing ports everywhere looked roughly the same, with small, neat cottages grouped about the cheerful center of activity. Many of the cottages were color-washed blue, white and pink, interspaced with a latticework of yards and gardens where lobster-pots were stacked and the nets spread out to dry, and women, warmly clad, with colorful cotton scarves about their heads, gathered in their washing, or leaned, elbows on the walls, to gossip.

But the vaguely sensed familiarity of the scene served to remind her that this was not home. These people were strangers to her, and she was about to embark on a strange new chapter of her life.

Squaring her shoulders, she stared at the bumpy road behind the cart, listening to the steady clip-clop of the horse's hooves, noticing the hedgerows with their light, delicate brushwork of frost, catching the whiff of Godolphin's pipe tobacco, feeling the pressure of Kathy's body against hers, wondering what Rowan was really thinking as he conversed with the driver.

"I can only take you to the top of the lane," Godolphin

explained. "It's too narrow for the cart to go down. I go round the villages three times a week collecting orders and making deliveries." He knocked out his pipe against the side of the cart. "My brother runs the grocer's shop, so anything you want, just leave a note in the box at the lane end. Or, if you want to go into Polperro, I can pick you up Mondays, Wednesdays, and Fridays at two o'clock. Well, here we are."

The old man climbed down from his seat and hobbled round to the rear of the cart while the horse moved forward to crunch the rough grass at the entrance to a narrow, high-banked lane. "Come on, young 'un," Godolphin muttered, lifting down the excited, wriggling Kathy from the back. "Now you, missis."

"I can manage on my own, thanks," Charlotte said primly, as Rowan started heaving down the luggage.

How she bit back the words, "Let me help you with that," she would never know. She simply knew that she must not even attempt to prevent his doing whatever he felt capable of doing; never appoint herself his keeper. Gathering up a few smaller items of luggage, she started to walk along the lane, thinking no wonder the cart couldn't come down it. It was scarcely wide enough for two people walking abreast, steep and slippery; stone-littered, with firmly rooted hedgerows towering overhead, and ditches where the lumber of last year's leaves lay soggily in ice-crinkled water.

"Watch your step, Rowan," she called over her shoulder. "You too, Kathy." But the child, agog with excitement, skipped ahead, the pom-pom of her green tam-o'-shanter bouncing as she ran, until she stopped abruptly, and seemed to have been swallowed into thin air.

The tall, brooding hedgerows unnerved Charlotte as she stumbled breathlessly after the child. "Kathy," she called, "where are you?" What have we done, she thought despairingly. We should have stayed at Grey Wethers, not come all this way for nothing. In her mind's eye she saw her child spitted on the horns of an angry bull.

Close to tears at the sheer frustration of arriving, cold and exhausted, in the middle of nowhere, Charlotte thought what a sight she must look with her hair blowing untidily about her face, her hat askew; skirt muddied at the hem, her hands full of bits and bobs of string bags. And where on earth had Kathy got to?

And then she noticed a gate set between the hedges, and saw her willful child standing on tiptoe to gaze into one of the downstairs rooms of the cottage. Relief flooded through her, but anxiety had made her short-tempered. "Kathy, come here this minute!" She might as well have spoken to a brick wall.

She turned to wait for Rowan, then. "Are you all right?" she asked anxiously, going against her better judgment.

"I'm fine!"

But he didn't look fine, arms straining at the sockets, his forehead beaded with perspiration. Oh God, she thought, we can't keep on pretending everything's fine when it isn't.

"Where's the key, darling? The sooner we get indoors, the better," Rowan reminded her.

She found the key in her purse, and stood nervously, near the gate, worrying about Kathy, brushing back stray tendrils of hair with her gloved fingers. She had not even noticed the cottage.

"Well, what do you think of it?" Rowan asked.

She realized, afterward, that she had scarcely given a thought to the place where she and Rowan would live together as man and wife. If she had thought about the cottage at all, she had imagined a kind of fisherman's dwelling, perched, like a seagull, on some wild, inhospitable cliff top.

Now, turning to look at it, a cry of pleasure escaped her lips. Built of rough Cornish stone, the cottage seemed to have sprung, without human aid, from the rich, moist earth of Cornwall; a long, low building, with a tiled roof inset with peaked dormer windows, the walls a mass of clambering ivy; the porch hung with shrivelled fronds of clematis, the garden full of gnarled apple trees whose branches wove a delicate tracery against the pale winter sky.

"Feeling better now?" Rowan raised a quizzical eyebrow.

She felt suddenly, deeply ashamed of herself. "Much better. I'm sorry. I was worrying about Kathy, that's all."

"Perhaps she needs a modicum of independence, too," Rowan said quietly.

"But she's only three years old!" Charlotte paused, not knowing how to put into words that it would not be easy for her to relax the responsibility she felt towards her child after three years of caring for her alone.

"What are you thinking?" Rowan asked.

"Oh, nothing. Listen! I can hear the sea in the distance . . ." Every other day would not be like this one, she thought. Warmer air would soon bring the apple trees into flower; the lilacs would burst into blossom, filling the air with their fragrance; birds would begin to nest in the ivy, swallows skim the skies, and great gulls wheel inland from the sea. Lifting her head, holding her breath, enchanted, she caught the familiar tang of seaweed on the wind.

"The key, sweetheart!"

"Oh yes, of course." She pressed it into the palm of his outstretched hand. "I—I'd better see what Kathy's up to!"

"I'm just playing," the child said hostilely, pulling away from her mother's restraining hand.

"But it's cold out, and Dadda and I are going indoors now."

"No! I want to play!" Kathy's bottom lip went out. She had that stubborn, defiant look about her that Charlotte knew so well, the prelude to a tantrum.

"Very well, but you must promise not to leave the garden; to come in when you are called. Promise?"

"Yes," Kathy said reluctantly, and Charlotte knew that she would keep her word.

Rowan had lifted the luggage indoors when she returned. "Well?" he asked, an amused smile playing about his lips.

"Our daughter has a mind of her own," Charlotte said sharply.

"So I've noticed!" Suddenly, unexpectedly, he lifted her up in his arms, and carried her across the threshold of the cottage.

"Welcome home, darling," he whispered.

It was a much bigger house than she had anticipated, with rooms to right and left of the hall with its polished staircase, the walls of which were hung with good, original oil paintings of ships in sail; the hall table embellished with a massive handbell with a stout wooden handle, which she attempted to pick up, and then set down again, because it was so heavy.

"Curfew shall not ring tonight," she said laughing, not understanding the significance of that bell.

The room to the left must be the "best" parlor, Charlotte mused, thinking suddenly of Kitty Tanquillan and Gilbert Stapleford, wondering if it were there they had talked together of the future, and come to terms with the past; she noticed that a fire had been laid in the grate, awaiting the touch of a match.

"Look, darling, a piano!" Rowan opened the lid and ran his fingers lightly over the keys. Music! He had missed that more than anything else, apart from Charlotte. More than china cups, more than food and hot baths, books, and clean clothing. Music was as essential to him as breathing. He had felt lost and empty, drained, without it.

Suddenly, the war, and memories of his imprisonment, seemed further away from him here, in this quiet room, with the woman he loved beside him. Bending down, he put a match to the fire, thinking that he and Charlotte might sit here, later, when Kathy had been tucked into bed.

The room across the hall was much smaller. Cosier, less formally arranged, it was a woman's room, with rose-papered walls, and chintz-curtained windows overlooking a sloping lawn girdled with a growth of pines and birches bordering the garden's edge.

Swiftly crossing the room to look out of the window, Charlotte saw, with infinite pleasure, the faint line of the horizon where sea and sky met; heard, with joy, the mysterious song of the sea in the distance, the crooning of the wind among the trees.

Godolphin had spoken of loneliness, the lack of close neighbors to pass the time of day with, but Charlotte knew that she could never feel lonely here, with the sea close by; watching the ever-changing patterns of clouds and gulls' wings; seeing the slow passage of ships far out at sea.

She clasped Rowan's hand tightly in hers. "It's almost like being on the deck of a ship," she murmured.

"Yes, it is rather," he said, thinking how lovely she was; how much he loved her. "Perhaps that is why the house is called 'Stella Maris.' "

"Stella Maris'?" she enquired, looking up at him. "Why? What does that mean?"

"Star of the Sea," he said gently.

"Oh, how lovely." She pulled off her hat and placed it carefully on a chair near a sampler frame on which was stretched a canvas stitched with petit-point roses. Scarlet geraniums were in flower on the deeply recessed windowsills. The shell-framed photographs on the mantelpiece, the rocking chair pulled up near the hearth, the pyramid of sticks and coal in the grate, the paraffin lamps with rosy glass shades dotted about the room, all enhanced the room's welcoming cosiness.

They wandered hand in hand along the passage to the kitchen where a tall white dresser, decked with rows of blue and white china plates, dishes and tureens, took pride of place alongside shelves of gleaming copper pans and earthenware storage jars, neatly labelled.

"Look, there's a note on the table!"

"What does it say?" Charlotte turned eagerly from her contemplation of the black-leaded range.

" 'Please make yourselves at home. There is plenty of kindling and coal in the shed, and Godolphin will bring you anything else you need. Meanwhile, I've left you enough food to keep you going for a day or two. I boiled you a ham, knowing it would keep all right in the pantry, and there's a dozen eggs in the larder; bread is in the breadbox, butter in the crock, and you'll find a can of milk on the back doorstep. (Mrs. Cilgerran's boy, Johnny, from the farm across the fields, would leave it there this morning). P.S. It's best to go into Polperro for meat, fish and vegetables. Market day's on Wednesday. I aired the beds before leaving the house, but put the bottles in again, to make sure. Oh, by the way, there's a little paraffin stove for cooking until you get the range going. With best wishes, yours truly, Lucy Tregaran.' "

Charlotte opened the back door to make sure the milk was there, catching a glimpse of Kathy as she did so, happily running in circles on the grass, bright curls in a tangled mass about her shoulders, cheeks stung to a healthy glow by the wind. "Shall I call her in now?" she asked anxiously.

'She'll come to no harm," Rowan said lightly. "Let's take a look upstairs."

Flushed and strangely nervous, Charlotte walked with him to the wide upper landing. The room above the parlor contained a bed, a glossy mahogany wardrobe, dressing-table and washstand. The windows were framed in chintz material faded by the sun to a soft blur of blues and greens. There were rose-patterned toilet accessories on the tiled washstand: pitcher, basin, soap dish, and a toothbrush holder; a polished brass can for hot water, and little shell-covered trinket boxes on the dressing-table. A rose-shaded Victorian lamp stood on the bedside table. The air smelt faintly of lavender and rose petals, a potpourri of summertime in a blue bowl on the windowsill.

"Where will Kathy sleep?" Charlotte asked the question instinctively. The little girl had always slept in the same room with her.

"There's another room through here." Rowan opened an adjoining door and peeped in. "Look, darling."

"It's just that she's never been alone at night before."

"There's a night light beside the bed, and she is a very independent little thing. Oh, Charlotte!"

Very gently, Rowan drew her into his arms and kissed her. She stood quietly, resting her head against his shoulder. Neither spoke. She remembered, hearing the beating of his heart against her cheek, that other room they had shared the night she went to London to be with him before his regiment sailed for France. She had been nervous then, too, knowing nothing of the physical act of love, content to let him teach her.

Now, at his kiss, feeling his arms about her, a thrill of desire ran through her. She wanted him now even more than she had then; wanted him with a desperate hunger born of the lonely days and years without him. She dared not think of a future without him. She longed to lie at peace with him, naked and unafraid, his lips on hers, hands warm on her body.

But the time for love was not now, not yet. The day had been too long and exhausting. They must eat first, and wash the dust of the journey from their bodies, be totally at peace with each other. Perhaps, after supper, Rowan would play to her, then the multitudinous memories and impressions of the day would be washed away, too.

She stirred in his arms. "It's getting dark," she said. "I must call Kathy to come indoors."

"Don't worry, darling, I'll find her." On an impulse, he touched her hair with the palm of his hand, then slid it gently down the curve of her cheek and lifted her face to his, noticing the way her hazel green eyes shone with desire beneath the delicately curved eyebrows, the soft dewiness of her lips, the way her hair escaped in gleaming red tendrils from the heavy chignon at the nape of her neck. And this was how he would always remember her, strangely vulnerable, yet strong.

"I love you," he said simply.

Dusk came quickly. Wearing a checked pinafore, Charlotte boiled eggs for herself and Kathy, and sliced the ham for Rowan. They ate in the kitchen. She had discovered a bag of potatoes in the pantry, and jars of homemade chutney alongside a note which read: "Please make use of these."

Rowan had lit the fire in the range, for warmth. Kathy almost nodded off, tired out by the long journey and the fresh Cornish air. "It seems a pity to risk waking her up too much," Charlotte said in a low voice. "Perhaps I'll just wash her hands and face tonight, and bath her properly in the morning."

"Yes, I should if I were you." He gathered up the child in his arms and carried her upstairs. The bathroom, they had discovered, was across the landing next to another bedroom, near an enclosed staircase to the attic, not yet explored.

Thankfully, Kathy was far too sleepy to demur at being put to bed in a strange room. Her head dropped onto the pillow like a rose on its stem.

70

Charlotte towelled herself dry. The water had not been very hot nor very deep, but she felt refreshed, dreamily relaxed. Sitting in front of the dressing-table, she brushed her hair with long, even strokes, letting it drift about her shoulders, hearing the sound of music from the room below.

Crossing to the window, she looked out at the night. Somewhere in the darkness shone a few pinpricks of light, belonging, perhaps, to the farmhouse Lucy Tregaran had mentioned in her letter. The sky was velvety dark, lit with a myriad frosty stars.

Standing quite still for a little while, she breathed in the essence of the night, comforted by the tiny sounds all around her, the rustling of the ivy, the scuttering of nocturnal creatures abroad in the garden, the screech of an owl, the distant barking of one of the farm dogs. She felt attuned to every sound and movement of life, as if her body were an empty vessel awaiting replenishment with new wine.

And now she was ready to go downstairs. Quietly opening the door, she noticed a piece of paper half-hidden by the bed valance. Picking it up, she stared at the red crest above the words "Buckingham Palace." Frowning slightly, she read:

"The Queen joins me in welcoming you on your release from the miseries and hardships which you have endured with so much patience and courage . . . We are thankful that this longed-for day has arrived, and that back in the Old Country you will be able once more to enjoy the happiness of a home and to see good days among those who anxiously looked for your return. George R.I."

Rowan was seated at the piano, playing softly. She slipped her arms round his neck and kissed the top of his head.

71

"God, but my fingers are stiff. I sound like an organ-grinder," he said harshly.

"No, darling, you mustn't belittle yourself. It sounds wonderful to me. What is it you're playing?"

"Elgar's 'Salut d'Amour.' "

"It's glorious, but sad somehow." She sensed Rowan's tenseness. "I know so little about music," she said, feeling shut out, wondering if she had been too optimistic in hoping that coming here to the cottage would miraculously make things right between them, draw them closer together.

To break the tension, she produced the letter. "I found this in the bedroom," she explained. "You must have dropped it."

"What is it?"

"A letter from the King, no less." She spoke teasingly.

"Give it to me!" He rose swiftly to his feet, snatched it from her, crumpled it savagely, and threw it on the fire.

"Rowan! How could you?" She stood appalled, watching it blaze.

"Don't you see? Don't you understand?" He turned on her, beside himself with anger. "This is the kind of crap they churned out by the thousand as a kind of sop, a palliative to the poor devils who lived through the horror of imprisonment. It's nothing short of an insult!"

"Rowan!" She had never seen him like this before, nor heard him speak with such scorn and bitterness. "I'm sorry the letter upset you so much . . ." But he wasn't listening. His face reflected all the pent-up misery of the past years, his eyes looked beyond her into some private hell of the mind. The barriers were up again. She felt excluded, shut out, powerless to help him.

"For God's sake, Rowan, tell me what's bothering you! Don't keep things bottled up inside you!"

"No! I don't want to talk about it. Not now. Not ever! I want to forget!"

"But you can't, can you? It's there all the time, festering like a canker in your mind, poisoning your life."

"My life!" He gave a short, bitter laugh. "What—life? I suppose you mean this charade I'm acting out, God knows to what purpose." He turned away from her, gripping the edge of the mantelpiece. "I did a very selfish thing in bringing you and Kathy to this place. I should have had the courage of my convictions that day in the park. I should have gone away then."

A flame of anger flickered in Charlotte's eyes. "You made the decision to come here," she said in a low voice, "but you might just as well have gone away somewhere by yourself, to nurse your grievances, if you are really just living a charade, acting out a lie. But that's no use to me. If there cannot be truth and understanding between us, we'd be better off apart."

There was nothing more to say. She walked out of the room, closing the door firmly behind her. Then, blinded with tears, she ran up to the bedroom and lay face down on the white bedspread. Joy in the house, in music, in the night sounds, the simple domestic tasks she had performed—setting the table, cutting the bread, peeling potatoes, boiling eggs, washing up the dishes afterward and rearranging them on Lucy Tregaran's dresser—all were dissipated now, gone, blown away like bright, fleeting bubbles in the harsh wind of reality.

Worse than that, she had gone to him so sure of his love, her hair loose about her shoulders, filled with desire for him, wanting him, needing his gentleness and compassion to bridge the long years of their separation. It would have taken all his understanding to break down her own natural barriers of shyness and reserve, to make their loving, when it happened, a thing of tenderness as well as passion. She wept because he had hurt her more than if he had struck her in the face. But a physical blow would have been easier to bear than his indifference, his admission that he was merely acting out a charade of loving.

God, what a fool she'd been. She bit her knuckles to keep from crying aloud. She was fast asleep when Rowan came up to beg her forgiveness, lying on the bedspread, her hair fanned out about her on the pillow, tears wet on her cheeks. With a low murmur of despair, he touched her hair lightly with his fingertips, then covering her with a warm blanket from the chest at the end of the bed, he bent over to kiss her, looked in at Kathy, and went downstairs to the fire to sit staring into the embers until the coal sank to a fine white powdery ash.

Charlotte woke to the light of gray morning filtering between the curtains. In the first moments of consciousness she scarcely remembered why she was lying on top of the bed wearing her dressing-gown. As memory slowly returned to her, so did the misery of last night; the anger and misunderstanding between herself and Rowan. And he had not even come to bed. Did he hate her so much then that he could not bear to be in the same room with her? Where was he? With a quick movement, she slid her feet to the ground, and began to dress haphazardly, her fingers trembling so that she could scarcely fasten her buttons and waistband. Scooping back her hair, she twisted it into a rough knot, not stopping to brush or comb it, securing it with a few hurriedly placed hairpins.

Kathy was still fast asleep. Charlotte tiptoed on to the landing. The house seemed to have stopped breathing. If Rowan were dead, how could she live with the thought that her last words to him had been spoken in anger?

Scarcely able to breathe, she pushed open the parlor door. Rowan had fallen asleep in the armchair. She could hear the slight exhalation of his breath between his lips. His head lay cradled against a cushion; hair rumpled, mouth slightly open. She wondered if she should wake him. No, she decided, better to let him sleep. She slipped back quietly to her room to find something to put over him. And then it dawned on her that she had fallen asleep uncovered, that the blanket on the bed had not been there then. He must have come up to her after all, and she had thought . . .

She laid the blanket across his knees. He stirred, like a child in its sleep, muttering uneasily, turning his cheek against the cushion. His right hand moved involuntarily. Gently, she tucked the blanket round his legs.

She let herself out of the cottage by the back door. It was scarcely light yet. A light film of frost lay on the grass. The gate felt icy to the touch as she opened it. The brittle sugar-frosting of ice crackled beneath her shoes as she made her way down the lane. The path to the beach was steep and difficult. Rough steps were edged with sagging strips of wood in places, slippery with mud near the over-hanging brambles which tore at her skirt.

Impatiently, she wrenched herself free of the snatching, out-flung tentacles, drawn on by the sound of waves wash-ing in on the shore, needing solitude and comfort, wanting to come close to some strong, eternal force beyond herself.

She stepped at last onto a fan-shaped wedge of sand. Light grew stronger on the horizon. Seagulls sliced the air with swiftly beating wings, uttering melancholy drawn-out cries, skimming the surface of the water in search of food. The shelving beach, protected by jutting outcrops of rock and boulders, lay wet and gleaming beyond the reach of the receding tide.

Huddled in a knitted jacket, head bare, Charlotte looked out at the gray line of the horizon, listening in-tently to the pulsating beat of the waves, the grating sound of their withdrawal, watching the tiny, curling edges of foam clawing at the sand. All around her were stranded sea shells, tiny sea creatures, and the curious jetsam the waves had left behind: a sea-bird's wing, a quivering star-fish, long trails of seaweed.

She began to pray wordlessly for strength, wondering if God would make sense of her jumbled thoughts, if thoughts even qualified as prayers. Or perhaps He would not listen to her at all, a human being who had so often thrown down the gauntlet at His feet.

Hugging her arms about her body, she strove to understand what she should do now, how to face the future. Time was slipping away from her as fast as the tide, beyond the power of human hands, or prayer, to hold back. But whatever time was left to herself and Rowan must not be squandered, made hollow with half-truths or false emotions.

She searched her heart for the true values; love, compassion, gentleness, understanding, courage. These were the only gifts she had to give him, whether or not he wanted them. Only he could decide that. If he did not want her any more, she must leave him, without bitterness or selfish pride.

Drawing in a deep breath, she lifted her face to the wind, then turned and walked back the way she had come.

Rowan sat bolt upright, staring wildly about him, crying out, not realizing where he was, that he had been dreaming. His body felt cold and stiff, and yet he was wet with a sticky, warm perspiration. "Jacko?" The boy whose name he uttered in a choked, hoarse voice was still with him, mouth gaping open and bloodied, body rigid with pain and fear, eyes glazing over, staring up at the circle of light above the operating table, while Shiltz, the butcher, calmly divested himself of his blood-smeared white coat, lips drawn back in a grinning satyr's smile.

"Rowan! What is it? What's wrong?" Charlotte ran into the room. He was sitting there, hands gripping the arms of the chair, his face twisted in horror. His jaw muscles were clenched, spasms of pain shuddered through his tensed-up body; he appeared to be undergoing a convulsion or an electric shock. "Jacko!" The name seemed wrenched from some dark pit of the soul.

76

"Rowan! It's all right! I'm here! You've been dreaming." She sank down on her knees beside him, clinging desperately to his hands.

"He was only a boy. Nineteen years old." Tears rained down Rowan's face. "A boy with toothache! Christ!" He covered his face with his hands, remembering that gaping, bloody, toothless mouth, the way the guards held him down, the writhing figure of the terrified youth, while Shiltz, the grinning butcher, wrenched every tooth from his head, without anesthetic. "The shock killed him." Rowan said brokenly. "The pain, the shock, the horror of what Shiltz did to him. Being held down like that. The brutality, the indignity . . ." He shuddered violently.

"A fine-looking boy with a bloody gaping hole in his face, his bottom lip torn away . . ."

"God! How horrible, horrible!" Charlotte's face whitened. She shared Rowan's sense of outrage at the torture of a defenseless boy. "But—surely—there's the Prisoner of War Code?"

"What code?" Rowan rubbed his hands wearily across his face. "We were in enemy territory, at the mercy of brutal, sadistic men. The women, too lost no opportunity of insulting us: fouling our drinking water, hurling abuse at us. Whenever we were herded into the cattle trucks, every time we stopped, the women would be there to jeer at us—even the wounded and dying—to spit at the men on stretchers. I have nightmares about them: the cruel pleasure they derived from their particular kind of torture, prodding dying men with sticks, tearing at their bandages, pelting the stretchers with every kind of nameless filth!

"I was sent to Nebendale because I spoke German, God help me! If that's what education does for a man, I wish to Christ I had been born a deaf mute! This bloody education of mine was less than useless when it came to preventing the death of Jacko, and others like him. Perhaps they thought my command of their language made me seem like one of them. It was my job to interpret orders.

Shiltz was the camp's medical officer, a slovenly pig of a man of subnormal intelligence. The men who were foolish enough to report sick were thrown into cells under lock and key, without food and water. But then, we were not officers, just the rank and file."

Charlotte's hands shook as she wiped his face with her handkerchief. Perspiration had dripped from his forehead to mingle with the tears on his cheeks. "You are cold. You must try to rest now. I'll get you a hot-water bottle. Please, darling, come to bed." His hands felt clammy to the touch. He was shaking in every limb. His voice came in hoarse, breathless gasps. She was desperately afraid for him now. He had begun to cough, a deep, hollow, racking, exhausting cough; a trace of blood-flecked saliva stained his lips.

She ran blindly to the kitchen to fetch water. He was on his feet when she returned, his body bent forward, hands gripping the edge of the mantelpiece.

"Drink this." She held the glass to his lips, but he turned his head aside.

"No!" He made a superhuman effort to pull himself together. The nightmare, the words he had spewed forth so bitterly last night, lay like a dead weight on his spirit. That he had made Charlotte suffer for his own inadequacies was unforgivable. To have made such issue of the letter, to have used it as a tool to punish the woman he loved, seemed akin to the cruelty he abhorred in others.

Charlotte was right. He had let the horror of his imprisonment poison his life. There was still so much he hadn't told her about: the coal mines at Semftenburg; the punishment camp at Menschburg, where the cold had seeped into his bones during that deadly winter of 1916; the slaughterhouse in the town where the prisoners' food was prepared from the carcasses of old, diseased, or wounded horses; the stink of death in the air.

He turned to her. "Can you ever forgive me?"

"Forgive you for what?" She laid her hands on his

78

shoulders. "You're a man, not a plaster saint. I understand now why you burned that letter."

"It was a stupid, pointless, unreasonable thing to do. I made an issue of it because I couldn't play the piano properly. I made you the butt of my anger, said things I didn't mean to salve my pride. I know how much I hurt you . . ."

She laid a finger across his lips. "I love you. Nothing has changed between us. But you must rest now."

"I have done nothing to deserve you, my love." He buried his face in her hair, inhaling the wholesome fragrance of her. "But things will be different from now on."

"Everything will be different, better, if we face—face what must be faced," her lips trembled, "in truth and honesty. No more lies or evasions . . ."

"When have I lied to you?"

"We have lied to each other all along." She looked at him compassionately. "Not deliberately. More by implication. You are not 'fine' and neither am I. How could we possibly be, faced with our situation?" She clasped his hands tightly in hers. "Rowan, are we so weak, so cowardly, that we cannot be totally honest with each other? If you don't want me, say so, and I'll go away, if this is all just a—charade."

"Oh, God. Charlotte, my darling!" Suddenly she was in his arms, his lips on hers, his tears warm on her cheeks. "If only you knew how much I want you . . ."

"Listen! Kathy's awake!" She smiled tremulously, "Don't say any more just now, darling. Come upstairs. Try to sleep."

Clinging together, they walked slowly to the foot of the stairs.

Chapter Six

March came in with sunshine and blustering winds, a feeling of freshness and freedom in the high-flying white clouds and watercolor skies. February seemed, to Charlotte, like a dusty, ragbound mummy trailing its shroud of wrinkled leaves. She had hated every moment of its damp grayness. Now, although she knew that March was often an unpredictable month, the air here was softer and warmer, and spring would come earlier to the pleasant, green countryside with its patchwork fields, secret lanes, and sea cliffs.

They drove to Polperro market on the first Wednesday of the month, riding once more on Godolphin's cart. Kathy needed new shoes, and Charlotte's housewifely instincts were honed to a sharp pleasure at the prospect of wandering among the market stalls of the old town to choose what she wanted of fish, meat and vegetables. She gripped the handles of a strong woven bag with one hand, and held onto the side of the cart with the other as they jounced along to the rhythm of Foxy's trotting hooves.

Kitty had generously insisted on paying a lump sum of money into a bank in Polperro. It was difficult to see how they could have managed otherwise. Rowan had forfeited his right to a government pension by his refusal to go into an Army sanitorium, and Charlotte had not two pennies to rub together.

Kitty had reminded Rowan, when he protested that he

could not possibly accept her money, that this was a matter of family pride. "Kathy is a growing child," she said, in her most imperious grande dame manner, "I want her to have whatever she needs by way of good food and clothing. Surely to goodness, Rowan, you would not deny an old woman the pleasure of providing a few necessities for her own flesh and blood?"

What an infinitely wise and sensitive old lady she was, Charlotte thought, to have made their child the object of her generosity. Her speech and manner had cut the ground from under Rowan's feet. He had felt obliged to accept, for Kathy's sake, what he must have refused for his own.

The market stalls were clustered, against a backdrop of splintering waves, near the curve of the harbor's sheltering arms.

On sale were fishermen's ganzies, remnants of materials, leather goods, garish hand-thrown pottery; glowing mounds of fruit and vegetables; gleaming fish, fresh from the docks; butter and cheeses brought in from the outlying farms.

The stalls wore brightly-colored striped awnings. The folk who rented them were jealous of their own territory; the bakers of homemade bread and pastries and hot mutton pies kept a distance between their stall and the butcher's with its trays of trotters, pease pudding, tripe and chitterlings. Rivalry ran high as the stall-holders shouted their wares.

The sight of the butcher's stall made Charlotte feel queasy. She had long ago decided not to eat meat—a resolution made in Scarborough, before the war, when the butcher's son at the shop round the corner had brutally chopped the paws off a rabbit and thrown one of them across the counter to her—"for luck."

Even so, she could not inflict her own vegetarianism on others, and she approached the stall bravely to buy some mutton for the stew she had planned for Rowan's supper.

It was then she noticed the dog, squatting on its

haunches, gazing up at the stall with hungry eyes. It was a sizeable animal, black with floppy ears, but the outline of its protruding ribs and the dustiness of its coat told their own story. The poor brute was obviously starving. There was a pathetic, lost look in its intelligent eyes.

"Dog," Kathy said, pointing to it. The creature moved its tail in acknowledgment.

"Yes, darling." Charlotte bent down to stroke it. "I wonder what his name is."

"Dog," Kathy reiterated.

"Yes, I know he's a dog," Charlotte said patiently, "but he must have a name. I wonder who he belongs to."

"Me!" Kathy sighed, amazed at the stupidity of grown-ups. "He's *my* dog!"

Rowan came up to them at that moment. He had been down to the bank to sign the necessary papers and draw out money, stopping on his way to the harbor at one of the stalls to buy some cheese. Charlotte smiled up at him. "We were just wondering who the dog belongs to," she explained. "The poor thing looks lost."

Undoing the parcel, he threw the dog a scrap of cheese, which it wolfed down in one bite. Frowning, he bought a slice of corned beef from the butcher. "Is that your dog?" he inquired, as he paid for the meat.

"Gawd no, sir," the man said indignantly. "That it ain't! The damned thing's been hanging around ever since I set my stall up. Go on! Get away! Damned mangy cur!"

The dog shambled away, its tail between it legs. Rowan threw the meat after it. When they turned to look, the meat had gone the same way as the cheese. "It probably lives round here somewhere," Rowan said comfortingly to Kathy who had begun to wail at the top of her voice.

"Come on, darling. We're going to buy you some new shoes," Charlotte said, tugging at her recalcitrant daughter's hand.

"Don't want new shoes," Kathy blubbed, "I want Dog!"

82

"I want, never gets," Charlotte said, remembering her mother's favorite saying. But she wasn't Filly, and she understood her daughter's misery all too well. God forbid that she should ever hide behind so trivial a sop to a child's heartbreak. "I'm sorry, love," she said, "but you see, he isn't your dog, or mine. We can't just take him away with us. That would be stealing."

Rowan said firmly, "Anyone capable of maltreating an animal doesn't deserve to own one." He cast an amused, sideways glance at Charlotte as they began to walk slowly up the hill into town.

"What do you think, then?" Charlotte frowned, biting her lip.

"The same as you," he laughed, "that we have an addition to our family."

"Dog!" Kathy cried ecstatically, flinging her arms round its neck, hugging it close to her.

"At least we don't have to worry about finding a name for it," Charlotte laughed, holding Rowan's hand.

As the days went by, she blessed Dog for giving point and purpose to Kathy's life. She had been lost and lonely without a child of her own age to play with, inclined to be tearful and pettish. Now that Dog had come into her life, she was her old, bright, laughing self again. She adored the animal, and the feeling was obviously mutual.

Perhaps she and Rowan had been too preoccupied, these past few weeks, too selfishly wrapped up in their rediscovery of each other to realize that their child was lonely and bored. Kathy had seemed contented enough, racing about in the garden or playing with her toys, while Charlotte got on with the housework, the cleaning and polishing, washing, cooking and ironing, and Rowan tended the range, or gathered up dead leaves for a bonfire. Charlotte blamed herself for ignoring the fact that what seemed new and exciting to them had not necessarily seemed so to a three-year-old.

Kathy had been alone in the garden, playing with her

83

humming top, when she and Rowan decided to explore the attic.

She had expected to find there the usual homogeneous collection of bric-a-brac, discarded furniture, packing cases, and broken ornaments common to most attics, but it was not like that at all. The room had been lived in. Used, perhaps, as a hideaway.

The dormer windows, looking out over the sea, were curtained with a light chintzy material, beneath which was drawn up a velvet chaise longue. It seemed that someone had been in the habit of lying there to watch the ships out at sea—if the binoculars on a low table beside the couch were anything to go by. The table also contained a pile of books, a worn tobacco-pouch, and a curved pipe with an amber bowl.

The floorboards had been scrubbed and waxed and covered with a medley of faded Persian rugs. Deep armchairs were drawn up beside the narrow iron fireplace. Above the mantel hung a picture which Rowan instantly recognized as belonging to Kitty Tanquillan—a scene depicting a shadowy road with the interlaced branches of leafless trees against a pale wash of moonlight—a picture which drew a deep sigh of pleasure from Charlotte as she looked at it.

"It's beautiful," she said, "I wonder who painted it."

"It's by John Atkinson Grimshaw," Rowan said reflectively. "It used to hang in Kitty's bedroom at Grey Wethers. I wondered what had become of it."

"Why do you suppose she brought it here?"

"To please a special guest?" Rowan suggested.

"You mean—Gilbert Stapleford?"

"It seems more than likely," Rowan said with some amusement, "unless my great-aunt has also taken to smoking a pipe."

"Oh yes, of course." Charlotte knew then that she had been wrong about the front room. It was here that Kitty and Gilbert had spent their last idyllic days together. She glanced at the brass double-railed bed with its multicolored patchwork quilt, and the table beside it, stacked with more books, cheek by jowl with a brass-chimneyed oil lamp.

Crossing the room, she picked up one of the books. "It's poetry," she said delightedly. "Elizabeth Barrett Browning."

"Aunt Kitty's favorite!" Rowan stood close beside her to read. " 'How I do love thee? Let me count the ways,' " he murmured, shaken suddenly by the hot tide of passion welling up inside him, the realization of how little time he had left in which to express his deep physical need of Charlotte.

He had worried, at first, that he might fail when it came to their physical union, and perhaps he had failed, inasmuch as he had never felt entirely at ease with her in the room, adjoining Kathy's. Nor, he guessed, had Charlotte felt at ease with him there, never totally relaxed as lovers should be when they made love.

Now, as he bent his head to kiss her, and felt the softness of her lips on his, the thudding of her heart against his chest, he swung her up in his arms and laid her gently on the bed, engulfed with the all-consuming tide of love he had felt for her that night in a London hotel room the night Kathy was conceived, before his battalion sailed for France.

And this, Charlotte thought dreamily, as she lay there, her head thrown back, hair streaming loose from its imprisoning hairpins, feeling Rowan's warm, gentle hands caressing her body, was what she had waited and hoped for, the moment when they would relive their first, passionate mating, when she would experience the utter joy and peace she had known then.

When their loving was over, and they lay together, warm and secure in each other's arms, Rowan said softly, urgently, "Let us sleep together here, occasionally. Would you mind very much, my darling?" knowing they could hear Kathy if she called to them.

"No, of course not." She knew what he meant. It seemed that here, in this attic room with its air of faded comfort and serenity, the words of love spoken by its former occupants hovered, like bright, warm ghosts in the very air surrounding them; as if here death held no dominion over happiness; that if only they could stay here, locked in each other's arms, they could shut out the rest of the world forever.

That evening, Rowan walked alone on the beach, before supper. The tide was on the turn, the sky, westward, tinged with the brilliant fading glory of a March sunset. The sea, holding the crystalline light of the fast-dying day, swam mysteriously before him, dappled with a myriad rapidly dissolving colors.

He stopped at the breakwater to look up at the sky, swamped with a searing despair, knowing that he must try to come to terms with his imminent departure from the world he had known and loved.

He was no coward, but never to hold Charlotte in his arms again, never to watch his Kathy grow to womanhood. He buried his face in his hands, remembering all the times he had chanted, unthinkingly, the words of the 23rd Psalm: "Yea, though I walk through the valley of the shadow of death, I will fear no evil, for Thou art with me. Thy rod and Thy staff they comfort me."

There seemed to be nothing left in the world to cling to now except memories: the sweet simplicity of youth when he had felt the stinging winds of winter against his cheek; the creak of the rocking-horse in his childhood nursery. Strange how those memories of early childhood still clung to him. Knowing that his parents did not love him had driven him to seek solace in the feel of the wind, the creak of his rocking-horse, the view of the square, seen from his lonely vantage point; the way the lamplight shone against the dusk of early winter evenings.

How different it had been at Grey Wethers, watching larks rise up, singing, from their nests in summertime meadows. He remembered the happiness he had known then, far away from the cold house in Eaton Square; how he had lain on his back watching great white clouds moving majestically against a checkered sky, knowing that rain would soon come to lance the shivering lake in Sweet Water Meadow with a million crystal spears. He recalled how he had sheltered from the rain in the old summerhouse, listening to the soft pitter-patter of the rain on the roof, his boy's belly churning with excitement.

Now the great warm tide of life was slowly ebbing away from him, and there was nothing he could do to prevent it.

What he most regretted was not having died silencing that enemy machine-gun. He had been prepared to die, then, in the slime and mud of the no-man's-land between the trenches; had known the risk he was taking in crawling steadily forward, wiping away the sweat and rain from his face with the back of his hand as he slithered along the ground like a snake. Inch by inch he had advanced inexorably towards that hill where the German gun raked the open ground with its merciless fire, mowing down his comrades at arms as a reaping machine cuts down a field of wheat.

But to die like this, through rottenness and a pair of diseased lungs, to cause so much pain and suffering to the woman he loved, seemed a travesty of his manhood.

He had paid lip service to religion all his life; had gone to church, every Sunday morning, with his unloving parents; had mouthed all the meaningless prayers. And yet— were they so meaningless, after all? Had there not always been a part of him which clung to the notion of rebirth? Had he ever doubted that winter would turn again to spring, that new generations of larks would rise up singing in the meadow near the old cricket pavilion?

Comforted, he turned homeward, knowing that Charlotte would be there, awaiting his return.

Sir Gervaise and Lady Tanquillan set out early to travel to Wiltshire. Dawn painted a rosy glow over the City of London, touching Wordsworth's "domes, theatres and temples" to an almost fairytale beauty.

But even as she got into the car, Rachel Tanquillan knew that going to Wiltshire to see her husband's Aunt Kitty would prove a complete waste of time. The old woman was mad, in her opinion, even more so than Alice. She must be, to have taken that wretched, mentally deficient girl under her wing, to have willed a valuable estate to her.

Of course, Kitty would never see reason as far as her husband's claim to that estate was concerned. Gervaise was a fool if he thought otherwise. But Rachel shared her husband's desire to find out what their son was up to, and Kitty would know all about that, since Rowan had always gone snivelling to his great-aunt at the first opportunity.

Rowan was back in England, that much they knew, due to Gervaise's propensity for string-pulling. The fact that their son had not taken the trouble, or possessed the common courtesy to get in touch with them, had seemed like a slap in the face to Rachel, and enraged his father. They had believed, quite reasonably, that when the war was over, and Rowan had proved his independence in going off the way he did to join the Army, and had got out of his system what they could only suppose was a strange temporary aberration in leaving the Company, his wife and son, to play at being a soldier, he would return home, chastened by his years of imprisonment, to beg their forgiveness for his incomprehensible behavior.

Rachel had decided that when their son did come to his

senses she would act to the hilt her role of wise, understanding mother, not pausing to consider that it had been
her lack of wisdom and understanding which had influ-
enced Rowan's decision to join the Army in the first place.

She knew how desperately Gervaise wanted Rowan back
in the Company. He also wanted Grey Wethers and the
five hundred acres of rich farmland surrounding it, which
he considered his rightful inheritance.

Gervaise, in one of his dominant moods, was a force to
be reckoned with. His anger and resentment about Rowan,
and Grey Wethers, had finally boiled over, culminating in
this sudden decision of his to confront his Aunt Kitty and
bully her into telling him his son's whereabouts, and
changing her will. Even so, Rachel still believed their
journey would prove fruitless. Kitty Tanquillan was a
force to be reckoned with, too.

"Don't be so damned stubborn, Kitty," Gervaise
muttered, rounding on his aunt with renewed ferocity,
clenching and unclenching his hands on the polished
dining-table. Then, realizing that he was getting nowhere,
he tried another tack. "I'm sorry, Aunt, but you must
understand my feelings in these matters . . ."

Rachel stepped in adroitly. "You mustn't be too hard
on Gervaise," she said, shooting him a warning glance
over the wineglasses, "he is naturally upset, as I am, that
Rowan has not been in touch with us yet." She toyed
restlessly with the pearls at her throat. "Of course we do
not blame Rowan for doing as he saw fit, at the outbreak
of war, but the war is over now." She smiled frostily.
"Doesn't it seem strange to you, Kitty, that he hasn't
bothered to let us know his whereabouts?"

"Not particularly," Kitty said abruptly. "Since neither
of you has ever cared a brass farthing for him; never even
bothered to find out what he wanted from life."

"How could the young fool possibly have known what he wanted from life?" Gervaise put in sullenly.

"Exactly," Kitty said triumphantly, "since you thwarted him at every turn! What about his music?"

"Music? Pah!" Gervaise mopped his forehead with his handkerchief, eased his collar, and glanced longingly at the whisky decanter on the sideboard. "What the hell use is music?"

"You simply *must* tell us where he is," Rachel said persuasively.

"I did not invite you here," Kitty retorted. "Civility compelled me to ask you to stay to lunch, but I refuse to be told what I *must* do at my own table." She cast a withering glance at her nephew. "Oh, for heaven's sake, man, pour yourself a drink if you want to, though you should drink less, in my opinion." The red veins on Gervaise's cheeks were beginning to invade his nostrils, she noticed with a feeling of revulsion. Inevitably, Gervaise had rubbed his aunt the wrong way.

Rachel tried yet again to pour oil on troubled waters. "Rowan was ever wayward," she commented, scornful of her husband's dwindling support and self-possession.

"Perhaps it is time, then, that you considered the reason for his so-called 'waywardness,' " Kitty said coolly, leaning back in her chair, "the reasons why he has failed to get in touch with you. Will you never learn that human beings cannot be manipulated like the pieces on a chessboard? Have you ever stopped to consider how much he resented being forced to marry a girl he was not in love with? Are you really surprised that his marriage did not work out the way you intended? What a fine pair of fools you are, to be sure!"

Rachel rose hurriedly to her feet. "We are leaving now," she said icily. "We shall not stay here to be insulted. Come, Gervaise."

But Kitty had not finished with them yet. "Sit down,"

90

she said. "Hear me out! At least allow me the courtesy of rising first from my own table."

Rachel sank down again in her chair.

"Do you imagine I don't know what you are up to?" Kitty flung at them contemptuously. "You would stop at nothing to force Rowan back into the Company. Yes, even emotional blackmail. You've tried it before. No doubt you'll try it again! Isn't it true, Gervaise, that you own the mortgage on Emily Beresford's house in Eaton Square? The woman was a fool to allow you to handle her affairs! But then, I suppose she trusted you, since her daughter had married your son . . ."

"I don't know what you mean," Gervaise muttered sullenly.

"Come on, don't play the innocent with me!" Kitty tapped the table with her fingertips. "You know damned well that you would not hesitate to threaten Emily with bankruptcy, if you believed for one moment that that would give you the necessary leverage to force Rowan to toe the Company line, to go back to his wife and child. Well, it won't do!"

Kitty trembled slightly, her flow of adrenalin halted by a sudden weariness. "You've always been a greedy man, Gervaise," she said, "but you can rest assured that you will never have Grey Wethers, and you will never have Rowan, either." Her voice shook with emotion. "He has found happiness now with the woman he loves. That is all I intend telling you." She got up slowly from her chair. "You may leave now," she said dully.

Chapter Seven

As the days lengthened, they spent more time outdoors together. Rowan had decided to cut back the brambles which lay heavily against the fence from the lane side; to clear the steps to the beach of their overhanging tentacles.

Kathy loved the garden, the beach, the narrow Cornish lanes, their weekly visits to Polperro, above all, Dog. But she was possessed of a child's natural curiosity about the farmhouse across the fields, whose chimneys could be clearly seen from her bedroom window.

Whenever young Johnny Cilgerran called for the milk money, which was usually on Saturday morning, Kathy was sure to be there, hanging about in the kitchen, lolling against the table, one leg crossed behind the other, watching the transaction, staring owlishly at the lad who would blush to the roots of his hair and scoot off up the lane as quickly as possible after mumbling his thanks for the threepence extra Charlotte gave him to buy himself some sweets.

One day, "Why can't we go to the farm to pay the milk money?" Kathy asked wistfully, swinging on the gate as she spoke.

"Why not, indeed?" Rowan cast a quizzical look at Charlotte, who was busily raking up the brambles for a bonfire. "What do you think, darling?"

She leaned on the rake, and pushed back the hair from

92

her forehead. Her thoughts had been miles away. "What did you say? I'm sorry, I wasn't listening."

"Kathy wants to visit the farm." It occurred to Rowan that they had, perhaps, kept too much to themselves, that it might be as well to make friends of the neighbors. Time was slipping away.

"Oh yes," she said, "they must think it rather odd that we haven't introduced ourselves yet."

"Fine, then. We'll call there this afternoon, and pay our milk money at the same time," Rowan promised the delighted Kathy.

They walked up the lane and took a path to the right through the farm gate.

"We had better put Dog on his lead," Rowan said. "We don't want him frightening the life out of the cows."

Kathy giggled. Charlotte picked up her skirts; the field path was muddy after a shower of rain.

The air smelt sweet and fresh. The sky was a pale, watercolor blue, dotted with pure white clouds; the farmhouse stood solidly, a long, low building of natural Cornish stone, weathered by centuries of storms and salt winds blowing in from the sea. A cluster of leaning pine trees bore silent testimony to the strength of those storms.

The farm was set out in the usual chunky pattern of house, barns, cow sheds and outbuildings grouped round a straw-littered cobbled yard, with a scattering of scratching, flapping hens, and the pink snouts of grunting pigs thrust through the bars of their sty.

As they approached, they sniffed in the richly blended odors of damp earth, manure, straw, swill and mire, which reminded Rowan of the farmyard and stables at Grey Wethers. Memories arose of holidays spent there in his childhood when, clad in thick rubber boots and disreputable trousers, he had lingered happily round the stackyard and sheep-pens, leading the soft-muzzled Shire horses to the drinking trough, inhaling the thrilling scents of hide and harnesses.

A line of washing flapped madly in the farmhouse garden. Suddenly an elderly woman enveloped in a flowered pinafore emerged from the back door, wiping her chapped hands down her ample thighs to dry them, obviously in a flurry at the arrival of unexpected visitors. A child of about Kathy's age hung back in her shadow, a girl with brown hair tied with scarlet ribbons, wearing a brown smock and black laced-up boots. She stared at Kathy, trailing a battered doll by one of its legs as she did so.

"Well," the woman said, "you'll have to excuse my appearance, this being washday. You'll be from Mrs. Tregaran's, I suppose? Name of Tanquillan? Godolphin told me about you, and Johnny, of course. He's my grandson who brings the milk. He's nine, going on ten, my eldest son's boy. That one's three, going on four. Helen, come and say, 'how do you do' to the lady and gentleman." A pause for breath. "You'll have to excuse her, she ain't used to strangers. I'm Adeline Cilgerran." Her round, apple face puckered in a smile, a mixture of consternation and pleasure. "Well, come in, do, though you'll have to excuse the state of things, what with the washing, and Hannah, she's my daughter-in-law, busy doing a bit of baking."

She had taken in the quality of the folk she was speaking to at a glance. The young man looked poorly, she thought, but she knew a gentleman when she saw one. It had to do with the way they wore their clothes, no matter how shabby; the way the squire wore his when he was busy about his land, or the parson, when he came to call. Funny how gentlemen always dressed down, and common folk dressed up.

His wife had the bearing of a lady, too, with her head set so proudly on her shoulders. Adeline Cilgerran thought what a lovely face she had, and the little girl was the spit and image of her mother.

94

They followed the farmer's wife indoors. The air was spiced with the scent of freshly-baked bread and teacakes. A sharp-featured young woman with brown hair tucked under a blue cap and wearing a voluminous pinafore, her arms nearly up to the elbows in flour, reminded Charlotte of her mother in the kitchen of the old house in St. Martin's Square, when she and Maggie were children. That kitchen had smelt exactly the same on baking days.

This kitchen reminded her, too, of the farm kitchen at Grey Wethers, when she was married to Will Oakleigh. It had been the center and hub of the house, with its stone-flagged floor and deep window recesses; a litter of wellington boots in the corner; sides of bacon hanging from hooks driven into the beams; the wide fireplace with its generous sideovens; the square, scoured central table littered with baskets of eggs, pots of jam, and stone jars containing salt and sugar, with pollen drifting from hazel branches stuck carelessly in a jam jar.

"This is my son's wife, Hannah. Helen and Johnny's mother," said the farmer's wife by way of introduction. "Hannah, these are the folk who've come to stay at Mrs. Tregaran's for a spell."

Hannah gave them a brief nod, and went on with her kneading. A mongrel bitch rose from its place near the fire and approached Dog, who was straining at his lead, furiously wagging his tail.

"I'm sorry, Mrs. Cilgerran," Rowan said, "I'd better tie our dog up outside. I should have known better than to bring him indoors in the first place."

"Bless you," Adeline laughed, "that don't matter. We've more dogs here than we can shake a stick at. One more won't matter. Sit you down and take a cup of tea with us." She cleared a space at the table. "Hannah! Are those tea-cakes ready yet? I'll just get the cups and saucers; the kettle's always on the boil here. Well, this is a sweet little girl of yours. What's your name, my dearie?"

95

"Shelley Katherine Oakleigh," Kathy replied, with careless, innocent candor.

"We call her Kathy," Rowan said easily.

It was bound to happen, sooner or later; an innocent remark to set people wondering and gossiping. Perhaps they had made a mistake in coming here, in making contact with people who had lived, generation after generation, in one place, uneasy with strangers. But Rowan had suffered the mental shackles of imprisonment long enough. Strange how impending death made a mockery of all else.

He said, "Kathy is our child. We are very proud of her."

Adeline Cilgerran's face puckered suddenly with understanding. "There's those that mind other people's business, and those who mind their own," she said, as little Helen sidled up to Kathy to show her the doll. "Seems to me that the young ones have more sense than the rest of us put together at times. They've been sizing each other up while we grown-ups have been talking fiddle-faddle."

She looked Charlotte straight in the face. "You must bring your little girl over here to play with Helen any time you've a mind to, Mrs. Tanquillan. It will be a pleasure to see you. Now, what about that tea?"

"Thank you, Mrs. Cilgerran." Charlotte stretched out her hand impulsively, blinded with tears of gratitude.

"Ah well," Adeline murmured, "living close to the land, as we do, teaches far better than all the books in those newfangled libraries."

She smiled awkwardly, taking Charlotte's trembling hand in her own knobby, workworn fingers. "It don't take books to make me know a real lady when I meet one, nor a real gentleman neither."

Human beings never ceased to amaze Rowan, their innate kindness or deceit, their basic natures which prompted them to act as angels or devils.

Gratitude for Adeline Cilgerran and her kind welled up in him as he, Charlotte, Kathy, and Dog walked slowly back to the cottage. Of one thing he was very sure, that he would bless this day on which his child had found a friend in little Helen Cilgerran, a home from home in the gray farmhouse across the fields.

At Kathy's insistent pleading, they took a different path from the way they had come. Dog, released from the bondage of his lead, raced ahead of them down a cutting leading to the cliff top.

A little way along the deeply rutted lane, behind a barrier of interlaced alder and pussy willow, they came upon an open space; grass, thickly strewn with clumps of dying snowdrops and monkshood, just as thickly strewn with budding primroses. There, the last vestiges of winter seemed dispelled by new growth, the soft bloom of pollen dusted catkins in the hedgerows.

In the center of the clearing lay a small lake of pure, shining water.

Suddenly, "Look, darling," Charlotte whispered, gripping Rowan's arm. "Swans!"

They stood stock still, holding Kathy and Dog in check as the two creatures swam majestically into the middle of the lake, their proud heads and curving necks reflected in the wind-rippled water.

"Oh, aren't they simply—glorious?" Charlotte rested her head against Rowan's shoulder as the cob and its mate glided along to the little island of twigs where they were building their nest.

"Swans remain faithful partners all their lives," Rowan said softly, "did you know that?"

"No."

"It's true. That lovely intertwining of their necks is their mating ritual."

Closing his eyes, he prayed that he would still be alive to see the fluffy cygnets swimming on the lake. But his breath was becoming more and more labored as time went by. Even now, beads of perspiration were standing out on his forehead despite the cool breeze blowing in from the sea.

Charlotte worried a great deal about Rowan's son. Time was slipping past so quickly. There was so much to say, so little time to say it. She watched, despairingly, day by day, Rowan's attempts to breathe naturally. So, minute by minute grew her love and admiration for him; for that proud spirit which would not admit defeat.

When she suggested that he should see a doctor, he would not hear of it. "I'm feeling much better, much stronger," he said, and she had to admit that he looked better. Freedom, comparative peace of mind, fresh sea air, and good food, had at least taken away the haunted look about him. And yet she was not easy in her mind. She had to know the truth about Berry, how he really felt about the child he might never see again.

Her chance came one evening when they had put Kathy to bed. When the little girl was asleep, clutching her doll, Charlotte said wistfully, "Rowan, do you ever regret leaving your son?"

The room was very still, very quiet, dark save for the night light winking in its saucer of water beside Kathy's bed.

Rowan's hand tightened on her shoulder. "In one sense, of course I do," he said in a low voice. "What kind of man would I be if I did not?"

"Darling, I'm sorry, I didn't mean to pry . . ." Charlotte ran her fingers through her hair, resting the palms of her hands against her aching forehead. Motherhood had brought her an acute realization of the unbreakable bonds between parents and their children. "It's just that . . ."

"No need to explain. I understand." He held her in a tight embrace. "All I can say is, I reached a decision about—my son—a long time ago. The choice was mine to make. I chose you. Berry is better off with his mother."

She stared up at him. "But you must have some regrets . . ."

"Not about Romilly," he said. "Not about my wife. The only person I really regret losing is Emily Beresford, Romilly's mother."

He paused, thinking of the tall, dark-haired, compassionate woman. At times, he had felt a strange, almost physical desire to hold her in his arms.

"Were you in love with her?" Charlotte asked, making a wild, unfounded guess.

"No, not 'in love with.' I simply loved her," he said. "There is a difference . . ."

"But she was in love with you?"

Rowan shook his head bemusedly. "Nothing is ever as cut and dried as all that, my darling. I know Emily cared a great deal for me, that I cared a great deal for her. It does sometimes happen, I suppose, that inexplicable rapport between two people of different ages, different generations."

In the years to come, Charlotte would remember those words with a blinding realization of their truth.

One bright April morning, they took a picnic lunch to the cliff top. Kathy had gone to the farmhouse across the field to spend the day with the Cilgerrans.

Rowan lay on his back in the sunshine, looking up at the sky, breathing in the essence of the day, the scent of earth and grass, the ripening thickets of gorse soon to break out in great clusters of golden blossom.

Here, in the warm climate of Cornwall, nature seemed aglow with the promise of a lilac, gold, and clover-colored springtime.

He felt that, if he could simply lie there, not moving, Death, the old Artificer, might pass him by, unnoticed.

If only he might live long enough to see the gorse in bloom; feel the full strength of the summer sun on his body.

How curious, he thought, that although his limbs were gradually growing weaker, his breathing more labored, his brain had never felt more alive. Nor had he ever been more in love, not just with Charlotte, but life itself.

Life had never seemed so good to him before, so worth the living. It seemed that, in the face of death, the loveliness of each passing moment was branded firmly on his heart. He supposed that men, with time to spare, with endless years before them, never thinking of death, let time slip away from them, uncaring.

Now, he drank in the beauty of the world, the great expanse of blue water beyond the rough, tall grass at the cliff edge. Sitting up, he noticed the way the sea foamed in on the rocks below, bursting in clouds of spray which caught the brilliance of the sun in their wild, convoluted dance of freedom, sparkling like showers of diamonds in the clean, fresh air.

He wanted to stand strong on his feet then, to confront God, to shout aloud to the winds of heaven, "If You are the Creator of life, the giver of life, give me *my* life!"

"What are you thinking?" Charlotte was kneeling beside him, her hands full of wild grasses, the curious, brown-tipped blades she thought of as bows and arrows, and the delicate kind which reminded her of Quaker ladies at a prayer meeting.

Rowan turned on his elbow. "I was questioning God. Strange, isn't it, questioning a Being I scarcely believe in?"

"I've often questioned Him myself," Charlotte said. "I've done worse than that. I cursed Him the day Annie's baby was born." She paused. "For what it's worth, one must feel pretty certain that there is a Being, somewhere, to curse or question, or why bother?"

"Yes, of course. I hadn't thought of that." Rowan clasped her hands tightly in his.

"Now you've made me drop my grasses."

"So I have. I'm sorry." He began weaving a small circle from a Quaker lady. "Do you really believe in God, Charlotte?"

"You've asked me that question before. The answer is still the same, sometimes yes, sometimes no. But I believed in Him very strongly when Kathy was born." She stared out to sea. "When I heard that you were missing, believed dead, I stopped fighting. I lay there, in the labor ward, thinking of Scarborough, imagining that I was drifting out to sea.

"Bridie told me afterward that she had prayed for a miracle to happen. A miracle *did* happen. Harry and Jenny appeared out of the blue. When the nurse told me, I knew I was not alone after all. That's when I started fighting, for your sake, and Kathy's."

Watching Rowan fashioning the circle of grass, she continued, "That should have taught me a lesson. It didn't. There's so much in life I feel incapable of accepting without question, but there's nothing to be done about it. I believe the pattern of our lives is woven at our birth."

"I had no idea that you were a fatalist," Rowan said.

"Neither had I until this minute. But then, I had no idea that I sympathized with the suffragettes until Jenny dragged me into the thick of that demonstration in Trafalgar Square. Suddenly, there I was, waving a placard. The trouble with me is, I'm not clever enough to reason things out. I act on impulse. Perhaps that's the only way to live, doing what seems right at the time; worrying about it afterward."

Taking her hand, Rowan slipped onto her finger the tiny circle of grass he had woven. "With this ring, I thee wed," he said solemnly. "I wish we could have been married, in church, my darling, with you in a white dress, and the congregation singing 'O Perfect Love.' " He kissed her finger where the ring of plaited grass rested.

"But we had Westminster Abbey, and Bach's Toccata and Fugue in D Minor," she whispered. "Remember? You bought me a bunch of roses from a flower-seller's barrow for my wedding bouquet?"

She lay quietly against his fast-beating heart. Suddenly, a low cry of delight escaped her lips. "Look, darling," she murmured.

"What is it, sweetheart?"

"Just under the bank there, hidden away from the wind. The first violets!"

She gazed at them joyfully. Sitting up, she touched the tiny, fragile things gently with her fingertips.

Chapter Eight

Rowan lay on the chaise longue, looking up at the stars.

Unable to sleep, he had grown weary of bed. Getting up, he drew back the curtains, intending to read for a while, but the night, so still and beautiful, drew him to the quiet contemplation of the intricate yet ordered patterns of the stars burning in the dark vault of the sky; Orion's belt, the Pleiades, the solitary shining jewel of the great North Star, eclipsing all the rest.

When he was a boy, he had longed each year for the first day of his visit to Grey Wethers, keeping the agony of waiting a closely guarded secret. Whom, after all, could he have confided in? Certainly not his parents who considered his annual vacations with his Aunt Kitty a bad influence upon an impressionable youngster. He suspected in later years, that they had given their grudging consent to his visits for reasons of diplomacy. And so he had held his excitement achingly to himself, counting the days, the hours, the minutes until at last he was on his way to Paddington station, and safely aboard the huge, green, grunting, steaming monster which would carry him westward—to freedom. But, ah God, the agony of waiting.

He felt the same way now, waiting to die. Not knowing how long the torment would last seemed far worse to him than the actuality of dying. In the trenches he had waited, heart pounding, for the sharp command to go over the top, willing away the slowly crawling minutes, filled with an intense, burning desire to get on with the job in hand, to face what must be faced as quickly as possible.

Scrambling out of the trench, running madly to meet the enemy had seemed less terrible to him than the dragging moments preceding the attack. If only he could run, now, to face his final enemy.

Charlotte was sleeping downstairs. Kathy had been restless since she'd come back from the farm, snuffling with cold, weepy at bedtime. "I think I'd better stay with her," she said. And, "Yes," he'd replied, smiling, glad that she had not discerned his unsettled state, his aching need to be alone for a while.

He had played the piano before coming to bed, Elgar's "Salut d'Amour," the music unleashing a host of unbearably sweet memories of Charlotte as he had first known her, how she had run to him through the early morning mist of a springtime meadow long ago, wearing a green and white cotton dress pintucked to a narrow waist, swinging her broad-brimmed straw hat by its emerald green ribbons, the skirt of her dress dusted with buttercup pollen, her hair a burning flame about her face.

He had known then that he should have refused to succumb to his mother's emotional blackmail. He seemed, now, to stand a little apart from himself, wishing he had done certain things differently: that he had found the courage to break with his family long before he did; refused to marry Romilly; told his mother to go to hell. Too late now.

He ran his fingers distractedly through his hair. How quiet everything was. He could hear the soft wash of the tide on the shore. The sea would be wide and full and deep, now, beneath the velvet-dark arch of the sky. He thought, with a sense of blessed release, of the feel of cold, cleansing water upon his skin, the supreme glory of going out to meet the enemy on his own terms; swimming out towards the horizon until his arms were weary, until the water enfolded him in a final caress.

It had been a perfect day in the sense that he had never seemed closer to any living being than he had to Charlotte, there on the cliff top. What more could they give to each other that had not already been given in full measure?

Two people who had touched, however briefly, the pinnacle of love and understanding?

Nothing, not Romilly, his son, nor his social background, not even conscience could override the deep abiding love he felt for Charlotte, the power of which had enriched his life. Whenever he was with her he experienced a tremendous sense of release, of fulfillment. He had found in her arms the man he had wished himself to be, untrammelled by wealth, free to express his hopes and dreams as an ordinary man, not the privileged son of unloving parents.

Charlotte's courage had been his lodestar: the courage of a tender young woman who had dared to flout convention for his sake, to go against those hammered-home precepts of right and wrong to which most girls of her age and upbringing were inured, who had once come through a hail of bursting shells to be with him.

He knew now that to take the coward's way out was unthinkable. There must be no weakening, no shame. The future would be hard enough for her to face without that.

Suddenly he heard a movement: footsteps on the stairs. She entered the room quietly, in white, hair loose about her shoulders, a glimmering apparition in the darkness.

"I sensed that you were awake . . ."

He held out his arms to her. She sat down beside him, cradling her head against his shoulder. Finding her mouth with his lips, he stroked back her long, bright hair, seeing by starlight the pale, upturned oval of her face, feeling the swift beating of her heart against his, the slight trembling of her body beneath the white nightdress.

Overwhelmed with desire for her, he felt the sudden, urgent hardening of his flesh, and knew that this loving would be like no other they had experienced together. It would be more than physical union: an act of unsurpassing tenderness as well as passion, born of their desperate need, filled with the spiritual grace and joy of their love for each other.

When the final moment came, Rowan heard the gentle sobbing of her indrawn breath and felt a warm tide of peace flooding through him, engulfing him, spreading through him like sweet September wine. The wine, longest stored, which had the most flavor.

"Charlotte," he said, when he had covered her gently with her shawl, "I want you to promise me, when—when the time comes, that you will go back to your own people; to Annie and Joe, who love you and will take care of you. Promise me that you will make a new life for yourself and Kathy."

He held her close to his heart, knowing that she was silently weeping. "No, you mustn't cry," he said tenderly. "Whatever happens now, we have known the best that life has to offer." He smiled, remembering Kitty Tanquillan. "Our 'brief springtime of the heart.' When that springtime is over, I want you, not to forget, but to go on, proudly, with your head held high. One thing more, don't trouble Kathy with—all this. Let her go on being Katherine Oakleigh. She will not remember, in any case. She's far too young. Promise?"

"I *want* her to remember you! I shall always want that!"

"But have you thought that it might not be fair to burden a child with that kind of knowledge? No, far better to leave things as they are. You heard her tell Adeline Cilgerran that her name is Kathy Oakleigh. Let her go on believing that."

They fell asleep, eventually, in each other's arms, and slept until the light of a new day flooded the room.

They went down to the cove that afternoon, she and Rowan hand in hand. Dog and Kathy racing ahead of them.

Kathy had just become the proud owner of a red rubber ball given to her by Adeline Cilgerran, so that she and Helen wouldn't "fall out" as she put it, over whose turn it was when it came to "bouncing."

Adeline's turn of phrase had vastly amused both children, who had promptly started bouncing up and down on the old horsehair sofa in the farmhouse kitchen, making the springs twang alarmingly.

"Kathy! You mustn't do that!" Charlotte had admonished her bouncing offspring. But Adeline had merely laughed. "Eh, there's nothing to hurt here, bless your heart, and children must work off steam somehow."

Later that day, Charlotte had made tentative inquiries about the local doctor.

"You'll be asking about him on account of your husband, I suppose?" Adeline said, sympathetically. "I'm not one to pry, but I could see he wasn't well the moment I set eyes on him."

"The trouble is, he won't see a doctor," Charlotte said quietly.

Adeline screwed up her eyes thoughtfully. "Have you ever noticed that big brass bell on the hall table?" she asked. "Well, if ever you need help, ring it in the garden. You'd be surprised how the sound carries! Lucy Tregaran uses it as a kind of distress signal, the way she did when she hurt her leg last summer."

Today, Charlotte had brought scones and apples to eat on the beach, knowing Kathy's love of picnicking. Rowan held her hand firmly as they negotiated the steps to the cove.

A sharp east wind ruffled the surface of the sea. Foam creamed and splintered about the rocks with their brilliant patchwork of green. Fountains of spray jetted up near the breakwater where Kathy and Dog were playing with the ball.

Charlotte set down the picnic basket on the sand at the base of the cliffs. It was sheltered there, away from the wind. Rowan spread out his limbs in a relaxed attitude and lifted his face to the sun, eyes closed, savoring the peace and the quietude with the woman he loved beside him.

There was no presentiment of danger; nothing to ruffle his calm feeling of happiness and fulfillment.

Kathy had never before ventured beyond the breakwater where the rocks were piled high and jagged, slippery with sea-moss, interspersed with deep pools of bubbling, sucking water. Now, suddenly, they heard the child's shrill scream of anguish.

Charlotte rose instantly to her feet, uttering a sharp cry of terror. Rowan was immediately beside her, running with her towards the figure of the child clinging to the far side of the breakwater.

All they could see clearly was the top of her head, and her fingers holding onto the sloping wooden structure built of piles driven deep into the sand. Its crosspieces were slimed over with moss and encrusted with a jagged mosaic of seashells.

Even as they pounded towards Kathy, they could see that her fingers were slipping. She cried out, "Dadda! Dadda! Mama!"

"Hold on!" Fear lent a hoarse, rasping note to Rowan's voice. That same fear lent a curious strength to his legs as he raced towards the breakwater. With a final burst of speed, he lunged forward to seize the child's wrists, and hauled her to safety.

But Kathy would not be held. Writhing and screaming, face distorted with anguish, she pointed at Dog, struggling in the water, paws threshing helplessly against the strong undertow which was carrying him further and further away from the shore.

"Here, take Kathy," Rowan said briefly, handing her to Charlotte.

She heard the sound of her own voice, shrill with fear. "What are you going to do?" But she knew quite well what he intended. "Rowan! You can't! You *mustn't!*" she screamed.

"Kathy would never forgive me!" He smiled at her briefly, then stripped off his jacket and went into the water.

He waded out until, waist deep, he began to swim. The icy cold current struck him as forcibly as an electric shock, seizing up his muscles with a pain akin to cramp. Lifting his head, he drew in searing gulps of air. His body felt like a worn-out machine, rusty with neglect, and yet he knew he must go on; that he must save Dog for his child's sake. Anything else was unthinkable. He had not stopped to wonder if he could do it. He *had* to do it.

Now he could see the dog's black head above the churning water, but the remorseless grip of the current swirling about his legs seemed intent on sucking him down.

Christ! He had never realized that water could be so implacably icy. An overwhelming loneliness assailed him. He was well out of his depth now; the great weight of the sea pressed in on him, draining him of what little strength he had left.

He had lost sight of the dog momentarily, now he saw it again, heard the threshing of its paws only a few feet away. Swimming blindly, stretching out his hand, he caught hold of its collar.

The poor creature seemed to understand that he was trying to help it. Rowan trod water. There was no time to lose. Somehow he must get back to dry land before the water numbed him completely, before his starved lungs refused to draw in more air.

Gasping, gulping, scarcely able to breathe, he turned on his back, briefly, to rest; floated momentarily, threshing the water with his free arm, clinging to Dog with the other. Staring up at the sky, he thought how remote the clouds seemed, like great ships with the wind in their sails.

Now it was time for the final, supreme effort. He prayed silently for strength enough to battle against the tide. Thrusting self-doubt to the back of his mind, he began, painfully, to swim, keeping tight hold of the dog's collar, swallowing water as he paddled back slowly toward the beach.

Dog, saved from its blind, blundering panic, pointed its nose towards land and swam with him, churning up the water in quick, furious bursts, tongue lolling, uttering curious half growls and whimpers, thrusting its eager body forward towards the child and woman on the shore.

Now Rowan could feel the shells beneath his feet, and began wading, clawing for breath, water streaming from his hair and clothing.

With a low whine, the dog crawled up on the sand, making a half-hearted attempt to shake itself free of water, faintly wagging its tail.

White-faced with shock and horror, Charlotte waded into the sea to help Rowan, while Kathy ran forward to make a fuss of her pet, not understanding what had happened until she saw Dadda lying motionless on the sand and her mother bending over him, weeping, attempting to mop up the bloodstained rivulets of water running down his face with her handkerchief.

Kathy would not remember, in the years to come, the terror which assailed her now, but her life would always be colored by it. In future years, she would wake up suddenly from deeply troubled sleep, to a dreadful sense of loss, of utter loneliness.

Charlotte stared wildly about her, knowing she must get help quickly, that Kathy would impede her progress. It was a dreadful decision to make, leaving her child on the beach with a desperately ill man and a half-drowned dog, but she had no other choice.

"I want you to stay here, Kathy," she said. "Promise not to move! *Promise!*"

The child began to cry, but Charlotte had no time to comfort her. Hampered by her wet skirts, she stumbled frantically up the steps to the cottage, intent on the bell. The bell that would bring help from the farmhouse across the fields.

She rang it until her arms ached. Standing in the garden, she swung the bell until the air around her head was filled with its noisy clamor; rang it until the sky was filled with the noisy cawing of nesting crows, and the sinister flapping of their jet black wings.

Then, racing indoors, she hurried upstairs to tear an armful of blankets from the bed, which she lashed with twine from the kitchen, and kicked down the steps to the beach, with only one thought in mind, to cover Rowan's half-frozen body.

Kneeling beside him, she began warming his hands, massaging his back, pushing instinctively against his ribcage to expel as much seawater as possible; saw, with a terrible fascination, the rush of blood and water from his mouth.

He was icy cold, his face the color of putty. Frenziedly, she tucked the blankets closer about him, and huddled over him, praying; attempting to impart the warmth of her own body to his.

Suddenly, his eyelids flickered open. He smiled drowsily. She felt the touch of his fingers on hers. "Better this way," he murmured. "No regrets . . ."

She kissed his lips, laid her head wearily on his breast, and waited.

Men from the farm carried him up the steps to the cottage, and laid him gently on the parlor sofa.

Adeline Cilgerran was there. Hannah took charge of Kathy and the dog.

Charlotte knew he was dead by the way the farmhands stood, caps doffed, hands dangling uselessly by their sides. Adeline slipped a comforting arm round her waist, not speaking. After all, Charlotte thought, what was there left to say?

111

Looking at Rowan's face in repose, she thought that she had lived through grief before, when Will died, her brother Frank, and Dadda, but nothing would ever hurt so much again as this sudden blotting-out of happiness at a time when she had known the full tide of fulfillment in the arms of the man she loved. And yet she knew what Rowan meant when he said, "Better this way. No regrets."

Rowan had quit the world, not ingloriously, but bravely, as befitted a man of his caliber. He had left it with a fine disregard of his own safety; her eternal squire at arms, her defender, her lover. Her love. The love of her life.

Behind all the heartbreak, she was glad that he would never have to suffer the indignity of that slow death he had so despised.

Remembering all that he had meant to her, she must not fail him now.

Slowly, she moved away from the circle of Adeline's arm, and went upstairs to the room where they had spent their last night together.

Very quietly, she smoothed the cushions where their heads had rested.

Glancing down at the low table beside the couch, she noticed a book, lying open, and picked it up to read.

It was the volume of Elizabeth Barrett Browning poems. Rowan had used a tiny bunch of wild violets as a bookmark.

She read, smiling through her tears,

I love thee with the passion put to use
In my old griefs, and with my childhood's faith.
I love thee with a love I seemed to lose
With my lost saints,—I love thee with the breath,
Smiles, tears, of all my life!—and, if God choose,
I shall but love thee better after death.

Part Two

Chapter Nine

She walked quickly along Queen Street, past the Central Hall where John Wesley had once preached, and turned into Newborough, glancing up at the buildings as she went, noticing the way the October sunlight washed the facades of the tall houses; drawing in deep breaths of cool autumn air to steady her nerves.

Her heels tap-tapped with a steady rhythm on the leaf-swept pavements. Fallen leaves swirled in a scurrying dance at the swish of her skirts.

Signs of the bombardment were still clearly in evidence; that brief holocaust of 1914 when German shells ripped into the town had left behind a legacy of pitted stonework and patched repairs. Charlotte could not rid herself of the notion that the war had left an aftermath of broken pieces to be mended. Her pitying glance fell on a shuffling figure coming toward her, a tray of bootlaces round his neck, obviously one of the thousands of ex-servicemen scraping a living by what seemed tantamount to begging.

As poor as they were, Annie had taken pity on such a man only a few days ago, a young fellow down on his luck selling matches from door to door, his face pinched with cold and hunger. Before long he had been sitting in the kitchen drinking scalding broth, telling them the story of his misfortunes without a trace of self-pity, in a quietly cultured voice. His story was a familiar one. With no trade at his fingertips, his studies interrupted by the war, he preferred to sell matches rather than admit to being unemployed or turn to petty crime as a means of livelihood as so many others had done.

Annie had sent him on his way with a parcel of bread and cheese and a jacket of Joe's. When the man demurred, Annie said, "Take it, and welcome. My husband has a fire to keep him warm."

"He has much more than that, ma'am, if you ask me!" the man said, and Charlotte had caught the glint of tears in his eyes.

As she turned the corner into St. Nicholas Street, Charlotte thought of the days when she and Maggie had worked at Mrs. Hollister's fashion emporium as seamstresses, sitting over their sewing machines in the cobwebby workroom above the salon.

Maggie had left there in the April before the war broke out, to marry Bob Masters. Charlotte had left a few weeks later to become Alice Tanquillan's companion.

Mrs. Hollister's business had been in poor shape even then. The wonder was that it had survived the war years and the bombardment, for St. Nicholas Street had been well in the line of the German guns. The Royal Hotel, close by, had been holed, the beams, laths, plaster and costly furnishings spilling from the wreckage like entrails from an open wound.

Charlotte had wasted no time in reaching a decision once the idea had entered her head. It had seemed an opportunity too good to miss when Annie had read aloud from the evening paper that Agnes Hollister's business was about to go into liquidation.

"It does seem a shame," Annie sighed. "Poor Mrs. Hollister! She dreaded going bankrupt. Now it has happened, I wonder what she'll do?" Then, frowning slightly as she caught sight of Charlotte's face, flushed with excitement, she laid down the paper. "Why, what's the matter?"

"I just thought . . . Wouldn't it be wonderful if . . . ?"

116

Charlotte clasped her hands together to keep them from trembling. The idea seemed so right, so feasible, almost inspirational. She'd clenched her knuckles to her lips and stared past Annie, her imagination working overtime.

"I wish you'd tell me what's going on in that head of yours," Annie said mildly, surprised and amused at Charlotte's comical expression.

"It has just occurred to me. You know how busy I am at the moment, how hard up for space . . . ?"

Annie knew well enough. Since Charlotte's return from Cornwall, the small front room had proved inadequate to cope with the rush of customers wanting new clothes. Every chair, table, and even the floor, was snowed under with materials, patterns, clippings, pins and thread, and the trestle table on which Charlotte did the cutting-out effectively blocked the entrance so that there was scarcely room for the customers to edge past it to be fitted. The dummy had to be waltzed from pillar to post to make room for them, and the curtains drawn to obscure from the street the sight of ladies standing in their underwear.

"You mean that you . . . ?" Annie said breathlessly, catching Charlotte's excitement.

"Yes. Why not? I have more work than I can cope with, Mrs. Hollister needs help. So do I. Perhaps we could come to some arrangement. What do you think? What do *you* think, Joey?" Charlotte had looked anxiously across the table at her brother.

"It's a fine idea," Annie laughed. "Isn't it, Joe?"

"Yes." Joe nodded enthusiastically, glad that Charlotte and Kathy were home again where they belonged. The house had seemed empty without them. Now he felt much stronger, more alive, part of life again. Although he still had trouble with his speech and was incapable of stringing long sentences together, his mind was much clearer, and his limbs shook less often than they used to. The other day he had managed to walk as far as the end of the street, with Annie's help.

117

"I'll go and see her, first thing in the morning then," Charlotte had said decisively.

Now she could see that the lace curtains of the salon hung listlessly from brass rods sadly in need of polish. The windows were filmed over with dust and caked salt, and the side door leading to the workrooms and Mrs. Hollister's private apartment was firmly closed.

If she stopped to think, she might lose her nerve. And so she rang the bell, and waited. Glancing up, she caught the movement of a curtain at an upstairs window.

She could hear shuffling footsteps behind the closed door. When it opened, after much fumbling with locks and chains, she could scarcely prevent a cry of horror escaping her lips at Mrs. Hollister's appearance. The once proud and domineering old Jewess, with her pendulous breasts and towering pompadour hairstyle, seemed to have shrunk to half her normal size. Her cheeks were pasty and flabby, hair gray at the parting, her mouth slack. A kind of dull apathy hung about her. "Yes, what is it?" she asked abruptly.

"Don't you know me? It's Charlotte. Charlotte—Grayler."

"Charlotte Grayler?" There was no flicker of recognition in the lacklustre eyes of the old woman.

"I used to work for you before the war. My sister Maggie worked here, too," Charlotte reminded her.

"Oh yes, you left me for Lady Tanquillan." Mrs. Hollister's mouth worked as if she were about to cry. "The best seamstress I ever had." She spoke in a slurred voice, and Charlotte knew she was in that maudlin state of self-pity common to people who drank too much.

The girls she had worked with before the war always said that "Old Aggie" as they called her, kept a bottle hidden away in her private apartment. "You can always tell," one of them said nastily, "by the whiff of her breath

118

when she's giving you a talking to! Old bitch!" But Charlotte, seventeen at the time, had been more interested in romantic poetry than the unpleasant facts of life; she had ignored sly innuendo, and the aimless gossip the others indulged in when they felt mistreated. And most of them had felt mistreated when "Aggie" came rattling downstairs in a temper, or when the stove in the workroom remained unlit on cold winter mornings. Maggie, especially had vowed and declared she couldn't wait to leave to get married.

But, whatever Mrs. Hollister's shortcomings, Charlotte had always respected her ability as a dressmaker. The shop, in its heyday, had boasted a clientele of the town's most fashionable and wealthy women, including Lady Tanquillan. Now, Charlotte felt desperately sorry to see the once proud, independent woman down on her luck.

"Please, may I come in and talk to you?" she said quietly.

"Talk? What is there to talk about?" Agnes hiccupped slightly, fiddled up the sleeve of her dress for a grubby hanky, and blew her nose, discreetly turning the hiccup into a cough.

"May I come indoors for a few minutes?"

"Oh, very well." The old woman turned away wearily, defeated by Charlotte's youth and energy. "We'll go upstairs to my apartment."

Charlotte glanced round, remembering the old days, when she and the other girls had clattered up to the workroom, stamping their feet against the cold wind or rain, complaining in loud voices about the state of the place, the grimy windows and the recalcitrant black stove sulking in the corner. Sometimes they had gossiped about where they had been the night before, what their boyfriends had said to them. Laughing and pulling faces, they had taken the covers off the machines and settled down to earn their living. They had passed sweets along the row, cursing when a thread snapped or a needle broke, falling silent when their employer swept into the room to

119

survey them with an eagle eye, and took them to task for a crooked seam or a badly inset sleeve.

The door of the workroom stood open. If the girls had seen fit to complain then, heaven alone knew what they would think of it now. A fine film of dust covered the machines; a desolate air of finale hung about the place. Cobwebs were draped thicker than ever.

With a fast-beating heart, Charlotte envisioned the workroom as it might be, with all the machines humming merrily again; the shelves in the cutting-out room, which had been Mrs. Hollister's special and personal preserve, filled with bolts of colorful materials; windows shining; stove alight and glowing.

"You'll have to excuse the mess," Mrs. Hollister muttered, pushing open the door of her apartment. "I'm packing up."

Charlotte stood dismayed at the chaos. The sitting-room looked as if a bomb had hit it. Every spare inch of space was filled with a tumbled assortment of clothes, out-of-date fashion magazines, coat-hangers, paper patterns, empty whisky bottles, discarded newspapers, bills, letters and photographs: the sad paraphernalia of a woman who had long since ceased to care for herself or the world she inhabited.

"Go on, take a good look!" Agnes cried despairingly, giving way to tears and hiccups, sinking down in a sagging armchair filled with scraps of torn paper and bursting cushions." "Oh, my God, my God! I'm finished! Done for!"

"No, Mrs. Hollister, you are not! Not yet! Please listen to me! I'd like you to help me, if you will."

"Help *you?*" Agnes stared up blearily. "You want *me* to help *you?* What the hell are you talking about? Take a look at that stack of bills over there on the desk. That's how much I owe! Three hundred pounds!" Her teeth chattered suddenly with cold. "If you look in my purse, you'll see that I have less than five pence!" She covered her face with her hands, sobbing harshly, shoulders heaving.

"Please, Mrs. Hollister. I'm here to help you." Charlotte knelt down beside her. "I have a plan. Oh, it may not work, but it's worth a try."

"Plan? What—plan?" Agnes looked up—her eyelids were swollen and tearstained.

"Do you remember that you once asked me to go into partnership with you?" Charlotte spoke as gently and persuasively as if she were addressing Kathy or Laurie. "Well, that may be possible now. I have more sewing on hand than I know how to cope with and not enough space to do it in."

"You don't understand." Agnes shook her head heavily. "I'm bankrupt. They'll make me move out; take my sewing machines . . ."

"Perhaps not," Charlotte interrupted eagerly, "if we could pay off the creditors at so much a week. I don't know how these things work out, but I daresay the people you owe money to would rather have it paid back in full than turn you out of house and home."

A tinge of color stained Agnes Hollister's flaccid cheeks, a sharp, watchful expression came into her eyes. "There must be a catch in it," she said with the air of one who knew all there was to know about snags in the fabric of life. "Where would I come into this plan of yours?"

"I'd need your help with the sewing," Charlotte replied carefully, remembering the old woman's fierce pride and uncertain temper.

Agnes snorted suddenly. *You'd* need my help!" Her pride had been stung. "Are you suggesting that you would be in charge of *my* business?"

Charlotte squared her shoulders. "Yes. I'd need a free hand in the salon and workroom. There would have to be changes. But I could bring you plenty of customers and I would work hard to make a success of things. It could be a new beginning for both of us."

The old woman regarded her scornfully. "How dare you come here with such a proposition? It's insulting. A woman of my experience relegated to the role of a seamstress! You had better leave now!"

Charlotte rose to her feet. "I'm sorry. I had no intention of insulting you. I simply hoped that we might have something worth saving." She smiled, despite her bitter disappointment. "Well, good-bye Mrs. Hollister."

Her hand was on the doorknob when Agnes heaved herself from the depths of the armchair. "No! Wait!" she cried. "You mean that I could continue to live here?"

"Yes, of course."

Turning back into the room, Charlotte knew that she had won.

"Three hundred pounds!" Annie said incredulously. "You mean to say you've saddled yourself with three hundred pounds worth of debt?"

Her mind reeled at the thought. Three hundred pounds was a small fortune.

"Well, not yet," Charlotte said consolingly, "it rests with the creditors. They may not accept the idea."

Annie sat down heavily on a kitchen chair, half ashamed of hoping that "they" would not agree to the plan. She could scarcely bear the thought of Charlotte taking on so much hard work and worry. And what if she failed to meet those weekly payments? Then, glancing at Charlotte's forlorn face, she realized that what her sister-in-law needed now was help and support, and all the encouragement she could give her.

Lifting her chin, smiling, Annie said, "I could pawn my mother's gold locket again, if that would help!"

"Oh, Annie. Annie darling!" Charlotte skimmed across the room to throw her arms round Annie's frail shoulders.

"And I'll come down with a mop and bucket and clean

the place up for you," Annie said as Charlotte swung her into a waltz.

"You really think I stand a chance, then?" Charlotte asked, misty-eyed with hope.

"Of course you stand a chance. All you have to do is make those creditors see sense. What have you got to lose? More to the point, what have they got to lose? If they clamp down hard on Mrs. Hollister, they haven't the ghost of a chance of recouping their losses. This way, they'll all get paid in time." Eyes shining, Annie said, "Go on, darling, do it! I have such faith in you, Charlotte. But you'll need a name for your shop, something eye-catching and—kind of French, if you know what I mean. What about Madame Fifi?" She laughed delightedly.

"Or Carlotta? Jenny always called me that!"

"That's exactly right!" Enthusiasm was catching. The pair of them sat down together at the kitchen table to make plans. When Joe came into the room, he found his wife and sister kneeling up at the table like a couple of schoolgirls, making notes on the back of a notebook.

"Oh, Joey, come and help," Charlotte said. "Give us the benefit of your expert advice." Joe had passed an accountancy exam before the war, when he worked at the harbormaster's office.

"Don't forget," Annie said, "that you have some money in the china teapot."

"That's for the Club man," Charlotte frowned. "I can't very well put that into the business." She laughed at the absurd idea of putting ten shillings and sixpence into anything. The Club man called on a Monday morning with his cards and clothing checks in a battered suitcase. Everyone in the street paid into the Club. It was one way of getting new shoes and warm underclothing for the children.

"But you have money owing to you for work already done," Joe reminded her, in his halting way.

"Yes, of course I have. I'd forgotten that." Charlotte

squeezed her brother's arm affectionately, thinking how wonderful it was that Joe was able to participate once more in family matters after the terrible years he had spent locked away in the darkness of his mind.

Clenching her hands, she prayed suddenly that she would make a success of this wild, outrageous plan of hers, that she would make those creditors see sense, not for her sake, but Annie's, and Joe's, and the children's.

Maggie's husband came home the same day that Charlotte went, heart in mouth, to meet Mrs. Hollister's creditors. Bob was one of the men referred to in an editorial in the *Daily Mail* complaining that "Demobilization is proceeding with a leisurely step, when it ought to go into a quick march."

"There is a clog in the pipes somewhere," the editorial went on, "the machine must be speeded up." This was accompanied by a series of bitter cartoons depicting soldiers tied to a wharf by "red tape."

Bob had been one of the thousands destined to await the pleasure of His Majesty's Government's decision to speed up the demobilization process; he had spent a year kicking his heels in Dover with the rest of his battalion, awaiting the word to go home.

Not that Bob kidded himself Maggie would be waiting, open-armed, to receive him back into the bosom of his family. He and Maggie had parted coolly as a result of his mother-in-law's presence in the house, and Maggie's dread of getting pregnant again.

He hadn't even told her he was going to join up. Fed up to the teeth with the constant wrangling, he had simply gone out one morning to take the King's shilling, coming in at dinnertime wearing his Green Howard's uniform and clutching his travel warrant.

Maggie had been shocked and horrified then at his perfidy, weeping and wailing at what she called his selfish-

124

ness in leaving her alone with an old woman and a child to look after. But Bob had long become inured to the fact that whatever he did would be wrong in his wife's eyes. His usual simple, placid good nature had been undermined by her outbursts of temper and flat refusal to allow him his conjugal rights. Bitterness had crept in. The only thing he deeply regretted was leaving his daughter, his Peggy, the apple of his eye.

In one sense, he had gone off to war as a protest against the usurpation of his rights as a husband, father and householder. He would have had to go, sooner or later, in any case, he'd reckoned. Choosing to go sooner had at least restored his self-respect.

Now, walking down Garibaldi Street with his kit-bag over his shoulder, he viewed his homecoming with certain misgivings, his mouth set in a grim line of stubborn determination to make his voice heard in his own house this time.

It had been hell, waiting in Dover for the past twelve months. It would be equally hellish going back to the same set of circumstances that had driven him away in the first place. But a returning soldier had rights, he told himself firmly; and if Maggie refused him his conjugal rights tonight, by hell, he'd know the reason why.

He thought of Peggy, and the grim set of his lips relaxed a little. What a song and dance Maggie had made about having the kid. But why did she marry him in the first place if she didn't want his children? Then, when her mother came to live with them, she wouldn't let him touch her in case the old girl heard the creaking of the bedsprings.

"Stop it!" Maggie muttered, every time he tried to make love to her. "Ma'll hear us!"

Well, he wouldn't "stop it" tonight, even if the blinking bed collapsed under them. He'd fought damned hard for his country, now he intended to be master in his own house.

Charlotte's meeting with the creditors took place in the bank manager's office. Mr. Burridge, who had arranged the meeting, hoped that the affair would reach a swift and satisfactory conclusion, having been plagued with his unsatisfactory client, Mrs. Hollister, for more years than he cared to remember. Personally, he considered that the five claimants would be extremely foolish to turn down young Mrs. Oakleigh's offer to pay back the money Agnes Hollister owed them, on a weekly basis, but Robert Wade, the main claimant, who believed a woman's place was in the home, might prove a tough nut to crack.

Burridge silently approved the manner in which Mrs. Oakleigh had dressed for the interview, in a simple gray suit and white blouse, and a black hat with an artificial pink rose perched on the brim. He noticed the impact her youth and beauty had made on the claimants, who rose to their feet as she and Mrs. Hollister came into the office. He also noticed that despite her outwardly calm appearance, the girl's hands trembled slightly on the large black handbag she carried.

The introductions made, Burridge cleared his throat and said a few words relevant to the meeting, touching briefly on Mrs. Hollister's overdraft, which had necessitated calling in her bank loan, and Mrs. Oakleigh's proposal of injecting new life into the business and guaranteeing the payment of the outstanding debts over an agreed period of time.

Robert Wade, Mr. Burridge noted, seemed unimpressed by the offer, and continued to stare at Mrs. Oakleigh with unfriendly eyes. "That's all very well," he said, "but how many orders has Mrs. Oakleigh on hand at the moment, and what has she to offer by way of hard cash to back up her guarantee?"

"Will this do for a start?" Charlotte unfastened her handbag and laid twenty crisp one-pound notes on the desk. "And here is a list of my orders." Thank heaven for Joe, she thought, who had sent polite requests for payment to all the people who owed *her* money. She smiled inwardly. The hard-headed Yorkshire businessmen seated in Mr. Burridge's office would never know what she, Annie and Joe had had to resort to in order to raise the money. Annie's gold locket was back in the pawn shop, even the Club money teapot had been denuded.

Taking advantage of the silence, she went on, "I realize that I may seem very young and inexperienced to you gentlemen, but I'm not afraid of hard work, and I know my trade inside out. I'm turning away work at the moment through lack of space. Think what I could do with a shop in a prime position."

"A somewhat run-down shop, and a very expensive one to maintain," Wade retorted. "Have you considered precisely how much a week you will need to earn to cover the cost of rates and lighting alone, apart from the debts? And what about stock? Material and so forth, which, I imagine, does not grow on trees."

"I make up my clients' own material," Charlotte said. "I don't think you need worry that I am going into this venture blindfolded. My brother has studied accountancy. We have gone into everything very carefully."

But Wade hadn't finished with her yet. "Perhaps you would care to explain why you feel it necessary to take on a bankrupt business," he said. "If all you've told us is true, you'd be better off renting shop elsewhere."

Charlotte flushed at his implication that she was lying. "Mrs. Hollister taught me all I know about dressmaking," she replied coolly. How *dared* he have said what he did? But she had no intention of knuckling down. "She is a mistress of her craft who once had the fashionable women of Scarborough flocking to her salon."

"Oh, very well, Mrs. Oakleigh." Wade waved his hand dismissively. "But I warn you, if you default, I shall not reconsider for one moment putting you out of business. Is that clear?"

"Very clear." She lifted her chin proudly. "Don't worry, Mr. Wade, I shall not default." Wade had taught her a lesson well worth the learning, that to survive in a man's world, women must use their own brains and initiative.

It was up to her now to beat the Robert Wades of this world at their own game. She found, to her surprise, that she relished the challenge.

It was just as Bob had imagined it would be. Maggie's mother had not improved. He had never exactly hit it off with her; had always felt dumb and stupid in her presence. Now, with her under the same roof, the old pressures returned as soon as he set foot across the threshold. And Maggie hadn't exactly given him a hero's welcome either. Had it not been for Peggy, who had snuggled up in his arms and crowed with delight at seeing him again, he might have felt inclined to catch the next train back to Dover.

Surely a man had a right to talk to his wife alone after being away for so long? And any other woman but his mother-in-law would have made some excuse to leave the room. But no! There she sat, as large as life, in her chair by the living-room fire, listening to every word. Not that Maggie had said very much worth listening to. In fact, she had scarcely uttered two sentences together since he had dumped his satchel in the hall.

As he'd anticipated, he had begun to feel lusty at the sight of his wife bustling about the room, setting the table, her plump waist nipped in with her pinafore, her sagging breasts wobbling to the movement of her arms, the outlines of her nipples clearly defined because she wasn't wearing a bra.

Catching Filly's eye, he blushed furiously, knowing by the prim expression on her face that she had read his mind.

128

Suddenly, the smell of burnt sausages assailed his nostrils. As Maggie shrieked, and hurried through to the pantry, Filly said, "Well, I suppose you'll be going round to Cowling's first thing tomorrow morning, to see about getting your old job back."

"Yeah, I suppose so," He spoke laconically, but he was boiling inside. God's truth, he thought angrily, I ain't been home five minutes and already she's yammering on about me getting a job. Well, suppose he didn't want his old job back straight off? "I'd like a bit of a rest first, though," he muttered.

"Rest?" Filly pursed her lips. "I thought you'd have had enough rest to be going on with—doing nothing these past twelve months."

"Doing nothing!" He could have burst with the injustice of it. As if it was his bleeding fault he'd been kicking his heels in Dover! As for being kept busy, the Army saw to that! When they'd finished marching you up hill and down dale till your blinking feet were ready to drop off, they set you to peeling potatoes, and cleaning your kit till your arms were ready to drop off, too.

"Supper's ready!" Maggie shoved the plates on the table. "The sausages are burnt a bit."

She'd never been much of a cook. Bob thought. Even so, burnt offerings on his first night home! And the potatoes were lumpy, with little hard knobs which she hadn't bothered to mash properly. He felt aggrieved, and yet he was still eager, thinking about bedtime, and Maggie letting her hair down.

A starchy, hastily put-together pudding followed the main course. Having eaten that, he felt obliged to unfasten his belt. Rocking back in his chair, he asked what had been happening while he was away. Neither he nor Maggie were much use when it came to letter-writing. His letters home had usually run: "Dear Wife, I hope you are well, as this leaves me at present." Hers to him: "Dear

129

Bob, I thought you said you had sent me some money, but the postal order has not arrived yet . . ."

Maggie and her mother exchanged glances. Bob said the first thing that came into his head, "How's Charlotte?"

"Ha!" Maggie snorted. "No better than she should be! Going off the way she did to live with that fancy bloke of hers!"

"Eh?" Bob asked, mystified. "When? Where?"

"God only knows, and *He* won't tell!" Maggie said scathingly. "Off she went, last November, taking Kathy with her. But she soon came down off her high horse, didn't she Ma?" Maggie nodded with grim satisfaction. "Oh yes, she's back home now, looking like death warmed over! S'pect they had some kind of quarrel, and serves her damn well right!"

"I think I'll have a smoke," he said, unearthing a squashed package of Woodbines. Bob liked Charlotte, had always liked her. He didn't want to listen to anything against her.

"You never used to smoke," Filly said accusingly.

"Well, I do now," Bob snapped, sticking a cigarette between his lips. "There's a lot of things I do now that I never used to do!" The old, sour feelings of not being master in his own home washed over him as he lit up.

"No one in our family has ever smoked," Filly said, coughing.

"Frank did," Bob reminded her, listening to the sloshing of washing-up water in the kitchen, the clatter of pots and pans; wishing his mother-in-law would get herself off to bed. It was coming to something when a man couldn't even enjoy a smoke in peace.

The black marble clock on the mantelpiece inched toward ten before Filly stuffed her knitting into her hold-all, stood up, and said it was no use wasting more coal and gas. "You coming, Maggie?" she asked.

"Yes, Ma," Maggie said reluctantly. She had been dreading this moment all evening; the thought of getting into bed with this man who seemed a stranger to her. God, what if he wanted to make love? Memories of her wedding night flooded back to her: all that awful poking and prying; having to lie flat on her back with her legs open. It wasn't decent in her opinion. It certainly wouldn't be decent with little Peggy in the same room with them, and she'd tell him so if he dared lay a finger on her.

The candle wobbled in her hand as she set it down on the chest of drawers, and Bob closed the door behind them. She watched him nervously as he stripped down to his vest, his lips puckered in a silent whistle.

He took his shoes off next, very quietly, setting them side by side under the bed, on his side, so as not to disturb the sleeping child in her cot.

"Oh, by the way, I've brought you this," he said, rummaging through his satchel which he had brought upstairs with him.

"What is it?" Maggie glanced fearfully at the small package.

"Well, go on, open it. It won't bite you. It's genuine French perfume. I bought it for you in Le Havre."

Maggie unstoppered the bottle. "Ugh! It's too strong!" She made a face. "You know I only like eau de cologne and lavender water!"

"Never mind about that, put some on," Bob said, in a low voice.

"No, I won't! I don't want to!" Maggie stood, trembling, near the chest of drawers. "I know why you want me to wear it, though! You've been eying me up and down all evening! I've never felt so embarrassed in all my life, with Ma watching! But I'm telling you straight, Bob Masters, I don't want any more babies! If you think I'm

putting up with your damned nonsense, you've got another thing coming!"

Bob crossed the room silently on his bare feet. "Oh, is
that so? Well, we'll see about that! I'm your husband, in
case you've forgotten, and I'll damn well prove it!" He
laughed quietly. "And there's no need to worry about the
bedsprings. They do it this way in France!"

Wedging Maggie firmly between the wall and the chest
of drawers, he began, slowly and deliberately, to let down
her hair.

Chapter Ten

She awoke from her nightmare with an icy feeling of terror, the same feeling she had experienced when the nightmare really happened, just after Rowan's death.

Her dream brought back acutely the sense of confusion and unreality she had felt then: not knowing what to do for the best, moving about the cottage like an automaton, hearing soft footsteps retreating as the men who had brought Rowan's body from the beach went silently away to get on with their own lives. And then the doctor had come, and Adeline Cilgerran had told her, very gently, that there would have to be an enquiry into the cause of Rowan's death, and asked her if there was anyone who should be informed of the tragedy, and she had said that she didn't know, because she couldn't think clearly any more.

And later, much later, she had thought that Kitty Tanquillan must be told. But Kitty, who did not believe in new-fangled inventions, did not possess a telephone, and so Adeline had walked all the way to the post office to send her a telegram. And then a telegraph boy had come to the cottage; a mere lad, whistling because he was young and alive on that peerless morning in May. She remembered envying that telegraph boy his carefree acceptance of life.

And then, because Rowan's Aunt Kitty was ill with a chest infection, Thomas Rivers and his sister, Lucy Tregaran, had come to the cottage to be with her, to help her through the dreadful days that lay ahead. And all the time she had wondered if she shouldn't have sent for Rowan's parents and his wife, Romilly.

But no, she had decided. He wouldn't have wanted that.

Then came the question of where Rowan should be buried, and she had spent quite a lot of time with the obsequious undertaker, who appeared to be wearing felt slippers, so quiet were his footsteps.

And she had known, from somewhere at the back of her mind, that Rowan would want to be buried in the graveyard of the little gray stone church near Talland Bay, with the sound of the sea close by, and the cliffs with their great golden thickets of gorse in full bloom, and the swans on the lake.

And then, one day came a thundering knock on the cottage door, and there were Sir Gervaise and Lady Tanquillan, demanding to see their son.

They must have walked down the lane, she thought. Not even their sleek limousine could have nosed its way past the tall, blossoming bushes.

She had stood aside, then, quietly, in her black dress, to admit them, trying to find the words to tell them what had happened, but they would not listen. Gervaise had run true to form, pushing past her, insensitive and blundering, rushing in where angels might fear to tread.

"Well, where is he?"

And, "Please," she had said, "you don't understand. There is something I must tell you."

And, "Get out of my way, you—harlot!" Gervaise said, pushing her roughly aside. "I wish to speak to my son, at once, and alone!"

"I'm afraid that is not possible."

"Not possible? How *dare* you? Where is he? In there?"

"No! *Please* don't go in there! You don't understand! Please listen . . ."

She had watched, in horror, his blundering approach to

the sitting-room door. "No!" she cried out, but he had almost knocked her over with the force of his powerfully built body, his determination to have his own way at any cost.

Flinging open the door, he stormed into the room, closely followed by the slim, rustling figure of his wife with her haughtily held head and cold, seagull eyes.

Rowan's coffin was mounted on trestles. The curtains were drawn. The room was delicately scented with the lilac she had gathered for him that morning.

"*Christ!*" The cry of shocked horror seemed wrenched from the old man. A long drawn-out, bubbling sigh of disbelief escaped from his wife's lips.

"I—I'm so sorry. I did try to warn you." She had closed the door very quietly behind her, leaving them alone with their son.

Everything was quiet in her nightmare. Far too quiet, and in slow motion. People were moving their lips and saying nothing. Lady Tanquillan's face was a white blur, mouthing hatred, screaming at her that she was responsible for her son's death. But no sound came.

It was only when Charlotte awakened from her nightmare that she knew it was true, that it really all happened, just the way she had dreamt it. And then the agony of that day had to be lived through all over again.

Not content to leave their son to be put to rest with quiet dignity in the churchyard near Talland Bay, they had felt it incumbent on themselves to make hasty arrangements for the removal of Rowan's body to London for burial. And nothing she could say or do would prevent them having their own way.

They had treated her as a loose, wanton woman who had wrecked their son's life; had treated her as a pariah, an outcast. Numb with grief, Charlotte had not even attempted to defend herself against their torrent of abuse.

In the early hours of next morning, she had said her final farewell to Rowan, then she had walked, in her black dress, up the lane and across the fields to the Cilgerran house, knowing that her time with Rowan was over and done with, that she had no part to play in what was about to happen. She would not have been able to watch the men from London arrive to remove his coffin from the cottage.

Later that day, she had travelled with Kathy, Rivers and Dog to Grey Wethers; a lonely, distraught woman sadly in need of Kitty's help and comfort, the sharing of grief.

She must have cried out during her nightmare, for suddenly Kathy was awake too, and scrambled out of her own bed, saying she was cold, wanting to get in beside her mother, wriggling like a worm beneath the covers.

In those first moments of wakefulness, with the awfulness of her dream still clear in her mind, Charlotte cuddled up close to the child, and remembered that this was New Year's Day. The year was 1920.

Kathy's feet were like blocks of ice. No wonder. When it was time to get up, Charlotte saw that the water on the washstand was frozen solid, and their breath had frozen into patterns on the windowpanes. She moved quietly about the room, opening drawers, finding her things by the light of a candle, rubbing the window to see what it was like outside. She might have guessed. There had been a heavy snowfall in the night. Kathy would love that. Annie would probably take the children to the Castle Hill, tobogganing, later on. Meanwhile, she had work to do.

Glancing at the mound in the bed, she saw that Kathy was fast asleep, and smiled on her way downstairs to fill the kettle. Thank God her child was happy again. Rowan was right in wanting her to come home to her own people. He had known that life must go on, that children soon forget.

Kathy had missed Rowan terribly at first, had cried heartbrokenly and wanted to know why Dadda could not go with them to Grey Wethers, and she had not known how to explain death to a three-year-old child, nor had she thought it advisable to attempt doing so. She had simply said that Dadda had had to go away for a little while, but he still loved them.

For a long time, it had been all Dadda. "Where has he gone to?" "When is he coming back?" And then they came home to Scarborough, and the child's anguish had gradually been dispelled once she was back with her Aunt Annie, Uncle Joe, and Laurie.

Christmas had proved a blessing, with women flocking to the shop for new clothes. Fashions were changing, skirts were shorter. A decade before they had swept the ground. Now women dared show their ankles for the first time.

Peace had brought with it a general dissatisfaction with making do. Women were restless for change. Now they wore their skirts eight or nine inches above their shoes.

Looking through some of Agnes Hollister's old fashion magazines had proved an eye opener to Charlotte. Living in Cornwall, cut off from the world of fashion, she had neither known nor cared what women were wearing at Ascot last year: lace skirts, broad satin sashes, scooped-out necklines, buckled shoes, romantic organza-brimmed hats crowned with ornamental feathers; furs, foaming lace jabots, velvet ribbons; bandeaux worn at eye-level beneath elaborate hairstyles.

Some of the older women still clung to the mode of dressing favored by Queen Mary, and the Queen Mother, Alexandra, whose long-skirted Edwardian elegance retained close links with the pre-war years. But for every long dress she was called on to make nowadays, Charlotte cut out and sewed three in the new, shorter style, and to every garment she made she added a certain flair and passion for detail, born of her painstaking, perfectionist approach to her work.

* * *

The banks and most of the shops in town would be closed today, but as soon as she had breakfasted and got Kathy ready, she would be off to St. Nicholas Street to cut out and tack the January orders, to sweep and dust the workroom and polish the brass window rods. She was kitted out in a flowered overall, with a scarf pulled down over her distinctive red hair, so that no one passing the shop would equate the skivvy doing the polishing with "Madam Carlotta."

She could not rest easy in her mind until every penny of the money due to the creditors was paid off—particularly the debt owed to the skeptical Mr. Wade.

She felt at times as if she had been cut in half by the sword of Damocles, and the two halves were scurrying around in different directions. The Christmas rush had been gratifying, and uplifting in one sense, but she had never worked so hard in her life. Mrs. Hollister, she quickly realized, was not dependable. Years of worry and heavy drinking had taken their toll, and the old woman was intolerant of instruction from Charlotte, whom she still regarded as her employee.

Charlotte had guessed this might happen, but she could not be too hard on her. Had it not been for Mrs. Hollister, "Carlotta" might still have been making up garments, for a pittance, in Annie's front room. Perhaps she was paying too high a price for the extra space. The other five sewing-machines still remained idle. Her mind seemed shredded with tiredness, and her body ached with the mental and physical effort involved in sewing, cutting, measuring, fitting, pressing; doing the accounts; sweeping, dusting and polishing besides.

Agnes had appointed herself receptionist in the shop with its threadbare plum velvet curtains, tatty gold-painted chairs, and listless potted palms, maintaining her dignified hauteur as owner of the establishment.

"That's all very well," Annie said, "but she's just wasting time, leaving you to do all the scutwork."

"I know," Charlotte sighed, "but that is better than

nothing. I thought she'd help out with the sewing, but . . ." She shrugged helplessly, "I'm afraid that was asking too much." She added generously, "At least she's doing what she's best at, showing the clients into the fitting rooms, keeping them talking until I have time to see to them." She paused guiltily. "The fact is, I don't really want her to do the fittings . . ."

"What you need," Annie said thoughtfully, "is a good assistant. Someone you could rely on to get on with the work while you are busy with other things."

"I know. But who? Besides, I can't afford to employ a full-time seamstress, not until the debts are paid off."

"What about Maggie?" Annie made the suggestion tentatively, knowing the state of affairs between the two sisters. "I just thought, now that Bob's at home most of the time, and with Filly there to look after Peggy and see to the meals, Maggie might be glad of a few hours' employment now and then."

"Maggie would bite my head off if I suggested it."

"Yes, she probably would, but at least you'd have tried, and it must have been rotten for poor Bob, being turned down by his old firm. Fancy a skilled carpenter like him having to take a part-time job sweeping up at the market hall."

"Well, if you think so," Charlotte said doubtfully.

"And I'm coming down to clean up for you at the weekends," Annie said firmly, waving aside Charlotte's protestations that she had enough to do without that. "I'd come every morning," Annie went on, "if it didn't mean leaving Joe on his own, and never quite knowing how he'll be. But if I give the shop and workroom a good cleaning on a Saturday it will save your hands." She laughed merrily, a happy woman despite Joe's uncertain health, and having to scrape to make ends meet. "It won't do if your hands get so rough they catch up the threads in the material. One snag could ruin a whole garment."

She rose from the table and started washing up the supper things, neat and plain in her old-fashioned long skirt and spotless white pinafore, her ash-blond hair drawn back from her thin face with its enormous blue eyes. "I just can't help wishing that Mrs. Hollister would buckle down more."

Charlotte went to see Maggie the next evening after work, taking with her a few sweets for Peggy, and a bunch of snowdrops for her mother.

Bob answered the door in his shirtsleeves. He looked tired and frustrated. Poor Bob, whom she had always liked as a decent, ordinary young fellow.

His face lit up when he saw her; he was as smitten now as he had always been by her beauty and her air of intrinsic kindness. Charlotte he had always seen as a cut above himself, an almost fairytale creature who reminded him of the illustrations in a book he'd read as a boy, the kind of woman a man would slay dragons to possess.

How wonderful she looked, as fresh and neat as a rose, her cheeks stung crimson with the cold, hair tucked back beneath a plaid tam-o'-shanter.

"Come in," he said, aware that his difficult wife and sanctimonious mother-in-law would scarcely welcome her presence under their roof.

"Are you sure it will be all right? I know I don't exactly belong here, but I'd like to speak to Maggie . . ."

Filly's curious voice issued forth from the living room. "Who is it? Why are you standing out there so long?"

Damn and blast the old crone, Bob thought furiously as Charlotte stepped forward clutching the bunch of snowdrops.

Filly pursed her lips primly at the sight of her younger daughter standing nervously in the doorway. "Well, what do you want?" she asked, crinkling her forehead.

"I thought you might like these." Charlotte handed her

mother the snowdrops, which Filly threw aside with a gasp of horror.

"I've told you before," she snapped, "it's unlucky to bring snowdrops into the house!"

"I'm sorry," Charlotte said bleakly, "I thought that was bluebells."

"Bluebells *and* snowdrops—May blossom, too!" Filly mouthed her superstitions with a fearful glee, pushing the snowdrops away from her as if their presence in the room might bring down a thunderbolt on her unlucky head. "They're a sign of sickness," she shuddered, drawing her shawl more closely about her shoulders.

"Don't be crazy," Bob interposed angrily, as little Peggy came through from the kitchen, crowing with delight at seeing her Aunt Charlotte again, her night-black hair tortured into a pipe-cleaner-induced frizz by her mother.

Peggy was five years old now, almost ready for school, along with Kathy. How quickly the years passed, how quickly children grew up, Charlotte thought, bending down to kiss her. She felt Peggy's warm little hands clasped jubilantly at the nape of her neck, aware, as she held the child in her arms, how much she loved Maggie's daughter, with her sweet, outgoing nature and startlingly beautiful face.

Then Maggie came in, fat, untidy, and out of temper, smelling of cooking; cheeks aflame with the aggravation of a panful of burnt liver and onions. "Well, what do *you* want?" she muttered angrily, glaring at her sister.

Charlotte felt inclined to laugh at the absurdity of the situation. "Oh, for heaven's sake, Maggie," she said, "isn't it about time we dropped this ridiculous animosity? You too, Mother! Can't we let bygones be bygones?" She sighed faintly with irritation. "I've come to offer you a job, Maggie." Charlotte held out her hands appealingly. "I want you to come in with me as an equal partner; to share in the profits. Oh, Maggie, dear, please say yes."

141

Maggie drew in a deep, snorting breath of anger, laced with pent-up jealousy and frustration. "No," she snapped, "I don't want your damned help—you *whore!*"

"*Maggie!*" Filly stared at her open-mouthed. Bob stepped forward angrily. "And Peggy doesn't want your bloody sweets, neither," panted the irate Maggie, snatching them away from her, making the child cry. "As for you, Bob Masters, you can get your own rotten supper!" She stared at him with something approaching hatred. Her cheeks were nearly scarlet with unbecoming spider veins. "I'm sick and tired of everything! I wish I were dead!" Maggie flung herself at the door, slammed it shut behind her, and clattered upstairs to the bedroom.

Filly stared after her daughter as if she had taken leave of her senses. "She's going to kill herself," she wailed hysterically. "Well, don't just stand there, Bob, go after her!"

"It's all my fault," Charlotte said in a low voice. "I shouldn't have come here. I'm sorry, Mother. I never will again."

"No, it wasn't your fault," Filly said unexpectedly, ashamed of Maggie's outburst. "I wish your father was here. He'd know what to do." Life had never been the same since Albert died. She felt old and useless, overcome with worry. Then she remembered, with a resurgence of hope, that the clairvoyant had warned her about the dark clouds gathering around her before the Truth, in all its glory, would be revealed to her, and had told her that death was nothing but a veil which briefly separated the living from their dear departed.

"The Valley of the Shadow," the clairvoyant had called it, rolling up her eyes. Then would emerge the "Life Beyond the Shadow." All Mrs. Grayler had to do was to come regularly to her sittings in the front parlor, and wait for the Truth to be made plain.

Bob ran upstairs. Maggie was lying across the bed, her shoulders heaving.

"What the hell's got into you?" He was roughly unsympathetic, angry over her treatment of Charlotte and Peggy.

Maggie drew in a deep, rasping breath as she sat up to confront him. "I'll tell you what's got into me, Bob Masters! Another bloody baby!"

His anger evaporated. He grinned. "Well, that isn't the end of the world, is it?"

"It is to me," she screeched. "It makes me feel sick, the way you did it! Making me wear that rotten, stinking scent, as if I was some kind of French floozie! And that's another thing. You must have been with one, or how would you have known? No, don't touch me. Get off! Get away from me!" Her anger was at full heat now. "I wish to hell I'd never married you!"

He struck her a stinging blow across the face; watched her collapse suddenly like a deflated balloon. "Well, you did marry me," he said harshly, "for better or worse, and we're going to stay married, whether you like it or not. I'll tell you something else while I'm about it. As soon as I can find a decent job away from here, I'm going to take it, and you and Peggy are coming with me!"

She stared up at him tearfully. "But what about Ma?"

"Oh no! She's your mother, not mine. The sooner we're shot of her the better. She's caused nothing but trouble between us ever since she came to live here, and I'm fed up with her!"

Charlotte quickly walked back to Friar's Way. It had started snowing again, the new snow lightly dusting the cleared patches of pavement fronting the houses.

The scene at Maggie's had upset her. Above all, she felt worried about Peggy, whose natural charm and bright, outgoing personality stood in danger of eclipse if the pattern of her days was not soon altered. Only the children mattered now; their young lives must not be made miserable by the quarrels and misunderstandings of their parents' generation. And yet there seemed no solution to the misunderstandings between herself and Maggie. She had thought that, in time, would come a softening of her attitude, and Filly's, a spark of warmth, and forgiveness, instead of which they appeared to have reached an impasse.

Feeling in her handbag for her key, she wondered if she had done right in not telling them about Rowan's death, then knew that she could not have borne it if Maggie had said something cruel or derogatory about him. And so she had decided to say nothing. Only Annie and Joe knew what really had happened. And yet, as she stepped into the narrow passageway, and pushed back the chenille curtain behind the door, placed there by Annie to keep out the draught, she felt keenly the division of a once happy, united family.

Annie appeared from the back room the moment she heard the door close. Gaslight shone on her pale, heart-shaped face. She looked very serious. "This came for you," she said blankly, holding out a telegram. "I'm sorry, I had to open it, the boy wanted to know if there was any reply."

"Who is it from? What does it say?" Charlotte's voice came in almost a whisper.

"It's from Alice Tanquillan," Annie said gently. "Miss Kitty is dying. She wants to see you."

Chapter Eleven

Alice Tanquillan had grown from a skinny, dark-haired girl into a surprisingly handsome young woman, very tall and slender. She was not beautiful by any means, but striking, with pale, creamy skin and passionate dark eyes beneath heavy, uptilted brows, her hair cut daringly short at the back and lying in thick, straight bangs on her forehead.

She had recently taken up smoking, to Claude Latimer's intense displeasure. The tall, elderly psychiatrist, at whose London clinic Alice had spent a great deal of time during the past years, frowned on smoking as an obnoxious, harmful habit he would prefer her not to pursue. Not that his opinion made a jot of difference to Alice, who had always possessed an uncanny knack of getting her own way with him.

Even as a child, she knew that she had intrigued him with her odd turn of phrase and disarming flirtation, her devastating intelligence and pathetic lapses into confusion; had often pretended to be confused when she was feeling particularly in command of herself; laughing inwardly because he, not she, appeared to be the more confused of the two of them. She was not blind. She knew quite well, as time went by, that he had become more and more intrigued by her obvious physical attractions, her long, slender legs and shapely breasts. She enjoyed her feeling of power over him.

And so she continued to smoke, tucking the long Russian cigarettes she preferred into a jade holder, saying sweetly that smoking made her feel more sophisticated and gave her something to do with her hands.

"Please don't be angry with me, Tim," she would say appealingly, "I couldn't bear it if you were." And all the time she was shaking with suppressed laughter at his gullibility so far as she was concerned.

It was just a game to her, using her blossoming womanhood as a weapon to charm men. It had all happened quite suddenly, the exciting awareness of her own body, the soft feel of it beneath the stunning clothes she wore; the way men looked with open admiration at her slim waist, her pointed, proudly upthrust breasts; the way she walked, swaying her hips, the startling black and white etching of her gypsy face beneath the cropped-off bangs.

She also knew, as she stared out of the window at the wide sweep of gravelled drive fronting Grey Wethers, that she not give a damn for any of the men she came in contact with here or in London. The only man she had ever loved was dead. Now, the knowledge that she would never have what she had most wanted—Rowan's physical love—filled her with a searing frustration. Never once had she brought that bloody, condescending cousin of hers to his knees: Rowan, whose very presence in a room had made her body ache with a febrile, urgent desire to have him touch her, to make love to her.

Now, the woman who had taken him away from her was coming to Grey Wethers; coming closer and closer with every turn of the car wheels. Charlotte Oakleigh, her one-time companion. God, how she hated her.

Charlotte did not immediately recognize the tall, grayhaired man standing erect near the station barrier, and felt a strange aversion toward him as he walked forward, unsmiling, to carry her case.

She knew she had seen him somewhere before, a long time ago, that her vague dislike of him dated back to some previous encounter. And then, as he preceded her to the car, she suddenly remembered. Of course . . . he had been a guest at her marriage to Will Oakleigh. Claude Latimer, the distinguished London psychiatrist, a friend of Kitty Tanquillan.

Watching his fussy preoccupation with his driving gloves, which he pulled on carefully and proceeded to smooth, finger by finger, over his somewhat effeminate hands, she wondered how such a cold fish had ever succeeded in a profession which had to do primarily with human kindness and understanding.

Perhaps he was a different person when it came to receiving generous payment for his services. Yes, of course, that would make a world of difference to his approach.

She could fairly see him as he must appear to the foolish, wealthy women flocking to his clinic for advice: a godlike figure in an immaculately tailored suit, a carnation in his buttonhole; deep-set gray eyes hypnotic beneath somewhat bushy eyebrows, a charming smile playing about his full, sensuous lips.

But Charlotte was far too level-headed to suppose that Latimer saw herself as anything other than one of the servant class. As the car moved forward, she felt like a delinquent adolescent in the presence of a magistrate.

A lump rose up in her throat as she thought of her journey's end, her last meeting with Kitty Tanquillan. She saw, through a haze of tears, the tall chimneys of Grey Wethers rising up before her, its roof covered with a light dusting of snow, smoke from its fires rising straight up in the foggy, twilit air.

As the car drew up near the steps to the terrace, she caught the flutter of a lace curtain at the drawing-room window. Then Alice emerged, running lightly along the terrace, hands outstretched in welcome. Watching her, Charlotte thought how much she had changed and ma-

147

tured in the past few years, and how elegant she looked in one of the new shorter dresses in a soft shade of green, with a square-cut neckline, and a rope of scintillating green glass beads which swayed from side to side as she ran.

She had naturally assumed that Alice was running to her, but she was mistaken. The girl hurried past her in a deliberately insulting manner, pointedly ignoring her. And yet Charlotte knew she was looking at her covertly as she seized Latimer's hands, and held up her face to be kissed; Alice was gaining pleasure from her discomfort.

Feeling as if she had received a slap in the face, Charlotte turned away from them and walked, head up, to the front door which Rivers had opened when he heard the car arrive.

"Thank goodness you've come," he said hoarsely. "Will you go up right away? The mistress is waiting for you."

"How is she?"

"Very ill." His mouth worked awkwardly. "I never thought I'd live to see this day."

Suddenly, Alice was beside them, eyes blazing. "What are you two muttering about?" Her voice was shrill with anger. "You, Rivers, go and fetch the luggage, and tell Simpson to put the car away. Hurry, man. *Hurry!*"

"Yes, Miss Alice." The old fellow trotted off down the steps, shaking his head bemusedly.

Charlotte's anger was aroused at last, not because she cared tuppence about herself, but she did care very much about Thomas Rivers, and Alice was not the mistress of Grey Wethers yet. "So you had noticed me?" she said coolly, keeping her temper well under control. "I thought that I had suddenly become invisible!"

Alice merely smiled. "Oh, how are you, Charlotte? Shall we go indoors? Tea's almost ready. We'll have it in the study."

"I don't want any tea, thank you. I've come all this way to see Miss Kitty, and I intend to do just that!"

"You can't see her now, she's resting." Alice stood close to Latimer. "You may see her tomorrow."

Their eyes met. The clear hazel eyes of the redhead and the hostile eyes of the brunette; the former companion, and the future mistress of Grey Wethers, with no love lost between them.

"I'm going up to her now," Charlotte said.

Kitty Tanquillan knew she was dying. The cold she had caught a month ago had not cleared up as the doctor had expected. He had known Kitty ever since she had come to Grey Wethers as a young woman; had often told her that she possessed the constitution of an ox. But this time his old friend appeared to have no reserves of strength left to fight the infection. It seemed, almost, that she had lost the will to live.

The cold had quickly developed into a high fever, with prolonged bouts of coughing which racked her frail body, weakening her heart and lungs, sapping her powers of endurance.

Faraday had begged her to go into a nursing-home, but Kitty would not hear of it. "I intend to die here," she said obdurately, "in my own home."

"Die? Who said anything about dying?" Faraday retorted.

"Oh, get on with you, man," Kitty replied wearily, "the truth is, I'm ready to go now. I'm so very tired. Just a worn-out bundle of brittle bones covered in flesh. It's high time I moved on." She'd closed her eyes suddenly; painfully. "If only I could feel certain that Alice . . ." Seized with a sudden bout of coughing, she had been unable to finish the sentence. Later, she had asked Faraday to send a message to Claude Latimer. Charlotte entered the room very quietly. It was the most beautiful room in the house, with mullioned windows overlooking the garden and the distant hills, the windows curtained with deep, glowing red velvet, and screens drawn round the vast bed where the old woman lay.

Old age and illness had wreaked havoc upon Kitty's delicate, thin frame, but even rapidly approaching death had not conquered her valiant spirit, nor dulled her razor-sharp intellect.

"Don't ask me how I am," she said, with a faint smile. "I'm dying. No, don't grieve for me. I've lived my life to the full. I have no regrets, except . . ." Her voice faltered as she struggled for breath. When the spasm was over, "Prop me a little higher," she said to the nurse. "Thank you. You may leave us now."

When the woman had rustled away, she continued, "Except that you would not allow me to help you financially after Rowan died. Why did you never ask me?" Her wrinkled old face softened suddenly in a smile. "But I know why not, because you and I were cut from the same length of cloth: proud and stubborn, the pair of us. But I must know the truth now. This business venture you wrote to me about, is it a viable proposition?"

"Perhaps not quite at the moment, but it will be, given time. I know I can make a success of it."

"I wish that you and Rowan could have been married. He was so proud of you. But life is often cruelly unfair . . ."

"I never looked at it in that light," Charlotte said softly. "We loved each other. That was enough. But you must rest now."

"Rest?" Kitty snorted. "There'll be all the time in the world for me to rest soon. I intend making the most of the little time left to me. There are certain things I want to make clear to you. First of all, I have left Kathy, and Rowan's son, Berry, a little money in my will, which I have decided they will receive when they are eighteen." She waved Charlotte's thanks aside. "Now, about Alice. I know her faults and failings better than most. She is wild, stubborn, troublesome and unpredictable, and you

150

have reason enough to hate her, but I want you to promise that you will always be her friend . . ."

The old woman was breathing rapidly, shallowly now, but her eyes still burned with their former fierce, indomitable light. "I have elected Latimer and my solicitor, Alfred Cunningham, to stand as her guardians until she comes of age, but they are men, and the day will come when Alice will need a woman friend she can turn to."

She seemed to wander a little then. "Latimer will stand between Alice and Gervaise Tanquillan. Grey Wethers must never fall into his hands! I should never rest quietly in my grave if it did!" Kitty was becoming agitated now, her sunken cheeks were flushed with two high-spots of unnaturally bright color. Her hands picked restlessly at the covers as she said, in a low, hoarse voice. "Promise me that you will always be Alice's friend. *Promise?*"

"Very well, I promise."

The nurse came into the room at that moment, and signalled Charlotte to leave.

On an impulse, she leaned over to kiss Kitty Tanquillan's withered cheek. Then she picked up her gloves and handbag from a nearby chair and walked slowly downstairs.

Thankfully, there was no sign of Alice or Latimer. Lost and lonely, in the grip of an overwhelming grief, she saw Rivers emerge from the door at the end of the passage. "I think I'd like to go to my room now," she said.

He looked suddenly ashamed. "It isn't your old room, I'm afraid. Miss Alice gave orders that you were to have a room at the back of the house, overlooking the stables." Tears filled his eyes. "The mistress would have a fit if she knew."

"She mustn't know, then, Thomas. In any event, it doesn't matter. It isn't important."

When he opened the door, she said softly, "Where will you go, Thomas, what will you do when all this is—over?"

"To my sister in Cornwall. I've saved a little money for

my old age . . ." He smiled ruefully. "Sounds silly, doesn't it? I've been old for a very long time now, but that never seemed to matter, as long as my lady needed me."

"I'm glad you are going to Lucy," Charlotte said. "I'm glad I met her. You'll be happy together, I know."

Alice toyed moodily with the keys of the grand piano. The lamps had been lit and a log fire spread a warm glow over walls and ceiling.

Latimer watched her, a deep frown between his eyebrows. He knew, of course, that the tune she was playing held a deep significance for her: "Sur le pont d'Avignon," the old French nursery rhyme she closely associated with her dead cousin, Rowan Tanquillan.

It occurred to him as he listened that he ought to know everything there was to know about Alice, after all the years he had treated her, but he did not. She still remained to him an enigma, so that he felt he had never even come close to discovering the real Alice Tanquillan.

One moment she would make advances to him, playing the part of the flirt, driving him frantic with her coy questions: did he like her new dress, shoes, hat, hairstyle? The next minute she would seem to him nothing more than a lost and lonely little girl, crying on his shoulder; a child in desperate need of love and reassurance, wanting nothing more from him than a fatherly pat on the head, a gentle arm about her shoulders. He could never decide whether she was play-acting or not. Alice was a consummate actress.

She appeared to be brooding now, and sullen, as she picked away at the piano. Her anger over Charlotte's flouting of her wishes had not burst forth in a pyrotechnic display of wrath as he had expected, but had, apparently, turned more dangerously inward. Or was this simply another facet of her play-acting?

Whichever, his sympathy lay entirely with her, because

he was head over heels in love with her, and she knew it. Moreover, the poor child had been called upon to endure a great deal of mental suffering in the past few days, and she would be called upon to endure a great deal more in the days to come. The old lady's life was slowly ebbing away, Dr. Faraday had warned him.

Suddenly, Alice turned away from the piano, and slammed down the lid on the row of grinning ivory keys.

Latimer rose to his feet as she stumbled towards him, weeping, and held her closely in his arms as she sobbed helplessly against his chest. "Alice, my dear," he murmured.

"Kiss me," she whispered hoarsely, lifting her face to his. "Oh, God, Tim, please kiss me! Tell me you love me!"

"I do love you, Alice! You know that I do! I have always loved you!"

"Then prove it! Prove it now!"

Latimer felt the tight clasp of her hands at the nape of his neck as she drew him down on to the cushioned sofa in front of the fire, and spread out her body beneath his, flickering her tongue between his lips, like a snake, begging him to make love to her.

He pulled suddenly away from her. "No," he said harshly, "not like this. Not here. Not now!"

"You don't really want me, then?" she asked dully.

"Want you? Of course I want you!" He groaned slightly, feeling the sapping of his will power, and leaned forward to kiss her again.

Charlotte walked into the room at that moment and saw, with a feeling of disgust, the two figures on the sofa.

Not a bit abashed, Alice sat up and said, "I see we have an audience!" She threw back her head and laughed. "My God, Charlotte, if you could see your face!"

Deeply shocked, Charlotte turned and ran, out of the house into the clean, fresh air, scarcely knowing where she was running to, until she found herself in the lane leading down to the farmhouse where she had once lived with Will Oakleigh. Icy cold and shivering, she stumbled toward the farmyard, disbelieving of the scene she had just witnessed: the so-called "eminent psychiatrist," Claude Latimer, behaving like a schoolboy, Alice lying there in his arms, an expression of triumph on her dark, gypsy face.

A scream escaped her lips as she ran full tilt into the arms of a man whose figure loomed at her suddenly through the dusk.

"Hey, now," said a soft, lilting Irish voice, "no need to yell your head off! I'll not harm you. But who are you, and where did you come from?" He pulled her into the square of light framed by the farmhouse window. "Well, now," he said admiringly.

She saw, as she looked up at him, that he was young, well-built, with a mane of dark hair, wearing leather gaiters, corduroy trousers, and a patched jacket, the kind of clothes Will Oakleigh used to wear around the farm.

"What are you up to?" he asked with a faintly amused smile. "It's scarcely a night for a woman to go walking alone, now, is it? Especially a woman without a coat and hat. You'll have come from the main house, I suppose?" He shoved open the farmhouse door. "Come inside. You must be frozen stiff." He held the door for her and eyed her quizzically as she hesitated on the threshold. "What's wrong?" he asked. "Isn't my house good enough for you?"

"No, it isn't that. It's just that I once lived here, a long time ago." She smiled at him, ashamed of running away. "My—husband was once Miss Tanquillan's farm manager."

"You don't look like a farmer's wife," he said, noticing the softness of her hands as she held them to the fire, and the beauty of her face framed with curling, mist-damp strands of auburn hair. "My name's Rory O'Neill. What's yours?"

"Charlotte. Charlotte Oakleigh."

"Sorry things are in a bit of a muddle," he said apologetically, "that's because I'm a loner, without a wife to take care of me." He grinned suddenly, engagingly. "What about a drop of brandy? No, I insist! I thought you were going to faint for a moment, out there. I realize that a pale skin usually goes with red hair, but you are as white as a sheet!"

He produced a bottle from the corner cupboard and poured her a good dose. "Drink it," he ordered. "I'm not at all sure I'd know how to cope with a fainting female."

"Thank you." Her hand shook slightly as she lifted the glass to her lips. "Do you mind if I sit down for a minute?"

"Of course not! How boorish of me! I'll join you in a drink, if you don't mind. I've been up to the sheep pasture these past six hours, playing midwife. But I daresay you'll know all about that."

"Yes," she said slowly, "I do."

He gave her a long, searching glance as he tried to remember where he had heard the name Oakleigh before. Suddenly he did remember: there had been a Will Oakleigh, a kind of local hero who had been killed stopping a runaway horse. They had even put up a memorial tablet to him in the local church, the poor devil.

No wonder his widow had been so reluctant to reenter the house.

"For what it's worth," he said, "I'm sorry the old lady is dying. I have a great deal of respect for her kind: rather less for that niece of hers." He swallowed his drink in one gulp.

"I'd better be going now," Charlotte said, getting up from her chair.

"I'll walk back to the house with you."

"No, I'd rather go by myself."

"I hope we'll meet again," he said, in a low voice.

"I think that is hardly likely," she replied. "Now, if you wouldn't mind letting go of my hand . . ."

"Sorry! Perhaps I was hoping that you would stay with me for a little while longer." He smiled wickedly. "I think you are the most beautiful woman I have ever seen in the whole of my life, Charlotte Oakleigh, and I'd give my eye teeth to make love to you."

"I don't think that you would be quite as conceited, without your eye teeth," she said primly, biting her lip to keep from laughing. "Goodnight, Mr. O'Neill." At least he had cheered her up.

"Goodnight, Mrs. Oakleigh."

He watched her retreating figure until it was swallowed up by the darkness.

Kitty Tanquillan died later that night.

"No, I don't want to look at her," Alice cried hysterically, burying her face against Latimer's shoulder. "Don't make me look at her! I couldn't bear it!"

Alone in her room, the thought of the house with a dead woman lying at its center unnerved her. She could not stand the sound of soft footsteps coming and going, the still, heavy air of mourning, the whispering voices. She was repelled by the scent of morticians' fluids and hothouse flowers: the solemn awfulness of death.

Nor could she bear the strange shadows cast by the flickering candles and fireglow. She lay in bed as tense as a coiled spring, staring fearfully at the shadowy ceiling, imagining the tiny, shrunken, lifeless figure of her Aunt Kitty in the room across the landing.

If only she had not listened, as a child, outside the kitchen door, to the cook and her crony, the district nurse, talking about death; what they did to people once the life had gone out of them: such terrible, terrible things. . . .

Knuckling her fists against her mouth, she sat bolt upright, staring wildly around the shadowy bedroom.

Suddenly, she twisted her legs out of bed, slipped into her dressing gown, and fled along the corridor to Latimer's room. Not bothering to knock, she flung open the door and stood breathlessly on the threshold, her face the color of wax. "Oh Tim," she cried, "help me! For God's sake, help me!"

Latimer turned, silver-backed hairbrush in hand, startled by her appearance.

"Alice, darling!" Throwing the brush aside, he strode quickly towards her.

"Hold me," she cried, "I'm so—frightened!"

"I know, I know," he murmured, stroking her hair, "but there's no need. Death is inevitable. Just try to think that your aunt lived a full and happy life . . ."

"You don't understand," she whispered hoarsely, "it isn't Aunt Kitty I'm worried about, it's—*myself!* I'm scared of what they'll do to me when I am dead! If they stuff my nose with cottonwool, I shan't be able to breathe properly!" Her eyes widened with terror, and this time she was not play-acting. "Oh, Tim! Help me!"

"For Christ's sake, Alice, calm yourself!"

Badly shaken, Latimer felt the jerking of her body beneath its covering of thin nightclothes. Fearing some kind of fit, he held her tightly until she sagged, a dead weight, in his arms.

Suddenly, she lifted her tear-stained face to his and said despairingly, "Won't you make love to me now? I swear I'll die if you don't!"

"Yes, yes," he muttered, fastening his lips on hers; moving his mouth slowly, searchingly, up the column of her throat, forgetting everything in the overwhelming passion he felt for her, this slim, lovely child–woman whom he intended to marry.

She moaned softly with erotic pleasure as he swept her up in his arms and carried her to bed.

"Don't stop," she cried, but the pain and the ectasy

ended suddenly when Latimer rolled away from her, exhausted, leaving her unfulfilled.

Tears of disappointment welled up in Alice's eyes. On the brink of some wild, pagan discovery of absolute joy, the chalice had been snatched from her lips, flung down, drained, summarily emptied.

He's too old, she thought dully, noticing for the first time the slackness of his flesh, so different from that of the young men who worked about the farm in summertime, stripped to the waist, their bodies glistening with sweat, arm muscles rippling in the sun. So different from—Rowan.

They buried Kitty Tanquillan in the churchyard at Cloud Merridon and laid her coffin to rest beneath the bare branches of an elm tree on a cold January morning.

The service over, Charlotte straightened her shoulders and walked away from the grave.

On an impulse, she turned near the gate to look back, to bid her personal, silent farewell to the woman she had loved.

Words from the Scriptures came into her mind.

Christ being raised from the dead dieth no more;

Death hath no more dominion. . . .

Chapter Twelve

Easter brought a burgeoning of daffodils and new green leaves, and a feeling of freshness and purpose to Charlotte as she hurried about, cutting, tacking, and stitching for her steadily increasing clientele. The money she earned from this latest influx of trade would pay Mrs. Hollister's creditors. Then she could turn her mind to other matters, such as much-needed improvements to the shop and workroom. She was determined to get rid of Agatha's moth-eaten potted palm for a start, and to buy new curtains for the cubicles, and glass lamps for the workroom.

Bending over her accounts one Saturday night in Annie's warm kitchen, she worked out her finances to the last ha'penny. Annie, seated on her chair near the fire, was doing the mending. Joe, opposite, smiled at his wife whenever she looked up from her work. Dog, lying blissfully between them, pointed nose on paws, provided a black hearthrug for Annie's foot, and sighed deeply with contentment as she rubbed her toe absentmindedly along his sleek black flank.

As the clock struck eight, Charlotte threw down her pen. "Well, that's it!" she said triumphantly. "I've been over the figures three times, and we're out of the red at last!"

"Oh darling, that's wonderful news!" Annie rose swiftly to give her a hug. "Isn't it marvellous, Joe? I feel like celebrating!"

159

"I—I'll put the kettle on," Joe said. He had arrived at the stage of doing small household chores: helping Annie prepare the vegetables, bringing in coal from the yard, clearing the grate. He worked at his own pace, encouraged by his wife and sister, inevitably accompanied by Dog, who followed him like a shadow.

Watching Joe walk through to the kitchen, Charlotte realized the importance of the dog in Joe's recovery. His interest in the shop, too, had helped clear his head. For a while, his hitherto bright, intelligent face had worn the mask of a man old before his time. Now he often accompanied Annie on her weekly cleaning visits to the salon, where he would help her to wash the windows and swish the dust from the fittings. Gradually the mask began to peel away, the lines of suffering erased by his renewed interest in life, and the laughter which Annie spun about her like a shining silken thread.

Charlotte had started clearing away her account books to leave the table free for supper when a loud knock came at the front door, followed by a series of smaller knocks, like the hammering of a woodpecker on a tree.

"Who on earth can that be?" Frowning, Annie rushed to find out.

Seconds later, the distraught figure of Filly appeared, hat askew, coat wrongly buttoned, clasping a worn handbag in her shaking fingers, with tears running down her cheeks. She almost fell into Annie's chair by the fire.

"I never thought I'd live to see this day," she sobbed, pushing away Dog's inquisitive nose as she fumbled in her bag for a handkerchief.

Joe came in at that moment. "What's the matter, Mother?" He gripped the edge of the mantelpiece, disturbed by her appearance.

"I've been turned out of house and home, that's what! Bob's got himself a job in Darlington. He's selling up, and Maggie's 'that way' again!"

Annie held on to Joe's arm, understanding the distress

160

signals. "Sit down, darling," she said quietly. "Don't upset yourself. We'll sort things out."

Filly glared up at her with red-rimmed eyes. "I'm glad you think so," she snapped.

Charlotte stepped quietly into the arena. "Whatever you have to say, Mother, try to say it without losing your temper!"

"Huh!" Filly stared up at her daughter momentarily, bosom heaving, then she lay back, crying quietly, sapped of energy and will power. "After all I've done for them," she sobbed. "But where shall I go now? Where? That's what I want to know. I've been given my marching orders! Bob says they won't have room for me where they're going! As if I'd want to go where I'm not welcome!"

"I suppose we could put you up for a few days," said the ever-helpful and sympathetic Annie. "But it wouldn't be permanent. There just isn't room. There's five of us in the house already. Joe and me and Laurie in the front bedroom, Charlotte and Kathy in the back. So you see—Mother . . ."

"Oh yes, I see," Filly said bitterly. "A woman gives up her whole life to bringing up her family, then, when she's old and worn out, nobody wants her any longer."

"It isn't a question of not wanting you," Charlotte said patiently. "It's a matter of space."

"It's all Bob's fault," Filly said tearfully, "getting our Maggie in the family way again, and putting in for some job or other in another town."

"You mustn't blame Bob for that," Charlotte said firmly. "He's only done what any sensible may would do in the circumstances. It's up to him to provide a living for his wife and family."

"But I'm part of his family," Filly retorted. "At least I thought I was until he gave me the boot!"

"Don't worry about that, Mrs. Grayler," Annie said—somehow she had always found it hard to call her "Mother"—"we'll take care of you somehow. Tell Bob and Maggie it's all right, we'll do our best to look after you, won't we, Joe?"

Filly got up, settling her hat, attempting to smooth the wrinkles from her wrongly buttoned coat, stuffing the handkerchief back in her handbag.

"Just a second, you've got your coat buttoned all wrong," Charlotte said, rectifying the mistake, feeling a warm rush of sympathy for her mother as she did so, half expecting Filly to draw away at her touch.

Instead, to her surprise, Filly smiled. "Funny, isn't it?" she said ambiguously.

"What's—funny?" Annie asked, bewildered by the turn of events, more concerned about her husband than his mother.

"Oh, you know," Filly shrugged self-consciously. "I haven't been exactly close to all of you recently, but I knew where to come when I needed help."

She turned in the doorway. "I'm sorry if I've upset you, son." Suddenly she moved forward to kiss him. "I'm sorry about a lot of things. I—I don't know whatever came over me. . . ."

Annie said kindly, "That doesn't matter now, Mrs. Grayler. When you're ready, bring your things round here. All we can offer you is the sofa, but you're welcome to that until we can sort things out."

"You're a good lass, Annie Crystal," Filly said softly, unexpectedly. "Our Joe's a lucky lad to have you for a wife."

When she had gone, "It's no use," Charlotte said. "Kathy and I can't stay here any longer if Mother is coming to live with you," realizing, as she spoke, that Filly had a way of becoming a permanent fixture. It wasn't just the overcrowding she dreaded, but her mother's overpowering and dictatorial personality. Four adults and two small children would be unthinkable under Annie's roof, with Joe still needing peace and quiet.

"What? And break up the family? No, I couldn't bear

162

that," Annie said with a catch in her voice. "Whatever happens, I don't want to be parted from you and Kathy. Why, we've been like sisters all these years. No! What we need is a bigger place, somewhere we wouldn't all be on top of each other. What do you say, Joe?"

"You're right," he replied, thinking the same as Charlotte, that his mother would soon take over the entire house. "Let's look at the ads in the evening paper."

Charlotte and Annie began a wearying tour of the estate agents' offices. Some of the houses they looked at were far too expensive. Often, rushing straight out, after tea, to answer a likely advertisement, they would find that the house had already been rented. Most of them wouldn't have been much good anyway, being too far away from the shops, or with massive gardens. Some were no bigger than the house in Friar's Way.

And then, one day—a Saturday it was—an estate agent, leafing through his list of properties to rent, told them that there was a house going in Abbey Crescent, in the town center, a very desirable property indeed, at an amazingly low rent.

"Why? What's the matter with it?" asked the perspicacious Annie.

The estate agent blushed a little. "There's nothing actually the *matter* with it, except that it's a little run-down, in need of decoration, that kind of thing. . . ." he waved his hand vaguely. The house in Abbey Crescent had been on his books for several months now, because no one, so far, had wanted to tackle it. "Why don't you take the key?" he suggested. "It's in a very nice location." He glanced at his register. "Two sitting rooms, four bedrooms, plus two spacious attics; kitchen and bathroom, with a small garden in front, and a yard to the rear."

Annie noticed that his voice faltered a little at the word

"kitchen." "Anything else we should know about it?" she asked suspiciously.

"As I said before," the estate agent muttered desperately, "it's in a very nice location. Well, I mean to say, you must know Abbey Crescent quite well. The house overlooks the Baptist church, and a very nice, well-kept garden owned by the church council."

"That's what's worrying me," Annie said flatly, "if it is such a desirable residence, why is it going so cheap?"

Charlotte gave Annie a gentle poke in the ribs. "We'll take the key," she said, charmingly, to the man. "Come on, Annie!"

The house, No. 16, was on the flat side of the crescent. The front garden resembled a pocket handkerchief, fronted with tall black iron railings stamped with a fleur-de-lys pattern, and filled with spotted laurel bushes.

But Abbey Crescent itself was certainly impressive, with its sweeping curves of fine Victorian houses, and the Baptist church, set in the middle like a cream and red jewel in a diadem, commanding the church council's garden: a half-moon of grass surrounded with flowering lilac bushes, with trees, and seats, railings and gates, securely locked.

Annie's face fell when she caught sight of those padlocks. "Well, would you believe it," she said indignantly, "what's the use of a garden that size if the kids can't play in it?"

"I expect the church elders want to keep it sacrosanct," Charlotte laughed. "But we haven't come to look at the garden. It's the house that really matters; whether we like it or not."

"I have the strangest feeling you've made up your mind about it already," Annie said teasingly. "Well, go on, open the door."

They stepped into a small vestibule with a half-glass

inner door. Beyond lay an L-shaped hall and to their left, the door of the "front" room.

"Ye gods," Annie said, "it looks like the bottom of a stagnant pool!"

The room swam in a kind of greenish light because the blinds covering the bay window were drawn down.

Charlotte tugged impatiently at the blinds with their dangling acorns, flooding the room with the light of a sun-shiny May morning. "Now how does it look?" she asked triumphantly.

"Terrible," Annie replied, with a slight shudder. "No wonder this house is going cheap. It will need a small fortune spending on it, if this room is anything to go by. Look at the width of the base boards for a start—all that ugly brown paint—and have you thought how much curtain material we'd need to cover this one bay window alone?"

"You don't like it very much, do you?" Charlotte said despondently. "We'd better go. . . ."

"I didn't say that," Annie replied, "I was simply trying to be practical. But you obviously like it a great deal. I wonder why."

"Because—oh, it's hard to explain—because I feel I *belong* here; because it reminds me of the old house in St. Martin's Square, with the church and the garden. . . ."

"Let's have a look at the rest of it," Annie suggested, squeezing Charlotte's hand. "Take no notice of me, I'm just playing the devil's advocate. I don't want you to bite off more than you can chew, that's all." Her voice faltered. "Besides, it just looks so enormous after our own little place. . . ."

"Oh, Annie, I'm sorry." Charlotte knew how much Annie's "little place" meant to her, the house where she was born, where she had lived with her parents until they had died; the home she had created, with so much love, for all of them—Joe, Kathy and herself.

"Don't be crazy," Annie said, swallowing the lump in her throat. "Let's take a look at the rest of the house."

The second sitting room, beyond the L-shaped hall, led into the kitchen. And what a kitchen!

"Annie, it's—dreadful," Charlotte admitted, staring in dismay at the flaking dark green walls, the shelves coated thickly with grease and mouse-droppings, the cracked stone sink, rotting draining boards, and the kitchen range contained within a slimy alcove. "Oh, come on, let's go. We'd never make this right in a thousand years!"

"No," Annie replied firmly, "all it needs is lots of hot, strong water, soda, and elbow grease. Besides, I rather liked the second reception room, despite the piles of soot in the hearth." Her eyes twinkled merrily. "One thing's for sure, we wouldn't keep tripping over each other in a place this size. . . . Let's take a look upstairs!"

Together they walked up the creaking staircase. On the landing they stared, laughing, into a high, wide and handsome gilt-framed mirror lit by shafts of sunlight shining down from the cupola on the top landing, far above their heads. Laughingly, Annie curtseyed to Charlotte's reflection in the glass.

The massive bay-windowed front bedroom overlooked the church, and this room, thankfully, would need little in the way of new decoration. "Joe would love this room," Annie said wistfully, "being able to sit in the window watching the world go by. Come on, let's take a look at the bathroom! Just imagine not having to fill that old zinc tub of ours any more." They scurried along the passage.

"Lord," she said, staring at the bath supported with claw feet, "and what a 'throne'! But just you wait until I've finished polishing that seat, and given those tiles a good going-over with soap and water!"

"Come on, Annie, there's more stairs to climb yet," Charlotte laughed, realizing that her sister-in-law had suddenly changed tenses.

The whole house seemed awash with sunlight now. The

higher they went, the more sunshine and fresh air seemed to invade the house.

At last they came to the closed-off attic stairs leading from the uppermost landing. Suddenly, Charlotte was gripped with a feeling of intense, shivery excitement.

"What is it? What's the matter?" Annie asked, mystified by her expression. "Go on, you can tell me."

"I don't really know, it's just that . . ."

"What?"

"I just have the strangest feeling that we are about to see something—special."

"Ugh," Annie gasped, staring into the front attic with its narrow, push-open skylight window. "Well, this certainly isn't it! It's absolutely beasty! Filthy dirty, and covered with cobwebs!"

But Charlotte wasn't listening. She could not have explained in a million years why her heart beat so fast as she pushed open the door of the back attic. It was as if she had known all along that this would be the most beautiful room in the entire house.

Standing completely still on the threshold, she clasped her hands together, then walked, almost in a dream, to the wide dormer windows commanding a breathtaking view of the sea beyond the main street with its shining slate roofs and apricot chimneys.

The room was flooded with sunlight. Light was trapped in every corner of it, spilling energetically over dusty walls and sloping ceilings.

"Oh, *Charlotte!*" Annie was lost for words as she looked out at sea shimmering on the sun-drenched horizon.

"You think we should take the house, then?" Charlotte asked softly.

"Yes! Oh yes! Of course we must!" A tinge of color stained Annie's pale cheeks. "But Joe and I can't just go on taking from you and giving nothing in return. What I'd really like is to let off rooms to summer visitors. I could cook for them; look after them. I'd love that, so

167

would Joe. The money we earned would help with the upkeep. What do you think?"

"It's a wonderful idea! Oh, Annie! Let's go and tell the house agent right away!"

Chapter Thirteen

Kathy and Peggy were destined not to start school together. Bob and Maggie moved to Darlington in the summer of 1920, putting their house up for sale, leaving Filly to bemoan her fate. "Turning their backs on me," she said bitterly when she arrived at Annie's house, her meager belongings piled up on a hired hand-cart pushed by a doddering old man who charged her one and six for the privilege—to Filly's indignation.

Annie had cleared the front room to accommodate her mother-in-law and her bits and pieces: pictures, ornaments, and a glossy leaved plant in a fancy pot. Meanwhile, work on the house in Abbey Crescent proceeded quickly.

Joe and Annie spent most of their free time there, Annie busy with the scrubbing brush and buckets of scalding hot water in which she dissolved rough lumps of grease-dispelling soda while Joe painted the surfaces she had prepared for him, whistling happily between his teeth, utterly absorbed in his new occupation.

The resourceful Annie had borrowed a trestle table for the wallpapering from one of the neighbors in Friar's Way. She and Joe had decided to tackle one room at a time, paying for materials as they went along. When the front room had been painted, Joe sat on an upturned crate to trim the paper, to Kathy and Laurie's delight. The two little girls adorned themselves with the cut edges as they curled away in ringlets from the scissors.

Every evening, after work, Charlotte would hurry over to admire Joe's handiwork, to don an apron and help Annie with the scouring. Joe would smile with pleasure that his efforts had met with her approval. He had seldom been as happy before, working steadily at his own pace with Annie and the children beside him, and Dog padding in and out, his collar festooned with paper ringlets. With Annie's encouragement Joe had even managed to climb the stepladder without turning giddy, although Filly nearly had a fit when she saw him.

"Eh, son, you're never going up that ladder?" she wailed. "What if you fall off?"

"He won't, if you don't unnerve him," Annie retorted, grabbing Filly's elbow and hustling her out of the room.

In the kitchen, Filly said, "It's funny, but this place reminds me of when Albert and I went to look at the house in St. Martin's Square, before Joe and Maggie and Charlotte were born. A right mess that was in, too. I told Albert straight there was too much hard work and expense involved. But he wanted the shop and the warehouse, so I had to make the best of a bad job."

Charlotte looked up from scraping grease from the cooker. Dèjá vu! Was it possible that somehow, before she was born, she had intercepted her mother's thought patterns regarding an old house in need of repair? The possibility intrigued her.

Joe loved the house. Between spells of decorating, he would sit near the bay window in the upstairs sitting-room, breathing in the scent of early summer, noticing the way the church spire probed the sky like a pointing finger.

The war, the trenches, the barbed wire, the horror of

the shelling were slowly beginning to fade from his mind, held at bay by this new, hazy feeling of contentment.

Strange how this house reminded him of St. Martin's Square. There was a central garden there, too, busy with birds, with lilac trees and flowering bushes, and a church across the way. How happy and carefree they had all been then, with Mother and Dad the fulcrum on which had swung the tender years of their growing up.

He dared not probe too closely the reason why their happiness had terminated so abruptly. Annie had patiently taught him not to dwell on the war; the death of his brother Frank. "It won't be easy, Joe," she had said, "but try to think of the present—the future." Darling Annie, to whom he owed his life and his sanity.

Kathy Oakleigh surveyed the dilapidated rocking horse in the classroom with a jaundiced eye; opened her mouth, and screamed, at the top of her lungs, because her mother had left her in this strange wilderness of a room, with nothing to hang on to except the sparse, wiry hair on the horse's neck.

The teacher, Miss Plum, a plain, decent, nicely brought-up woman in her early forties, wondered, not for the first time, why she had ever entered the teaching profession, as she caught hold of her recalcitrant pupil by the waist and dragged her over to the sand-tray abutting the blackboard, where her other, more amenable charges had arranged a Bedouin village consisting of tents made of cones of brown paper, and palm trees plucked from their mothers' ferns.

"Now, Kathy," the teacher muttered desperately, "do remember that we are all your friends here. Look at this lovely sand-tray, dear. If you are a good girl, I'll let you decide our next project."

"I don't like you," Kathy said succinctly. "I want to go home to my mother!"

Oh, God, the teacher thought, fiddling in her desk for an aspirin to relieve her throbbing headache. "Well, you can't go home," she retorted, "not until the bell rings."

When the bell went, Kathy bounded out of the school gates like a young antelope, straight into her mother's arms.

"I've done it," she sobbed. "I've stuck my day at school, I needn't go back there any more now, need I, Mama?"

With a sinking heart, Charlotte explained to her child that this first day at school was merely the start. They walked hand in hand to the little shop at the end of the street which sold everything from vinegar to charcoal, cooked ham to corn plasters, and looked in the window. Pressing her nose to the glass, Kathy viewed, through troubled eyes, the licorice, lollipops and chalky sweet "Woodbines" with glowing tips.

Suddenly, hurrying along the pavement came an explosion of "Mixed Infants" from the high spiked gate of the playground, the bigger lads whooping like Red Indians, tugging the girls' hair as they ran.

"Can I have some sweets?" Kathy asked mournfully, squeezing out another tear or two.

"Yes, what would you like?"

"Five Woodbines." She added craftily, "I wouldn't mind going to school so much if I could have a penny-worth of sweets every day."

Bribery and corruption, Charlotte thought as they entered the shop. "But you can't—smoke—them on the way home," she admonished, torn between pity and uncontrollable laughter, trying hard to keep a straight face as Kathy pranced along by her side, telling her all about the rocking horse and the sand-tray, which had secretly made a great impression on her, along with the squeaky sound the chalk made on the blackboard, the brightly-colored bead-frames, and "ah, buh, cuh, duh."

"Buh, again. Buh, again. Buh, again," she chanted,

hop, skipping and jumping in rhythm to the words the teacher had taught her.

After tea, Annie tugged Charlotte's sleeve. "Just take a look," she whispered, her face puckered with amusement. They peeped into the kitchen where Kathy was busy teaching Laurie the alphabet, perfectly imitating the distraught Miss Plum, clapping her hand to her forehead, crying, "Now, repeat after me. Buh, again. Buh, again. Buh, again . . . no, you silly girl, you may *not* leave the room until the bell rings!"

"Only nine more years to go," Charlotte laughed. "I wonder who'll go gray-haired first, me or Miss Plum!"

At last the house in Abbey Crescent was almost finished. It had taken all summer to clean and decorate every room. Even working nonstop at the salon, Charlotte had been hard pressed to find enough money for the rent and rates of two places, paint and wallpaper for Abbey Crescent, and wages. She had been obliged to take on, for the busy summer months, a student at the salon, a bright-eyed, intelligent girl with a flair for sewing. Not that she begrudged Prue Mayhew her five shillings a week. The girl was a treasure, able to work well without constant supervision.

But money was tight, the world of business harshly competitive, and the news was depressing, as if the shadows cast by the Great War still hovered over them like a dark cloud. The papers were full of Sir Edwin Lutyens' Cenotaph, to be unveiled by His Majesty the King on the anniversary of the Armistice; the bringing home, to England, of the body of an unknown soldier from the battlefields of Flanders, to be buried in Westminster Abbey.

Was there no end, Charlotte wondered, to the raking over of old coals? The truth was, she could not bear to relive the sadness, the empty pomp and circumstance of war which had robbed a generation of its heroic young men. Her throat ached with tears, remembering the past.

173

Yet who could deny the right of those men who had died to a nation's grateful homage?

Apart from all that, Filly was proving difficult. Her mother's personality had suffered a big change since the death of her husband and eldest son, and what she still saw as Bob and Maggie's cruelty in leaving her behind to make their own way in another town. Besides which, neither Kathy nor Laurie had taken to their grandmother, whose presence in the narrow confines of the house in Friar's Way had brought into their hitherto carefree lives a kind of hypercritical, ramrod figure, emerging all too often from her sitting room either to lay down the law or embark on long-winded tales of what she did when she was young.

"Mama, when is Grandma going back to where she belongs?" Kathy asked one night at bedtime. "I don't like it when she kisses me goodnight, she has a whisker on her chin. Besides, I'm frightened of her."

"*Frightened?*" Charlotte sat on the edge of the bed. "What do you mean?"

"Because she told me she was in touch with Grandpa Grayler, and he's dead."

Oh God, Charlotte thought angrily, Filly would have to be tackled about this. How *dared* she frighten a child with such nonsense, as if the loving spirits of the dead could be conjured up in a fraudulent medium's sitting room!

She had it out with her mother at once, marching straight through to Annie's front room where Filly was tidying away some clothes in the chest of drawers. "This has to stop," she said in a vibrant, ringing voice.

"Eh?" Filly stared at her aghast. "What has to stop? I was only clearing up a bit."

"If you must dabble in spiritualism, I can't prevent you. But if you ever dare to frighten my daughter again, I warn you, you won't be welcome in the new house!"

"*Dabble* in spiritualism!" Filly's voice was harsh. "I've heard your father! He spoke to me. I *heard* him, I tell

174

you. He said he was well and happy. If you think you can deny me that comfort, you're wrong!"

"I don't wish to deny you anything, Mother. That's not the point. I'm simply telling you to keep your beliefs to yourself in future. Kathy's far too young and impressionable to be burdened with grown-up matters."

"You don't believe in anything, that's your trouble. . . ."

"That's where you're wrong." Charlotte bit her lip. "I believe that those people I loved are still part of the pattern of our lives. What I don't believe in is that they conveniently gather to speak to us in Mrs. Marsden's parlor at a shilling a visit."

Annie and Joe heard the altercation. Annie stood, white-faced, fingertips pressed to her lips, eyes round and worried.

"I'm sorry. I had to say it!" Charlotte walked past them, upstairs to her bedroom. Kathy was asleep.

Despite herself, Charlotte felt sympathy for her mother, drawn by desperation and loneliness to seek the solace of messages from the "other side," in company with other desolate women.

The house in Abbey Crescent was ready to move into by the end of September. Annie and Joe had decided to occupy the back bedroom on the first landing, and let Filly have the big front room, so that she could stare at passers-by to her heart's content, while Charlotte and Kathy had opted for the back attic with its gently sloping ceilings and sweeping dormer window.

"You'll freeze to death up there," Filly grumbled. The words struck a chord in Charlotte's memory. Her mother had said the same thing when she had elected to sleep in the attic in St. Martin's Square. "I can't think why you always want to be stuck away at the top of the house."

Charlotte laughed. She and Annie had had a fine old

175

time sitting in auction houses, bidding for carpets and furniture: comfy sofas and chairs, and a big, polished table. A thrill of excitement flooded through her when she saw the great van at the front door and watched the removal men carrying in their belongings. "Mind you don't scratch that sideboard," Filly warned them.

Annie was in her element, flitting from room to room, directing operations, while Charlotte, Joe and Filly unpacked the tea chests. Joe had color-washed the kitchen a light spring green and edged the shelves with oiled paper. The doors stood wide open to admit the moving men and the pale, warm sunlight of a mild September Saturday morning.

Kathy and Laurie busily folded up discarded newspapers and ran out with them to the garbage can, while Dog, tired of padding about after them, lay in the yard in a patch of sunshine.

Filly said her room was "grand." At last she had been able to take her old furniture from St. Martin's Square out of store. She uttered sharp little cries of pleasure at its reappearance in her life, and wept, too, overcome with the memories it evoked. All her housewifely pride shone as she set about dusting her ornaments. She felt alive again, filled with a new sense of purpose, more like the woman she used to be.

By the time Christmas came round, the house had become a home. At first, Annie said, she had felt like a pea rattling round in a drum, in the spacious rooms. Now she was mistress of her domain—the kitchen. And when Christmas arrived, and the downstairs fires were all aglow, the tree decorated with bulbs and little wax candles, and the goose in the oven, she had no regrets about leaving the house in Friar's Way.

When New Year came, with sleet driving horizontally against the attic windows, Charlotte wondered where the old year had gone to. So many events: the shop, the death of Kitty Tanquillan, this house. It seemed that time had telescoped. She could not believe that so much had happened in what seemed such a short interval between one new year and the next. She saw, in her imagination, the leaves of a calendar fluttering away like snowflakes in the wind.

Howard Ryder stared out of the window at the man-made lake sparkling in the light of a pale, sunshiny January morning.

High Tor, built of solid gray stone, might have gone unnoticed by a casual observer crossing the valley with its rough grass and stone walls. Glancing up at the towering granite precipices of the Pennine Range, a stranger to the area might think that the turrets of the house were merely a part of the landscape, for who in his right senses would ever have built a house on a high, unprotected ridge of rock, in the uncompromisingly harsh West Riding neighborhood of Yorkshire?

Turning restlessly from the window, Ryder caught sight of his reflection in an ornate full-length mirror brought to the house by his grandmother on the occasion of her wedding to Silas Ryder. Just seventeen at the time, pretty and delicate, as her portrait over the mantelpiece in the drawing-room suggested, Arabella Janvier Tremayne had travelled up from her home in Cornwall after her wedding. Newly married to a bluff, hard-headed Yorkshire man old enough to be her father, she brought with her her dowry of fine china, linen, pictures, tapestries, and furniture, to High Tor, a house she had never seen.

Poor little Arabella, Howard thought. No wonder she had withered early and died young away from her native Cornwall! He had often speculated on her first reaction to the house with its solid oak staircases, long draughty passages, and high-ceilinged rooms. Her pictures, furniture and ornaments must have seemed dwarfed here, out of place in Silas Ryder's folly, built at a time when the size and grandeur of houses reflected their owners' wealth and position in society, and the flamboyant taste of the architects given carte blanche to build "high, wide and handsome," with no expense spared.

At any rate, Ryder thought, he had been glad enough of his grandfather's money to smooth his own path. Now, after the boredom of a traditional family Christmas spent with his mother, sisters and his brother Julian, it was high time he returned to London to take up his own pursuits again.

He would stay at his bachelor flat near Eaton Square, visit his tailor, stroll along Bond Street, indulge his amateur taste in purchasing works of art. He must telephone at once, tell his butler to expect him the day after tomorrow.

Pausing briefly to glance at his reflected image, he smoothed back his hair, thinking it was time he paid a visit to M. Audibert, his London barber. Was it his imagination, or was his hair beginning to recede a little at the temples? Damnation! Frowning, he considered his face in the mirror; ran his hand contemplatively over his clean-shaven chin. Hair had a way of sprouting like the devil where it didn't matter. Perhaps he'd better grow a beard.

At least he could find nothing to fault in his lean, well-muscled body, the cut and fit of his dark gray suit and monogrammed silk shirt. The fit of his skin, come to that. A dedicated sun-worshipper, he had whiled away the summer in Greece; in Athens, which he considered to be the most civilized and beautiful city in the world, apart from Paris. There he had acquired his deep suntan, faded now to a pale honey.

Slamming the door behind him, he hurried down to the telephone in the hall, taking the stairs two at a time, almost colliding with his brother's wheelchair.

"Why the hell can't you look where you're going?" Julian's face darkened with anger as he swung the chair round by its wheels.

"Sorry, old chap. Here, let me give you a hand."

"Leave me alone." Julian's dark, brooding eyes swept contemptuously over Howard's lean body. "Prancing around like a damned gazelle!"

No one would have taken them for brothers, the insouciant, fair-haired Howard, and the dark-haired Julian hunched in his invalid chair.

"Christ, but you're a bad-tempered devil," Howard remarked. "How Mother and the girls put up with you, I can't imagine. Thank God I'll be out of this bloody tomb the day after tomorrow!" He spoke without undue rancor. It wasn't Julian's fault he'd been smashed up on the Somme. Must be rotten for the poor bastard losing the use of his legs, having to be hauled out of bed by a servant every morning. Even so, there was no need for him to behave like a bear with a sore head. After all, Julian, as the elder brother, had inherited the "tomb" and the greater share of the income from the mills.

Howard flushed with annoyance, knowing all too well his brother's low opinion of him. It wasn't his fault he'd missed the war. The blind spot in his right eye had made it impossible for him to join the Army.

Julian should be grateful he'd been left at home to look after the business and increase the family wealth by turning out miles of reclaimed wool for the fighting forces. Instead, his brother had castigated him violently on his return from convalescent hospital, for what he termed "bastardization" of the mills in weaving, at a profit, poor quality fabric to clothe the men in the front-line trenches.

"That's not fair," Howard had retaliated. "What else could I have done under the circumstances? Well, run thing your own way from now on! Let me get on with my life!"

"Yes, do so by all means, for what it's worth," Julian said bitterly.

179

"Seems to me you should be glad of that wheelchair, if only to prove yourself a better man than I am, however handicapped you may be," Howard replied heatedly.

Since then, there had been no love lost between them.

Oh God, Howard thought, let him get back to London and the tender ministrations of his servant—a veritable Jeeves—who knew his taste in food, wine, and women, and asked no questions.

What he most needed, after this wretched, boring family Christmas, was a new exciting love affair.

As chance would have it, Howard's servant reported, on the telephone, the failure of the flat's heating system during the holidays, resulting in a series of burst pipes which had flooded the master bedroom and ruined the decorations.

"The cleaners are at work now, sir," the man said. "I hoped to have everything shipshape by the time you returned, but I'm afraid that will not be possible."

"Never mind, Flinton," Howard said absently, wondering where the devil he could go for a few days until his bedroom was fixed up. Suddenly he had a great idea. "I'll go over to Scarborough for a spell. Get in touch with me at the Royal when the mess is cleared up."

"Very good, sir."

The Royal Hotel! He'd enjoy a few days' peace and quiet there. The maître d'hôtel and he were old friends who enjoyed a shared appreciation of good food and wine. Food, as well as works of art and beautiful women, ranked high with Howard Ryder, who considered the Royal's cuisine, especially the chef's carbonnade de boeuf á la flamande, the best he had ever tasted. He left High Tor with scarcely a backward glance.

Unfortunately the weather was bad, and his friend the maître d'hôtel was down with flu. Perhaps he had made a mistake in coming here after all.

Out of season, the town seemed withdrawn, introverted as an elderly hypochondriac nursing her aches and pains.

Turning up his collar, Howard gazed with lackluster eyes into shop windows, at the dreary hats, gloves, shoes, and fancy goods on display.

And then he noticed, with a sharp flicker of interest, a bridal gown in a salon halfway along the street, a thing of grace and beauty, as white as a swan's feathers, beautifully hand-sewn, with scallops of fine lace at the neckline and hem; the kind of dress that would cause a sensation in a Bond Street window.

Screwing up his blind right eye, he read with some difficulty the hand-printed card beside the dress. "Designed by Carlotta. Orders executed with care and attention. Own materials made up. Reasonable charges."

My God, he thought. The woman must be a fool, with her talent, advertising that way. Reasonable charges, indeed! In London, Carlotta would have clients flocking to her shop, demanding her services at any price.

On an impulse, he opened the door and entered the shop.

"Yes?" The woman blocking his way was an elderly Jewess with dark, suspicious eyes.

"Are you—the proprietress?"

"Yes. What can I do for you?" Mrs. Hollister said aggressively.

"I couldn't help noticing the wedding dress in the window."

"Ah, the wedding dress. You wish to buy it?"

"No, simply to congratulate you on its creation, Madam Carlotta."

Agnes Hollister shrugged her heavy shoulders in a gesture of resignation. "I am not Madam Carlotta," she admitted. "But this *is* my salon. Ask anyone you like; they will all tell you the same thing. I founded this business years ago." She lifted her head proudly. "I will tell Carlotta you called—pass on your message."

"I prefer to pass on the message personally, if you have no objection," Ryder said courteously.

181

"She's very busy."

"Even so, perhaps you would give her my card?"

Agnes raised her glasses to see what was printed on it. Had she been tricked?

"Howard Ryder. Dealer in Fine Arts," she read, glancing at the London address in the right-hand corner, covertly taking in his impeccably tailored overcoat and hand-made shoes. He was a handsome young devil, she considered, with a certain air of wealth and breeding about him, now that she could see him more clearly.

"Oh, very well." Conceding defeat, she pressed the bell connecting the salon with the workroom. "Carlotta will be down in a minute."

Hat in hand, Ryder examined the other dresses on display. A good layout, he thought. This shop was in a prime position in one of the town's busiest thoroughfares. But Carlotta, whoever she was, must be wanting in business acumen in allowing a hostile old Jewess to act as her receptionist. Accustomed to the finer things in life, he could not help noticing the poor quality of the fittings. The place was obviously suffering from lack of money. Possibly Madam Carlotta was some old harpy with a face like a horse. But that did not seem to fit with the wedding dress.

"You wished to see me?"

He turned. A tall, slim young woman with red hair and the face of a Botticelli angel stood before him. Feeling as if he had received a stunning blow, he stared at her with such intensity that her pale cheeks flamed suddenly to wild-rose pink. "Are *you*—Carlotta?" he asked.

"No, not exactly. What I mean to say is, Carlotta is simply a trade name. My real name is Charlotte Oakleigh."

"I am staying at the Royal Hotel for a few days," he said. "I wonder if you would care to have dinner with me tonight? Say, eight o'clock? I'll send a car for you."

"Dinner? But—why?" Charlotte had had no experience of strange men who literally walked in from the street, and suggested dining out, within minutes.

"Apart from the fact that I would enjoy your company very much, I should like to discuss business with you," Ryder said easily. "It could be to our mutual advantage. Perhaps I should mention that, apart from my interest in fine art, my family are mill owners in West Riding. It occurred to me that someone with your talent for dressmaking and designing should cast your net much wider than Scarborough."

"I see." Charlotte considered him carefully, with a certain amount of trepidation. And yet, if what he said was true, if, as he had suggested, their meeting at dinner could be advantageous, what had she to lose? "Very well, Mr. Ryder," she said quietly, glancing at his card, "I *will* have dinner with you. Thank you for asking me."

Chapter Fourteen

London shimmered in the warmth of a perfect May morning. Horse Guards clattered along The Mall, sun glistening on their breastplates, harness jingling against the rippling flanks of the horses.

Charlotte had left the hotel early to walk beneath the trees in St. James's Park, where the grass was wet with dew.

Ryder had taken a great deal of trouble to introduce her to the doyens of the great London and Continental fashion houses, to wangle her an invitation to the Spring Fashion Show at the Grosvenor Hotel, but she felt out of place there among the famous haute couturiers with their sharp eyes and blatant insincerities. Coming from a largely undemonstrative family, she could not get used to people falling on each other's necks the way they did, and calling each other "darling."

"My dear, where on earth have you been?" Ryder hurried forward to meet her outside the hotel.

"In the park. It's such a lovely morning I thought I'd go for a walk."

"Have you had breakfast?" He looked anxious; slightly put-out.

"No, the dining-room wasn't open when I went out."

"Come along, then. You must at least have some toast and coffee. There's a long morning ahead of us." Taking her arm, he led her briskly into the restaurant where the waiters were serving breakfast. The noise was appalling. The place seemed filled with brightly colored birds of paradise: even at this early hour, the women were heavily made-up, immaculately coiffed, elegantly, even bizarrely dressed, with long earrings and ropes of beads, and gauzy scarves wrapped across their brows, the ends floating loosely about their shoulders.

The scene bewildered her. Her feet felt as if they were sinking into the carpet as Ryder led her to a table near an ornate centerpiece of hothouse flowers in a massive marble urn. She must look as out-of-place here as a sparrow in a cage of hummingbirds, she thought, wearing a simple green dress unrelieved by any kind of jewelry, her face innocent of makeup. She wished, as the waiter deftly pulled back her chair, that she had at least worn some lipstick.

She realized, of course, that Ryder had not taken all this trouble simply because he admired her skill with a sewing machine, although he had gone to enormous lengths to advise her in the matter of the clothes she should create to make the most impact on her audience. At his instigation, she had brought along the wedding dress he had noticed in the window of her salon, plus a selection of afternoon frocks, and three evening gowns which she had especially designed and created for the event. Even so, every woman possesses an instinct about men's motives, and she knew that Howard Ryder, given half a chance, would do his best to seduce her.

Glancing at him across the menu, she wondered why she was keeping him at arm's length. He was young; remarkably good-looking and attentive; charming and helpful. And yet she remained acutely aware of the fact that it was, perhaps, for those very reasons that she mistrusted him, although she could not help liking him.

Ryder was being equally cagey, remembering the night he had taken her to dinner at the Royal Hotel, the way people had turned to stare at her as he escorted her to

185

their table near the dance floor; he had felt piqued because she had scarcely seemed aware of him as a potential suitor.

Damn the woman, he'd thought irritably, why didn't she flirt with him a little? And then, afterward, because he possessed a sense of humor, he'd thought that, had she done so, he would probably have dropped her like a hot potato. The charm of Charlotte Oakleigh—Madam Carlotta—lay in the intriguing fact that she had *not* attempted to flirt with him. Nor, apparently, despite her stunning beauty and dressmaking skill, did she hold any great opinion of her own potential.

When he had broached the idea of this spring fashion show, she had said, quite sincerely, "But no one has ever heard of me."

"No, but they have heard of *me*," he'd said persuasively. "You needn't worry, I'll guide you every inch of the way."

"No, I couldn't possibly . . ."

"Of course you could! You must have more faith in your own ability." He'd enlarged on his theme. "Of course, most of the Paris fashion houses will be showing, and we could not expect to get a peak showing-time in the main salon, but there are lots of rooms available to the smaller collections, and buyers are forever on the lookout for new talent. So you see, it could be done."

"But what about models?"

"The big houses bring their own, of course," he'd said, "but it is possible to hire models from a London agency. I see no difficulty in that, and I would attend to all the other details: accessories, lighting, music, and so forth." He'd watched her intently over the rim of his brandy glass, vastly intrigued by her patent innocence and self-doubt. Now, diving into eggs and bacon, he realized that she was still an enigma to him.

Ever since they arrived at the hotel yesterday afternoon,

186

she had seemed withdrawn and sad, rather than nervous and excited at the prospect of her first fashion show.

Most other women he knew would have been in a state of near-hysteria. Not so Carla, as he chose to call her. And why had she been out walking in the park so early? Had she, perhaps, a secret lover tucked away somewhere in London?

They had been allocated one of the smoking rooms as the venue for the showing. Ryder had hired three tall girls from Madam Sophia's agency to do the modelling. Behind the partition, Charlotte came, for the first time, upon a scene of unbelievable chaos, with the girls' clothes strewn everywhere. The girls themselves were sitting, half-naked, at a table littered with makeup, adding more rouge to their already overly pink complexions. A stout little woman, who reminded Charlotte of Mrs. Hollister, arranged the clothes they were about to model, in order, on a metal rail, a frown of concentration between her painted eyebrows.

Ryder could not help laughing at the bewildered expression on Charlotte's face. "Don't worry," he said, "everything's under control. Look, here are the accessories."

Suddenly one of the girls uttered a scream of delight, and launched herself, and her frilly corset, into his arms, to Ryder's chagrin.

"For God's sake, Bella," Sophia snapped, "leave all that till later! We haven't got all day! The rest of you: one trace of makeup on any of these dresses, and you'll have me to contend with. Understood?"

They merely grinned, and straightened the seams of the sheer silk stockings adorning their long slender legs.

"Look," Ryder said to Charlotte, "why don't you go and sit in the audience?"

She moved nervously toward the partition to watch the buyers come in. Most of them, she noticed, were elderly men and women with shrewd, worldly eyes, whose approval might be hard to win.

When they were seated, and the chatter had died away, a young man appeared holding a placard inscribed with the words, "Gowns by Carlotta." He was a very small boy, Charlotte noticed, almost as nervous as herself by the look of him. Her heart went out to him as he put down the placard, picked up a basket of carnations, and moved stiffly up the aisles, handing a flower to every lady in the audience.

Watching the poor little lad, she thought of Rowan's son, Berry: remembered her walk in the park that morning. So many memories had crowded in on her there, beneath the trees. She had thought, not only of Rowan's son, but of Rowan's grave in the Highgate cemetery, which she had not yet visited.

She slipped into a chair in the front row. Presently, Ryder took his place beside her. A door opened, and three musicians seated themselves near the runway to begin playing a Chopin waltz.

Charlotte realized how well Ryder had managed the whole affair, making a production of what she had assumed would be nothing more than a dull parade of her dresses in a dark side room.

But Ryder had flooded the room with light; had brought in baskets of spring flowers, daffodils, jonquil, and narcissus, arranged against boughs of unfolding greenery.

Sitting, hands clenched in her lap, she watched the models walk onto the runway, turning this way and that to show off the details of the light wool dresses. The clothes were enhanced by the accessories Ryder had chosen to complement them: soft fur necklets and elegant shoes, sparkling beads and brooches.

The war had forced the closing of many of the great Paris fashion houses, Worth, Doeuillet and Bechoff-David among them, although Madame Cheruit had declared that women needed clothes, war or no war, and she would continue to make what she could.

Now Charlotte experienced for the first time the thrill of the occasion, warmed by the thought that, somehow, despite the war, the creators had survived: the artists, writers, musicians, and the designers of women's clothes. Although she had never regarded clothes as being of supreme importance, she felt privileged to be here as one of the survivors.

Only she knew how many hours she had put in, night after night, after the salon closed for the day. She had worked against time, hunched over her sewing machine, to create her collection, after her basic commitments to her clients had been fulfilled.

For Howard Ryder she felt deep admiration and gratitude—he who had gone to so much trouble to promote what she still regarded as her small talent for sewing. Without his backing, she would have been swamped in this alien world of haute couture. But then, had it not been for Ryder's encouragement, she would never have even attempted to enter it in the first place.

The girls were now modelling her evening gowns, moving gracefully along the runway dressed in the soft, shimmering fabrics she had chosen to reflect the coming of spring. She listened, with a fast-beating heart, to the ripple of applause as the girls swayed and turned to the beat of the music. The models knew each trick by heart, just as Charlotte knew each stitch in her gowns.

She smiled to herself. The green silk dress sewn with crystal beads had been created from her memories of a springtime meadow. Mist overlying a field of buttercups had inspired the diaphanous gold and gray dress Bella wore, while the white frock, flaring to a delicate pink hemline, had been suggested by unfolding daisy petals at daybreak.

Charlotte could not believe what she had heard: someone in the audience had shouted "Bravo!"

When Bella appeared again on the runway wearing the wedding gown, her dark hair tucked demurely beneath a floating white veil, holding a curved bouquet of orange blossom, and swirling this way and that to show off the petalled, snowdrop design of the skirt, an elegantly dressed Frenchwoman cried out ecstatically, "Charmant—trés, trés, charmant, n'est-ce pas?"

Ryder laughed delightedly, clapping the palms of his hands on his knees. "Well, Carla, stand up and take a bow! You've done it, my dear! But then, I knew you would!"

"I couldn't have done it without you," Charlotte said breathlessly, smiling at him. "How can I possibly thank you?"

"Leave that until later," he suggested. "This is your big moment. Make the most of it."

Success brought with it a strange, heady sense of relief, a feeling of utter exhaustion. Charlotte's legs seemed to have turned to jelly. As the buyers crowded round to congratulate her, Ryder slipped his hands supportively beneath her elbow, sensing her bewilderment in face of so much adulation, so many questions and compliments. He took charge of the situation as skillfully as he had done the management of the show.

Grateful for his presence, she knew that she could rely on him to deal with the business side of things, that he would sell her collection at the most favorable price; settle advantageously the matter of copyright. She neither knew nor cared about the financial deals; what mattered most to her was the thrill of creation, the feel of the fabrics she handled, the wonderful colors of tweed, silk, and satin. She had often wondered if poets felt the same way in creating a poem: that incredible moment of joy and fulfillment she experienced when an idea blossomed into reality.

Ryder continued to hold her arm as they made their

way through the throng to the hotel foyer where he lavishly ordered champagne for the dozen or so buyers who had detached themselves from the rest to follow in their wake.

Seated at a circular table, waiting for the champagne, Ryder remarked, under his breath, to Charlotte that these were the ones eager to discuss business. Not that they would do so at the moment, of course, but invitations would be forthcoming, cards exchanged, appointments made. This subtle game of cat-and-mouse delighted Howard, he was so used to auction sales where a raised eyebrow, a slight nod or shake of the head, a casual movement of a catalogue in an experienced hand, meant success or failure to a prospective buyer.

Raising his glass, he proposed a toast. "To Carlotta! Happiness and success always!"

People were drifting away from the hotel. The show had been a triumph. Now the foyer was stacked with luggage; a steady stream of cars and taxis flowed to and from the revolving doors; there were high-pitched cries of "Goodbye darling," as the participants in the thrilling events of the weekend kissed and clung to each other, vowing eternal love and friendship.

The women, Charlotte thought, as she stood on the edge of the crowd, looked tired and jaded beneath their carefully applied makeup. Late nights and too much champagne told their own story, and yet despite their hangovers they remained determinedly ebullient and charming, fluttering their hands and smiling; chattering nineteen to the dozen on the way to their cars; shrieking that they had mislaid a case, a handbag, a glove, an address book.

When Ryder asked Charlotte if she would care to return with him to his flat, she declined with thanks. "I have a friend in London," she said. "I promised to be there in time for tea."

Ryder masked his disappointment with a charming smile. "Oh, come now," he said winningly, "I can give you tea, or something stronger if you prefer."

"No. It's very kind of you, but I'm going back to Scarborough first thing in the morning. I shan't have much time with my friend as it is."

"Very well," he said coolly, "but at least promise me that you will soon visit my home in West Riding." He added quickly, "I'd like you to meet my family, they've heard so much about you."

"Yes, I'd like that very much." She felt inordinately relieved that she had managed to sidestep going to Ryder's flat.

Striding briskly to the door, he tipped the bellman to hail a taxi; helped Charlotte into it, made sure that she had all her belongings with her, and stood on the curb to wave her good-bye, a handsome, debonair figure, his fair hair slightly ruffled by the breeze.

Charlotte went first to Bridie's. Later, by taxi, to the Highgate cemetery.

Outside the gates, she bought flowers from a barrow, three bunches of daffodils, and a posy of violets bound up with ribbon.

The gatekeeper consulted his map, and pointed out the path she should take.

She came upon the stone quite suddenly.

ROWAN TANQUILLAN. 1892—1919. ONLY SON OF GERVAISE AND RACHEL TANQUILLAN. REST IN PEACE.

At least they had not added "beloved" to the inscription.

No one, apparently, had been near the grave in some time. The chrysanthemums in the vase were dead and brittle, the water stagnant.

Charlotte replenished the vase from a nearby tap; arranged the daffodils and placed them near the headstone. The violet stalks were too short, and so she held them in her hands.

Staring at the flowers, she thought that Rowan was not beneath the earth at all, but there beside her watching her, an amused smile on his lips. So strong was the impression that she turned her head quickly, half-expecting to catch a glimpse of him. At that moment, a thrush perched on the gravestone and began singing. She could see the movement of its speckled breast, almost discern the heartbeat. When it flew away, a soft brown feather floated gently on the breeze, and came to rest in the palm of her hand.

Something odd happened at King's Cross: she was just about to go through the barrier when she saw Alice Tanquillan talking earnestly to a tall, dark-haired man who was obviously about to leave on the same train as herself. Departure time was drawing near. Already the guard, with his whistle and green flag, was pacing the platform, glancing at his pocket watch.

Suddenly, the dark-haired man drew Alice into his arms and kissed her passionately. Charlotte could clearly see the whiteness of Alice's face, the trembling of her lips as the man turned away and hurried through the barrier.

At that moment, Alice noticed Charlotte standing there, ticket in hand, waiting to go onto the platform. Her reaction was extraordinary. Without hesitation, she said in a low, hoarse voice, "For God's sake, don't tell anyone you saw me here! Tim mustn't find out! He'd kill me if he did!"

"That is hardly likely," Charlotte replied coolly. "I'm sorry, I haven't time to talk now or I'll miss my train."

"No, *please*, you don't understand. I must have your solemn promise!" There was a dark, frantic look about

Alice; her old cocksureness had disappeared. She looked strained: ill.

"Very well, you have my promise." Charlotte's heart softened towards her. "What's wrong? Are you in trouble?"

"You could call it that. I—I'm going to have a baby!" She laid her hand beseechingly on Charlotte's arm; a thick gold wedding ring gleamed on her finger. "Tim and I married just after Aunt Kitty died," she explained dully. She moistened her lips with her tongue and Charlotte noticed that her hand was shaking. "I must tell you, I'm sorry about what happened! The way I treated you! Will you forgive me?"

Impulsively, Charlotte leaned forward to kiss her, remembering how much she and Alice had once meant to each other. "Of course I forgive you. But I must go now." Quickly, she handed Alice one of her business cards. "If ever you need me . . . Good-bye, dear, and don't worry."

Home! The lights of home shining through the dusk to welcome her. Who needed fame or riches! She had stepped, momentarily, out of her own environment. Now, the thrill of homecoming far outweighed her success at the fashion show.

Annie was bathing the children; Laurie was seated at one end of the tub, Kathy at the other. Flaxen-haired Laurie was laughing, Kathy was not. Normally, her little wild-rose face would have been wreathed in smiles at seeing her mother again. Instead, she was pretending hard not to have noticed her; playing at throwing the soap into the water, and losing it; exasperating the usually placid Annie with her naughtiness.

"I don't know what's come over her," Annie sighed, lifting Laurie out of the bath and bundling her up in a towel; signalling to Charlotte with her eyes that she would take Laurie downstairs to dry her.

"Are you upset because I went away?" Charlotte asked Kathy when they were alone together.

"No." Kathy smacked the water hard with the flat of her hand, half drenching her mother.

"Then why are you behaving like this?"

"Because I—because I'm a . . ."

"Because you're a *what?*"

Tears rolled down Kathy's cheeks. "What the girls at school called me." A sob shook the child's body. "They said I must be one because . . ."

Suddenly Charlotte knew exactly what those cruel, thoughtless schoolchildren had called Kathy. They had called her a bastard, because she hadn't a father.

The child stared up at her. "Mama," she wept, heartbrokenly, "I *did* have a daddy, didn't I?"

Very gently, Charlotte lifted her out of the bath and wrapped her in a soft, warm towel. "Of course you did," she said, burying her face in her child's bright auburn hair, "the finest, bravest father in all the world." She paused, struggling to hold back her own tears. "Don't you remember him?"

Kathy shook her head decisively.

Children's memories remained sharp and clear for a while, Charlotte thought bleakly, then blurred and faded to make room for new, day-to-day impressions.

Life, for the very young, was not a thing of memories, and that was as it should be. Memories were for the very old, not happy, growing children.

She could not help wondering, as she held her child comfortingly in her arms, if this was the right moment to tell her the facts about her birth. And then she knew that Kathy was far too young to be burdened with the truth. How right Rowan had been when he said: "Don't trouble Kathy with all this. Let her go on being Katherine Oakleigh. She will not remember in any case. . . ."

How wise of Rowan.

Kathy had started to smile now, her distress all forgotten. "Just wait till I see them on Monday morning," she said. "Wait till I tell them my father was the finest, bravest man in all the world." She giggled suddenly. "I'll poke Jane Freeman in the eye, you see if I don't, if she calls me a 'custard' again!"

Charlotte had tucked the soft brown thrush's feather safely inside her handbag. Looking at it much later, when Kathy was fast asleep, she thought that in order to survive, one must never allow oneself to become swamped by grief, or hopeless longing, for a past over and done with.

She trembled with the enormity of what she had undertaken; starting out alone in her own frail craft of silks and satins; attempting to breathe new life into a bankrupt business; raising her own small flag of independence in the face of almost insurmountable odds.

Thank God she had this flair, this talent for creation. Staring out of her attic window at the night sky hung with a myriad stars, she wondered what life would have been like for herself, and those dependent on her for happiness, had she been obliged to earn her living as—a typist, or a waitress.

She had not cared much for her initiation into the false word of haute couture, and yet she knew, with her inborn sense of survival, that this was where her future lay, if only she could persuade herself that starlight would not eventually turn to stardust in her eyes.

Smoothing the feather in her hand, she knew that her visit to the Highgate Cemetery had moved her intensely; she recalled the feeling she'd had there of coming close to Rowan again.

If he had lived, they would, in time, have been married. But her longing for him was all part of the stardust. Somehow, she had never stopped to face the reality that he would never come back to her. She had always hoped—believed, however foolishly—that one day, they would meet again; that she would walk into a room to find him there, waiting for her; holding out his hands to her to draw her back into the safe, secure world of their loving.

She wondered, looking up at the stars, what the future held in store for her.

Chapter Fifteen

Julian Ryder glanced out at the lake with its fleshy lily-pads and reeds glistening beneath an early morning sky. From somewhere in the garden came the sound of shears trimming a bush. Topiary had been his late father's overwhelming passion.

Early mornings were Julian's angry times. All that business of being "attended to" filled him with disgust at his disability. He knew he gave his servant, Bennison, a rough ride for the first hour or so until he'd been dressed and helped to his wheelchair.

Bennison would be in soon to shave him, a task which he insisted on performing, possibly for the sense of superiority it gave him, Julian thought wryly; more probably because he doesn't trust me with the bloody razor. He knew his hands weren't too steady at times, but hated to admit it. He'd once accused Bennison of reading too much Wodehouse, of trying to out-Jeeves Jeeves.

His mother walked along the terrace dressed in white, wearing a broad-brimmed straw hat tied with blue ribbons, a pair of pruning shears in one hand, a basket in the other, on her way to gather roses for the house. She smiled when she saw Julian, whose rooms were on the ground floor, and fluttered, like a white moth, to the open window to bid him good morning.

"You're out early, Mother," he said, struck anew by

her air of almost childlike innocence, the soft pinkness of her skin, the honesty of her faded blue eyes.

"It's such a beautiful morning," she sighed blissfully, "besides, there's a lot to do. Howard is bringing his friend for the weekend. Had you forgotten?"

"No, I hadn't forgotten." Julian frowned. "Another of his conquests, I suppose?"

Amelia Ryder sighed, less blissfully this time, wishing that Julian would not scowl so. She used to say to her children when they were small, "You mustn't make faces. If the wind changes, it'll stay like that," and Julian had been such a handsome little boy, with his dark hair and laughing brown eyes. It troubled her deeply to see him like this, a helpless cripple, confined to a wheelchair, his face lined with suffering, lips set in a grim line. Very occasionally a smile would crinkle the corners of his eyes, and she could glimpse something of the old Julian behind the new stern facade.

She said mildly, "I don't know, I'm sure. Howard mentioned in his letter that he and Mrs. Oakleigh are business associates, that's all. She's the person he met in Scarborough, do you remember? The one who is such a talented dress designer."

"That's a refreshing change," Julian said sarcastically. "Howard's friends are not usually endowed with talent."

Amelia Ryder tilted her head a little to one side perplexedly. Was Julian joking or not? She hoped he was. She could not bear the atmosphere in the house when he was in one of his moods.

A gentle, uncomplicated woman who lived for her children, she had not been able to come to terms with the changes in her elder son's once bright, outgoing personality. Amelia often wept, secretly, in her room at bedtime, because the Army had taken a straight-limbed active young man, and sent back to her a crippled hero, old before his time.

"You will have tea with us today dear, won't you?" she

199

asked, knowing Julian's preference for eating alone in his room. "It's a lovely day, and I do so want to make Mrs. Oakleigh feel welcome."

"I'm sorry, Mother, I'm afraid not. I don't feel up to it." Julian tightened his lips. The last thing he wanted was to appear in front of Howard and his latest woman, in his wheelchair.

God damn Howard to hell, Julian thought, closing the window, why did he bring those simpering, idiotic girls of his to High Tor? Was it done deliberately to humiliate him?

Bennison, who had been his sergeant during the war, a wiry ex-soldier of the West Yorkshire Regiment, came in at that moment to shave him.

"Now, sir," he said in that slightly aggressive way of his which meant a lot to Julian Ryder, "you'd better hold still, unless you want your throat cut."

"Would it matter very much if I did?" Julian grinned, tilting his chin.

"Not to me, sir, it wouldn't," Bennison said drily, "except it might be hard for me to find another job as thankless as this one." He paused, lathering Julian's chin. "Begging your pardon, sir, but I couldn't help overhearing just now. Why not have tea with them? You're a bit rough on Mrs. Ryder at times, if you ask me."

"Just get on with your job," Julian snapped, "and keep your opinions to yourself."

Bennison was not easily defeated. "At least give them a treat at dinner," he said, stropping the razor, "show his lordship and his fancy woman what a hero looks like."

Bennison would never have admitted in a thousand years the pride he took in caring for Julian Ryder. Any other man who had been with the major when he earned his Distinguished Service Order would have felt the same.

When the shaving ritual was over, he wheeled Julian's chair along the terrace to his favorite spot overlooking the rose garden and a sweeping view of the valley beyond, rising to windswept heights in the far distance.

A small gazebo had been built there to accommodate the wheelchair, a place where he could sit both winter and summer to read or listen to music. Bennison knew how much it meant to Ryder, how much he valued his privacy away from the house, although it seemed to Bennison that his master spent too much time alone with his pride.

He reckoned he knew what was biting the major this morning, the arrival of his brother with his latest woman friend.

Howard helped Charlotte from the car. "Well, what do you think of it? Pretty ghastly, isn't it?"

He spoke deprecatingly about his home, but he was secretly quite proud of it, especially on a day like this, with sunlight gilding the terrace. The velvety lawns were neatly mown, the deep borders massed with flowers, and the scent of roses drifted up from his mother's carefully tended blossoms.

Charlotte held onto her hat as she stared up at the sprawling facade of High Tor. Building this house must have been tantamount to building a pyramid, she thought, imagining the effort involved in bringing the heavy masonry from the quarries to the hilltop. The solid stone doorstep alone must weigh a ton.

"I don't know about ghastly," she smiled, "it's certainly imposing."

"Wait till you see inside," Howard laughed. "It's like a museum."

He was right about that, Charlotte thought. The hall, with its frowning portraits, weaponry, and massive oak staircase slightly depressed her. This would be a grim place in winter, with all these high draughty rooms. But today, with the sun spilling in through the mullioned windows, masses of flowers in the wide stone hearth, and sunshine lightening the atmosphere, she was able to dispel from her mind thoughts of dark days when the terrace would be piled high with snow, and the rooms freezing cold.

Suddenly Howard's mother appeared at the head of the stairs, hands extended to welcome. "Howard," she cried, hurrying down to kiss him, "I'm so pleased to see you! And this must be Mrs. Oakleigh."

"Please call me Charlotte."

"Yes, of course. But I thought your name was Carlotta?"

"That is the name I adopted for business reasons, but I often wish I hadn't," Charlotte explained.

"Never mind, a rose by any other name . . ." Amelia laughed delightedly, relieved that she and this new friend of Howard's had struck up an instant rapport. She had scarcely known what to say to most of Howard's girlfriends with all their airs and graces. But this girl was not only beautiful, she was charming, Amelia thought, leading the way to the drawing room where two young women, almost identical in appearance, were sitting near an open window.

The introductions made, Mrs. Ryder confided in Charlotte that Tansy and Sorrel had recently become engaged to be married, and were planning a double wedding, the date of which had not yet been decided.

Pouring out the tea, Amelia cast a meaningful look at her son, and Howard knew what was going through her mind. When was he going to get married and settle down?

Watching Charlotte intently over his teacup, Howard realized that she would make him an excellent wife if only he could break through that cool, daunting facade of hers. Damn it all, he had never even kissed her, but he wanted to. If only she would talk about her past life; confide in him. So far, all he knew was that she had a five-year-old daughter and that her husband had been killed in some kind of riding accident.

Charlotte said, in answer to a question from his mother, "I was born in Scarborough. My father was a grocer."

"How interesting, my dear," Amelia Ryder said, smiling. "Mine was a mill-hand. I was fortunate enough to marry the owner's son! Sadly, my husband died four years ago."

Charlotte and Howard spent the afternoon walking about the grounds of High Tor together.

"The London weekend was a great financial success," Ryder said enthusiastically. "You received my check? I meant to come to Scarborough, but I was kept busy in London, attending sales. I have a small gallery in Knightsbridge and my clients have come to trust my judgment."

He seemed as eager as a boy, Charlotte noticed, talking about his interest in fine arts; the authentic Goyas, the Picassos and Monets he had managed to spot and buy at a fraction of their real worth, besides all the antique furniture and silverware he acquired at auction. As he spoke, he brushed his soft fair hair from his forehead with the back of his hand. Charlotte liked him far better now than she had ever before. He seemed more natural and human than he had at the spring fashion show.

"But we must press on, Carla," he said, smiling down at her, holding her hand warmly in his. "You must come to Paris with me next spring! Carla, I want you to dream up the loveliest gowns imaginable! Let your imagination run riot! Promise me that you will!"

He thought that he had never seen a lovelier face than hers, nor met anyone more suitable to become his wife. His mother and his sisters were obviously charmed with her; moreover, he believed himself to be falling deeply in love.

"That is very flattering," she replied, "but I'm not sure that I want to go to Paris. I'd feel out of place there."

"How can you say that? You, of all people? Think,

Carla, you are on the verge of making a name for yourself! You can't turn your back on the future. Think of your daughter. Don't you want the best possible schooling for her?"

Slowly freeing her hands, she turned to watch the lake quivering gently in the late afternoon sunshine, remembering the day Laurie was born; how she had stood in the kitchen of Annie's house, and declared before God her intention of putting an end to the kind of poverty they were forced to endure then. She thought, too, of Kitty Tanquillan, who had put so much faith in her ability to succeed.

Was she being cowardly in throwing away this chance of success? There was still so much that needed to be done for her family, and she wanted to refurbish her salon, to sweep away all the dowdy fitting rooms and modernize the property, perhaps even *buy* the property! She had not thought about that before. Perhaps, if she worked hard enough, she might, in time, be able to afford to buy the house in Abbey Crescent. And Howard was right when he suggested that she would want the best schooling for Kathy.

But it would not be easy for her to enter the claustrophobic world of haute couture. She was afraid of losing more than she gained in the long run. Her business was thriving without the worry of another spring collection.

If she went along with Howard's plans for the future, she might end up like those herons and kingfishers down there on the lake, not realizing in their search for food, that theirs was not a natural habitat at all, but an ornamental setting created by human hands.

At that moment, Mrs. Ryder appeared on the terrace. "Julian is joining us for dinner," she said happily. "I'm sorry to interrupt your tête-á-tête, but it is almost time to get ready."

* * *

Charlotte walked down the long staircase, wearing a simple green evening gown, her hand resting lightly on the banister, pausing now and then to look at the portraits in their heavy gilt frames.

The family and their guests would gather in the drawing room for sherry before dinner, and Clive Antrobus and James Wentworth-Pryce, the twins' fiancés, would be present, Amelia told Charlotte as they went upstairs to dress. "I'm sure you'll enjoy meeting them, and Julian," she said.

Now, hearing the faint hum of voices and laughter from the drawing room, she hesitated momentarily on the bottom step, not relishing the thought of making a belated entrance, uncertain of Howard's motive in asking her here to meet his family. She could not help feeling that she was being very charmingly sized up, and she had not failed to notice Mrs. Ryder's meaningful glance at Howard, across the teacups, at the mention of weddings.

Deep in thought, Charlotte did fail to notice the man in the wheelchair until she bumped into him.

"I'm so sorry," she said quickly, "I wasn't looking where I was going. You must be Julian. Please let me help you." She grasped the chair handles as she spoke, a natural enough gesture which the crippled man obviously resented.

"What the hell do you think you are doing?" Julian Ryder muttered in a hoarse voice. "When I need help, I'll ask for it!"

He caught a glimpse of red hair framing a pale, cameo face, a slim figure in a green dress, an outstretched hand, as he swung his chair round and wheeled it savagely toward the drawing room.

Charlotte watched as he blundered into the room. His rudeness almost decided her to go back upstairs, to plead a sudden headache. But she was a guest in the Ryders' home. It would be insulting to her hostess if she failed to make an appearance at dinner.

Frowning, she followed in Julian Ryder's wake. Amelia hurried forward to greet her. "Oh, my dear, how charming you look. May I introduce you? This is my son, Julian."

"We have already met," Charlotte said coldly, "we bumped into each other in the hall a few minutes ago."

At that moment was born her resolve to go to Paris with Howard Ryder, to stand on her own two feet as a woman with a career. She still had a great deal to learn about survival in what seemed to her a male-oriented world, but survive she would.

She set about creating next spring's fashions with a zeal approaching fanaticism. Violet would be the predominant color. Her evening gowns would reflect the delicacy of her favorite flowers, violets and purple lilac.

She thought, as she sketched out the details, and snipped purposefully at the shimmering fabrics beneath her shears, of violets pinned to a fur necklet, of lilac blossoms in a Cornish garden, of an amazing sunset she had once seen. She visualized amethysts, and the bloom on purple grapes.

Laurie started school in September, and went off hand-in-hand with Kathy, a penny for sweets in a little purse Annie had made her. It matched the one she had given Kathy, and the two children wore them on strings around their necks.

"You mustn't start yelling when Miss Plum sits you on the rocking horse," Kathy said, as one who had weathered the storm. "And you must tell the teacher when you want to go to the lavatory, otherwise you'll do it on the floor, like Nellie Swailes. And don't push beads up your nose like she did, or you won't be able to breathe."

Laurie, who had never even thought of such a thing, said carelessly, "Shall if I want to!"

Annie, walking along beside them, gasped anxiously. "Pushed beads up her nose? Oh, my goodness! Where did she get them from?"

"Her bead-frame broke," Kathy said airily, "so she stuffed them up her nose, in her ears, and in her mouth, and then she wet the floor. The teacher had ever such a time with her."

Oh, God, Annie thought, I shall never know a moment's peace of mind from now on. She watched the children prance through the schoolyard gate set in a high ornamental brick wall, with a feeling of panic. Laurie hadn't even shed a tear, but Annie did, on her way home. She knew she was being silly, but her tender mother's heart yearned after her child; no longer her baby but a name on a school register, her bright fair hair sticking out in two pathetic pigtails under her red tam-o'-shanter.

Charlotte stretched her arms to ease her aching shoulders and neck muscles. She had worked late into the night to finish the violet chiffon evening dress resting on a muslin-swathed hanger in her sewing room.

All six machines were humming merrily now. At last she had been able to afford the extra help she needed. Her first employee, Prudence Mayhew, had proved a born dressmaker, eager and willing to learn. She reminded Charlotte of herself at the same age, under Mrs. Hollister's tutelage.

The rest of the girls, older than Prue, had been carefully selected by Charlotte on their merits as experienced seamstresses. All had proved satisfactory: ordinary, conscientious young women happy to have employment. All of them were the breadwinners in families hard hit by the war.

Mary Nicholson's husband had lost a leg at Ypres, Dora

Smith's husband both arms in Mons; Helen Bowen and her sister Phyllis had lost their husbands in the first Battle of the Somme; Anne Steadman had an ailing mother to provide for since her father's ship was lost at sea.

Charlotte had also engaged, as an alteration assistant, an elderly, slightly acerbic woman, Miss Louise Jennings, who said little, but knew her job inside out. There was little love between Miss Jennings and Agnes Hollister, but the old Jewess was becoming increasingly difficult to please these days.

Charlotte thought, as she looked out of the window at the street below, washed with bright October sunshine, that it was time Mrs. Hollister retired. The prospect of suggesting it filled her with misgivings. Despite her age, Agnes was still a force to be reckoned with, but her short-tempered hauteur was upsetting the staff, and interfering with the smooth running of the salon.

Pondering the problem, Charlotte scarcely noticed, at first, a stiffly erect woman walking along the pavement on the opposite side of the street, holding a child by the hand.

Then, with a quickening heartbeat, she realized that the woman was Rachel Tanquillan, and the boy beside her, Rowan's son, Berry.

There was no mistaking the resemblance. The boy was the image of his father.

"Is anything the matter, Mrs. Oakleigh?" Prudence Mayhew paused on her way to the ironing board with a customer's garment.

"No, I'm just a bit tired, that's all," Charlotte smiled.

"You've been working too hard," Prue said sympathetically, "but the dresses are lovely."

"Oh, Rowan, my darling! I have just seen your son!" The words were locked away in Charlotte's heart, spoken silently to the man she loved. "You would be so proud of him. He has your eyes, your hair, your smile."

She made tiredness the excuse to go home early. She

needed peace, solace, Annie's comforting presence, Dog's warm tongue on her hand.

But peace, it seemed, was at a premium. As she entered the house, Annie handed her the telegram which had just arrived.

"Who is it from?" Charlotte asked.

"Alice Tanquillan. She must be in trouble. She wants you to go down to Grey Wethers at once! It sounds urgent!"

Chapter Sixteen

Glowing October color washed in a red-gold tide over the peaceful Wiltshire countryside; cottage gardens blazed flame and crimson with dahlias, great bright swathes of multicolored daisies and snapdragons, late flowering roses and flaring hollyhocks. The fields, shorn of their harvest of wheat, lay warmly naked in the crystal clear air.

There was something different about Grey Wethers, but Charlotte could not immediately put her finger on what it was until she noticed sprouting grass between the paving stones, weeds in the terrace border. A servant opened the door to her. She had half-expected to see Thomas Rivers, but this man was much younger, a stranger in what now seemed to her an unfamiliar setting. Then she noticed that the copper jugs which had been Kitty's pride and joy were missing from the windowsills, and a film of dust lay over the furniture.

Signs of neglect were everywhere. A saying of Filly's crossed Charlotte's mind—a bad mistress makes a bad servant. "Where is Mrs. Latimer?" she asked, taking off her gloves.

The man smirked unpleasantly. "Upstairs in her room. She's having one of her off days."

Restraining her anger at his insolence, she hurried upstairs. The door of Alice's room stood slightly ajar. She knocked and went in. The curtains were half-drawn. Alice was sitting in front of the dressing-table mirror, wearing a dressing gown, hair lank about her shoulders, rocking to and fro like a baby monkey robbed of its mother.

"What is it? What's wrong? I came as quickly as I could." Looking at her, Charlotte could scarcely believe that this was the proud, fashionable woman of her previous visit.

"I knew you'd come," Alice said. "I'm glad you did. I'm quite alone now, you see. Tim has finished with me."

"At a time like this?" Charlotte said indignantly. "What can he be thinking of when you're having his child!"

"But I'm not. It isn't his child." Alice spoke in a monotone, betraying no sign of her usual hysteria. "He was so angry when he found out. You see," she continued dully, "I pretended for his sake that he had satisfied me, but he never did. Not once. But I do love him a kind of way because I need him to take care of me." She grasped Charlotte's hand. "But I wanted more than that. I had to have more. All my life I have wanted love, and never found it. Oh, I know my father loved me, and Aunt Kitty. When they died, there was no one to turn to except Tim." She gave a short, bitter laugh. "I thought once that Rowan loved me, but he didn't. I tried so hard to make him love me, but it was always you he wanted."

"I'm so sorry," Charlotte said compassionately. "I never meant to hurt you."

"I know that now, but I was crazy with jealousy at the time. I'm not jealous any longer, just so tired of everything."

"What you need is a good rest," Charlotte said. "You look worn out. Why don't you get into bed? We'll talk later."

"No, I want to talk now. That is why I sent for you to tell you how wicked I've been, to ask your forgiveness."

"There's nothing to forgive." Charlotte fingered the girl's hair, thinking what a pity it was that she had let it grow out of the style which had suited her so well. "We had a misunderstanding, that's all, but I think you always knew that I was your friend."

"But I treated you shamefully. I didn't even trouble to say good-bye to you after Aunt Kitty's funeral."

"I know, but that's in the past. Do you imagine I'd have come all this way if I bore a grudge against you?"

Alice appeared not to have heard. "Tim and I slept together on the night Aunt Kitty died. That was wicked, wasn't it? I went to his room. I was so frightened. I made him do it. I begged him to make love to me. He tried, but it was no use. I knew as well as he did that he could never have fathered a child. I knew then that he was too old for me."

"I don't think you should tell me any more," Charlotte said gently, feeling that Alice might regret divulging her most intimate secrets.

"But I want to. I must. Don't you see? How can you forgive me if you don't know what I've done—how wicked I really am?" She was becoming agitated. "That's when Tim started to hate me, when I told him I was pregnant. His pride was hurt. I think he guessed who had fathered my baby. I'd been coming down here from London at every opportunity, you see; making excuses, saying I had things to attend to.

"Of course I knew that Rory O'Neill didn't really love me. It was all just a game with him. But the more I had, the more I wanted. It was like a drug. I couldn't think of anything else. He was so different from Tim. Young, strong, virile. I think he bewitched me with those blue eyes, and that soft Irish accent of his. Besides, he made me laugh, and I needed to laugh. I would go down to the farmhouse late at night, and . . ."

"Don't! Please don't say any more!"

"Have I shocked you? I'm sorry, I just wanted you to understand how it was between us. You know, the thrill of it all, that lovely, warm exciting feeling when you know what is going to happen, and when it does, the wild, reck-

212

less feeling that nothing else matters; the sensation of joy and absolute fulfillment. And yet, afterward, I would think about Tim, and know how much I needed him too, because he is the only man who has ever really understood me, who understands why I do mad things at times." She screwed up her face suddenly; tears flooded down her cheeks. "Am I mad, Charlotte? Am I really hopelessly insane as my poor mother was?"

"No, of course not." Charlotte held Alice's hands tightly as if to draw her back from the brink of insanity. And who could say for certain that she was mad? She had always been highly strung, over-imaginative; moody, as Charlotte knew, but she had often seen the funny side of Alice, and the sad child beneath the willful exterior; the lost, lonely little girl crying out for love and attention.

"Come on, into bed with you now," she said firmly. "You must get some sleep." Tucking her in, she bent over to kiss her. "I'll call you in time for dinner."

"I'm glad you came," Alice said quietly. "I knew you'd make things all right again." She nestled down. "I feel all warm and safe now, as if I had just been to church." She gave a little sigh. "I love you, Charlotte."

"And I love you. Sleep well, darling."

The bright October day had faded to a pearly dusk when she went to call Alice.

The bed was empty, the dressing-gown she had worn lay crumpled on the carpet, the wardrobe doors stood wide open. A feeling of unease washed over Charlotte as she picked up the robe and laid it neatly over a chair. But of course, Alice must have decided to bathe before dinner. The feeling of unease deepened when she saw that the bathroom door was open, the room empty.

The servant was setting the table for dinner. "Have you seen Mrs. Latimer?" she asked, keeping her voice casual.

"No, haven't. But it isn't my business to follow the lady

213

of the house." He smiled cheekily. "Perhaps she's gone down to the farm, she often does."

Slipping on her coat, Charlotte walked quickly down the lane and knocked at the farmhouse door, tense, her heart beating fast. At first there was no reply, and so she hammered on the door with her clenched fist, wondering if Alice and O'Neill were together in the house and did not want to answer her summons.

Suddenly she heard a footstep behind the door. O'Neill called out, "All right, all right, I'm coming."

He appeared, stripped to the waist, holding a towel, his hair wet. He grinned when he saw her, and looked her up and down. "Well, if it isn't Mrs. Oakleigh. I thought it might have been someone else."

"Alice, you mean?" She regarded him scornfully. "Is she here? Are you hiding her?"

"Now, why in the name of all that's holy would I want to do that?" He began towelling his hair. "You'd better come in, or the neighbors will start talking." He grinned at her discomfiture. "With me half-naked, I mean, and you so beautiful."

"Don't talk rubbish!" But she stepped inside. They could hardly carry on a conversation on the doorstep, and one of the farmhands was crossing the yard. As much as Charlotte disliked the man for the harm he had done Alice, she could not help understanding why she had found him so attractive. He had a kind of animal magnetism about him, a cocksureness and conceit which had to do with the way he looked and talked. His eyelashes were so long and so dark that his eyes, half closed, seemed almost black against the warm, tanned skin of a man out in all weathers, and his voice with its soft Irish burr had a way of making his words sound like a caress.

"Now, what's all this about?" he asked, pulling on his shirt. "Oh, I get it. She's been blabbing, has she? And you've come to read me the riot act." He grinned unashamedly. "A bit like locking the stable door after the horse has gone, isn't it?"

"Alice is missing," she said coldly, "that's why I came, to ask if you had seen her."

"Missing?" He gave a low whistle, and raised his eyebrows, regarding her quizzically, not taking her seriously. "You mean she's run off somewhere? Well, well . . ."

"Oh, for God's sake! She could scarcely 'run' anywhere, in her condition. She's not in the house, she's not here. Where can she be?"

"Yeah, I see what you mean." He stopped smiling. "Perhaps we'd better start looking for her. I'll call the men—search the lane and the woods. You'd better wait here."

Shrugging into his jacket, he strode to the door, calling to his dogs. She watched him from the window, striding across the yard to the stables, then to the cottages at the end of the lane. She saw the men emerge, carrying lanterns, followed by their wives, anxious to know what was happening. She could see their pinafores gleaming whitely in the twilight.

Sitting in a chair near the fire, she listened to the slow, solemn ticking of the clock, the crackle of the flames on the hearth, her hands clenched on the arms of her chair.

Alice walked across Sweet Water Meadow, swinging her broad-brimmed straw hat by its scarlet ribbons, breathing in the scents of an October evening, the faint tang of a bonfire, burning leaves, the bittersweet fragrance of dying flowers blended with damp earth and wet grass.

She had dressed herself with special care for the occasion, in a loose white dress with a long skirt. She moved like a shimmering ghost across the meadow, calm and happy, knowing that she was not mad after all, but acutely, wonderfully sane at last, seeing the world as it

215

really was, not as some dark image in a shattered looking glass.

> Out flew the web and floated wide;
> The mirror crack'd from side to side;
> "The curse is come upon me," cried
> The Lady of Shalott.

She smiled, remembering the poem Jenny Carfax had taught her in those far-off days in Scarborough. The poor Lady of Shalott, she thought, pausing to gather a cluster of dying flowers from the long grass, to have died for love, to have been so cursed.

But she, Alice Tanquillan, was not cursed. She was free and happy and light-hearted. Strange that she still thought of herself as Alice Tanquillan, not Alice Latimer, married to a man who no longer wanted her, who no longer loved her.

But my father loved me, she thought, pressing the flowers to her cheek in an agony of affection for the poor, half-dead things, and I think Rowan loved me too, in his own way.

Perhaps he was waiting for her near the landing stage. She started to hurry, scattering the flowers in her wake, anxious not to keep Rowan waiting too long; remembering that pretty pink parasol with the lace ruffles, and the green dress with the pointed lace collar she had worn that day they went rowing together.

She could see Rowan quite clearly now, smiling at her through the mists of time. Her thoughts made a daisy chain as she stumbled through the dewy grass. "He loves me, he loves me not. He loves me . . ."

"Hush, little baby, do not cry, and I will sing a lullaby." Crooning softly, she stepped into the boat, untied the rope, and pushed away from the jetty.

How beautiful the sky looked, with nebulous clouds melting away to a deepening twilight; how deep and dark the water, gliding along beneath her. She listened delightedly to the chuckling, slapping sound it made washing against the sides of the boat.

Water to wash away the sins of the world, she thought, and tried to remember the words the parson had spoken at Aunt Kitty's funeral. "The mountains also shall bring peace: and the little hills righteousness unto the people." Yes, that was exactly right. But her dress was getting wet. Her lovely green dress with the pointed lace collar, the one Charlotte had made for her a long time ago.

She began singing the words of an old French nursery rhyme as the boat drifted silently towards the center of the lake.

She wondered if Will Oakleigh was right when he said that the lake was bottomless. Poor Will. But she was not afraid of legends. For the first time in her life she was not afraid of anything. Love, after all, casts out fear.

She continued to sing a song to her baby. "Sur le pont d'Avignon, l'on y danse, l'on y danse."

They found her early next morning, trapped in the reeds near the water's edge, her hair floating gently, like seaweed.

The tired men doffed their caps. O'Neill knelt beside her swollen body and covered it as best he could with his jacket, and stayed with her while the men went back to the farm to fetch a wagon. All his ebullience had left him now. He wondered how this thing had happened. In the spreading dawn of a new day, he noticed that the boat was missing.

Charlotte knew, by his face, the whiteness of his lips, the tired lines beneath his eyes, what had happened; knew that Alice was dead. All the laughter had faded from those

Irish blue eyes of his. He seemed stunned; shocked, bewildered.

"It was an accident," he said briefly. "It must have been an accident. The boat was rotten. She didn't know. I should have told her, but I never dreamed . . . Why? Holy Mother of God, what made her take that boat on the lake in the first place? Why did she do it?"

Charlotte shook her head dumbly, unable to speak; trembling from head to foot; numb and frozen with grief and shock.

"Here, have some brandy! Sit down before you fall down!" He sounded angry. "I know what you're thinking, that it was my fault! I should have told her about that bloody boat. But I'll tell the police; tell them everything! Oh, my Christ!"

"No!" Charlotte's head came up sharply. "You can tell them about the boat if you like, but nothing else. No one must know about. . . ." She began to sob, harshly. "Leave her some dignity. She had suffered enough. Let her rest in peace."

"Don't be a fool," O'Neill said roughly. "Latimer knows damn fine well the kid isn't—wasn't—his."

"Perhaps," she said fiercely, "but his pride will never let him admit it."

"Oh, Jesus! All right, then. I'll do whatever you think best." His voice roughened with tears. "Don't forget it was my kid, too."

"Yes," she said bleakly. "I'm sorry." Suddenly, she needed to know the truth. "Did you love Alice?"

"Ah, sure I did, in a way. There was something about her." He swallowed awkwardly. "I think I made her happy. She needed someone. But there was no future in it. I have a wife in Ireland. Besides, I wasn't the only one . . ."

"I see."

"When all this is over," he said, staring out of the win-

218

dow, "all the things that need to be done, I'll be on my
way. I hate this bloody place now."

The police had taken charge, moving ponderously about
the house, asking questions. They had taken Alice's body
to the mortuary in Devizes. The servant and his wife, the
cook, said little, wanting to keep out of trouble. Charlotte
had been worried that the man would mention Alice's
habit of visiting the farmhouse, but he said nothing.

She had sent for Latimer, and Kitty's elderly lawyer,
Alfred Cunningham, whom she had met briefly at the old
lady's funeral—a man she liked and trusted, a tall, quiet,
gray-haired man, impeccably dressed, with shrewd gray
eyes that missed nothing. She also sent telegrams to Annie
and Joe, Bridie McKenna, and Howard Ryder, explaining what had happened, saying she must stay on at Grey
Wethers until after the inquest and the funeral.

Cunningham and Latimer would be on the last train from
Paddington. Charlotte took charge of the arrangements,
making sure their rooms would be ready, planning what
to serve them for dinner. Life must go on, and there was
no one else to see to things now.

Latimer remained coldly aloof throughout the meal,
taking no part in the conversation, eating practically nothing, betraying no sign of grief that his wife was dead.

Cunningham, on the other hand, could not have been
more charming or solicitous. Charlotte kept on thinking,
over the food that nobody really wanted, that all this, the
house, the farms, the land, belonged to Latimer now; that
he would probably sell them to the highest bidder. In her
overwrought state of mind she remembered Kitty
Tanquillan's pride in her home, and seemed to see her
there, in her old place at the head of the table, her eyes

219

brightly challenging, hair aureoled about her thin, humorous face.

After coffee in the drawing-room, she excused herself, pleading tiredness. "I'm sure you'll have things to discuss," she added, wondering if she was the reason for Latimer's moody silence. Perhaps he had felt it beneath his dignity to eat with one of the "lower orders."

"Please stay," Cunningham said, "what I have to say now, concerns you." He took a sheaf of papers from the document case near his chair. "I am speaking of Mrs. Latimer's will." He glanced at Latimer. "It may surprise you to learn that your wife came to my office, several weeks ago, to settle her affairs."

Latimer shrugged his shoulders disinterestedly. "Nothing my late wife did would surprise me in the least."

"I'm relieved to hear it. Then it will come as no great shock to you to hear that Mrs. Latimer left her entire estate to Mrs. Oakleigh."

"What? *What* did you say?" Latimer stood up, almost speechless with anger. "But this is—outrageous!"

"Alice has left Grey Wethers to me?" Charlotte frowned disbelievingly. "But that is not possible."

"I assure you that it is." Cunningham smiled. "She also requested that I should deliver this letter to you personally in the event of her death." The old lawyer nodded his satisfaction. "Congratulations, my dear. May I say how delighted I am?" Glancing up at Latimer, whom he obviously disliked, he asked, "Have you anything more to say, sir?"

"Simply this. I don't give a damn about this place, or the woman I married. I am more than relieved to be rid of both. I married—a slut!"

Anger flooded through Charlotte, a deep, cleansing anger, a fierce, burning contempt for a man who had shown so little compassion for Alice when she was alive, and dared to denigrate her now that she was dead. Standing up to confront him, she said in a clear, ringing voice, "No,

Mr. Latimer, you married an unhappy child young enough to be your granddaughter. In my opinion, you should have known better! One thing is certain, if you had cared more for her and less for yourself, she might well be alive now!"

Latimer strode from the room, his face contorted with anger.

Alone in her room, she opened Alice's letter.

Dear Charlotte,

I have been to London today to see Mr. Cunningham. When you read this, you will know why. I have been troubled that if anything happens to me, Tim would automatically inherit Grey Wethers. I don't want that to happen.

Tim doesn't care for Grey Wethers. He has told me so often enough, but I know that you do. Above all things, I never want it to fall into the hands of my Uncle Gervaise, who was so unkind to my father and me.

I also visited Dr. Faraday for the results of certain tests. As I suspected, my baby is lying wrongly. I am not afraid of dying, but if I were to die, giving birth, I could not bear to think of my baby alone in the world. And, if my baby died and I was spared, how could I bear to go on living without my child?

Please accept Grey Wethers as my gift to you, a token of my deep and abiding gratitude for all that you have meant to me; a continuance of my love for you and Rowan.

Alice

Chapter Seventeen

The inquest on Alice was held in a dusty schoolroom near the Devizes Corn Exchange. The coroner recorded a verdict of accidental death.

When it was over, Charlotte left on Cunningham's arm. "Thank God," she murmured. "Thank God."

He patted her hand. "It was an entirely fair verdict. The coroner could have reached no other conclusion in view of the evidence."

Thank heaven, the old man thought, for Latimer's stiff-necked conceit which led him to state, under oath, that his wife had been well-balanced, though of a slightly nervous disposition. The evidence of a man of his standing had carried considerable weight.

It had been a long drawn-out proceeding, hot and stuffy, in the makeshift courtroom. The coroner had gone into all the evidence very thoroughly, especially that concerning the condition of the boat.

Asked why he had not drawn the deceased's attention to the fact that the boat stood in need of repair, O'Neill said that he and the other farm workers had been busy with the harvest. In any case, he was not the estate manager. There had been no one in that position for some time past, but he had drawn Constable Drury's attention to the fact that the boat was missing, after Mrs. Latimer's body had been recovered.

So it went on.

When all the evidence had been heard, and weighed, the coroner said that here was a tragic case of a young mother-to-be who had suddenly found herself in dire circumstances in the middle of a lake in a leaking boat. His sympathy lay with the bereaved husband, and all concerned with the tragedy.

Later, Charlotte and Cunningham walked together about the estate, noticing signs of neglect everywhere.

Charlotte, who had learned a little about farming when she was married to Will Oakleigh, knew that things were not as they should be, that an estate of this size needed a firm, guiding hand at the helm. She attached no blame to Alice, who knew even less about running an estate than she did.

In the midst of all the confusion connected with Alice's death, and the inquest, she had not stopped to think of her new role as the mistress of Grey Wethers. The enormity of the situation overwhelmed her suddenly: the fact that she could not keep Grey Wethers, manage it by herself, and run a dressmaking business at the same time. It simply was not possible.

O'Neill, she knew, had meant what he said about leaving. Who, then, would manage the farm?

After dinner, when she and Cunningham were alone in the drawing room, she told him that she could not keep Grey Wethers.

"That possibility had occurred to me," the lawyer said.

"It isn't just the estate," she explained wearily, "the actual land, and the farms, but the house itself. I honestly couldn't go away and leave it as things stand at the moment." She was thinking of the servant and his wife; what might happen to Grey Wethers if it was left in their care. "On the other hand, I can't stay here indefinitely. I have my own work to see to. . . ."

"Yes, I can see all the problems." Cunningham nodded

his head sympathetically. "Of course, my dear, you are very tired at the moment. This has been a trying time for you, and you have held up quite splendidly. As I see it, what you need is someone you could trust implicitly to act as your agent. Two people, perhaps. Someone to run the estate, and a capable woman to look after the house. Think about it, Charlotte. That is the best advice I have to offer."

They buried Alice next to Kitty Tanquillan on a rosy October morning.

The farm workers and their wives had turned out en masse, as they had done at Kitty's funeral. Perhaps they had never taken Alice to their hearts in quite the same way, but they had gathered as a mark of respect to the girl who had married in their midst only a short while ago, wearing a white dress and carrying a bouquet of crimson roses.

Some had thought it scandalous of Kitty Tanquillan's niece to marry so soon after the old lady's death; others had seen the bride as a symbol of hope for the future, as the mother of sons who would grow up to farm the land as Kitty had farmed it. In any event, they had not been able to resist the spectacle of a bride on her wedding day, a real county wedding, or the huge party Alice had treated them to afterward in the village hall, with plenty of good food, and all the beer the men could drink.

In the church, during the parson's address, Charlotte's eyes rested on the coffin. How tiny it looked. Blinking back tears, she looked up at the memorial tablets on the walls to ease the ache in her throat, and noticed one that she had not seen before:

To the memory of William Oakleigh. Greater love hath no man. Placed here by Alice Tanquillan Latimer, whose life he saved. Deo Gratias.

At least Latimer had possessed enough common decency to attend his wife's funeral, not that Charlotte deluded herself into thinking he had done so for any other reason than to silence the wagging tongues of the villagers, but he had icily declined her invitation to return to Grey Wethers for luncheon afterward. The minute the service was over, he strode to his car without a backward glance.

O'Neill was at the graveside, too, eyes puckered to blackness in his downcast face. She wondered briefly if he would stay on, if she asked him, but he had already given his notice and made arrangements to have his personal belongings removed from the farmhouse.

And now it was all over, the funeral, the seemingly interminable luncheon at which she had presided as Lady of the Manor, keeping her thoughts and feelings to herself as befitted her new, "exalted" station in life, a role for which she felt herself to be singulary unsuitable. What would all these gentry folk think, she wondered, if they knew that she intended to sell Grey Wethers to the highest bidder?

And yet her heart ached at the thought of it. What would Kitty say if she knew? And Alice, who had proved to be, in the final analysis, both sagacious and caring. The memorial tablet to Will Oakleigh had touched Charlotte deeply. She asked Cunningham about it when her guests had gone.

"It was her own idea," he said gently. "Her way of making reparation for the wrong she had done him. Poor Alice."

In the ensuing silence, they heard the far-off ringing of the doorbell, voices in the hall. The servant knocked, and came into the room. "There's someone here to see you," he said offhandedly.

"I'd better go and see who it is." Charlotte rose to her feet. The doorbell had scarcely been silent these past few days, what with the undertaker's men, and people calling with messages of sympathy, bringing flowers; some genuinely sorry that Alice was dead, others avid to take a look inside the house.

The last people she had expected to see were Sir Gervaise and Lady Tanquillan.

Apparently, the last person they expected to see was herself.

Charlotte froze suddenly. This was something she had not anticipated. But her hesitation was momentary. As much as she might wish to turn and run, she had a duty to fulfill: that of the new mistress of Grey Wethers. Remembering the old mistress of Grey Wethers, Kitty Tanquillan, she drew back her shoulders and walked proudly toward them.

Gervaise's jaw sagged suddenly. "What are you doing here?"

Charlotte smiled faintly. "More to the point, Sir Gervaise, what are *you* doing here?"

"I want to see Latimer," he said shortly. "The matter is urgent."

"I'm afraid that is not possible . . ."

"Not possible! Not possible!" Clenching her hands, Charlotte remembered that she had said those very words to Gervaise Tanquillan a long time ago—the day he pushed past her at the cottage in Cornwall, intent on seeing his son. The memory of that day rose up suddenly before her. The humiliation she had suffered was impossible to forget: the way he and his wife had walked in to accuse her of ruining their son's life, calling her a wanton woman. They had not paused for one moment to consider her feelings, her agony at having lost the man she loved, but had brushed her aside as if she did not exist.

226

Drawing in a deep breath, she continued, "Mr. Latimer is not here. He left after the funeral."

"But I *must* see him," Tanquillan said doggedly. "I've a business proposition to put to him, where can I find him?"

"I really couldn't say."

"Come along, Gervaise," Rachel Tanquillan said, butting into the conversation. "We are simply wasting our time here, talking to a servant." She considered Charlotte coolly, insultingly. "But, of course, your niece was ever fond of making friends with the lower orders."

At that moment, Alfred Cunningham entered the arena. Smiling pleasantly, he said, "Perhaps I can be of help? You remember me, don't you, Sir Gervaise? I was your great-aunt's solicitor."

"Oh, yes," Gervaise said briefly.

"But we can't talk here, in the hall. Won't you come into the drawing room, and sit down?"

"That's more like it!" Gervaise snapped. "My wife and I have driven all the way from London to make Latimer an offer for my great-aunt's estate; an offer he can scarcely refuse if he has any brains in his head!"

'Oh, really?" Cunningham paused on the threshold of the drawing room. "Then you've come all this way for nothing. I'm afraid Mr. Latimer does not own the property."

"Eh?" Gervaise's chin came up sharply. "Then—who does?"

Cunningham smiled. "Perhaps I'd better introduce you, though I believe you have met before." He laid his hand on Charlotte's arm. "My dear, you have just heard that Sir Gervaise has an interesting, and no doubt lucrative, offer to put before you. He wishes to buy you out. Are you willing to sell?"

"No," Charlotte said quietly, making up her mind in a split second. "I am not!"

"You!" Rachel Tanquillan turned on her in a fury.

"Why, you scheming little hussy." Her body trembled with unrestrained anger. "You've played your cards well, haven't you? First my son; now—all this!" Her lips curled contemptuously. "But there's one thing you'll never have! The thing you wanted most of all! The name Tanquillan!"

"Will you please leave my house, now?" Charlotte said wearily, "and, please, never come back. You are not welcome here."

The die was cast. Later, Charlotte sobbed until she felt her heart would break.

In the early hours of next morning, she woke up with a start, her mind as clear as a bell.

Of course. Why hadn't she thought of it sooner? Someone she could trust implicitly, who knew all about farming.

Harry! Her brother Harry! Dear, dependable Harry who had taken up farming as a career, after the war.

She came down to breakfast, smiling. Cunningham was in the dining room, helping himself to bacon and eggs. His train was due to leave Devizes at eleven o'clock.

"You look positively radiant this morning, my dear," he said. "Any particular reason?"

"Yes. I've just sent a telegram to my brother, who knows all there is to know about farming. I'm sure he'll come! He's family, you see."

"And the house? Any ideas about that?" Cunningham raised a quizzical eyebrow.

"No, not yet. But something will turn up."

Charlotte stood with the old lawyer on the terrace, awaiting the arrival of his taxi.

"You've been so marvelous to me, I'll never be able to thank you enough," she said quietly, gripping his hand.

"Ah, here's my car now."

But it was not his car that drew up in the gravelled drive.

They watched silently as the driver got out and helped his passenger to disembark. A slightly bizarre figure emerged, wearing a wide-brimmed hat with strands of gray hair blowing untidily about her face. She gave explicit directions to the driver about her luggage, in a lilting Scottish accent.

"Bridie!" Charlotte ran down the steps to her, arms outstretched. "Oh, Bridie! I'm so glad you've come! But—*why?*"

"I just had the feeling you needed me! I've told you before, Scots people know about such things!"

She frowned suddenly at the servant who was dragging her suitcase. "Here," she snapped, "that won't do! Pick it up and carry it properly!"

"Yes, ma'am," he said respectfully.

Part Three

Chapter Eighteen

Emily Beresford's heart missed a beat as she watched her grandson playing the piano. How like his father he was.

Fifteen now, Berry was even taller than Rowan had been at the same age, and just as handsome, possessing his father's characteristics of inner strength and determination.

Emily could see where that determination might lead to, knowing that Berry would one day rebel against Tanquillan's domination. The boy had confided to her his dread of entering the Company. "I told Grandfather I want to become a musician," he said, "but he lost his temper and told me never to mention it again."

Gervaise had not changed over the years. The loss of his son, and the reasons for that loss, had taught Tanquillan nothing of kindness, tolerance, or compassion. Berry was already being prepared, like a sacrificial lamb, for his future as heir apparent of the Tanquillan Company. Gervaise would take Berry with him to France and Italy, during the school vacation, to visit the Continental warehouses at Marseilles and Genoa.

Berry sighed as he closed the piano. He had Emily to thank for his secret music lessons. Now it was time for him to go home. He would not see her again for several weeks.

"I'll miss you, Madre," Berry said, using his special name for her. "A whole month . . ."

"It will soon pass, darling."

He pulled a face. "It won't be any fun with Grandfather. He'll make me practice my French and Italian."

Smiling, Emily kissed her grandson good-bye, and watched from the drawing-room window as he ran up the steps of the house next door. Poor Berry, she thought. Like father, like son. The pattern was about to repeat itself.

She missed Rowan every day of her life. Had she really been in love with him? Was it possible for a woman of her age to fall in love with a man young enough to be her son?

"Excuse me, madam, will you take supper in the dining room?"

Emily started; she had not noticed the servant. "I think not, Julia. I feel rather tired. Will you bring a tray to my room?"

"Of course, madam."

I'm just a foolish, ghost-ridden old woman, Emily thought, walking slowly upstairs. The year is 1930, and I'm still living in the past; hanging onto this house which no longer belongs to me, for its memories of happier times.

Glancing down at the shadowy hall, she could almost see people crowding in through the open door the night of Romilly's coming-of-age party, and hear their laughter, the music of a tango from the lantern-lit conservatory. She remembered Romilly skimming downstairs like a white silk butterfly, hands outstretched to greet Rowan, inviting him to dance with her, in that high-pitched, girlish voice of hers.

That was almost seventeen years ago. Emily sighed. Now Romilly was married to David McClean, the mother of his two unattractive children, James and Fiona, who had inherited their father's prominent nose and high coloring. Emily knew that Romilly cared more for them than she did for Berry, whom she had packed off to school in London at an early age.

Seated at her dressing-table, Emily saw in the mirror

the streaks of gray at her temples, and wondered where the years had flown. It seemed no time at all since she was a young woman with a husband and a growing daughter to care for; she had been a brilliant hostess, involved in living.

She felt that she had outlived her purpose in life, and yet there was still one battle left to fight. The battle for Berry's happiness.

Laurie Grayler inched forward to the edge of her seat, staring up at the screen, living every moment of the story.

Rio Rita, Senorita
Here is my heart.

This was romance with a capital R.

"That reminds me," Filly said, giving her a nudge with her elbow, "you haven't had your Saturday night senna pods. Remind me when we get home."

"*Senna pods?*" Laurie turned her flaxen head to stare disbelievingly at her grandmother. "What made you think of that?" How could anyone possibly think of senna pods when John Boles was singing his heart out?

" 'Senna Rita,' " Filly nodded sagely.

"I *hate* senna tea," Laurie cried mutinously, screwing up her face, "it makes me feel sick! I can't even bear the smell of it!"

"I'll nip your nose then," Filly threatened. "Besides, you'll feel a lot worse if you get plugged up!"

"Oh, all right." Laurie sighed: it was no use arguing with Gran. But she'd bet any money that film stars never had such a problem. Her sensitive soul felt lacerated by life and senna pods.

She almost wished that Gran had stuck to her spooks.

It was all that medium's fault. Why hadn't she got in touch with her from the spirit world as she said she would? Laurie didn't think much of people who didn't keep their promises. Just one groan from the "other side" would have sufficed. But then, if she *had* groaned, or let out a yell, Laurie thought philosophically, Gran might not have given up spiritualism in disgust and turned to the silver screen as an alternative, and *she* might never have fallen in love with Ramon Novarro in *The Pagan,* or Rod la Rocque, the "Prince of Adventure."

Now, Laurie thought, lying in bed listening to her inner rumblings, she was head over heels in love with John Boles. Did that mean she was fickle? She sighed. What a lovely word, fickle. It reminded her of a tiny slip of a new moon, all bright and shiny.

"Oh, *crumbs!*" Suddenly she leapt out of bed and rushed downstairs to the lavatory.

Back in bed she thought, with a sudden thrill of pleasure, that Peggy would be coming from Darlington next week to help her mother with the visitors; that her schooldays were almost over. The long weeks of summer stretched invitingly ahead.

Charlotte woke to the sound of birdsong. For one blissful moment she thought she was back in Scarborough.

Why was it that one never remembered dreams very clearly afterward, only the mood they evoked?

Whatever she had dreamed last night had brought her a longing to go back in time. But would she even recognize the girl she used to be, the Charlotte Grayler of long ago, grasping the handles of a cart, during the war, to deliver her father's groceries?

Turning on her back, she thought about the day Laurie was born, the day she had thrown down the gauntlet to God. How did the saying go? "Take what you want, saith the Lord, take it and pay for it."

At least Kathy would be home from boarding school soon, bringing with her a feeling of youth and freshness.

Glancing at her bedside clock, Charlotte realized she would be late for her ten o'clock appointment if she did not hurry. Ringing for the maid to run her bath, she got up and crossed to the wardrobe to choose what she would wear for the day.

When she was ready, she hurried downstairs to breakfast in the room overlooking the park, dressed in a deceptively simply gray georgette dress, her hair drawn back from her face in one of the new, shorter styles.

Strange how light-headed, almost naked she had felt without the heavy chignon at the nape of her neck, but there were compensations. She had no time to waste in lengthy sessions at the hairdresser's.

The post was lying on a silver salver under the Venetian hall mirror as Charlotte paused to pull on a scarlet hat, stabbed through with a gray feather, to complement her dress and matching elbow-length gloves. Riffling through the letters, she put aside the ones she would read later, and picked out one with a York postmark, addressed in Kathy's sloping handwriting.

A frown of disappointment puckered her forehead as she skimmed through it:

Dear Mother,
Would you mind very much if I went to Scarborough for the next two or three weeks? Peggy will be coming from Darlington. There's nothing much to do in London and I hardly ever see you . . .

Charlotte understood her daughter's reluctance to spend her vacation in London when she could be on the sands with her cousins, and Dog—although the poor creature, by human standards, was very old now.

Would things have been different if she had allowed Kathy to bring her pet to London with her six years ago?

With a word to the servant that she would be back at six o'clock, and a reminder to Cook that Mr. Ryder was coming to dinner, Charlotte hastened down the steps to the car, glancing back at the house as the chauffeur drew them smoothly away from the curb.

She had always liked Georgian architecture, serene and unchangeable in a fast-changing world: high-windowed houses, fluted fanlights, curving staircases, light panelling, delicate moldings; the feeling of space and elegance encompassed within four walls. But loneliness, too, could be trapped within four walls.

Buying the house and the Bond Street premises was Ryder's idea when it became obvious that Madam Carlotta was fast becoming a force to be reckoned with in the world of haute couture, and that travelling constantly to and from Scarborough to attend the London and Continental fashion shows was both exhausting and impractical.

"You can afford to indulge yourself now, my dear Carla," Ryder said, after their brilliantly successful trip to Paris in the spring of 1922. "You are, after all, a very wealthy woman."

"Maybe I am, but I don't wish to squander money," Charlotte replied, "I'm not used to it." She had not felt close enough to the imperturbable Svengali figure who had become her mentor and business advisor to admit that she was worried sick about Annie and Joe, fearing that her inheritance might drive a wedge between them. "Besides," she added stubbornly, "there's my Scarborough salon to think of. I'm not turning my back on that, or my family."

"Your loyalty does you credit," Ryder said lightly, "but there's no reason why you should relinquish either. Prue Mayhew has proved herself capable of managing the salon, and your brother Joe, and his wife, are happily settled." He paused. "You are the one I feel concerned about, running yourself ragged when there's no need."

238

"I suppose you are right, it's just that . . ."

"I know exactly what you're thinking," Ryder said persuasively, "you're afraid of underwriting your business with the money from your inheritance; throwing good money after bad, as we say in Yorkshire. But that doesn't apply in your case. Even without Mrs. Latimer's money, you could afford to expand. Carla, you've *earned* your success!"

"Hmm," she'd said doubtfully. It was difficult to explain to a man like Ryder, who had always had plenty of money, that the sight of one five-pound note meant more to her than all the stocks and bonds that Alice had left her. She still remembered having to scrape to raise that twenty pounds to pay Mrs. Hollister's creditors, and woke up in a cold sweat, at times, wondering if she really had bitten off more than she could chew: opening a salon in the West End; buying a house in Glamorgan Square.

But there was more to it than that. She had seemed to be losing touch with her own daughter, whom she had left with Annie and Joe until the house was ready to move into. And she could never quite get it into her head that Grey Wethers actually belonged to her, that everything was running smoothly there, thanks to Harry and Bridie. Above all, she had wanted Kathy in London with her, but even that presented problems. She had found a charming private school for her, scarcely a stone's throw from Glamorgan Square, but she would have to engage someone, a companion-cum-nanny, to take Kathy to school, bring her home safely, and see to her during the holidays.

She did not really want to do this, but there was no other alternative. As much as she wanted to look after Kathy herself, she could not be with her all the time.

Another set of problems had arisen on the day of Kathy's arrival in London. When the child realized that the strange house was to be her home, she burst into floods of tears.

"What is it, darling? What's the matter?"

239

"I want to go home," Kathy sobbed.

"But, sweetheart, this *is* your home."

"No it isn't! I want my Auntie Annie—and Dog!" Face wet with tears, she'd gulped miserably, "Why couldn't Dog have come with me?"

"I'm sorry, love. I know how much Dog means to you, but he wouldn't be very happy here, with nowhere to run about. But you can see him whenever you go back to Scarborough, and Aunt Annie and Uncle Joe are sure to take him to Grey Wethers with them for the summer holidays.

But Kathy would not be comforted, and although time had taken the sharp edge from her misery, and she had quite liked the small private school her mother had chosen for her, Charlotte could not help feeling that Kathy had never entirely forgiven her over Dog.

She hadn't liked Howard Ryder very much, however, whom she treated with cold disdain. But Kathy had eventually gone away to boarding school, thus easing the situation.

The car nosed gently into Bond Street and drew up outside the salon with its discreet "House of Carlotta" sign.

Now, drawn into the busy world of her own creation, with softly carpeted floors, oyster satin draperies, shining crystal chandeliers, and great white planters of early summer flowers. Charlotte remembered, with pleasure, that Howard was coming to dinner. She had not seen him for some time.

"My dear Carla, how stunning you look!" Ryder kissed her lightly on the cheek. But he could not help thinking, as she smiled up at him, that he had never kissed her the way he wanted to. And yet he had believed, in that dazzling spring of 1922, when he had first shown her Paris with the may trees in blossom in the Tuileries gardens, and walked with her beside the Seine, pausing now and then to watch the bateaux-mouches passing beneath the bridges of the Ile de la Citè, that she was beginning to fall in love with him at last, but . . .

"You are looking well, too, Howard. But so you should, after a month in Greece. Did you enjoy your trip? Tell me all about it . . ."

He remembered the way her eyes sparkled, her transparent joy as the great city unfolded before her, her childlike pleasure in everything she saw, the way she had reverently bound her shining red hair with a green silk scarf as they entered Notre Dame.

"I always enjoy Greece," he said, "but Athens is becoming rather too filled with tourists for my liking. The Acropolis was never intended as a picnic area . . ."

"Shall we go in to dinner?" she laid her hand affectionately on his arm. The table was set for two; crystal goblets sparkled by candlelight. She had chosen white daisies for the centerpiece.

Exactly when had he lost his chance with her, he wondered. That night by the Seine, looking down into the twilit water after the excitement of the fashion show?

She had been standing, very quietly, eyes downcast, her arms resting on the parapet. When he'd asked her what she was thinking about, she had said, simply, "About London—the Embankment, the river Thames," and he had known that these were only a part of what she was thinking, that she was remembering—someone. Someone she had loved a long time ago, whose memory was always with her, blotting out the present, and he had felt suddenly bitterly jealous, and angry, because of that someone who seemed always to stand in the way of his coming closer to her.

He should have kept quiet, but he didn't. He said, in a harsh voice, "Why go on living in the past? Forget the past! We are here, together, now! Life is for living! I love you. I'm asking you to marry me!"

"I owe you more than I can ever repay," she said gently, "but I'm not in love with you, Howard."

"You could be, if you'd let yourself," he'd flung at her, "if you'd forget—whoever it is you are in love with."

"I wish I could forget . . ."

* * *

Over coffee in the drawing room, she said, "I had a letter from Kathy this morning. She doesn't want to come home yet. I can't blame her."

"She doesn't like me very much, does she? Treading on dangerous ground, but would you have changed your mind about marrying me, if she had?"

"I can't honestly answer that."

"Have you thought that ours could be a good marriage? We have a lot in common, and I have waited a long time, hoping that one day . . ."

"And if I refuse your offer, does that mean an end of our partnership?"

"Certainly not. I would rather have you for a friend than not at all." He paused. "It is simply that I am tired of a bachelor existence. I'd like to marry—have a son, before it's too late."

"And you've met someone you wish to marry, is that it?" Charlotte glanced across at him. The room was shadowy, with pools of light on the carpet; the glow of the fire in the basket grate; white shutters folded back to admit the last rays of the setting sun.

He smiled ruefully. "We met in Athens. Her name is Virginia Lees-Smith. She is young, beautiful, intelligent, and, well, we saw quite a lot of each other; travelled home together on the same boat."

"And you'd like my blessing? Oh, Howard, I couldn't be more delighted."

"I wanted to make perfectly certain that you hadn't changed your mind," he said.

"No, I haven't. I'm sorry. But thank you for asking."

Perhaps he would ask Virginia to marry him, Howard thought. But he would never stop wanting Carla. He remembered the lights of Paris shining down into the river; lovers walking hand in hand; the mingled scents of lilacs and Gauloises cigarettes. How angry he had been that night.

"You know what's wrong with you, Carla? You are nothing more than a shell of a woman! If you don't soon wake up to reality, you'll find that love has passed you by. Is that what you want?"

He would never forget the pain in her eyes, the softness of her voice as she said, "I have no other choice."

Chapter Nineteen

The three girls perched on the promenade railings to dry their feet. They had been what Peggy termed "splodging," wading ankle deep where the sea frilled in on the sand; kicking up the water, feeling its delicious coolness between their toes.

The clear, warm afternoon was filled with the sounds of laughter, the thin, high-pitched screams of children building castles in the wet sand left by the receding tide, or clinging to the saddles of the donkeys patiently trotting along, in the charge of urchins brandishing bamboo canes.

Laurie pushed back her flaxen hair from her sunburned forehead, and sighed deeply with regret for her lost donkey-riding days. It had been a bitter pill to swallow, standing there with her threepence clasped in her hot little hand, being turned away by the "donkey man" with the cutting comment that he wasn't risking having their backs broken by fat lumps like her.

The insult still rankled. Glancing down at her bare legs, holding them out for inspection, she said wistfully, 'I'm not all that fat, am I?" It was a question she asked ten times a week.

"It's only baby fat," Kathy said comfortingly, lifting her face to the sun, eyes closed, "you'll soon run it off when you start work in September."

Kathy was tall and slim like her mother, with bobbed auburn hair caught back with a tortoiseshell barrette. At fifteen she possessed Charlotte's grace and coloring, but her features were slightly heavier, mouth wider, eyes less green, almost the color of topaz.

Waving her feet to dry them so she could brush off the sand, Laurie wished she could sell ice-cream at one of the green canvas stalls dotted along the beach. She was consumed with a passionate longing to slather it on one of those metal gadgets they used for making ice-cream sandwiches, or to dip a wooden spoon in the container bobbing up and down in its sheath of packed ice, and stuff it into the cones.

She had begged her mother to let her become an ice-cream vendor, but she wouldn't hear of it. "You'd eat all the profits," Annie laughed, "besides, last week you wanted to work in a sweet shop so you could crack toffee with a hammer; the week before that you wanted to be a butter maker at the Meadow Dairy. No, my mind's made up, you'll be far better off learning hairdressing. In any case, it's all settled. Your dad and I have paid the fifty pounds for your indentures."

"*Indentures,*" Laurie said disgustedly. "Sounds like a set of false teeth! Besides, I didn't like Madam Hart very much. She'll make me have my hair cut, and I'll look all bottom and legs then."

"Nonsense," Annie replied briskly. "Madam Hart's salon is the best in Scarborough. You were lucky to get in there, and a bit of discipline will do you good." Her face had softened, then, at Laurie's woebegone expression. "The thing is, Daddy and I want you to learn a worthwhile job that will stand you in good stead. We wouldn't want you to waste your time stamping cows on blocks of butter."

"What's up with you?" Peggy demanded, nudging Laurie with her elbow, sticking out her own shapely legs; bending forward to give her feet a clout to dislodge the sand between her toes, nearly toppling off the railings as she did so, giggling as she grabbed at Kathy for support, her shoulder-length black hair fanning about her face in a cloud.

"I was just thinking about being a hairdresser," Laurie said with dignity, wondering why it was that Kathy and Peggy weren't larded with baby fat.

"You're not practicing on *me*," Peggy laughed, regaining her balance.

Somewhat offended, Laurie thought that Peggy never took anything seriously. Her dark-haired cousin would laugh to see a pudding cool, while Kathy just sat there, elegantly slim and self-contained, which had to do, Laurie supposed, with her being educated at a boarding school: learning French and German, and having riding lessons. For all that, Kathy did not seem very happy at times. Laurie was secretly rather glad that her mother had turned down Aunt Charlotte's offer of paying for her own education at that snobby boarding school near York.

She knew for a fact that her aunt had also offered to pay for Peggy's education, but nothing had come of it. She could just imagine her belligerent Aunt Maggie's reaction to *that* offer. She pictured her all hot and cross, saying she needed Peggy at home to help her look after her younger brothers and sisters: Daniel—a nasty-tempered little devil with a way of nipping your bottom when you weren't looking—Stu, Ernie, Ada, and the new baby, Clara.

The wonder was that Aunt Maggie allowed Peggy to spend her summers in Scarborough, helping Mother with the visitors, but Laurie thought she knew the reason for that. Peggy earned good tips for dusting, making beds, and serving the visitors' food; she returned to Darlington fattened up and fit for the winter, ready to cope with the housework, her mother's migraines, or yet another addition to the Masters' household.

Laurie, the innocent, vague about the facts of life, often wondered where all her Aunt Maggie's children came from.

She sighed. Suddenly her anguish over these problems floated away as she listened to the music of her life: the hoarse cries of the fishermen inviting visitors out to their boats for a trip round the bay; the tinny rattle of tambourines from the puppet show farther along the promenade; the queer, squeaky balloon voice of Mr. Punch; the muted roar of the sea in the distance; the cries of the gulls sweeping down over the harbor in search of food.

At that moment, Laurie felt herself to be on a warm secure pinnacle of happiness. Come September, she would begin her hairdressing apprenticeship, but that was just a kind of bridge between childhood and growing up, before she became a film star. She had read all about Hollywood in sixpenny film magazines from Woolworth's: about Malibu, where the stars lived. One day her own image would flicker down from the silver screens of the world, her eager footsteps would kick up the sand on the beach at Malibu.

Laurie's clear blue eyes—Annie's eyes—starred about with thick black lashes, gazed serenely into her special, magical world of dreams.

Gran was taking the three of them to see Garbo and Gilbert in *A Woman of Affairs* tonight. Sitting in the cinema, breathing in the pungent odor of disinfectant, Laurie would commit to memory every gesture of the enigmatic Swedish film star to re-enact in front of the swing mirror in the attic where she and Kathy and Peggy slept during the hot summer months. Kathy and Peggy occupied the double brass bed with a billowing feather mattress, and she had a narrow single bed set beneath an angle of the sloping ceiling. The windows were flung open wide to the warm night air. The sounds of the cinema, whose rear doors opened into the lane, rose excitingly toward them through the sweet-scented dusk of summer nights lit with brilliant stars.

Not that she would practice her acting in front of the other two, her dreams were too special and private for that, as secret as her diary and the exercise book into which she copied her favorite poems.

"We'd best be shoving off, now," Peggy said, craning her neck to look at the parish church clock, "the visitors will be in for their teas at five, an' me Aunt Annie'll skin me alive if I don't get the tables set in time."

Inching down from her perch, she slipped her bare feet into her sandals, followed reluctantly by the other two. "When you going home, then, Kathy?" Peggy asked, as they wandered arm-in-arm along the crowded foreshore.

"The day after tomorrow, I'm afraid." Kathy made a face, staring at the sea rocking gently beneath the azure blue of the sky, the little pleasure boats bobbing along, the green cliffs girdling the bay. She was thinking how much she would hate going back to the claustrophobic confines of the hot London streets, the loneliness of the elegant Georgian house in Glamorgan Square; how much she would miss her cousins, and Dog.

The thought of leaving him brought a lump to her throat. Dog had always been a part of her life, although she could not remember exactly when, or how, he had entered it, but it was tacitly understood that the poor old thing really belonged to her, despite the fact that he lived with Aunt Annie and Uncle Joe. Now Dog could barely walk on his arthritic legs, his muzzle was flecked with white, and he spent most of his time asleep in his wooden box under the kitchen table.

"If you're worrying about Dog, don't," said the perspicacious Laurie, squeezing Kathy's arm. "I'll take good care of him for you." But even Laurie, who had never come up against death in her fourteen years on earth, had the awful feeling that poor Dog would not be here for very much longer. For weeks now she had watched him growing weaker, with the same sad intensity that she watched the patient, gentle-eyed donkeys trotting along the beach under a hot summer sun, being whacked on the rump with those rotten little bamboo sticks. A great lump rose up in her throat at the thought of it.

Why was it, she wondered, biting her lip, that one could be so happy one minute, and so miserable the next? She had been ecstatically happy back there on the railings. Now, despite the laughing crowds thronging the beach, the exciting clamor of the trams dinging merrily along the seafront, the smartly dressed men and women paying their sixpences at the tollhouse at the entrance of the Spa walk, the distant sound of the band playing a march in the open-air bandstand, she knew that the trinity would soon be broken.

She wished Peggy hadn't asked Kathy when she was going away. Nothing would be quite the same when she was gone. She dreaded the thought of saying good-bye to her; watching the train growing smaller and smaller, remembering that her gran said it was unlucky to watch a train out of sight, and yet it seemed so disloyal to Kathy not to keep on waving until the very last minute.

Worse still would be waking up to find Kathy's half of the featherbed empty, her bits of makeup gone from the dressing table, her clothes removed from the makeshift wardrobe. But it was more than that, even. It was the feeling she had that Kathy was growing away from her. She could not have put her feelings into words, but it had to do with—change; growing older; realizing that changes were inevitable. But she didn't want things to alter. She wanted the world to stay exactly as it was, for ever and ever.

Charlotte had booked tickets for *The Three Musketeers* at Drury Lane. Kathy loved the theater. They had already seen *The Swan* at St. James's, *The Barretts of Wimpole Street*, and *Private Lives* with Noel Coward and Gertrude Lawrence.

How strange it was, Charlotte thought, that whenever

Kathy came home she felt it necessary to fill her every waking moment with excitement and treats, as if she were a guest in the house instead of her own daughter.

Sometimes they would have supper at the Ritz, or the Grosvenor, before driving to the heart of theaterland with its panorama of lights and swiftly moving traffic. If they did not go out together, the girl would simply make some excuse to spend the evening alone in her room, not wanting to meet her mother's business associates, whom she felt duty-bound to entertain to dinner once in a while. Charlotte had discovered, to her dismay, that fame had its price. Ryder's fault, not hers. He would call up and say, "Carla, darling, there's someone you simply must meet, who is dying to meet you." But Kathy abhorred those business dinners; would have no part in them. "All those dreadful men and women with pounds, shillings, and pence signs in their eyes," she would say contemptuously.

Charlotte supposed that most adolescent girls underwent the metamorphosis of growing up in a series of fits and starts: bubbling over one minute, introspective the next. Not that Kathy ever bubbled over, in London, as she did in Scarborough. Her attitude toward her mother was often restrained, at times faintly resentful, especially when Howard came to dinner, or accompanied them to the theater. She remained totally impervious to his charm, his gifts of chocolates and corsages. "Well, really, Mother! He does lay it on a bit thick, doesn't he?" And Charlotte secretly thought that he did.

Tonight, on their way to Drury Lane, Kathy seemed more natural, not exactly effervescent, but less withdrawn than usual, gazing out of the car windows at the passing parade of theater and cinema-goers, a faint smile of anticipation hovering about her lips.

Suddenly, a memory of Kathy running full-tilt into Rowan's arms on the beach in Cornwall invaded Charlotte's mind. Turning her head to hide her tears, she knew that she would trade all her wealth, all her success, the house in Glamorgan Square, her Bond Street salon, and Grey Wethers, to go back in time, to be with Rowan again, with Kathy a laughing child, her tumbled auburn curls blowing about her vivid, happy little face.

So much that was important in the child's life had been pushed into the background as a matter of expediency. She had grown up with the belief that Will Oakleigh was her father. But Charlotte knew that as long as the lie remained, she could never really come close to her daughter, that one day, at no matter what cost to herself, she must tell her the truth. She *must!*

The car halted momentarily near Piccadilly Circus where the crowds were thickest, thronging the pavements, wandering across the road toward the flower sellers and news vendors plying their trade beneath the poised figure of Eros.

Eyes aglow, Kathy leaned forward to read the placards. "Look, Mother," she cried eagerly. "Amy Johnson has arrived at Croydon Airport! Isn't that wonderful? Just think of a woman flying all that way, alone! I must buy a paper! I won't be a minute!"

Before Charlotte could stop her, Kathy was out of the car, dodging the traffic with all the careless impetuosity of youth, while the chauffeur, swearing softly under his breath, slid the car to the curb to wait for her.

The car door slammed. Kathy was back, eyes alight as she spread out the newspaper. "It says here that Amy Johnson was given a heroine's welcome. Crowds thronged the tarmac to cheer her! Oh, isn't that simply splendid! I wish I could have been there! Not just as an onlooker, but writing the story for other people to read!" Charlotte was destined to remember that night for a very long time afterward, the warmth of the theater, the hurrying crowds; stars shining down from a black velvet sky; the fragrance of the bowl of gardenias on the hall table as Kathy kissed her goodnight.

She had turned then to the pile of unopened letters beneath the Venetian mirror, one of them with a Scarborough postmark, and tears had flooded down her cheeks as she went slowly upstairs to Kathy's room to tell her that Dog had died, very quietly, in his sleep.

Chapter Twenty

Ryder had not exaggerated when he said that Virginia was beautiful. Enormous heavy-lidded blue eyes lent a dreamy expression to her piquant, heart-shaped face. Her skin reminded Charlotte of fine Chinese porcelain, but Virginia would be the first to admit that she owed her complexion to the hours she spent in a beauty parlor. She was brightly modern, as quick and lively as a bird. Her hair resembled dark birds' wings, lying smooth and glossy against her curving cheekbones.

Her father, Sir Thomas Lees-Smith, wealthy head of a Leeds biscuit firm, owner of a fine stone mansion set in an acre of neatly mown grass, flowerbeds, and tennis courts, had seen to it that news of his daughter's engagement to Howard Ryder received full coverage in the Yorkshire papers. He and his vivacious wife, Constance, obligingly posed for the press photographers and reporters who flocked to the house at his invitation. Sir Thomas had come up the hard way and didn't mind who knew it. Bluff and hearty, he handled the press very much as he handled his employees: "Now, we'll have a photograph of my daughter standing near the window, then another near the fireplace looking up at the portrait of my wife," he commanded jovially.

The press did as it was bid. It wasn't every day their job was made so easy for them, with beer and sandwiches provided.

She and her husband were delighted by the engagement, Lady Lees-Smith told the reporters. It was all so romantic, a fairy tale come true, the way the couple had met in Greece, to discover later they lived only a few miles apart. She smiled blissfully and delicately fluttered her chiffon hanky. Yes, they were planning a big wedding in Moortown parish church where Virginia had attended Sunday School as a child. "I have some photographs here," she said helpfully.

Virginia took it all in her stride. Daddy was like an overgrown schoolboy, and Mummy in her element posing for the county magazine photographer. Her parents would do all the donkey work and foot the bills, while she had already made up her mind exactly the kind of dress she would wear, how many bridesmaids she wanted, and where she and Howard would go on their honeymoon: Paris first, then the Mediterranean. Carla would, of course, create her trousseau. That was six months ago.

In May, Charlotte and Ryder travelled to Yorkshire together by train, Howard was as nervous as a kitten up a tree. "God, I wish it was all over and done with," he said, glancing at his watch for the umpteenth time. "I might feel marginally better knowing things were running smoothly at home, but that surly bastard Julian has ruined things, as usual. He refused point blank when I asked him to be best man, and now the ungracious brute has told Mother he won't even come to the wedding. She was in tears when I telephoned her last night."

Charlotte kept to herself the thought that Julian probably derived grim pleasure from ruining things. The man was a selfish boor. Tactfully, she changed the subject. "I'm looking forward to seeing your mother again," she said. "It was kind of her to invite me to High Tor for the weekend." Albeit to dress Virginia, she thought.

Howard sighed. "It'll be bloody chaos there. Mother

has invited relations I never even knew existed." He grinned ruefully. "She's throwing a party this evening, a buffet with champagne, caviar, and stuffed quails under glass, I shouldn't wonder."

"Surely not?" Charlotte laughed.

"No, I'm exaggerating." He frowned suddenly. "Carla, if it had been you and me, getting married, I mean, would you have wanted all this fuss?"

"But it isn't you and me," Charlotte replied quietly, "it's you and Virginia. In any case, I never waste time answering hypothetical questions."

She thought suddenly that all she had to remind her of Rowan was a tiny circle of dried grass, a few pressed flowers, a bird's feather, and a child who had very little need of her now.

Howard was right about the chaos. High Tor was the scene of feverish activity, with servants hurrying to and fro carrying trays of silver and glassware to the conservatory where buffet tables had been set up for the party, the starched white cloths looped with ivy, dotted with superb flower arrangements.

Amelia Ryder appeared in the hall, a small, worried ghost holding a pad and pencil. "Has Carlton brought in the hothouse flowers for the hall yet?" she asked the housekeeper. "We really must hurry. Everything must be ready before the guests start arriving. Are you sure Cook has baked plenty of scones and fruitcake for tea? Is there plenty of lamb? If not, we must order another leg."

Amelia had not even noticed the arrival of Howard and Charlotte until Howard stepped forward, laughing, to hug her.

"I've heard of killing the fatted calf, but this is ridiculous," he quipped. "Behold, the bridegroom cometh!"

"Oh, my dears!" Mrs. Ryder's face cleared. "How lovely it is to see you again, Charlotte. You must excuse all the mess. Come through to the drawing room. I'll ask Mrs. Carlton to send in some tea. The twins should be here at any moment to lend a hand."

"Perhaps I could lend a hand, too?" Charlotte suggested.

"Really? You wouldn't mind?" Amelia smiled. "Well, I could do with help arranging the flowers. Carlton left them until the last minute to make sure they were fresh for the weekend. They're in the garden room."

"Oh, they're beautiful—exquisite," Charlotte said, gazing with pleasure at the massed carnations and long-stemmed roses.

Filling the vases, Amelia remarked wistfully, "I know I shouldn't say this. Virginia's a nice girl, and I'm fond of her, but I had rather hoped that you and Howard . . ." She paused. "That you might learn to care for my son."

"I *do* care for him a great deal, Mrs. Ryder, but not in the way you mean."

"Are you happy, Charlotte?" Amelia placed the vase she had filled on the table. "You look rather tired. Oh, I know how hard you must have worked to achieve your success, but there are other things in life. Have you ever thought of remarrying?"

"No, I haven't."

"I didn't mean to pry," Amelia sighed, "it just seems such a waste of a beautiful woman. I often wonder if a career is enough for you. Tell me, do you see much of your little girl?"

"Kathy's scarcely that now, Mrs. Ryder. She's at boarding school at the moment, but we'll be spending some time together in Wiltshire during the summer holidays."

"I often wish that children need never grow up." Amelia turned her head away. "I'm sorry, I was thinking of Julian. I can't bear to see him the way he is now." She blinked, and smiled. "To be truthful, I'm not really looking forward to the wedding. I did so hope that he would make an effort to go—to be Howard's best man."

Charlotte wandered onto the terrace to breathe in the cool night air. The party was in full swing. Music floated through the open drawing-room windows. Resting her hands on the balustrade, she gazed down at the lake shimmering faintly in the starlight. May, not April, was the "cruellest month." The scent of lilac, almost unbearably sweet, sent her mind skittering down the alleyway of time to another Maytime, long ago.

Turning, she saw the glow of a cigarette in the shadows at the far end of the terrace, the humped outline of a man seated in a wheelchair. Her first impulse was to go back indoors, but it was cool and peaceful out here. Her long taffeta skirt made a rustling noise on the paving stones as she walked slowly towards Julian Ryder.

"Good evening," she said quietly.

"What the devil!" Ryder swung round to face her.

"I'm sorry if I startled you." She hesitated, wondering what had prompted her to attempt a conversation with him in the first place. "I came out for a breath of air. It's such a lovely night."

"It was," he said pointedly, throwing down his half-smoked cigarette.

Touched to the quick by his rudeness, angry with herself, Charlotte's temper rose, curbed only by her determination not to let him see how upset she was. She seldom resorted to sarcasm, but the words came out before she could prevent them.

"Tell me, Major Ryder," she said, "are you naturally insulting, or has practice made perfect in your case?"

"What the hell . . . ?"

"No, allow me to finish!" Charlotte was trembling now. "I realize that you had a bad time during the war, but so did a lot of other men, my brother Joe among them, who was wounded and shellshocked. My eldest brother fared even worse: he was killed outright. The man I loved came

257

home to die after three years in German hands. They all deserved a medal for valor, in my opinion. Perhaps they pinned yours on the wrong uniform!"

"If you were a man, and I were not confined to this bloody wheelchair, I'd knock you down for saying that," Ryder muttered hoarsely.

"If you were a man," Charlotte said passionately, "you would not use that chair as an excuse to make the people who care for you so unhappy! I suppose you imagine yourself an object of pity. The truth is, Major, the only person who pities you is yourself!"

Turning abruptly, she hurried back along the terrace and into the house.

What on earth had possessed her to say such dreadful things to a helpless cripple? Then suddenly she remembered her seamstress, Dora Smith's husband, Bill, who had lost both arms during the war; the valiant way he had fought to overcome his disability; the agony he had endured when the artificial arms were fitted. Dora used to weep about it over her sewing machine. But Bill had learned to type with his bare feet, to use his toes as fingers; had opened a little general shop in the front room of their home.

Tomorrow would be a trying day. Charlotte had arranged to drive to the bride's home first thing in the morning to supervise the dressing of Virginia and her bridesmaids. After the reception she would make her excuses to Mrs. Ryder. She could not bear the thought of bumping into Julian again.

Brilliant colors from the stained-glass windows dappled the altar lilies. The church was packed; the organist softly played Mozart's "Ave Verum," the music an accompaniment to the hum of conversation, the rustle of dresses and hymnbooks.

The Bishop of Leeds, who would perform the ceremony, had entered the body of the church; choirboys, white-surpliced, had filed in like a troupe of angels, and were now sitting, as if butter wouldn't melt in their mouths, doing "swops," Charlotte suspected, behind the high-fronted choirstalls.

Weddings vaguely depressed her, especially the ostentatious kind, when all that really mattered was two people, standing alone together, making their solemn vows to each other.

Perhaps she was just overtired. It had been a trying business making the last-minute adjustments to the bride's dress in a room full of chattering bridesmaids. She wished the whole thing over and done with, and thought that, as soon as possible, she would catch a train to Scarborough to see Annie.

She scarcely realized, at first, why the volume of whispers had suddenly increased, and the congregation seemed to be straining forward slightly, without being too obvious about it. Then she saw Julian's servant pushing in his wheelchair from the vestry. Well, she thought, wonders would never cease. So he had changed his mind about being Howard's best man after all.

She sensed, rather than heard the arrival of the bride, and turned to see Virginia, composed, smiling, utterly confident, a vision of loveliness in white silk organza sewn with crystal paillettes, bouffant veil held in place by a diamond tiara. One gloved hand rested lightly on her father's arm, the other held a bouquet of white gardenias and lilies-of-the-valley.

A marquee had been erected on Sir Thomas's smoothly-mown lawn to accommodate the overspill of wedding guests. Hired waiters moved deftly, serving champagne. Howard and Virginia were standing together in the hall to receive their congratulatory kisses and handshakes. Lady Lees-Smith fluttered, like a blue silk butterfly, among her guests, saying all the charming, meaningless things that the bride's mother usually says on her daughter's wedding day.

"Oh yes, Lady Dalrymple. So fortunate the weather held. Happy the bride the sun shines on, they say . . ."

Face pink with excitement, she went on scattering her little gems of conversation. "Oh, Mrs. McClean! Yes, she does look radiant, doesn't she? Her gown? Yes, it is stunning, isn't it? Designed by my son's business associate, Madam Carlotta. Yes, of course I'll introduce you. She's over there, by the window. She's not cheap, mind you."

Charlotte was standing alone, looking out at the sea of colorful hats and the penguin figures of the waiters. Half-suffocated by the heat, she was wondering how soon she could make her escape when she heard the high-pitched, girlish voice of Virginia's mother at her elbow. "Oh, there you are, Carla. There's someone I'd like you to meet. A friend of Ginny's, Romilly McClean."

Never, in her wildest dreams, had Charlotte expected to see Rowan's wife again, nor had Romilly expected to see her. The moment was electric. A dull flush mounted Romilly's cheeks.

"Have you two met before?" Lady Lees-Smith wished, at that moment, she possessed her husband's savoir-faire. Tommy always seemed to know how to handle crises of this sort, while she simply blundered on, making matters worse.

"Once, a long time ago," Romilly said stiffly.

"Really? How extraordinary!" Constance edged away from them. "Well, if you'll excuse me . . . you must have a lot to chat about."

When they were alone, Romilly said in a low passionate voice, "Is there no end to the humiliation you have caused me? But if you dare to breathe one word . . ."

"You need not worry about that."

The years had done nothing to enhance Romilly's persona. She still wore a fringe to conceal her slightly bulbous forehead. Now, motherhood had thickened her once-slender waistline, and years of discontent had etched premature lines about her mouth. She had been a petulant, spoiled girl. Now she was a petulant, spoiled woman, married to a wealthy Scottish landowner, anxious for her reputation; dreading the rattling of old skeletons in the family closet.

"Not *worry!*" How dare you say that to me? You, who ruined my life! But I warn you, if you so much as attempt to interfere in my life again, if a breath of scandal ever touches my marriage to David, or reaches the ears of my children . . ."

Charlotte frowned. "You mean you haven't told Berry about—about what happened?"

'Of course not! Do you take me for a complete fool? Berry thinks his father died in an Army sanitorium. He has never questioned that. Why should he? He need never question it, unless you choose to tell him differently."

"I'm sorry. I see no point in continuing this conversation. I'm leaving now. I have a train to catch." Charlotte felt suddenly faint, and slightly sick. Turning away, she hurried from the room. Her one thought was to go home to Annie.

Chapter Twenty-One

Laurie whisked around Madam Hart's private cubicle with a sawn-off sweeping brush, wiping snippets of gray hair from the floor into a dustpan. Kathy was right about baby fat, she thought. The wonder was that she had not worn her feet to her ankles with all the rushing around she had to do; dusting, making the tea, polishing basins and mirrors, washing gowns and towels, at the beck and call of the other assistants, not to mention Madam Hart. This lady put the fear of God into Laurie whenever she sailed into the shop like a Spanish galleon in full rig: stiffly corseted, dressed in black, and wearing a formidable black wig; a mountain of a woman whose coming could be heard a mile off by the creaking of stairs and floorboards. At the first creak, Laurie and the rest of the girls, would apply themselves to whatever they were supposed to be doing with unusual diligence.

The shop itself, just round the corner from her Aunt Charlotte's salon in St. Nicolas Street, facing St. Nicholas Square and the sea, with its ceiling-high showcases filled with perfumes and powders, delighted Laurie. She did not in the least mind dusting the glass-topped counter, and rearranging the goods on display there: diamantè-studded back-combs, huge drums of Coty dusting powder, compacts, and Lancôme face creams and lotions. But she did not much care for handling the long switches of human hair, and the pincurls mounted on wire stems, which made

262

her think of Indian scalping parties. She felt quite certain that she would never be able to master the complicated procedures of boardwork. The very sight of Madam's tackle in the back workshop, the clamps and brushes, and the hackle, resembling a fakir's bed of nails, filled her with dread.

But she liked, very much, the blended fragrances of green soft soap, violet oil, and Jean Patou's "Quelques Fleurs," which met her nostrils the minute she crossed the threshold, and she would linger, long and lovingly, over dusting Madam's private beauty parlor halfway up the stairs, unscrewing the jars and bottles to sniff the contents: Fuller's earth, astringent lotions, and cleansing creams.

At first she had puzzled over the queer machine with all those wires, and the cages of sharp little needles. Suddenly it dawned on her! She guessed why it was that so many of Madam's clients emerged from that private room with red chins, sans the whiskers they came in with. Perhaps all elderly women grew beards. Laurie had stopped dusting to stare anxiously at her own chin in the mirror.

What she did not like was standing silently beside Madam in the claustrophobic confines of her private cubicle on the ground floor. Most of Madam's clients were depressingly ancient, with waist-length gray hair, and talked about such boring things: bridge parties and sales of work, ailments and nursing homes.

Madam had hammered into Laurie's head that apprentices, like children, should be seen and not heard, but how could she tell what Madam would want handing to her next, without asking? She wasn't a mind-reader. Sighing, Laurie thought that what she really needed was a crystal ball.

The only way to overcome the boredom of a job she disliked intensely, Laurie discovered, was to pretend to be someone else, such as a Hollywood starlet awaiting discovery by Samuel Goldwyn. She imagined herself walking along the beach at Malibu.

What queer stuff henna was, to be sure. Leaves of some kind of Egyptian plant, ground to a fine pungent powder, Madam had told her. Laurie giggled as she mixed the powder with water and set it to cook in a double boiler, rather like vile-smelling porridge. Just fancy anyone being crazy enough to want it plastered, scalding hot, on their scalp with a paintbrush, and wrapped up afterward in brown paper.

When the henna was cooked, Laurie carried the double boiler carefully to Madam's cubicle where the customer awaited her ordeal.

In the middle of the operation Laurie's thoughts began to wander. Smiling, she imagined herself to be a Hollywood beautician, called to Sam Goldwyn's office to sign a contract—his latest discovery. She had just got to the part where Mr. Goldwyn had offered her a starring role, opposite Douglas Fairbanks Jr., when she caught Madam's eagle eye in the mirror above the washbasin. Suddenly the potful of henna trembled in her hands, and crashed to the floor, where the contents lay plastered on the linoleum.

"I'll speak to you later," Madam said coldly, "meanwhile you had better fetch a bucket of hot water and clear up the mess you've made."

Laurie's bottom lip quivered as she hurried through to the back room to fill a bucket. Now I'll really get it, she thought.

"Get it" she did. Later, Madam Hart surveyed her apprentice with the magisterial eye of a hanging judge regarding a prisoner found guilty of murder.

"To say that I am disappointed in you is putting it mildly," Madam said in a deep, throaty voice. "Wherever that butterfly mind of yours may be, it is certainly not on your work. I have my reputation to think of. I cannot afford to keep hangers-on in my line of business. You are dismissed, Miss Grayler. I shall write to your parents immediately."

"Oh, *please*, Madam Hart!" Fifty pounds down the drain! Laurie could not bear the thought of all that hard-earned money being wasted on a scatterbrained creature like herself.

Immediately, unselfconsciously, she went into her Mary Pickford act. She was suddenly Little Nell being driven out into the snow by a cruel landlord. "Oh, *please* don't make me leave," she wailed, wringing her hands, "I'll try to do better in future, really I will! My parents are just poor, honest working folk. It would kill my mother if she thought me a failure! *Please*, Madam Hart, remember just this once that the quality of mercy is not strained, but droppeth as the gentle rain from heaven." (Annie would have had a fit if she'd heard her.)

"Don't be ridiculous," Madam snapped, somewhat taken aback by Laurie's histrionics, secretly impressed by the girl's power of expression and her reference to *The Merchant of Venice*. "Oh, very well then. If you really promise to do better in future, I'll give you another chance." She cleared her throat. "But I want it clearly understood that I will not tolerate your standing in my cubicle with that silly smirk on your face."

Deeply offended, Laurie felt like telling her employer that the "silly smirk" she referred to happened to be her mysterious Greta Garbo smile. Injured to her very soul, she stalked away to put on her outdoor things in the back room, where the other girls were jostling each other for the best place in front of the spotted looking glass, busily applying their makeup and saying what they intended doing on their afternoon off.

"Well, what happened?" The speaker, a girl in her twenties called Freda, possessor of an enormous, suet-pudding face, with eyes like raisins, looked with mock pity at Laurie. Freda disliked Laurie intensely because of her naturally blond hair and that mysterious air of reserve which neither she, nor the rest of the girls, had ever been able to fathom. "Did Madam give you the sack?"

"No." Laurie shrugged on her coat as they all turned to stare at her.

"Well, I wouldn't be in your shoes now that Madam has got her knife into you," Freda said snidely.

"You could never fit into my shoes anyway," Laurie replied haughtily, not knowing what she really meant by that.

The minute she opened the side door, her feet started to run. She was free now, as free as a bird! A great tide of joy and relief surged through her. Gran was taking her to the pictures tonight. Oh, how she loved Saturday afternoons! All this and heaven, too! Tomorrow was Sunday, the month was May. How could anyone ever feel unhappy in Maytime?

Running home, Laurie thought about the words she liked best: ducks, scintillate, brilliant, brambles, lace, violet, enchantment. Little shivers of pleasure ran down her spine. The sweet-scented air, the familiar streets of home, the ineffable magic of youth filled her with a wild, singing happiness. Madam Hart, the stain on the cubicle floor, Freda's suet-pudding face, floated blissfully away from Laurie Grayler as she waltzed homeward.

This afternoon she would go out shopping with her mother. When they had been to the market, in St. Helen's Square, they would go to Rowntree's cafe in the main street and have tea together. There, she would eat two chocolate eclairs, or maybe two of those squashy flat biscuity cakes she thought of as "elephants' feet." And all the time she would be yearning towards the moment when her grandma paid their sixpences to enter the dark, fairytale world of dreams come true . . . the cinema.

She burst into the house in Abbey Crescent, as hungry as a hunter, to find her mother opening the telegram she had just received, saying that Charlotte would arrive on the four o'clock train.

266

"Oh, Mum! May I go to the station to meet her! *Please?*" Laurie cried ecstatically.

"We will both go to meet her," Annie replied. "Now, sit down and have your dinner before it gets cold! How did work go this morning?"

"Fine," Laurie mumbled, applying herself wholeheartedly to sausages and mashed potatoes, "leastways, I nearly got the sack, but Madam reinstated me."

"*What?*" Laurie's apparent unconcern confounded Annie. "What happened?"

When Laurie came to the part where she had wrung her hands and pleaded with Madam Hart, she dropped her knife and fork, got up and re-enacted the scene for her mother's benefit, adding a few embellishments, giving a faultless imitation of a silent screen actress, cowering and trembling and slapping her forehead, until Annie was obliged to wipe away her tears of mirth with the corner of her apron.

The old town lay warm and secure in the shadow of the castle, washed with sunlight and the sound of Sunday morning church bells.

Charlotte stood with Annie near the seafront railings, looking out across the bay at the shimmering sea; admiring the mother-of-pearl tints trapped in the wet sand near the water's edge, where Laurie was paddling, a sturdy figure in a cotton dress and cardigan, fair hair ruffled by the soft May breeze.

Charlotte thought how quickly the girl had grown; how fast all the children were growing, changing, as the world was changing, almost too rapidly. Her mind felt shredded with tiredness and worry. There came a time when the facets of one's life could not be compartmentalized, when human relationships became too complicated, weaving a design of bewildering complexity.

"I thought you were supposed to be staying at High Tor

over the weekend," Annie said, watching her daughter traipsing along happily, ankle-deep in water.

"I was. But I couldn't."

"Why? What happened?" Annie tucked her hand into Charlotte's elbow. "I have wondered," she said, "how you really felt about Howard marrying Virginia. Tell me to mind my own business if you want to, but you might have been happy together."

"Oh, come off it, Annie! You know I'm not in love with Howard Ryder. I'm not in love with anyone." She lifted her face to the sky, feeling the sun on her skin. "I doubt if I'll ever fall in love again." But Charlotte knew she owed Annie an explanation. "I met Romilly," she said quietly, "face to face. That was the last straw. I *had* to get away. Poor Mrs. Ryder. I meant to say good-bye to her properly. I didn't. I went back to the house, packed my things, left her a note, and—ran! Ran home to Scarborough. I simply didn't care what she or anyone else thought of me! I'd have suffocated if I'd stayed there any longer, at that ghastly wedding reception." She smiled ruefully. "But I don't suppose she even noticed I'd gone. She was so overjoyed about Julian being the best man after all."

"This—Julian," Annie said carefully, "what's he really like?"

"Oh, don't let's talk about *him!* Come on, let's walk on the beach for a little while." She squeezed Annie's fingers. "Oh, it's so good to be home!"

"All right, then. But it's nearly time I was seeing to the dinner!" Annie laughed. "Just think, the week after next I'll be up to my eyes in summer visitors again! They'll all be arriving with their parcels of fish and meat for me to cook, and Peggy will be coming over from Darlington to lend me a hand. Then we'll all be moving up into the attics."

They walked slowly, arm-in-arm, along the beach.

"There's really no need for you to work so hard," Char-

268

lotte said. "Not any longer. I worry about you slaving away in that kitchen, especially since you and Joe have paid off the mortgage on the house—which I would have done anyway, if only you'd let me."

"But don't you see, dearest, we didn't want that? Joe needed the challenge, just as you needed the challenge of paying off Mrs. Hollister's creditors!"

"Yes, I know. I understand." Charlotte suddenly stood still. "Annie, I'm going to tell Kathy the truth about her father! I don't know how, or when, but the truth could scarcely drive us farther apart than we are at the moment. I just have the awful feeling I'm losing her, that the past has put up an invisible barrier between us, and I—I can't bear it! Well, go on, tell me I'm wrong. Tell me I'm a fool!"

"But I don't think you are wrong," Annie said slowly. "I think there comes a time when children should be told the truth. How can they grow up otherwise?" Her eyes were very bright, very clear, shining with her own particular light of wisdom and understanding. "We were kept in ignorance of certain facts of life, and it didn't do us very much good."

It happened one Sunday, in the churchyard at Cloud Merridon. Charlotte had travelled from York, with Kathy, to deliver her safely into the hands of her "Aunt" Bridie and Uncle Harry, with whom she would spend two weeks of her vacation.

Charlotte intended to spend a long weekend with her daughter before returning to London. Even though it was high summer, the autumn collection had to be finalized, and ideas for winter discussed with Ryder.

Kathy liked Grey Wethers, where she could ride as often as she wished, and accompany Uncle Harry on his tours of the estate to find out what needed to be done to keep the farm cottages in good repair, the land in good heart. Everyone liked tall, handsome Harry Grayler who had taken the reins of Grey Wethers firmly in his capable hands, and the motherly Mrs. McKenna who did so much for the farmworkers' wives and children, acting as Charlotte's agent in discovering what they needed by way of warm winter clothing or proper medical treatment if they fell sick. Kathy also enjoyed being given a basket of home-baked bread, or maybe a few pots of Bridie's special homemade preserve, a quarter of tea, a dozen eggs, or a pound of butter, to take to the old people in the village.

The villagers approved the new regime at the manor house, feeling themselves more secure with a man at the helm, someone who knew farming like the back of his hand and spoke their language. Things had not been so settled or well-ordered since Kitty Tanquillan's time, when Will Oakleigh was in charge of the farms. A grand man, Will; a real hero. And now that his daughter was among them, they never tired of telling her what a fine man her father was, and that the memorial tablet in the church was no more than his due.

Kathy had taken to tending her father's grave whenever she came to Grey Wethers during her vacations: gathering fresh flowers to place in the stone vase, and trimming the grass. On this particular Sunday, after lunch, she set off down the village carrying a basket of roses and sweet peas.

When she had finished her task, she sat back on her heels, filled with a deep feeling of love, mingled with regret, for the father she had never known, wondering what her life would have been like had he lived. Deep in her reverie, she sensed, rather than heard, that someone had entered the churchyard. She turned her head to see her mother standing there, hands clasped, a curious expression on her face, a kind of wistfulness blended with gravity, as if tears were close to the surface.

"I've just finished," Kathy said. "The flowers look nice, don't they?"

"Yes, very nice . . ." Charlotte's voice faltered.

Kathy said, "I often wonder if my father knows I put flowers on his grave."

"Kathy . . ."

"What?" The girl scrambled to her feet, wondering why her mother was looking at her like that. She was impatient to be off, now that she had done what she came to do. It was time to change into her jodphurs and go riding with her Uncle Harry.

"I have been meaning to tell you for a long time," Charlotte said. "I suppose I should have told you years ago, but there were reasons . . ."

"Oh, dear," Kathy sighed impatiently, "tell me *what?*" she was half-expecting a lecture about something or other, though she couldn't for the life of her think what she had done wrong, apart from experimenting with her first cigarette in the privacy of her room. She went in feet first, believing attack to be the best method of defense. "If it's about smoking, I only had one, and I didn't like it. I gave the rest of the packet to one of the farmhands," she said defiantly.

"No, it's far more serious than that, I'm afraid. It's about—your father." Charlotte's knuckles showed white through the skin as she clenched her hands more tightly.

A wary expression came into Kathy's eyes. "What about my father? Because if you are going to tell me he wasn't a hero, I wouldn't believe you."

Charlotte closed her eyes momentarily. Now that the time had come, after she had screwed up her courage for this, she wondered if she was doing the right thing after all. Too late now. "Your father was a hero," she said, "but he was not Will Oakleigh. His name was Tanquillan. Rowan Tanquillan. We—we never married."

"I don't believe you!" Kathy turned on her mother in a fury. "You're just making it up because you know how much my father means to me, because you're jealous!" Tears flooded down her cheeks, tears of shocked horror and disbelief because her mother had lied to her.

271

"No, darling. No! Please listen!"

"I don't want to listen! I *won't* listen!" She ran blindly away from the graveside and stumbled along the path towards the gate, unable to take in what her mother had told her. Grief-stricken, she closed her eyes to Charlotte's distress, ignoring her plea that she must listen to her; let her explain.

Running, stumbling, weeping, Kathy fled into the house, brushing past Bridie, who was coming downstairs, almost knocking her over; not even noticing, not caring. Locking the door behind her, she flung herself on the bed, engulfed with misery, wetting the pillows with her tears. If it is true, she thought wildly, then I am what those girls at school called me. She knew the correct word now. The word was "bastard."

Nothing would persuade her to come down for dinner, or breakfast the next morning, to face her mother.

"I shouldn't have done it," Charlotte wept. "Rowan was right. I should have let her go on believing that Will was her father."

"But it would have had to come out sooner or later," Bridie pointed out. "Don't worry, Charlotte. Leave her to me. When you've gone back to London, I'll have Kathy to myself for a couple of weeks. I'll tell her the whole story, and I'll make quite certain she listens."

Chapter Twenty-Two

When Virginia Ryder suggested to her husband that it might be a good idea to have their baby christened, on Christmas Day, in the church where they were married, Howard leaned over in bed to kiss her, his beautiful Ginny who had made him the proudest, happiest man in the world. He forgot, as he held her slim body in his arms, his former dislike of family Christmases at High Tor.

Fatherhood had inbued him with a desire to show off his son to as wide an audience as possible, as a prince from the ramparts, to launch him on the sea of life with due ceremony. Virginia's impulsive notion to have the baptism at St. John's, Moortown, in the bosom of their respective families, with champagne toasts and a Fortnum and Mason christening cake, strongly appealed to Ryder, although they had previously toyed with the idea of having the ceremony performed in London in the New Year. And, of course, Carla must be the baby's godmother.

Once the broad outline of the plan had been settled between them, Virginia telephoned Howard's mother, and her own, delegating the hard work in her usual charming fashion. She mentioned the people she would like to invite, the buffet luncheon she envisioned, the flowers for the church. Leaving their respective mothers to make the arrangements, she said sweetly she knew she could rely on them to manage things beautifully between them.

Ryder had not considered the possibility that Charlotte

might demur. He found her, clad in a pencil-slim skirt and a short tailored smock, standing at her drawing board, putting the finishing touches to a wedding-dress design. He perched himself on a high stool, lit a small cigar, and launched into the plans for the christening, taking her enthusiasm for granted. He was surprised to hear her say, "I'm sorry, Howard, but you have sprung this on me too suddenly. I've made arrangements to spend Christmas in Scarborough."

"Damn it all, Carla," he said irritably, "this is a rather special occasion, surely you can see that?"

Charlotte laid down her pencil with a sigh, wishing that Howard had not interrupted her just then. He, of all people, should know what Christmas entailed: the last-minute rush to get the orders finished on time, and packed in long, tissue-paper lined boxes ready for delivery.

She had a thousand and one things to see to, and Christmas imposed the kind of deadline she dreaded, of the type which all professional people knew only too well, especially those catering to the needs of women who must have the new dress, or the new coiffure, as a matter of extreme urgency before the holiday got under way.

An hour since, she had been down in the workroom where the assistants were engaged in stitching intricate designs in crystal beads and sequins on to delicate fabrics: satin, chiffon, lace and organdy. The materials were spread in colorful swaths on the long central tables beneath the powerful electric lights. Charlotte had carefully checked the rows of completed garments hanging in immaculate array on muslin-covered hangers, ready for collection by the delivery men.

Apart from all that, there was Christmas shopping to do, and cards to write: literally hundreds of cards, to friends, family, business acquaintances, staff, and farm workers. She had promised faithfully to go to Scarborough on Christmas Eve, to be with her family, especially Kathy, whom she had not seen since that fateful day in the churchyard. Kathy, so Bridie had told her, had at last accepted the truth about her father and had now, at least, started writing to her again, from school; saying nothing of importance, never so much as mentioning their conversation, but at least writing. At Bridie's insistence, and Annie's, no doubt.

Perhaps, Charlotte had thought hopefully, this Christmas holiday would bring them closer together. She fervently hoped so, pushing to the back of her mind that stubborn streak Kathy had inherited from her Grandma Grayler. Now, here was Howard to complicate matters, taking it for granted that she would simply alter her arrangements to suit himself.

"Ah, darling," Howard said, trying another tack, "Virginia and I have our hearts set on you being our son's godmother, and I do think you owe it to my mother, after rushing away from our wedding reception the way you did. The poor soul feels, quite understandably, that she has offended you in some way." He smiled persuasively. "In any case, it would only be for one day. I give you my word of honor I'll drive you over to Scarborough on Boxing Day. I can't say fairer than that, can I?"

"No, I suppose not."

"Then you will come?"

"Oh, very well," she sighed, going against her better judgment. But she hated the thought of further upsetting Mrs. Ryder. "Now, will you leave me to get on with my work?"

"Yes, of course." Howard stubbed out his cigar, slipped down from his perch, lightly kissed her cheek, and walked to the door.

When he had gone, Charlotte walked over to the window to stare down at the mass of humanity scurrying, like ants, along Bond Street, intent on their Christmas shopping. She was aware, as the street lamps bloomed suddenly against the dusk of a winter afternoon, of the pulsing heartbeat of the House of Carlotta, the faint hum of sewing machines from the floor below, the soft whirr of the lift, the metallic closing of its gates. She wondered if Kathy would regard her absence on Christmas Day as yet another sign of her mother's indifference, disinterest, or neglect; whatever she chose to call it, or thought of it.

The trouble was, she no longer knew what Kathy really thought any more, and perhaps she didn't want to know. Perhaps she had given in to Ryder's emotional blackmail to put one more day between herself and her daughter, before finding out the truth.

And what if she read, in Kathy's eyes, none of those things, but something much worse? Disgust! What if her child had ranged herself firmly, if unknowingly, on her grandmother's side in thinking her immoral?

The terrace of High Tor was filmed over with a light sprinkling of snow, the lake with a layer of ice.

Inside the house, huge coal fires had been lit to dispel the gloom of a winter afternoon; lamps threw warm pools of light on thick Aubusson carpets and polished parquet. A huge Christmas tree, decorated with lights and shining purple, red, and green baubles gleamed at the foot of the great oak staircase; the air was redolent with the intermingled fragrances of spruce and fir. Arabella Janvier Tremayne's portrait above the high stone mantelpiece had been wreathed in holly, and the gleaming central table bore a centerpiece of scarlet poinsettias, massed in a towering silver centerpiece.

Crossing the threshold, hugging the collar of her tweed coat around her, Charlotte realized the enormous amount of trouble it must have taken to create this warm, shining atmosphere of welcome. And yet, given the courage, she would have turned on her heels and run away, as she had done from the wedding reception, dreading, as she did, a repeat performance of a similar family occasion. But Mrs. Ryder had already appeared at the head of the stairs, her face wreathed in smiles, hands extended to take hold of her grandchild lying asleep in his nurse's arms; risking the woman's displeasure in kissing the baby's cheek, and cuddling him; reacting, not as the lady of the house but the former mill-hand's daughter who believed that babies were born to be kissed and fussed over.

Watching her, Charlotte relaxed slightly, thinking that she had done the right thing in coming to High Tor, if only to please Howard's mother, to set things right between them. This feeling grew stronger when Mrs. Ryder, having come downstairs, relinquished the baby and turned, smiling, to take her hands, saying how pleased she was to see her again.

She was busy unpacking when Mrs. Ryder came up to her room to see if she had everything she required.

She had been given a south-facing room on the first floor, with a view of the garden, the lake, and the wide spreading valley beyond, a room filled with solid Victorian furniture: a massive wardrobe, dressing table and chests of drawers. A velvet chaise longue was drawn up to a crackling coal fire, and the enormous bed was covered by a soft crimson eiderdown.

"I have more than I require, or deserve," Charlotte said quietly. "I want to apologize for what happened on my last visit. You must have thought me very rude and ungracious."

"No, I didn't think that." Amelia straightened one of the lace dressing-table mats. "I thought I had upset you, saying what I did about your remarrying. I shouldn't have pried into your affairs the way I did."

Charlotte laid down the dress she had just unpacked. "My leaving the wedding reception so suddenly had nothing whatever to do with that," she said contritely. "I—I simply met someone I knew a long time ago. It was not a particularly happy meeting."

Amelia put her head a little to one side, recalling the incident. She had been standing near the French windows, intending to speak to Charlotte, when Virginia's mother had rustled across the room with someone in tow— a stiff, unpleasant-looking woman—a friend of Virginia's. What on earth was her name? Suddenly she remembered. "Oh, you mean Romilly McClean? How odd. She and her husband and children are coming here for Christmas. I believe that Virginia has also invited Mrs. McClean's mother. A Mrs. . . . Oh dear, I've forgotten her name."

"Beresford," Charlotte said slowly.

"Yes, that's right." Mrs. Ryder looked at Charlotte's stricken face. "Oh, my dear," she faltered, "how dreadful for you . I'm so sorry. I had no idea. I wouldn't have had this happen for the world! I don't even understand why Virginia asked them in the first place, except that my daughter-in-law has an unfortunate habit of collecting people who are out of the top drawer; socially speaking, that is."

Amelia's elderly child's face puckered unhappily. "I lied to you when I said that Virginia is a nice girl! She isn't! She's a snob, just like her father and mother; always on the lookout for people who will increase her social prestige! I gather that she and Romilly McClean met in Paris some time ago, and that McClean's former father-in-law is extremely grand: the owner of a shipping line, or some such, with a large house in Eton Square. Oh, what on earth is his name?"

"His name is Tanquillan. Sir Gervaise Tanquillan," Charlotte said, feeling suddenly cold and empty. "You see, Mrs. Ryder, I have good reasons to remember, and Romilly McClean has every reason to hate me. I had an affair with her husband: I bore his child."

"Oh, my dear." Amelia's bottom lip quivered.

"I'd better leave now," Charlotte said, "before I cause any more embarrassment."

"No," Amelia cried. "I won't let you! The very idea!

278

Now you listen to me, my girl! You are worth a dozen of that McClean woman! If you run now, you'll be running for the rest of your life!"

She tapped Charlotte lightly under the chin. "Tonight, you come down to dinner like a queen, with your head held high! Promise?"

Berry Tanquillan helped his grandmother from the car the Ryders had sent to the station to meet them.

"I'm still not quite certain why we were invited here," he said quietly as they went up the steps to the massive front door. 'Ye gods, what a house! It reminds me of Thornfield Hall in *Jane Eyre*.

Emily Beresford laughed a little nervously as she clung to Berry's arm. "Theirs not to reason why . . ."

"Theirs but to do or die," Berry added, squeezing her hand.

They chuckled quietly, and yet Mrs. Beresford felt suddenly afraid. When this Christmas holiday was over, she and her grandson would be separated, for months perhaps.

Romilly had made it quite clear that she wished her mother to spend the new year in Scotland with her younger grandchildren, and stay on at the house in the Trossachs, as their guardian, until the spring, while she and David went abroad for a holiday.

While Emily could tolerate her own circumstances, she could not tolerate so easily her grandson's banishment to Scarborough to take up his duties as his grandfather's agent.

If only she could have sent him to Paris, instead, to study music, but that was impossible. She had no money to call her own apart from the small annuity her husband had left her. Gervaise Tanquillan owned the house she lived in, and could bring her to the verge of bankruptcy if he chose to do so.

Emily had thought, when Grandmother Beresford died, that the turreted house in the Trossachs, along with old Mrs. Beresford's fortune, might have reverted to herself as her son's widow. But the old lady had left the house, its contents, and all her money to Romilly, who had grown more miserly with the passing years. She scarcely now regarded Romilly as her own daughter and actually disliked at times her children by David McClean.

She could not help wondering, when she was far away in Scotland, staying as a guest under her son-in-law's roof, how Berry would fare, alone in Scarborough, learning about the import of fish-manure and potatoes, as his father had been obliged to do before him. But she kept her thoughts to herself as they walked into the great hall of High Tor with its welcoming fire, bauble-decked Christmas tree, and the frowning holly-wreathed family portraits hung in a row on the staircase walls.

"I wonder if Mother and The Clan have arrived yet," Berry said, as a servant hurried away to find Mrs. Ryder.

Emily smiled sympathetically, knowing that Berry shared her own distaste for James and Fiona, his half-brother and sister; aware that he did not much care either, for David McClean, his mother's stuffy Scottish husband, who had never treated him with the same degree of affection that he showed towards his own offspring.

But Berry had thoughtfully concluded that, since David was not his real father, he could scarcely expect his love. And yet he could not help thinking of the other fellows at school, in the same boat as himself, whose mothers, widowed during the war, had remarried. These second husbands drew no strong demarcation line between their own and their stepchildren.

Glancing up at the painting above the mantelpiece, that of a sweet-faced young woman, the antithesis of the other portraits of grim old men and women with unsmiling lips, Berry could not help wondering what his life would have been like if his real father had not died in that Army sanatorium.

It seemed strange that his grandparents never mentioned his father's name, that, whenever he ventured to do so, there came what Berry thought of as a deathly hush: a tightening of Grandmother Tanquillan's lips, a guarded expression on his grandfather's face, as if their son's dying of consumption was something to be ashamed of. Had it not been for Madre keeping alive his memory, his father might never have existed.

Julian wrestled ineffectually with his bow tie. His mother must have taken leave of his senses, filling the house to bursting point with all these damned people simply to suit Howard and Virginia. Why couldn't they have had their brat christened in London?

"Oh curse this bloody tie! Bennison! Where the hell have you got to?" he shouted.

"Having a little trouble, are we, sir?" The ex-sergeant appeared, grinning. "Here, let me! There, how's that?"

"There are times when I'd like to wring your damned neck," Julian said darkly.

"All ready for the fray, sir?" Bennison refused to be put off by the thought of having his neck wrung, knowing full well why the old boy was in such a state of nerves. That redhead! "Shall I give your chair a push, or can you manage on your own?"

"I'm not going into dinner in my chair," Julian said tautly. "Hand me those sticks!"

Dressing for dinner, Charlotte thought longingly of home. Kathy would be there now. Perhaps Laurie had gone to the station to meet her. Christmas Eve. The time she loved best. Joe would have brought home and trimmed the tree, planting it carefully in a planter decorated with crinkled paper, while Annie would be doing the last-minute shopping, buying oranges—those flattened mandarins that Laurie liked so much—rosy Cox's apples, and boxes of sticky dates.

The shops in Westborough kept open until ten o'clock on Christmas Eve. She could picture it all exactly: haloed street lights shining onto icy pavements; people hurrying along, intent on buying last-minute presents; children singing carols for pennies; the Salvation Army band playing "Silent Night," girls dressed for dancing at the Olympia ballroom on the seafront; the elite rich walking up the steps of the Pavilion Hotel to dine; frosty stars shining down on the dark, restless sea. And here she was, dreading coming face to face with Romilly again, and Emily Beresford.

Talk about "alien corn." How did the lines go?

> Through the sad heart of Ruth, when, sick for home,
> She stood in tears amid the alien corn.

Ah well, no use standing here looking at herself in the mirror. Smoothing her dress, she walked downstairs to face what must be faced, and lingered for a moment in the hall to take a deep breath before entering the drawing room.

At that moment, Julian emerged from his private apartment, leaning heavily on his walking sticks. "Well," he snapped, "don't just stand there as if you'd seen a ghost."

"You're—walking," she said.

"Yes, well, that's rather obvious, isn't it? I've been practicing." He grinned suddenly, awkwardly. "Would you care to take my arm?"

"I'd be delighted. I could do with a strong arm to lean on tonight."

They walked slowly into the drawing room together. The buzz of conversation died down as they entered. Julian was painfully aware of Charlotte's supporting arm tucked into his elbow, the tensile strength of her body, the whispering of her blue dress on the polished floor, the soft cloud of fragrance which enveloped her, the sheen and luster of her short red hair.

"Oh, son!" Mrs. Ryder crossed the room swiftly, "this is the best Christmas present you could possibly have given me."

Charlotte relinquished her escort's arm. Smiling, she moved toward the slightly open French window leading onto the terrace.

Berry had gone out for a moment for a breath of air, feeling out of place among a crowd of strangers. As he stepped back into the room he saw Charlotte standing there and smiled at her, noticing the way her face lit up, as if she knew him. But he had never seen her before. He would have remembered if he had.

He was so like Rowan that Charlotte could scarcely prevent herself from speaking his name aloud. "Rowan! Rowan, oh, my darling! You are here at last! You have come back to me!"

A sudden feeling of joy flooded through her as she looked at Rowan's son. The room and all the people in it faded away, like a dim and distant dream, as she stood there, smiling up at him, eyes shining, as if she had been waiting for this moment throughout the long, lonely years of their separation.

Chapter Twenty-Three

"You must feel half-frozen," Charlotte said, "standing out there without a coat."

"Yes, but it was worth it just to look at the stars. Have you noticed, they always seem brighter on Christmas Eve?"

"Perhaps you were hoping to see that one special star?"

"There's always that possibility, isn't there?"

He looked so young and eager, the way Rowan must have looked when he was eighteen, before the years of imprisonment had taken their toll of his health and strength. She had the strangest feeling that this boy, with his cleanly chiselled features and dark expressive eyes, was Rowan made whole and vital again: Rowan reborn, with all the weariness of the war washed away.

She noticed that his shoulders were thin and angular, broad and lightly muscled, not yet fully developed, that his hands and wrists were slender. He possessed the touchingly vulnerable look of the very young, that kind of coltish grace when the limbs seem too long and somehow unmanageable, before the firm, heavier flesh of manhood has brought them into proportion. She felt an overwhelming tenderness for him.

"My name is Berry Tanquillan," he said with a smile. Rowan's smile.

"Mine is Charlotte. Charlotte Oakleigh."

"Are you a member of the family?"

"No, I came for the christening," she said confidingly, thinking how easy he was to talk to, unlike some youngsters of a similar age, who would have made an excuse to move away, disinterested in someone old enough to be their mother. But Berry was listening attentively, possessed of the same charm, the same inner grace as his father.

"As a matter of fact, I shouldn't really be here at all. I promised to go home to my family in Scarborough for Christmas. My brother and his wife live there, and my daughter, Kathy, will be there too." Your half-sister, she thought.

"How odd," he said, "I'm going to Scarborough. Not on Boxing Day, unfortunately, but shortly afterward. Oh, here's my grandmother!"

Charlotte noticed the eager way Berry stepped forward to take Emily Beresford's hand, the unmistakable bond of affection between them, as he made the introduction.

"Mrs. Oakleigh, this is my grandmother, Emily Beresford."

"I'm delighted to meet you, Mrs. Oakleigh."

Charlotte drew a deep breath of relief. She had half-feared a rebuff, coldness, on the part of Romilly's mother. But she should have known better. She remembered, as she shook Mrs. Beresford's hand, that Rowan had cared a great deal for this tall, sweet-faced woman. She should have trusted Rowan's judgment.

Smiling, Emily said, "Forgive me, Berry, for interrupting your conversation, but your mother and David have just arrived. Fiona was sick on the journey." She turned to Charlotte. "I'm so sorry. Just a small family problem. My daughter and her husband have travelled down from Scotland: a long journey for two small children to make. Fiona, Berry's half sister, and her brother James, are six and five. It's high time they were in bed, anyway."

* * *

Virginia, in scarlet chiffon, and Howard, immaculate in a faultlessly cut dinner jacket, occupied chairs on either side of Julian, while the Leeds-Smiths had been given places of honor next to their hostess.

Thankfully, Charlotte found herself ensconced between Uncle Arthur and Cousin Jeffrey, with the twins and their respective husbands seated opposite, and saw, with relief, that Romilly had been placed on the same side of the table as herself, three chairs away. So far, because of the confluence of guests round the dinner table, she and Romilly had not come face to face with each other. Their doing so later was inevitable, but Uncle Arthur, a man of considerable size, would prove an effective screen meanwhile.

Catching Mrs. Ryder's anxious look in her direction, Charlotte smiled and nodded, saying thank you with her eyes. Now, if only Virginia would not feel it necessary to draw attention to her as the baby's godmother, all would be well. But that was too much to hope for.

Virginia, in bubbling high spirits, and her mother, seemed to strike sparks from each other, like a well-rehearsed music-hall act. Constance Lees-Smith was fond of telling everyone that she and her daughter were often mistaken for sisters.

Glancing across the table at Emily, Charlotte noticed that she seemed acutely embarrassed by Lady Lees-Smith's continued angling for compliments, none of which were forthcoming from David McClean, whom Constance kept on nudging playfully with her elbow. The contingent of Ryders smiled gallantly through the soup, fish, and roast beef, feeling, perhaps, that the conversation was best left to the experts.

Julian seemed totally preoccupied with eating, his darkly handsome face puckered into a frown of concentration. Suddenly, Charlotte realized why. The man was in pain. Sitting upright in a carver must have thrown a considerable strain on his back muscles after years of being in a wheelchair. Howard, seated at his brother's right hand, remained impervious to the beads of perspiration gathering on Julian's forehead.

The inevitable happened. Leaning forward to speak to one of the Ryder cousins, Romilly caught sight of Charlotte.

At that moment, Constance Lees-Smith, who had drunk a considerable amount of wine, said in a high-pitched voice, "I'm really looking forward to this christening. Would you believe it, they're calling the baby William, after my hubby? Isn't that nice?" She wagged an admonitory finger at Charlotte. "Whatever you do, Carla, don't drop him in the font, will you?" She giggled inanely. "Not that I've ever heard of a godmother dropping the baby in the font, mind you, but there's got to be a first time for everything!"

"Don't be silly, Mother," Virginia retorted tipsily. "Carla never makes a mistake, do you, darling? Not so far as Howard is concerned, anyway! D'you know, I sometimes think that Howard married me because Carla wouldn't have him! Not that I blame him! She's so slim and beautiful, she'll outshine me any day now. But then, she hasn't just had a baby. I have!"

Virginia's mother rose immediately to the bait. "Nonsense, darling," she laughed, "just wait until everyone sees you in the new outfit Carla has designed for you. It's stunning, really magnificent, and so it should be, considering what it cost!"

In the ensuing silence, Romilly's voice could be clearly heard. "I have always thought," she said coldly, "that being a godparent to an innocent child carries a great deal of responsibility. Like marriage, it is not to be taken in hand lightly or wantonly. All I can say is that my husband and I were very careful, very particular, when it came to choosing godparents for our children!"

The implication was clear, the insult deliberate. *"Romilly!"* Emily said, in a shocked voice.

Cheeks burning with humiliation, Charlotte thought

that his was the worst moment she had ever been called upon to endure, with all eyes upon her; nobody knowing quite what to say or do to break the embarrassed silence.

Then Julian Ryder said, in a cool, positive voice, "I wonder if you would be kind enough to assist me to my room, Mrs. Oakleigh? I feel in need of a strong arm to lean on."

"Certainly, Major Ryder." She rose swiftly to her feet.

"With your permission, ladies and gentlemen," he said, with a correct, formal nod of the head, "my guest, Mrs. Oakleigh and I, wish you a very good night."

He could see that Charlotte was deeply upset. "That bloody woman should think herself lucky that I did not ask her to leave my house now, tonight," he said brusquely, when they were alone. "Who the hell is she anyway? Do you know her?"

"Yes, I know her."

"Come through to my apartment and have a drink," he suggested quietly. "I know I could do with one, and so, I suspect, could you. A stiff brandy and soda!"

"That's very kind of you, but I think I'll go to my room."

"Nonsense! I have something to say to you." He pushed open the door of his apartment. "Oh, damn these bloody sticks! Bennison, where are you? Give me a hand!" He turned at the door of his bedroom. "Make yourself at home, Mrs. Oakleigh. Put something on the phonograph. There's plenty to choose from: Brahms, Mozart, Beethoven. You'll find the records on the table."

She looked, with passive interest, round Julian's private sanctum, a comparatively small room, sparsely furnished in contrast with the rest of the house. It was very much a man's room, with its leather armchairs, rows of bookshelves, oil-paintings, and tables littered with books and newspapers.

The records were piled up, anyhow, beside a wind-up phonograph. The room bore the stamp of impatience. It was the room, she thought, of a solitary, edgy man who disliked frills; who, possibly also, disliked women. It was totally devoid of a woman's touch: no flowers, no plants. The air smelled slightly stale with cigarette smoke.

She chose Elgar's "Enigma Variations" from the pile of records, wound up the phonograph, and set the needle down carefully.

"Any particular reason for your choice?" Julian came into the room in his wheelchair, dressed casually in an open-neck shirt and pullover.

"Not really. I just happen to like Elgar."

"Yes, so do I, in moderation. But this is romantic stuff compared to his 'Dream of Gerontius.' "

"I'm surprised you bought it, then, Major Ryder."

"I didn't, as a matter of fact. It was a present from my mother." He wheeled himself to the fire. "Pour me a brandy and soda, would you?" he asked stiffly, "and one for yourself. You look as if you need it! Not still worried about that silly woman, are you?"

"If I said no, I'd be lying." Charlotte poured the drinks. "Perhaps she was right. I hadn't really thought about it before. Perhaps I am not a fit person to stand godmother to an—'innocent child.' " She twisted her lips into a faint smile.

Julian regarded her objectively. She was certainly beautiful, the most beautiful woman he had ever met. Beauty, he knew, was all too often skin deep, but this woman had lived—suffered. He could tell by her eyes. Most beautiful women, in his experience, were obsessed with their appearance, demanding constant approval of their looks, their charm. But not Charlotte Oakleigh.

He had never met a woman quite like her before: she was touched with a kind of—innocence—which he found totally refreshing, and curiously disturbing. That he had so often insulted her—particularly that night on the terrace—worried him a great deal.

Perhaps she had not realized that it was for her sake he

had changed his mind about being his brother's best man; that it was for her sake he had undergone so many painful sessions of physiotherapy and massage; so many ludicrous hours in the Bradford municipal swimming baths, bobbing in the water like a trained seal.

"Sit down," he said brusquely, when she had handed him his drink. "I have 'something to expiate—a pettiness.' "

He had not expected her to understand what he meant, but he should have known better.

"Oh, so you read D.H. Lawrence, too?" she replied, with a slight lifting of her eyebrows. "Though I think I prefer his 'Mountain Lion' to 'Snake.' "

"Little wonder you chose the 'Enigma Variations,' " he said. "That's the way I see you, Charlotte, as a total enigma! For God's sake, woman, I'm trying to apologize for my behavior toward you, and all you can do is sit there and say that you prefer 'Mountain Lion' to 'Snake.' Most other women would have looked at me with large round eyes, and asked what I meant. But not you! No, damn it, not you!"

"I knew exactly what you meant, Major Ryder." Charlotte's smile at last reached her eyes. "And since this seems to be the time for confessions, I'm sorry I said what I did about pinning the medal on the wrong uniform." She put down her glass and stood up, tall and forgiving; strangely moved by their encounter. "I'll never forget what you did for me tonight. It was a gallant gesture. They did not pin that medal on the wrong uniform, after all." She held out her hand. "I really must go now. Goodnight, Major Ryder."

Emily came to her room, later. "Charlotte, my dear," she said, "I'm so sorry about what happened. Romilly had no right. No right whatever! It was—unforgivable."

"Perhaps she *was* right," Charlotte said, "perhaps I am

not a fit person to make vows on behalf of an innocent child."

"Because of Rowan, you mean? Because you had the courage of your convictions? No, you must never think that! I knew, when he married my daughter, that he was not in love with her. I'm the one to blame for that."

"Does it really matter now who was to blame? It's all over and done with. All in the past."

"Is it? Do you really believe that?" Emily shivered. She felt suddenly very old and very tired. "It seems to me that the past can never be laid to rest, as it should be. Take Berry, for example. I know he has never quite accepted the idea that his father died in an Army sanatorium. I want so much to tell him the truth, but I can't, I don't dare!" She drew in a deep breath. "You see, Sir Gervaise Tanquillan holds the deeds of my house in Eaton Square. It happened just after the war started. My husband had died; his publishing business was in dire straits; I turned to Sir Gervaise for help . . . but that is *all* he owns. Nothing more!"

"Please don't upset yourself, Emily. You don't mind if I call you that?" Charlotte held the shaking woman in her arms. "I'm in the same situation, for what it's worth. I told Kathy the truth last summer. Now I think I've lost her love. Perhaps it is best that Berry should go on believing an untruth. I don't know. Who can say for certain what is right or wrong? All we can hope for is to get through tomorrow, and the next day, and the day after that as best we can."

Stepping away from Charlotte's comforting arms, Emily said quietly, "I always knew that you and Rowan were meant for each other. I—loved him so much. Romilly was never right for him, but you were! Oh yes, you were!"

She glanced at the clock. "It's almost midnight," she said, drying her eyes on a lace-edged handkerchief. "I'm sorry to have kept you up so late."

"You haven't," Charlotte replied, "I'm going to midnight service in the village church."

"Oh, really?" Emily smiled through her tears. "Berry's going too. He left a few minutes ago. He wanted me to go with him, but I felt too tired. One of the penalties of growing old, I suppose.

The air was sharp and frosty. Charlotte hurried down the hill to the village. The service was just about to start as she slipped into a pew near the door. A song began:

Once in Royal David's city . . .

Unable to sing properly because of the lump in her throat, Charlotte simply mouthed the words. If only she was at home now, safe and secure, with Annie and Joe, not having to think about how she would get through the christening service in Moortown parish church tomorrow, with everyone listening as she renounced the devil and all his works, the vain pomp and glory of this world, and the carnal desires of the flesh, on behalf of young William Ryder.

And yet, not to dare to stand up, not to dare take those vows on the child's behalf, would seem a slur on her love for Rowan: a denial of her belief that there was nothing wrong about a love affair which had stood the test, not only of time, but of condemnation, jealousy, and hatred.

Away in a manger . . .

She noticed Berry standing, tall and straight, in a pew near the communion rail; noticed that he was not singing, either; knew that he was just as lost and lonely as she was. Dear Berry, whom she loved as much as if he were her own son.

She waited for him after the service near the gate,

brushing away the first flakes of falling snow from her forehead, wishing that she had thought to bring her umbrella.

And then she remembered how once, a long time ago, she had loved walking in the snow, when she was young and carefree, before the world seemed so heavy with age and duties and responsibilities.

Then, as Berry came towards her, smiling his delight at seeing her there, in the shelter of the gate, she experienced once more all the old magic and rapture of youth, not caring tuppence about the falling snow, or that her feet were freezing, her fingers almost numb with the cold.

They walked, arms linked, back to High Tor, in a white world of falling snowflakes; laughing together; enjoying each other's company.

"All this reminds me," Berry said, "of *Wuthering Heights:* you know what I mean? As a Londoner, I've never come up against anything quite like this before: the old mills, the stone walls, the cobbled streets and ancient gas-lamps! It's simply marvelous! Don't you think so too, Mrs. Oakleigh?"

Charlotte scarcely knew what she thought as she clung to his arm, battling her way against what was now a blinding snowstorm.

Then, suddenly, Berry blurted, "I'm terribly sorry about what my mother said at the dinner table this evening! I'm sure she didn't mean to be so rude. She often does say things she doesn't mean, quite out of the blue, like that." He frowned perplexedly. "I only wish that I had been the one to act as your defender. I love my mother, of course, but she's not always the most tactful person in the world."

"It doesn't matter, Berry," Charlotte said. "In any case, that was yesterday. This is quite another day, Christmas Day!"

"So it is," he said thoughtfully.

293

"Then may I be the first to wish you a merry Christmas?"

They were standing together on the steep drive leading up to the house. Snowflakes whirled about them; pinpricks of light shone through the windows on the untrodden snow of the terrace. The air was still and heavy, every sound and movement muffled by the falling snow.

"Happy Christmas, Mrs. Oakleigh," Berry said quietly.

Standing on tiptoe, she brushed his cheek lightly with her lips, thinking of Rowan.

Chapter Twenty-Four

Filly Grayler nodded off to sleep after dinner. There was something about Christmas afternoon, a kind of drowsiness after a busy morning spent in the kitchen, and eating too much roast goose and plum pudding, which made staying awake impossible. There was a sense of anticlimax, too, after all the work entailed in the weeks leading up to Christmas, the polishing, washing, starching and bed-changing. Then the house had to be decorated with paper chains and holly—"But don't you bring that stuff into the house until Christmas Eve, you'll have bad luck if you do!" Another old ritual to be observed was the making of the cake and pudding a month beforehand.

Laurie had adored that Saturday afternoon pudding-making, with her mother and grandma washing the raisins, measuring the flour, and grating nutmeg, while she blanched the almonds, slipping the white kernels from the crinkled brown husks, peeled and cored the apples, and helped beat up the butter and sugar for the cake.

She loved the spicy aroma which invaded the house when the cake was nearly done, and the puddings bobbed merrily in simmering water on the stove; liked, most of all, the conclusion of the mixing ceremony, when everyone solemnly stirred the contents of the bowl three times, and made a wish. "And if you tell anyone what you've wished, it won't come true," Gran said in that severe tone of voice which Laurie always associated with her. Not that she minded. Gran was just—Gran, with her failing eyesight, wrinkles, and gray hair skewered into a knob at the back of her head.

Laurie loved Christmas afternoon, too, that safe, shadowy area of falling dusk and firelight, with the lights of the Christmas tree twinkling softly in the gloaming, when the familiar outlines of the furniture seemed faintly unreal in the twilight; when the fire burned brightly, and coals fell apart to reveal a glowing wonderland of pictures at its heart. She became agonizingly aware, then, of her love of home and her own folk, despite her Christmas pudding wish for fame and fortune, and a beach house at Malibu.

Sleepily, she stared into the fire, lolling beside Kathy on the sofa pulled up to the fire, her mind wandering mistily from dream to dream. But Kathy seemed restless and excitable, unable to settle.

Gran was fast asleep now, breathing heavily. Dad was asleep, too; Mum was sitting next to Kathy, at the other end of the sofa, her head against a cushion, eyes closed—not quite asleep, Laurie thought, just relaxing, thinking about getting the tea ready, perhaps.

When the time came for tea, everyone would protest that they didn't want any, could not eat another bite after the goose and roast potatoes, sprouts and stuffing, Christmas pudding and rum sauce. But when tea was on the table, all the succulent slices of boiled ham, sherry trifle, Christmas cake, and mince pies, appetites would be miraculously restored. I'll never get thin at this rate, Laurie thought despairingly.

She poked the restless Kathy with her elbow and muttered, "I wish you'd sit still. What's the matter with you?"

"I want to go out," Kathy said in a low voice. "I must go out. Will you come with me?"

"Me? Where to?"

"I don't know. Anywhere, just for a breath of fresh air!"

"Oh, suffering catfish!" Laurie heaved a reluctant sigh. "Oh, all right then, if you insist!"

Annie opened her eyes. "What did you say about going out?" she enquired sleepily.

"You don't mind, do you, Aunt Annie?" Kathy asked, getting up, "We won't be gone long."

"I didn't want to be gone at all," Laurie protested as they walked together to the seafront. "What *is* the matter with you? You've been acting strangely ever since you came. Is it because Aunt Charlotte isn't here?"

"Partly, I suppose," Kathy said, "but there's more to it than that. I can't stay at school any longer. I'm seventeen. I want to get out into the world and earn my own living!"

"But I thought . . . that is, I thought you were going into your mother's business when you left school."

Kathy snorted. "Can you see me as a dress designer? Making clothes for a lot of rich, silly women is the last thing on earth I want to do. No, I've made my mind up. I want to be a journalist—a writer, you know? I began to think seriously about it when I read about Amy Johnson flying to Australia. I thought then how wonderful it would be to be a news reporter, to travel the world in search of stories like that. Oh, Laurie, I'm so dreadfully unhappy as I am!"

Laurie raised her eyebrows. "*You*, unhappy? Blimey!" She walked on doggedly for a few minutes, anchored to Kathy's side by her hand on her arm. "I'm sorry. I always thought that you had everything you wanted."

"I suppose you mean money," Kathy said scornfully, "but that isn't everything!"

"It is if you haven't got any," Laurie reminded her. "But what if your mother won't let you be a journalist?"

"She can't really prevent me," Kathy said grimly. "I shall soon have that money Miss Tanquillan left me."

Laurie drew in a deep breath. She had never told anyone before, but as this seemed the time for unburdening the soul, she said, "I've made up *my* mind what I want to do, as well. I—I'm going to Hollywood when I've saved up enough for the fare. I'm going to be an actress."

They had reached the promenade railings by this time. "But if you want to be an actress," Kathy said seriously, "shouldn't you try to get a job with a repertory company, or try for a place at a school of dramatic art?"

"You don't understand," Laurie retorted frowning, looking at the sea running in on the sand. "I don't want to go on the stage, I want to be a—film star!"

"But surely acting is acting, wherever you want to do it," Kathy said. "I mean, it's something you'll have to learn how to do properly, just as I shall have to learn how to be a journalist."

"Do you really think so?" Laurie felt bewildered. Practicalities had never entered her head before. She simply believed that, once in Hollywood, having been discovered by Louis B. Mayer, she would be given a screen test and that would be that.

"Yes, honestly, Laurie. If you are really serious about this idea of yours, you should speak to Aunt Annie and Uncle Joe about it. You are simply wasting your time being a hairdresser."

"Ask Mum and Dad about going on the stage?" Laurie's heart fluttered alarmingly, "But they wouldn't let me. I know they wouldn't."

"You must stand up for what you believe in," Kathy said intently, "the way I'm going to stand up to my mother." They started to walk towards the harbor, past the shuttered singing hall, Evelyn's Cafe, St. Nicholas Cliff Gardens, and the Futurist cinema where Laurie and Gran had seen *Rio Rita*. The sky was faintly pink over the sea, Castle Hill gray in the afternoon light. "Laurie, have you heard—about me?" Kathy asked suddenly.

"Huh?" Laurie was thinking of the soft, warm sand at Malibu, with billowy breakers foaming in on the shore, and owning one of those beach houses with steps leading straight onto the sand, pondering what Kathy had said about becoming an actress. "Huh?" she repeated. "Heard *what* about you?"

"Do you know what a—bastard is?"

"Well, I know there's a lot of them about," Laurie replied carefully. "Why?"

"Because I'm one!" Kathy spoke defiantly, glad that she had said it at last—this thing which had been preying on her mind. "My mother told me last summer." Her eyes smarted with tears. "My father wasn't Will Oakleigh after all, just someone she had an affair with! Don't tell me you haven't heard."

"They wouldn't tell *me!* Nobody tells me anything worth knowing. I'm not even sure how babies come. Gran gets all peculiar if people start talking about it, specially since they opened that home for wayward girls across the road." Laurie twitched her nose. "I asked her once what a wayward girl was, and she told me to mind my own business. All I know is, they go in fat and come out with babies. In any case," she went on, "being one of—what you said—doesn't make you grow two heads or anything, does it?"

"Oh, *Laurie!* This is serious. How would you feel if you found out that Uncle Joe wasn't your real father?"

"I don't know." Laurie considered the question carefully. "It wouldn't stop me loving him. I say, you're not trying to break it to me that I'm one as well?"

"Don't be absurd! You're just so lucky, having a settled home with parents who love you . . ." Kathy blew her nose hard. "I've never known what it is to be like you; being shoved off to boarding-school because my mother hadn't time for me . . ."

"Hey, wait a minute," Laurie said, "Aunt Charlotte worships the ground you walk on. I know, because my mother said so. In any case, I think it's very romantic that she had a love affair." She remembered, dreamily, that film stars were always having love affairs: Greta

Garbo and John Gilbert, for instance. Now, *there* was a love affair if ever there was one. "I don't see what you're making such a fuss about anyway. Whoever your father was, he must have been someone very special to make Aunt Charlotte fall in love with him. If I were you, I'd want to find out all about him . . ."

"You, maybe, but I don't," Kathy said hoarsely. "I *hate* him! I don't want to know anything about him! It's all his fault for making me what I am!"

"Oh, come on, Kath," Laurie said sympathetically, "don't upset yourself." She knew, in a strange kind of way, that nothing lasts forever, not grief or despair, or even happiness—the wild, singing happiness of youth. They were all part of the mysterious business of growing up.

Charlotte knew, the moment she set eyes on her daughter's face, that she had not forgiven her. To make matters worse, she was deliberately rude to Howard Ryder, who had driven her over to Scarborough after the weighty occasion of his son's christening. No wonder he had left so abruptly, declining her invitation to stay for lunch.

On Boxing Day afternoon Annie, Joe, and Laurie went off together to watch a comic football match on the sands. Filly went to her own room to have a nap, and Charlotte and Kathy were left alone in the firelit sitting room. Not that Charlotte prided herself that Kathy had remained simply to enjoy her company. The girl obviously had something on her mind which she was determined to say at any cost.

"Mother! I've made up my mind to leave school! I want to be a journalist!" There it was out at last.

"And you thought I'd throw a dozen obstacles in your way, is that it? Oh, Kathy!"

"I don't know what I thought," Kathy said defensively. "I don't know what to think any more, not since . . ."

"Since I told you the truth about your father? But have you ever stopped to think what it cost me to tell you the truth? And what if I hadn't told you, and you had found out by accident? What would you have thought of me then?"

"I'm not interested in all that—mush! All I want to know is, have I your permission to leave school and go into journalism?"

"Yes, of course. But you must understand that going into journalism, as you put it, will not be all that easy. The best you can hope for is a job as a 'gofer', at first: making tea, emptying the reporters' ashtrays, that kind of thing." She smiled at her wayward daughter, "Where had you thought of going to, to start your career in journalism?"

"To Manchester," Kathy said in a businesslike way, feeling, somehow, that the wind had been taken out of her sails.

"Very well, then. Would you prefer to do it on your own, or may I be allowed to help a little?"

"I'd rather do it on my own," Kathy retorted.

"You really haven't forgiven me, then?" Charlotte said wistfully, gazing into the fire.

Something about the droop of her mothers's shoulders, the beauty of her face by fireglow, suddenly touched Kathy's heart. "I'll try to make you proud of me," she said.

"I have always been proud of you," Charlotte replied softly. "Your father would have been proud of you, too."

At that moment Annie, Joe, and Laurie came in.

"In the gloaming?" Annie laughed. "Do you mind if I turn the light on? It's time I was getting the tea ready. Where's Gran?"

"Upstairs, taking a nap," Kathy said, "and don't worry about the tea. Laurie and I will get it ready, won't we?"

"Yes," said Laurie reluctantly, following Kathy into the

301

kitchen, "but we'd better stamp our feet first to give the mouse time to get back to its hole!"

"Never mind the mouse," Kathy cried ecstatically. "Laurie, I asked Mother about being a journalist, and it's all right!" Catching hold of her cousin's waist, she swung her into a dance of joy, from the kitchen door to the sink.

Chapter Twenty-Five

Peggy stood up to lift her case down from the rack and gave a fleeting glance at herself in the oblong glass between the sepia prints of Cromer and Sandsend, to make sure her hat was on straight. It was the one she had paid two and eleven for in Barker's sale, a kind of pillbox covered with spotted veiling, which she wore perched atop her dark, frizzed hair.

Peggy was tall, slim, and beautiful, with hazel eyes, perfect teeth, a lively, enquiring face marred only, or possibly enhanced, by a slightly crooked chin, and a way of looking at men which first stunned, then captivated them entirely. She was also a great giggler.

Men glanced her way when the train stopped near the bookstall next to the ticket office, and she walked along the platform, lugging her case. One of them chanced his luck. "Here," he said, "let me give you a hand with that."

"Okay," Peggy replied, shoving the case at him, craning her neck to see the faces at the barrier.

"There she is," Laurie said breathlessly, filled with an overwhelming love for her funny, dark-haired cousin, running toward herself and Kathy as best she could on her three-inch heels.

"I see she's found a sucker to carry her case for her," Kathy remarked. But that was Peggy. Wherever she went, men fell over themselves to help her. Despite her cheap clothes, Peggy had style.

Laurie's heart swelled with happiness as Peggy kissed her and said, "Hello, petal! My, you're a lot thinner, aren't you?"

Peggy's coming added a new dimension to life, a kind of heady excitement which had to do with her sparkling, outgoing, fun-loving personality.

Tonight, Saturday night, Peggy would want to go dancing; would take Kathy and herself with her, against Annie and Joe's better judgment, perhaps, saying she would make sure that nothing bad happened to them, except that she wouldn't put it quite like that. Peggy wouldn't know what badness meant if it bounced up and hit her in the eye. She would simply say: "Don't worry, I'll take care of 'em, you see if I don't!"

She would, too. There was nothing promiscuous about Peggy. Perhaps that was why Laurie loved her so much. Peggy would flirt, to her heart's content, on the foreshore after dusk, with dozens of what she called "fellas" or "chaps." But just let one of them get out of hand, and Peggy would turn her back on him with a shrug of her slim shoulders, and march away, head in air, with herself and Kathy firmly in tow.

But, ah, the mystery and magic of those nights on the beach, with the lights strung round the bay reflected in the deep, shining water rolling in on the shore. Laurie felt that this summertime of the heart would never end, that it would last for ever, because they wanted it to; they were heedless of the coming autumn, and the first falling leaves at the end of this brief summertime of the very young.

The attic was hot and stuffy. Heat seemed trapped beneath the sloping ceiling, despite their dormer windows flung wide open to catch a breath of salt night air.

Lying flat on her back in her single bed, Laurie inhaled the curious dusty smell of the rose-patterned wallpaper inches away from her nostrils, and untucked the covers, revealing her ankles bound up like a racehorse's. She had read in a Hollywood magazine that bandaging one's ankles at bedtime and running upstairs on tiptoes would eventually produce marvelous slimming results. Not that she had so far noticed any difference, but what was good enough for Jeanette MacDonald was certainly good enough for her.

She could see, by starlight, and the strange translucent blueness of the sky, which never really grew dark at all in summertime, the humped outlines of Kathy and Peggy in the double bed opposite; the chest of drawers beneath the window, with its tilted mirror.

Gripped with a sudden feeling of clairvoyance, of premonition, Laurie knew that she would never forget this room, this night, this moment.

Tears sprang to her eyes and rolled silently down her cheeks at her inability to understand her mixed emotions. She simply felt that the world, "so various, so beautiful, so new," was fast spinning away from her. She thought, for as long as I live, I shall never forget our summer faces in that old looking glass. No matter how long or short our lives may be, whatever the future has in store for us, I shall always remember that we were once young together; that the world, with all its hopes and dreams, seemed a lovely place to be alive in.

Those summer nights seemed endless—simply a continuation of the long hot days which faded, imperceptibly, to a strange, clear darkness, a soft balminess when the heat of the day seemed trapped beneath the trees in the park, and in the dark water flowing under the Japanese bridge, leading to what Laurie always thought of as the enchanted island, crowned with a floodlit pagoda.

Every evening after tea, when Laurie came home from work, and Peggy had finished serving the visitors crab salad and strawberries-and-cream, everyone would lend a

305

hand with the washing up, and then the three girls would fly upstairs to the attic to get ready for off, jostling to look at themselves in the mirror.

What Laurie liked best was the sense of impermanence, as if summertime were a kind of play, the actors about to go onstage. Their dresses hung behind a curtain draped across an alcove, and the chest of drawers, which served as a dressing table, was littered with their pots of cream; lipsticks, sixpenny boxes of rouge, boxes of powder, eyebrow pencils, and mascara. Most of these cosmetics belonged to Peggy, bought during their Saturday afternoon dawdles round Woolworth's.

Peggy could not resist buying makeup. Most of her tips went on sixpenny tins of face cream, Maybelline mascara, vials of Jockey Club and California Poppy scent, or maybe a bottle of Evening in Paris if she felt rich. Laurie, starstruck, hankered after jars of Max Factor's Cleansing Cream, bottles of skin freshener, and the classier lipsticks, powders, and tinted foundation creams, advertised as the Makeup of the Stars, which she could not possibly afford to buy from her wages of seven and six a week, plus tips. Madam Hart's clients were not noted for their generosity when it came to tipping.

Peggy was fond of spending any leftover pocket-money on what she called trimmings: frothy lace collars, artificial flowers, or sequined necklaces, to enhance the one decent costume she possessed. This was a gray jacket and skirt of surprisingly good quality bought from last summer's tips, and chosen at Kathy's instigation. She wore it either all together or, in the very warm weather, the skirt without the jacket, with a variety of crisp cotton blouses. Whatever she wore, she always managed to appear stylish, which had to do, Laurie supposed with her tall slim figure, and the way she pranced along, jauntily, her head held upright on her thin shoulders, with perhaps a pink rose on her pillbox hat to match the one pinned to her lapel.

306

Wherever they went, on those summer evenings, they picked up, en route, a following of Peggy's admiring chaps. Kathy said Peggy reminded her of the Pied Piper. "Who's he when he's at home?" Peggy wanted to know.

Not that she ever took much notice of the youths she attracted on those evening strolls along the foreshore. "Pooh," she would say, tossing her head, "they're no use to me. When I get myself a chap, he'll have to look like a fillum star. I know exactly the kind of chap I want, with dark hair, a good set of teeth, and a snazzy car. I've had enough of scraping for money, and I don't want to end up like Ma, with a houseful of runny-nosed kids to look after."

"I don't intend to get married at all," Kathy said defiantly. "What about you, Laurie?"

"It all depends," Laurie said wistfully

"On what?" Kathy demanded.

"If anyone wants me, I suppose."

Laurie hated the talk of marriage, of things being different. Perhaps that was the reason for her tears in bed the other night, that the changes she dreaded had already begun. Kathy seemed absorbed, these days, with the idea of going to Manchester in the autumn to begin her training. Her mother, she said offhandedly, had made the necessary arrangements after all. She would start with the *Manchester Tribune*, as a "gofer" getting the feel of the place. She would take night classes in shorthand and typing and lodge at a cheap but comfortable boarding house the editor had recommended.

Later that evening, Peggy confessed that she already had her eye on a chap she'd met at the Darlington palace dance. They were leaning on the Japanese bridge at the time, looking down at the canoes floating beneath. Laurie had been thinking how lovely the colored lights were, reflected in the water, shimmering down into the dark mysterious lake, when Peggy dropped her bombshell.

"His name's Fred," she confided suddenly, "talk about

a looker! He's the spit and image of George Raft, and what a dancer!"

"Has he got a car?" Kathy asked.

"Well, yes and no. He drives his brother's. But he *will* have one of his own soon. He's got a very good job, you see. He's a gas fitter." Peggy giggled self-consciously. "I wouldn't mind betting we get engaged at Christmas, when he's saved enough for the ring." She nudged Laurie playfully with her elbow. "What's up with you? You look like a dying duck in a thunderstorm!"

Laurie could not have explained to anyone how she felt at that moment: as if her shining world had suddenly been shattered into fragments. The lights blurred through her tears. A gas fitter called Fred! Her Peggy married to a *gas fitter* called *Fred!*"

"You can't do it," she muttered in a frozen voice, shocked at Peggy's betrayal.

"Why not?" Peggy bridled. "What a funny kid you are! I thought you'd be pleased . . ."

"*Pleased!*" Laurie's mouth trembled. She turned and pushed her way thorough the visitors crossing the bridge to the enchanted island—except that it wasn't enchanted any more; it was cheap and false, all make-believe.

"I just don't know what to say, love." Annie glanced worriedly at her daughter's woebegone face. "I know you've always been keen on the pictures. But becoming an actress! Have you thought what that would entail?"

"No, not really," Laurie admitted. "Kathy said I should join a repertory company, or try for a place at a drama school. I thought maybe I would go along to see one of the summer show managers and ask his advice."

"But what about your job?" Annie bit her lip. "You're doing much better now, Madam Hart told me so when I went to see her about keeping you on."

"Doing *better!*" Laurie cried bitterly. "I *hate* hairdressing! Fiddling about perming hair, listening to the moans and groans when the machine starts getting hot! Honestly, Mother, it's deadly boring, standing about all day long saying the same things over and over again. 'No madam, I won't let the machine get too hot! Yes, madam, your perm has taken very well!' until I could scream!"

"I had no idea you felt like that." How strange, Annie thought, she had always felt so close to Laurie, and all the time the girl had been unhappy without her knowing. She guessed that something extraordinary must have happened to cause this outburst. Come to think of it, Laurie had dashed upstairs last night without stopping to say good-night, the minute she and Kathy and Peggy returned from their evening in Peasholm Park.

"I think you are exaggerating just a little about your job," Annie said carefully, feeling as if she was treading on eggshells. Very gently she placed her hands on Laurie's heaving shoulders. "You know you can tell me, darling."

"Oh," Laurie drew in a shuddering breath, searching frantically in the pocket of her polka-dot dress to find a handkerchief. "Oh, Mum, I'm so—*miserable!* Kathy's going to Manchester, and Peggy . . ."

"What about Peggy?" Annie drew Laurie down on the edge of the bed in the back attic. She had been dusting the dressing table when Laurie burst into the room to blurt out the news that she wanted to be an actress.

"She's going to marry a—a *gas fitter!*" Laurie sobbed, burying her head against her mother's shoulder.

"Peggy?" This was the first Annie had heard of it, but experience had taught her not to take Peggy's flirtations very seriously. The girl attracted boys as a flower attracts bees. Even so, the news was disturbing because of its effect on Laurie.

"Come on, darling," she said lightly, "you mustn't let it upset you. I daresay Peggy's mother will have something to say about that." Knowing Maggie, she would

309

have a great deal to say, most of it unpleasant. "What matters most to me is *your* future."

Annie understood, now, Laurie's restlessness. It was only natural. Her happiness had been undermined by the changes taking place in those she loved. Poor Laurie had not yet learned that dreams are one thing, reality another; that real happiness lay in the familiar setting of home, among the people she cared for. But it was no use telling her. She would have to discover that for herself.

Annie said slowly, "I'll talk to your father about this idea of yours. I daresay he will think the same as I, that if this is something you really want to do, and if you have enough talent to become a good actress, we shall not stand in your way."

"Oh, *Mum!*" Laurie looked up at Annie with stars in her eyes. "Thank you!"

"There's just one thing," Annie said firmly, "promise me you'll stick to hairdressing until things are settled one way or another. I'll write to Aunt Charlotte about it. Living in London, she may know someone who could give you proper advice."

"Yes, Mum, I promise," Laurie said ecstatically.

Now all Laurie had to do was to make up her quarrel with Peggy. She fairly waltzed downstairs to the kitchen, where her cousin was busy polishing the silver.

"I'm sorry about last night," she quavered. Peggy tilted her pointed chin in the air as if she hadn't heard. But Peggy could never keep up a quarrel for very long; sooner or later, the sun would break through the storm clouds.

If Laurie had been asked, at that moment, for a suitable adjective to sum up Peggy, she would have chosen maddening. No wonder boys fell so easily in love with her. Even hidebound Granma Grayler could not resist Peggy's charm for very long. No one could, Laurie thought fondly; her dark-haired cousin reminded her of a high-stepping thoroughbred filly, always seeing the funny side of life, drawing everyone into the orbit of her fun-loving personality.

"Eh, you're a queer 'un," Peggy said, capitulating almost immediately, "why ever did you get so hot and bothered in the first place? Anyone'd think I was getting married tomorrow, not next year, or the year after."

"But you will be getting married eventually, won't you?" Laurie asked bleakly, "to this Fred, or whatever his name is?"

"More than likely I shall," Peggy retorted, "but why all the fuss? I've never let him lay a finger on me, and I won't, not until we're married."

"What do you mean, 'lay a finger' on you?" Laurie asked fearfully.

"Well, you know—let him do what all men want to do with women," Peggy said uneasily. She laughed suddenly. "You're lucky! You'd soon learn a thing or two if you lived in our house, with Ma getting 'that way' all the time!" She drew her eyebrows together in a delicate frown. "I reckon it's time someone told you the facts of life."

Berry Tanquillan walked slowly toward the house in Chalice Walk, choosing the beach road with crowds of visitors thronging the amusement arcades, or strolling along to catch the warmth of the early summer evening.

This was the time of day Berry liked best, when he could shake the dust of the warehouse from his feet and feel himself part of the holiday scene, one of the crowd, except that, no matter how hard he tried, he felt separated from the rest of humanity by an invisible barrier of loneliness. Most of these people had probably just had tea, he thought, in comfortable, respectable digs where the landladies provided plates of fish and chips and piles of good thick bread and butter, while he would return home to a long dining table, one place-setting, polished silverware, crystal wineglass, crisply laundered napkins, and a soberly clad servant to bring in the soup, roast, and dessert.

Possibly, when he had had dinner, he would stroll down to the beach again, to watch the crowd flocking into Gala Land, that curious mock-Byzantine underground pleasure palace smelling of damp earth and ferns where, for the price of a sixpenny admission ticket, one might wander all day, if one felt so inclined, beneath the red and cream brick arches, trying to decide on a sideshow, or listening to a ladies' orchestra. The sideshows cost extra, of course: threepence to see Winnie, the Boxing Kangaroo; threepence for the Strong Man; a penny or tuppence for the children's rides and swings and roundabouts; threepence for the Ghost Train.

Alternatively, he might wander along to the Singing Hall, where a pianist, seated at a tinny upright, belted out the latest hit tunes. "Ramona," and "Shepherd of the Hills." But the uninhibited enjoyment of those around him, singing lustily to the rhythm of the "bouncing ball," would merely underline his feeling of isolation.

Things might be different if he enjoyed his work, or had a pal of his own age to knock about with. He had made a tentative suggestion to one of the apprentice warehousemen, one day, that the pair of them might take a trip on one of the pleasure steamers and have a bite to eat and a pint of beer afterward. He had known at once, by the embarrassed expression on the youth's face, that he had overstepped the invisible barrier between himself, the boss's grandson, and his employees, who respectfully called him "Mr. Berry" or "Sir"; never just Berry, or "hi, you!"

Possibly there were fellows of his own age and social background he could make friends with if he chose to join a cricket or tennis club, but Berry had no great liking for his own so-called class. He had, reprehensibly perhaps, managed to mislay the list of names his Grandmother

Tanquillan had handed to him on the eve of his departure for High Tor.

Walking homeward, Berry smiled to himself, remembering his adventure three weeks ago. At least, on that occasion, he had managed to break out of his shell. He had been sitting at a green-tiled table in Evelyn's Cafe on the foreshore, eating an ice-cream sundae, listening to the music played by a small, talented ladies' band. He was laughing at the antics of the lead accordionist, a bright extroverted comedienne with a raddled, attractively ugly face, when a timid voice at his elbow said, "Excuse me. Me mates and me couldn't help noticing you all alone. Would you mind if I ask you something? It's a bit cheeky, I know, but . . ."

"Oh." He rose to his feet as the girl, about his own age, with pale fluffy blond hair framing her sharp-featured face, slipped into the empty chair opposite. "I'm sorry," he said, "is there anything I can do for you?"

She giggled at that. "It all depends on whether you're willing. It's like this, you see, me mates and me—that's them over there at the table near the window . . ." She fluttered her hand in their direction. Her "mates," Berry saw, were two girls, one dark-haired, the other a dyed blonde, both of whom were smiling self-consciously. "Well, like I was saying, we're off dancing at the Olympia, an' the bloke I was going with has dropped out— made himself bad eating all them mussels, if you ask me." She sniffed disdainfully. "So I thought if you aren't doing anything special, you might like to come with us." She added hastily, "I'll pay for your ticket, of course—I mean, that'd only be fair, wouldn't it?"

The upshot was that he had found himself partnering the girl—Doreen, her name was—trying to remember the dance steps he had learned at school. He hadn't done too badly either, come to think of it, or Doreen, at least, didn't seem to think so, judging by the way she kept her head on his shoulder during the waltzes and slow foxtrots.

She told him, over coffee during the interval, that she came from Lancashire, and worked in a cotton mill; had saved up all winter to come to Scarborough for her holidays. She was eighteen, and nearly engaged to the bloke suffering from a surfeit of mussels. "An' what about you?" she asked. "Are you engaged—or anything?"

When Berry admitted that he was not, Doreen sighed heavily, and said, "Someone is in for a treat then. Wish it was me. No, honest, I've never met a bloke like you before. God, you ain't half good-looking. You wouldn't consider keeping touch with me, would you?"

"I don't think your fiancè would like that very much," Berry said gently.

"No, I don't suppose he would," Doreen admitted. "But we aren't *really* engaged. I mean, he hasn't given me a ring or anything."

When, after the dance, the mates and their respective boyfriends wandered off together, Berry found himself walking Doreen back to her digs by way of St. Nicholas Gardens: a maze of dark twisting paths and steps leading to the town center.

Suddenly, Doreen drew him into one of the shelters. Pressing her slight, eager little body closely to his. "Go on," she whispered urgently. "Kiss me! Jimmy'll never know."

A refusal often causes offense, Berry thought wryly, remembering a notice he had seen tacked up in a shop window, as he bent his lips to hers.

"Cor," said Doreen, when the kiss was over, "is that the best you can do? Anyone'd think you'd never kissed a girl before!"

"As a matter of fact, I haven't," Berry said meekly.

"Jimmy's a good kisser," Doreen remarked coldly. "Oh, come on, then. It's time I was in. The landlady locks up at midnight, besides, me feet are killing me."

Funny, he quite cherished that little adventure. At least he had felt alive in Doreen's company.

As he turned to walk along Valley Road, he almost bumped into three girls walking arm in arm; the middle one tall and dark, wearing a pillbox hat, the one on the right small and plump, with hair like spun gold, the third with dark chestnut hair, and clear, almost amber-colored eyes, whose face seemed vaguely familiar.

"I beg your pardon," he said, stepping aside to let them pass. "I wasn't looking where I was going."

"Now, that's what I call a handsome chap," Peggy said, turning her head to look over her shoulder; wishing she had worn her new lace collar, and pinned a rose to her hat.

Letting himself into the house with his latchkey, Berry suddenly knew whom the girl with the chestnut hair had reminded him of—Charlotte Oakleigh.

After his solitary dinner he went into the music room. Madre had told him about his father's piano. At least here, in this quiet room with French windows leading to the terrace, he could play to his heart's content; yet music was often a torment as well as a joy when he reflected that he would never be able to achieve his dearest wish. The future his grandfather had mapped out for him had wrecked his chances of becoming a musician.

He had wasted too much time already. The piano, as he wanted to play it, professionally, demanded hard, concentrated hours of study and practice. Madre had done her best to help him, but his music teacher, Professor Goldstein, had put it bluntly when he said there was little more he could do for him under the circumstances. "You play well, my boy," he said, "even brilliantly, but what you need now is the guidance of someone of the caliber of Monsieur Robillard of the Academy of Music in Paris, to take you under his wing, and hammer you into shape." The old man had spread out his hands in a gesture of resignation. "Alas, I have taught you all I know, and always there have been these impossible restrictions. Secret music lessons, bah! Music is the language of the universe. It should be shouted aloud, not whispered!"

If only he had the courage to break free, Berry thought. He had a little money of his own due in October: the legacy from his great-great-aunt Kitty. That should prove more than enough to take him to Paris in pursuit of his dream, and to pay for his tuition, provided he could live cheaply enough. He could find himself some kind of studio on the Left Bank and cook for himself, or eat out at those student cafes near the Sorbonne, where, for a few francs, one could purchase good, nourishing onion soup, bread, and delicious French coffee.

The dream seemed almost a reality as he seated himself at his father's piano and swept his hands over the keys.

He thought, as he played Debussy's "Clair de Lune," of a woman with red hair.

The relationship between Joe and Laurie was a tender loving affair of gentleness and shared laughter. Whenever his daughter walked into a room, the sun shone for Joe Grayler. The thought of losing her hung over him like a dark cloud, but he agreed with Annie that the girl must be given her chance in life. Laurie's happiness would always come first with him.

Filly, on the other hand, said the girl must be barmy wanting to be an actress. An *actress*, of all things! Acting, in her estimation, was tantamount to prostitution. "Do you mean to tell me, Joe Grayler, that you have actually given your consent to her going off to London to meet this—this stage-manager—or whoever he is? Well, you need your head examined, in my opinion! And that girl's as daft as you are." She added, "Laurie's not the type to be an actress. I'd have thought that was as plain as the nose on your face! Laurie's a homebody, always has been,

316

and always will be. She's not cut out for the—*theater!* Laurie's a dreamer, not a doer!"

Joe said, "I know that as well as you do, but it is something she must learn for herself. If Annie and I refuse to let her go, she might hold it against us for the rest of her life. I couldn't bear that."

"Nor I," Annie agreed. "In any case, it's all settled. Mr. Ryder has arranged the interview, and Charlotte is coming tomorrow to take Laurie back to London with her.

"Charlotte," Filly said bitterly, "trust her to have a finger in the pie!"

"You mustn't blame Charlotte for that," Annie said firmly, "after all, we did ask her."

Charlotte took Laurie aside. "If I were you," she said, "I should learn a passage of Shakespeare by heart. Nothing too dramatic. Choose something from one of the comedies: *A Midsummer Night's Dream*, perhaps, or *The Taming of the Shrew*. Above all, try to be natural."

"But if I *tried* to be natural, I wouldn't be natural at all," Laurie replied with a worried frown. "You see, Aunt Charlotte, I—I'm not a very disciplined person. I'm not very good at speaking lines written by other people, only at saying the words I hear in my head."

"You mean you prefer to write your own dialogue?"

"Oh, I don't write it. I just say it."

"Perhaps you should try writing it," Charlotte suggested thoughtfully. "I expect that's how people like Noel Coward got started."

"You mean I should be a playwright?" Laurie looked startled.

"It's a thought," Charlotte said, "after all, somebody has to write the lines for the actors to speak. You know, Laurie, you have a natural flair for comedy, the talent to make people laugh."

Laurie said gloomily, "But I don't want to make people

317

laugh. I want to be like Greta Garbo, all floaty and mysterious." She could not resist pulling her Garbo face and giving a near-perfect impression of that husky Swedish voice.

Charlotte laughed helplessly. "That's marvelous," she said, "perhaps you should do that at your audition."

The girl was bursting with talent, but whether a blasé London impresario would think it worth his while taking on a star-struck seventeen-year-old with no acting experience, was impossible to predict. Charlotte had been cooped up at the St. Nicholas Street salon all afternoon with a fussy client needing an extensive new wardrobe for an autumn cruise to the Bahamas. Thankfully making her escape, she walked quickly along St. Nicholas Street to the cliff gardens for a breath of sea air. She stood near the railings, looking down at the crowded beach, the little encampment of green bathing tents near Gala Land. Groups of people were playing sand cricket, others throwing beach balls; the sea edge was dotted with swimmers, not venturing far out. Taking off her hat, she let the warm breeze ruffle her hair and closed her eyes, hearing shrill cries of pleasure muted by distance, rising up to her from the teeming sand.

This was August, the height of the season, which was why she had offered to escort Laurie to London, knowing that neither Annie nor Joe could take time off from a houseful of visitors. Standing there, a slim elegant figure in her beige linen dress, she thought that Laurie might like to see Mary Ellis in *Music in the Air*.

Berry walked along the foreshore to the "zig-zag," a steep road which led, in a series of bends, to St. Nicholas Cliff. Planks had been placed horizontally to give purchase to the feet of those toiling up, or coming down it helter-skelter; girls in cotton dresses passed him, giggling hysterically as they ran.

"Sorry," one of them sang out blithely as she almost collided with him. Glancing up to see how many more

318

bends he must negotiate, his heart almost missed a beat. He would have known anywhere the slim woman with the shining auburn hair. He fairly raced the rest of the way to the top.

"Charlotte!" he said breathlessly, unaware, in his excitement, that he had used her Christian name.

"Berry!"

"I had almost given up hope of seeing you again."

"Where on earth have your sprung from?" They were both laughing.

"From the harbor, you know, where I work! I'm on my way home. Please won't you come with me? Have dinner with me? It isn't far to Chalice Walk."

The house in Chalice Walk, she thought. The house where her love affair with Rowan began, a place filled with haunting memories of the past. She had doubts about going there again.

"Please," Berry said persuasively, "you don't know how much it will mean to me."

"Very well, then. Of course I'll come."

Chapter Twenty-Six

The house was just as she remembered it. Only she was different, far removed from the gauche seventeen-year-old who brought Alice Tanquillan home to face the music the day she ran away from boarding-school.

Charlotte thought sadly that poor Alice had quite literally faced the music that day. Rowan was seated at the grand piano when the housekeeper showed them in. What was the woman's name? Ah yes, Mrs. Lomas. A sudden feeling of unease gripped Charlotte. What if Mrs. Lomas was still here; if she came face to face with her again? How could she explain to Berry that she, his guest, knew this house as well, perhaps better than he did?

Thankfully, a servant appeared from the staff quarters: a tall man, with strands of hair skillfully arranged to hide his balding pate. "Good evening, sir," he said deferentially. "Cook told me to say that dinner will be served in a quarter of an hour."

Berry replied cheerfully, "Thanks, Stevenson, perhaps you'll set another place for my guest, and tell Cook, with my compliments, there'll be one extra for dinner. What are we having by the way?"

Stevenson looked faintly shocked. "So far as I know, sir, Cook has prepared a cold dinner, on account of the weather being so warm."

"Fine," Berry said easily. Smiling, he asked Charlotte

is she would care to wash before the meal. "No," she replied, "but I don't mind waiting for you."

"Thanks awfully. Shan't be a tick. Warehouses are rather dusty places," Berry said, taking the stairs two at a time.

He was so young and eager, just as Rowan used to be, Charlotte thought, walking slowly to the open door of the music room. She was half-afraid of seeing the piano again, and the French windows leading to the terrace. On the threshold she seemed to hear the jingle of an old French nursery rhyme; to glimpse the ghost of a child in a navy school uniform and the silent, watchful figure of Romilly, standing in the shadows.

With a swiftly beating heart, she turned away from the door to wait for Berry. When he came downstairs they went into the long cool dining-room overlooking the lily pond, where the Venetian blinds were half-closed to keep out the sun. But this room, with its elegant Regency table, and Constable paintings in heavy gilt frames, had never been Charlotte's province. As Alice Tanquillan's companion she had spent most of her time in the schoolroom on the top floor, or the box-room, converted to her use as a bedroom.

If Sir Gervaise and Lady Tanquillan could see her now, she thought, a guest in their home. How little she realized, the day she brought Alice here all those years ago, that her involvement with the Tanquillans would run, like the recurring theme of a symphony, throughout her entire life.

"You are very quiet," Berry observed carefully. "I hope I didn't embarrass you, rushing up to you the way I did." He smiled shyly. "I've just remembered, in my excitement I called you Charlotte. I'm really very sorry."

"There's no need to apologize. I hope you'll continue to do so," Charlotte said smilingly. "Now, tell me how you're getting along. How's the job going?"

"Not very well," Berry admitted. "I don't seem quite cut out for it. I like working near the harbor, of course,

321

seeing the ships unloaded. There's a certain feeling of excitement then, but I'd rather be with the stevedores doing the unloading, than the owner's grandson, standing there watching!"

It might have been Rowan speaking through his son's lips. Charlotte said gently, "Given the choice, what would you rather be doing?"

An intense, yearning expression crossed Berry's face. "I want to be a musician," he said, "a concert pianist."

"Then why don't you?" Charlotte asked, in a low voice. "If that is really what you need to make you happy, why waste time doing a job you dislike?"

Berry shrugged. "You know how it is. My grandfather has his heart set on my becoming the head of the Tanquillan Company. He was terribly angry when I told him what I really want to do. I have Madre to thank for being able to play the piano at all. Grandfather would be furious if he knew about all those secret lessons. In any case, I've probably wasted too much time already. Professor Goldstein said that if I wished to make a career as a pianist, I should go to Paris to study. But you can see how impossible that would be."

Stevenson came in at that moment to serve the cold poached salmon, salad Nicoise, and tiny new potatoes cooked in their skin.

If only I dare tell Berry the truth, Charlotte thought, that his father faced the same emotional dilemma. Rowan had given up his dream of becoming a musician to please a power-hungry despot; how could she stand by, doing and saying nothing to prevent Tanquillan ruining his grandson's life also? She asked quietly, "Will you play for me after dinner?"

The windows leading to the terrace were wide open to the scent of stocks and lavender, curiously intermingled with

322

the tang of salt air; the indefinable fragrance of a warm summer evening drifted up from the garden.

As Berry seated himself at the piano, Charlotte remembered the times she had walked alone in that garden, in another summertime, long ago. It was May then, with other, different flowers in bloom. Often she had walked in the garden at dusk, seeing the lights of the house shining onto the terrace, striving hard to overcome her feelings of despair and jealousy, knowing that Rowan and Romilly were there together, on their honeymoon.

Sometimes she had heard the sound of music drifting down from the open French windows of the house. Occasionally she had seen Romilly standing on the terrace, resting her hands on the stone balustrade, a pale nebulous figure by starlight.

It seemed to Charlotte for one fleeting moment that the open windows had framed, in agonizing detail, a scene from the past, linked to all the uncertainty, jealousy, passion and heartbreak of youth. But the past was over and done with. What mattered now were the hopes, dreams and ambitions of the present generation. She and Rowan had lived their little time on earth together; their story was told; their children's just beginning.

Turning from the window, she moved silently toward the piano, to stand there, smiling at Berry, her hands resting lightly on the polished wood. His handsome young face, she noticed, was beaded with perspiration. "Don't be afraid," she said, understanding his nervousness, his mingled hopes and fears, "just play for yourself alone, as if no one else was listening. I'll sit there, near the fireplace." She remembered the ramrod figure of Lady Tanquillan seated upright in that very chair, the day she brought Alice home; the tap-tapping of Rachel's fingers on the chair arm; the cold sparkle of her diamond rings.

Berry ran his fingers over the keys. How strange, he thought, that "Clair de Lune" had somehow become linked, in his mind, with Charlotte's gentleness and beauty. He played it now as he had never played it before, aware of her quiet presence in the room, experiencing the strangest feeling that he was attempting to say to her, in music, all that lay hidden in his heart. Never a day had passed that he had not thought about her and longed to see her again.

When he met her today, so unexpectedly, he had suddenly felt as if that great barrier of loneliness between himself and the rest of humanity had melted like ice at the first touch of the sun.

When the last note of music died away, Charlotte came slowly to his side and stood there for a while, not speaking.

At last she said in a low, vibrant voice. "You must go to Paris, my dear. Life is so short, so precious: it must not be wasted."

The impresario's name was Peter Chandos, a short, stumpy, balding man of Turkish ancestry, with tufts of gray hair above his ears. To make up for the hair loss from his scalp, Chandos had cultivated a moustache of immense length and thickness which he frequently stroked upward with the back of his right hand. His sloe-dark eyes, beneath pouched eyelids, possessed all the keenness of a hawk hovering for prey. Chandos had amassed his fortune in theatrical enterprises, in London and the provinces, from his shrewdness in assessing and promoting talent.

He and Howard Ryder became acquainted as connoisseurs of antiques. Chandos's tastes, however, unlike Ryder's, veered towards the exotic. He collected Chinese lacquer screens and cabinets; Russian ikons; samovars; tapestries and weaponry, which he commissioned Ryder to purchase for him at auction. It was during one of their transactions that Howard mentioned a friend of his, and

Madam Carlotta's interest in arranging an audition for a promising young actress.

The name meant something to Chandos, whose wife spent a small fortune on clothes. "Bring the girl to the Alhambra Theatre on . . ." he consulted his diary, and mentioned the date. "I am doing a series of auditions on that day."

That day had now arrived, to Laurie's consternation. "It's no use, Aunt Charlotte," she said at breakfast, "I can't eat because I can't swallow properly. My mouth's all dried up inside."

Charlotte had suggested buying the budding Sarah Siddons a new outfit for the occasion, to give her confidence, but Laurie said she would rather wear her old things; she'd feel like a stranger otherwise—a sheep in wolf's clothing. Perhaps that *was* the most sensible approach, Charlotte considered. Laurie's fresh young beauty needed no embellishment.

Now she felt every bit as nervous as her niece as they walked together up the steps of the theater to find the door locked, the place apparently deserted. "Oh, Lord," Laurie groaned, "we must have come on the wrong day."

"Don't worry," Charlotte said, "we should have probably gone round the corner to the stage entrance. Yes, look, there's a sign. 'Auditions.' "

The stage-door keeper, a laconic man with a battered felt hat perched on the back of his head, gave them what Laurie termed the once-over, and led them down a long narrow passage to the auditorium where groups of people were standing aimlessly about, apparently awaiting the arrival of Mr. Chandos. A worried-looking young man with untidy fair hair ducked back and forth across the stage, giving directions about moving certain props to a couple of older men in shirtsleeves and braces.

Suddenly the doors to the rear of the auditorium were flung open, and in came the impresario, immaculately dressed in a lightweight brown suit, coffee-colored silk shirt, paisley tie, and wearing a white carnation in his buttonhole, followed by three other men—his entourage.

Without a word of greeting Mr. Chandos seated himself halfway down the stalls, and raised his fat beringed hand as a signal to the stage-manager to start the proceedings, in which he immediately appeared to lose all interest.

Laurie would remember for ever afterward that sick feeling that swept over her as she stood in the wings. She, who had never been on a stage in her life before, had always supposed that they were flat, but this one had a decided rake to it, and how queer and tawdry the scenery was, seen at close quarters. I can't do it, she thought desperately. I can't walk out onto that vast expanse of nothingness with everyone looking at me, and start acting.

It dawned on her, fearfully watching the others going through their paces, young men and women dressed outlandishly in a kind of stage uniform consisting of slacks and baggy jumpers, the women with their hair done up in colorful scarves or turbans, that all were professional actors to whom auditions were all part of a day's work; people who had trained hard and knew exactly how to project their personality across the footlights. Not that the footlights were switched on. Laurie might have felt better if they had been; if she had been able to sense a little magic in the air, that mysterious glamor of the theater the audience feels when the curtain goes up.

There was no magic here, merely a dusty stage, a depressing tangle of ropes and cables, and a vast, echoing auditorium which put her in mind of a Roman amphitheatre before the Christians came into the arena to tackle the lions.

"It's your turn now," the stage-manager hissed, propelling her forward a little, since she appeared to be rooted to the spot. "Laurie Grayler," he called to the four silent watchers in the stalls. "Katharina; *Taming of the Shrew;* Act five, scene two."

"Good luck, darling," Charlotte whispered, and

watched, hands clasped, heart in mouth, as Laurie, a forlorn figure in her blue cotton dress, walked to the center of the stage. How young she looked, and how vulnerable.

"Fie, fie! unknit that threatening unkind brow . . ." Laurie began, casting a nervous sideways look at Chandos.

"Tell her to speak up, we can't hear," one of the entourage interrupted.

Poor Laurie began again, forcing her voice unnaturally, stumbling through the long speech; too nervous to remember the inflections and gestures her Aunt Charlotte had taught her, wanting nothing more than to finish it without actually falling down in a dead faint. Then, suddenly, in a flash of audacity, thinking everything was lost anyway, she went into her perfect Garbo imitation.

"Well, that's that," she said when the ordeal was over. "Please let us go home now."

"But don't you want to hear what Mr. Chandos has to say to you? He promised Mr. Ryder that he would speak to us after the audition."

"I'd rather not, if you don't mind. I think I can guess what he'll have to say about me. I was terrible."

"Terrible? I thought you were marvelous." She daren't tell Laurie that she was a natural born comedienne. "Sit it the car if you want to. I'll wait for Mr. Chandos."

Laurie struggled with her conscience, not wishing to add cowardice to all her other shortcomings. "I'll wait, too," she said, "after all, he can't very well shoot me, I suppose." She smiled like a sunburst.

Charlotte had bought her a new outfit anyway, a soft blue dress and jacket suitable for a special occasion, and she had planned such an occasion tonight: dinner at the Grosvenor, then the theater, *The Late Christopher Bean*, starring Edith Evans and Cedric Hardwicke.

"I just can't take it all in," Laurie said bemusedly. "Pinch me to make sure I'm not dreaming."

Charlotte laughed. "My dear Laurie, I'm delighted for you."

"Mind you," Laurie sniffed, "Mr. Chandos wasn't very complimentary. Come to think of it, he wasn't very complimentary about anything. I can't think why he gave me that introduction to the London School of Dramatic Art."

"You know very well why," Charlotte said, "you just want to hear it again. Mr. Chandos said you had potential. I should think so, too. That Garbo impersonation rocked him back on his heels. Everyone loved it. Whatever made you think of it?"

"Ah well, I knew the Shakespeare hadn't gone down too well by the deathly hush, so I grabbed Greta out of the blue," Laurie admitted. She sighed. "Mum and Dad were so excited when I rang them, but I think they'll miss me, especially Dad. I worry about him, you know. I wish he was stronger. All the time he was saying how happy he was for me, I kept worrying about all the money they'll have to find for my fees . . ."

"Laurie, dear. You mustn't worry about that. Your parents were kind enough to agree to letting me pay for your tuition, and they know you'll be safe here, in London, with me."

"My cup runneth over," Laurie said softly, not believing that all this was really happening: sitting in the Grosvenor Grill, eating succulent fillet steak, wearing the prettiest dress she had ever owned, with her feet set on the first rung of the ladder of success. And yet at the back of her mind lingered a certain regret for all she would have to forego; the old music of her life, the unforgettable rapture of childhood.

Gervaise Tanquillan's face drained of color apart from the purplish network of broken veins covering his cheeks.

Berry could not help feeling a surge of pity for his grandfather. "I'm sorry," he said, "I realize this must

328

have come as a shock . . ." He was standing in front of Tanquillan's desk, being made to feel like an irresponsible schoolboy.

"Shock! You insolent young pup! How dare you speak to me of *shock?* It is more than shock I feel, it is disgust that my own grandson should have played traitor to the family name, the family honor!"

Berry frowned, thinking that this was going a bit too far. "I can't see what is dishonorable about wanting to become a concert pianist. In any case, I told you some time ago that this was what I wanted, but you wouldn't even listen."

"I have no intention of listening now," Gervaise thundered, bringing his fist down on his desk with such force that a vase containing a rose, placed near a photograph of his wife, suddenly toppled over. "I shall never listen to such bloody nonsense."

Berry watched, with a kind of fascination, the water dripping onto the carpet, feeling that he should, perhaps, do something about it.

"It isn't nonsense," he said quietly, standing his ground. "My mind is made up. I'm going to Paris to study music. Now, if you'll excuse me."

It seemed pointless to continue the argument. As he turned to the door, he found himself thinking not so much of the row with his grandfather as wondering how long the rose would survive without water. But Gervaise hadn't finished with him yet. "If you leave this house—throw away the future I have planned for you," he said in a cold, precise voice, "I shall have no hesitation whatever in foreclosing the mortgage on your grandmother's house, which I have owned for some considerable time."

Berry's hand hesitated on the doorknob he was about to turn. He had no choice other than to listen. Facing his grandfather, he said, "And to think it was you who spoke so glibly of family honor.

Gervaise said grimly, "Emily Beresford is not a member of my family. You are! A member of my own family would scarcely have had the temerity to do what she has done: encouraging my own flesh and blood to go behind my back in such a fashion." He uttered a short bark of derisive laughter. "Secret music lessons, indeed! Well, she who called the tune must pay the piper! If you go to Paris, I give you my word, Berry, I'll ruin that precious 'Madre' of yours! What have you to say to that?"

"What can I say, Grandfather, except that I shall hate you for the rest of my life," Berry said contemptuously, "not because of what you are doing to me, but what you can so easily contemplate doing to someone I love. Very well, Grandfather, you win! I'll go back to Scarborough tomorrow, after which, God willing, I shall never set foot in this house again!"

Somehow, he had to see Charlotte again, to talk to her; make her understand that he could not go to Paris after all.

In desperation, he telephoned the House of Carlotta.

"Who shall I say is calling, sir?"

"Just tell her, please, that Berry Tanquillan wishes to speak to her. It's really very urgent."

"Very well, sir. I'll put you through."

He had never felt so young, so inadequate, in all his life as he did then, waiting for the telephonist to connect him with Charlotte. What if she regarded him as little more than a nuisance, a foolish, ambitious boy, constantly in need of reassurance, of guidance? And why should she regard him as more than that? She must be a great deal older than himself, and yet he had never thought of the difference in their ages before; he had simply felt, from the moment they met, that there was little difference between them at all.

"Berry?" Charlotte's voice came to him across the wire. "Is anything the matter?"

330

Bitter disappointment welled up in him. "I'm not going to Paris after all."

"Not going? But I thought . . ."

"Something's happened, that's all. I'm going back to Scarborough tomorrow."

"Where are you now?"

"In London. I came to see my grandfather, I wondered if it would be possible to see you, to explain . . ."

"Why don't you have dinner with me tonight?" Charlotte suggested. "You know my address? 15 Glamorgan Square. I'll expect you about eight o'clock."

They had dinner together in Charlotte's elegant dining room overlooking the park. The trees, Berry noticed, betrayed the first unmistakable signs of autumn, a certain loss of fecundity, of bloom, shine and foliage, as if the leaves knew that September was here.

Afterward they went through to the drawing-room for coffee. Berry had said little so far, inhibited by the presence of the servant. Glancing at his handsome downcast young face as the servant brought in the tray, Charlotte thought that September had always been a season of change and upheaval. Laurie had gone back to Scarborough to collect the rest of her belongings; tomorrow Kathy would travel to Manchester to begin her training, whilst Peggy would be getting ready to return home to Darlington.

Charlotte remembered acutely that end of season feeling when the last of the summer visitors headed homeward, and the streets seemed strangely cleansed of the fever of summertime, curiously empty and peaceful again. And yet, linked to the initial beauty and quietude of falling leaves came a sense of decay, a loneliness of the heart. Now, here was Rowan's son, turning to her in the loneliness of his heart, not knowing, not understanding that he

331

was the son of the man she, Charlotte, had loved for what seemed like a million Septembers.

Berry told his tale haltingly. Charlotte let him speak, keeping silent, watching the play of firelight on his face, understanding his torment. Nothing about her outward appearance betrayed the bitter anger and resentment welling up inside her as she listened, hating Gervaise Tanquillan whose unscrupulous emotional blackmail had extinguished so effectively his grandson's shining hopes and dreams.

But this was nothing new. Tanquillan had always overridden those who threatened the great Company god he served. Rowan, Alice, his own brother, Oliver: all had known the pitiless despotism of this man. Now had come the time of reckoning. Charlotte knew she could not stand by to watch Tanquillan destroy his grandson and Emily Beresford.

"You talked of returning to Scarborough tomorrow," she said, when Berry had finished speaking.

"I have no other choice . . ."

"I think you have," Charlotte said. "Listen to me. Go home and pack your things. First thing tomorrow morning, go to Waterloo station and buy a one-way ticket to Paris."

"But . . ."

"No buts, you must do exactly as I say, and leave the rest to me. Will you trust me to take care of your grandmother? Tell her I'll come to the house tomorrow to see her."

Berry said quietly, "I would trust you with my life, Charlotte." He wanted to tell her the truth, but did not know how. "Because I love you."

Money and power lust lay at the heart of Gervaise Tanquillan's mentality like a cancerous growth, choking out human decency and compassion, Charlotte thought. Her

332

chauffeur-driven Rolls-Royce drew up outside Emily Beresford's house in Eaton Square and she stepped down from it, an immaculate figure in a lilac and gray costume, a double row of pearls at her throat.

She wondered, with a tightening of her lips, what Tanquillan's reaction would be when he knew that a former servant in his employ had every intention of buying the property next door to his.

She did not want or need the house. It would serve Sir Gervaise right if she turned it into a home for juvenile delinquents. A certain grim satisfaction lay in the thought.

She had discussed, at length, every aspect of the deal with her lawyer, Alfred Cunningham, as she had done when she had enlarged her Bond Street premises, and opened House of Carlotta shops in Bournemouth, Torquay, Bristol, York, and Edinburgh. She had also consulted him when she built a new school for the children at Cloud Merridon, updated the farm workers' cottages at Grey Wethers, and increased the farm acreage by carefully considered land speculation.

"Go ahead and buy the Eaton Square house, my dear," Cunningham said with a dry chuckle. "You can well afford to do so. *He* certainly cannot prevent you. If, as you say, Mrs. Beresford has not appointed Sir Gervaise her legal executor, it is a simple matter of refunding the amount he is dunning her for. But it seems unlikely that Mrs. Beresford would be able to stay on there, and even more unlikely that she would wish to do so, under the circumstances. Have you thought about that?"

"Yes," Charlotte smiled warmly at the old man, "I have a proposition to put to Mrs. Beresford."

"Madam is waiting for you in the library," the maid said, but Emily came out to meet her, hands extended, eyes shining. "Berry has just rung me from Dover," she said. "He's actually on his way to Paris! Oh, Charlotte, I don't give a damn what happens to me. This is what I have longed for, dreamed of. He told me what you've done. How can I possibly thank you?" Tears were close to the surface. Charlotte could feel the slight trembling of Emily's hands, and realized that she must be imagining the coming storm when Tanquillan found out that his grandson had slipped through the net, dreading the punishment he would mete out to her.

"May we got into the library? I have something to say to you." Charlotte smiled mysteriously. "You may wish to sit down when I tell you . . ."

"Tell me—what?" Emily closed the door behind them.

"With your permission, I'd like to buy this house. I've already spoken to my lawyer about it."

"Buy this . . . ?" Emily's cheeks paled, then flushed. "Yes, I think I should like to sit down." She seemed stunned, as if she could not quite take in what Charlotte had said to her. "But, my dear, you don't really want it, do you? I mean, what on earth would you do with it?"

"Several things have crossed my mind." She mentioned the home for juvenile delinquents to make Emily smile. "Wouldn't that be simply splendid? Can you imagine Sir Gervaise's face?"

"Oh, God," Emily said, "you wouldn't really do that . . . ?"

"Of course not, though it would serve him right if I did." Charlotte spoke more seriously then. "The thing I want most of all, for Berry's sake, is to get you away from here—to fix, once and for all, a situation which you must have found both frightening and humiliating over the past years. Emily, darling, you know how much I care for you, and Berry. I know how much Rowan cared for you. I simply thank God that it lies within my power to help you, if you'll let me."

"What do you want me to do?" Emily spoke coolly and Charlotte knew why. Mrs. Beresford had her pride.

"Nothing that you would be unwilling to do. This isn't a question of—charity—if that's what you are thinking. You must know that I love and admire you far too much

334

to insult you in that way. It simply occurred to me that you might feel happier away from—all this, now that Berry has gone to Paris."

She knelt at Emily's feet; looked up at her appealingly. "I'd like you to go home, to Grey Wethers. No, please listen! But for a quirk of fate, Grey Wethers might have belonged to Rowan. He loved it so much. I have never felt that any part of it really belongs to me. If things had been different, Rowan would have inherited Grey Wethers and would have handed it down to his son. That's the way it should have been, that's why I'm asking you to go there now!"

"Oh, Charlotte, my dear . . ." Tears flooded down Emily's cheeks.

"If you would prefer not to live in the house itself," Charlotte continued, "there's a cottage in the grounds. It isn't very big, admittedly, but I think you'd be happy there."

She smiled tenderly. "I'm sure Rowan would be happy to know you were there—a part of all he loved. Well, what do you think?"

Emily said, very quietly, "I think that it is high time I came home."

Part Four

Chapter Twenty-Seven

"It's really true, then, about the King and Mrs. Simpson," Kathy said, looking intently at the press agency report.

"He's been in love with her for ages, apparently," the operator said eagerly. "I wonder what he'll do now!"

"There's only one thing he *can* do, abdicate!"

"Oh, surely not! I mean to say, he *is* the King!"

"Yes, but the Cabinet will never agree to his marrying a divorced woman. He must have been crazy to get mixed up with her in the first place," Kathy observed coolly. "The King can't possibly marry Mrs. Simpson. My guess is, they'll try to make him give her up. He'll refuse, of course, then he'll be out on his ear, the darned fool!"

"I'm always amazed by the way you English denigrate your monarchy in public and get away with it. In my country, to refer to Hitler as a darned fool would be tantamount to signing one's own death warrant!"

Kathy looked up at the tall, bearish man with a mane of graying dark hair who had emerged in time to hear her remark. "Ah well, you're not in Germany now, Adam," she said, "there are no totalitarians in our corridors of power."

"I hope to God there never will be," Adam Bergmann's intelligent brown eyes clouded momentarily. The English joked about such matters because they had never heard those tyrants. He had. He heard them sometimes, even now, in nightmares.

"In any case," Kathy said levelly, "you weren't afraid to air your opinion of Hitler. You wouldn't be stuck here, otherwise."

Bergmann, she considered, had earned sanctuary in Britain. She held a deep admiration for this untidy Jewish giant whose hatred of the Nazi regime, forcibly expressed in his writings, had made it dangerous for him to remain in Germany.

Kathy wore her lustrous auburn hair in a very short crisp style nowadays. Adam liked the way she moved; the proud set of her head on her slim, erectly held shoulders; the plain but expensive clothes she wore, her lack of jewelry or heavily applied makeup; her slightly acerbic attitudes. She seemed to him an uncluttered young woman. Her reportage was equally uncluttered, straight to the point, accurate and neatly typed, requiring little or no help from his department.

Later that day he wandered through to the newsroom and asked if she would care to have dinner with him.

"Yes, I'd like that." Kathy had been hoping for some time that he would eventually get around to inviting her.

A great deal of fight had gone out of Maggie Masters in recent years. No wonder, she thought bitterly, being loaded with six kids to bring up, and feeling so poorly most of the time. Now, with Peggy engaged to be married, what would she do without her to help in the house—and to keep an eye on Ernie, Ada, and Clara, who were still at school?

Maggie, pregnant with Daniel the summer she and Bob moved to Darlington, had missed her mother "something terrible" when the baby was born. But no amount of harsh accusations of cruelty and selfishness would shake Bob's decision not to send for Filly. "You know as well as I do," he said adamantly, "if your mother set foot inside our front door again, we'd be stuck with her for good and all."

And so Maggie had moaned her way through the birth of her second child, and she had been moaning off and on ever since about life in general and the house in Cattermole Street in particular; a house backing onto the station goods yard, a facsimile, almost, of the one in Garibaldi Street, except that this one had three bedrooms and a bit of a garden to the rear, fenced off with rusty corrugated iron. She had moaned, too, about her husband's excessive sexual demands. It was nothing short of disgusting, in Maggie's opinion, the way in which Bob constantly demanded his conjugal rights, even on Sunday afternoons when the kids were at Sunday school.

Resentment against her sister Charlotte, who lived a life of luxury and had more money than she knew what to do with, cars, furs, jewels, and three houses as well, rose up like bile in Maggie, whenever she looked out of the back bedroom window at the rusty fence, or caught sight of herself in the mirror.

Maggie's never slim body had now run almost entirely to fat; her brown frizzy hair was flecked with gray at the temples, her chin had gone forth and multiplied. Thankfully, Bob seemed to have lost interest in his poking and prodding since the doctor had made it clear to him that another pregnancy, at his wife's age, might prove injurious to both mother and child. Now she resented the fact that he no longer wanted her.

When Peggy, her strength and stay, had announced her intention of getting married, next spring, to a man Maggie heartily detested, with brilliantined hair and a flashy style of dressing, a car salesman called Gee, short for George. "You must be out of your mind, our Peggy," she moaned. "The next thing you know, you'll be tied down with six kids, like me."

"Don't talk so daft, Ma," Peggy said defensively,

"there's no need for any woman to get tied down if she doesn't want to."

Suddenly all Maggie's frustration boiled over in a fury against Charlotte. "What have I done to deserve this?" she complained bitterly. "If your Aunt Charlotte had done her duty by you, by all of us, you wouldn't be throwing yourself away on a tuppence-ha'penny car salesman like Gee Jones . . ."

"Aw, shut up, Ma," Peggy said wearily. "It isn't Aunt Charlotte's fault! You know you hadn't a good word to say about her when she offered to pay for me to go the school. Dad was all for it, but not you! And what about all the invitations you've turned down for the kids to spend their summer holidays in Wiltshire? I wish you'd stop getting at Aunt Charlotte. It isn't her fault if you've got a potato where your head should be."

"Oh, that's right, blame me," Maggie snapped back at her. "It's always been the same—Charlotte could do no wrong! There was only your grandma and me who saw through her!" Maggie felt inclined to tell Peggy the truth, despite Bob's warning that she'd have him to answer to if she started raking over the past to the children—and Maggie had a healthy respect for Bob's temper, when aroused. Instead she said contemptuously, "Fine feathers don't always make fine birds, my girl. I could tell you things about your Aunt Charlotte that would make you change your opinion of her, right quick! Her and her fancy men!"

"The trouble with you, Ma," Peggy retorted, "you're as jealous as hell of her, and always have been. I'm not stupid, you know. I've known for a long time there was something to hush up, and I can guess what it is. But this is 1936, and people are more broad-minded now—all except you and Grandma! In any case, we weren't talking about Aunt Charlotte—we were talking about Gee and me getting married, and that's what we're going to do, whether you like it or not! At least I get a laugh when I'm with Gee, which is more than I get here!"

Peggy scarcely remembered Fred, the gas fitter she'd been crazy about in the summer of 1933: the inoffensive youth who had, unwittingly, been the cause of Laurie's entry into the London School of Dramatic Art.

Lauri'e baby fat had begun to melt away, like mist on a summer morning, the minute she started the intensive physical training regime considered necessary by her tutors. To them it was part and parcel of becoming an actress.

"Vell, you can zee for yourzelf, darlink," said Madame Kowlinska, a Russian Jewess by extraction, a tiny lady with hennaed hair, who believed wholeheartedly that as long as the body remained trim and graceful, the audience would not give a damn about facial defects. "Remember, darlink, acting has to do wiz illusion. If von so vishes von may change, in the tvinkling of an eye, a beautiful young girl into an old lady. On ze otter hand, it is qvite impossible to turn an old lady into a beautiful young girl, if she has too much the avoirdupois round ze hips, bust and midriff!" She had cast a troubled, expert eye over Laurie's avoirdupois. "And *you* have, darlink!" She added, "Remember, if you vish to become a screen actress, ze camera can be very cruel. Tventy pounds you are overveight; tventy pounds you must lose, at vonce—pouf, like a kiss from ze fingertips!"

"But I'm so hungry all the time, Madame Kowlinska," Laurie complained.

"Hungry? Vot matters ze hunger?" Madame Kowlinska replied, rolling up her eyes to heaven. "I gave up ze hunger years ago! Now I am zeventy long years removed from my mother's womb, and I have, still, ze body of ze angel. Zo must you give up ze hunger, if you vish to act! Laurie, my little von, verget ze vorms zat gnaw at ze stomach! Bend and stretch; bend and stretch! Ah, zat is good!"

Now Laurie scarcely recognized the svelte figure re-

343

flected in the rehearsal room mirrors as the girl she used to be. That last September in Scarborough, when she and Peggy and Kathy had walked, arms linked, along the beach, often came into her mind. She had realized, after that day, that everything would be changed, different. The brief flowering days of youth and childhood were over and done with. Despite their vows that nothing would ever change between the three of them, the changes had already begun.

That day had made a profound impression on Laurie; the long empty road before them, the sound of Sunday morning church bells dripping, like cleansing rain, down the twisting streets and alleyways of the old town in the lee of the castle, the roofs of the fishermen's cottages gilded with the clear September sunshine. She remembered the almost deserted stretch of sand curving between the rocks of the Children's Corner, the thin barking of a dog racing along near the water's edge, that end of summer feeling in the wide, sun-washed empty streets.

Later, they had gone up to the attic to close and latch the windows for the last time, and clear their clothes from the makeshift wardrobe. Closing the door on the faded rose-patterned wallpaper, after shrouding the furniture in dust-sheets, they left behind them the ghosts of the long-gone summertimes.

Turning at the door, before she closed it, Laurie had listened intently to the laughter which seemed trapped beneath the sloping ceiling, the whispered secrets, the music of the cinema which had drifted up through the warm, airless summer nights: "The Lullaby of Broadway," "Ah, Sweet Mystery of Life."

Looking at herself in the mirror, Laurie recalled the words of the poem she had written in her room that last September night, three years ago.

Never agin,
Acceptance of the Universe; stars

Familiar as baubles on a Christmas tree,
    Retreating, with tender, backward glance, I see
Perfection in retrospect,
Cloud-light, delightful in its purity.
The laughing child-phantom beckoning down the
    years . . .
Pitying me?

The view from his studio window never failed to excite
Berry, especially when darkness fell, and the lights of Paris
spread out, like a vast jewelled fan, beneath him; when
the sky, to the west, was flushed pink with the dying rays
of the sun, or heavy with rain clouds. Rain or sun, no
matter which, Berry's heart always rejoiced at the sudden
springing up of the lights in the city he loved.

He had been here almost three years now, studying music under the guidance of Maître Robillard at l'Academie
Municipale de Paris, living the way he had chosen to live,
frugally but excitingly. He enjoyed learning how to fend
for himself in his garret beneath the stars, shopping for
food in the busy streetmarkets on the Left Bank of the
Seine. He revelled in every minute of freedom: consciously
aware of it, as a gift to be treasured.

His room was spacious, all-purpose. The piano, his most
precious possession, bought from Aunt Kitty's legacy, occupied a dais near the windows opening onto a flat roof
where he grew herbs in Provencal pots, to flavor the stews
he cooked in the antiquated gas stove behind the screened-
off area which served as a kitchen. One stew, or "Ragout
Tanquillan" as he called it, would last him three days,
eaten with plenty of long French bread sticks from the
boulangerie in the street below, the Rue des Quatres Saisons.

His landlady, Madame Hotier, had thoughtfully provided him with a French recipe book and a selection
of copper pans, and taught him how to make sauces—

tartare, hollandaise, mousseline, and mayonnaise—taking under her ample wing the shy English boy with the gift for music. "You must eat well, mon cher," she would admonish him in the early days of his tenancy, "learn how to cook for yourself in the French style. You are far too thin but then you are still very young, like a spring chicken!"

Not that Mme. Hotier held the same opinion of her lodger nowadays. The passage of years had, inevitably, brought about changes in Berry's appearance. He had grown considerably taller, for one thing: his spare, boyish frame had filled out suddenly to a man's proportions, both broad-shouldered and muscular. Madame always knew whenever Berry entered the house in the Rue des Quatres Saisons. The front door would bang shut behind him and she would catch a glimpse of his long legs taking the stairs two at a time, whistling as he went. He dressed in orthodox English fashion, in plain serviceable trousers, shirt, and those soft cashmere sweaters his grandmother sent over from England on his birthday, or at Christmas, from her cottage in Wiltshire.

In the very bad weather Mme. Hotier's favorite lodger would wear something he called a Burberry, a somewhat disreputable raincoat which he wore with a belt tied in a knot. Winter or summer, he went hatless, and he wore his dark hair rather long because he could not afford to have it cut very often.

Madame knew why. Her Burberry as she affectionately called him, had been saving his money to buy the clothes he would need when he made his debut at l'Acadèmie Municipale's annual dinner, held in honor of those students about to graduate to a wider field of musical endeavor.

Whenever she went up to clean his room, Mme. Hotier would think, with regret, that she would never have another lodger like M. Tanquillan, with his charming English ways, his sense of fun, and oh, that smile of his!

"Ah, mon Dieu," she would mutter, "if I had been twenty years younger, I might have taught him more than French cookery."

One day, busy about her work, she picked up a scrap of paper on which was written "Charlotte" several times, as if the writer's mind had been preoccupied, or as if he had meant to begin writing a letter and decided not to. Mme. Hotier stared thoughtfully at the paper. What did it mean: "Faultless Poet, Andrea del Sarto. Charlotte, Charlotte, Charlotte. Ah, but a man's reach should exceed his grasp, or what's a heaven for"?

Emily had seldom been happier in her life. Her cottage, which she laughingly referred to as her "doll's house," occupied her time in a way which left no room for loneliness or regrets.

From her kitchen window she could see the roof and chimneys of Grey Wethers; at dusk, pinpricks of light shone through the trees. She had no servants now, to rattle about like peas in the shell of that great house in Eaton Square where she had so often felt shut way; isolated; no longer a part of the living world.

Now she cooked for herself and did her own housework and gardening, taking a particular pride in her vegetable plot where she grew green beans, lettuce, potatoes, and tomatoes in the neat little greenhouse near the garden fence. She had become part of the village life, going regularly to morning services with Bridie and Harry Grayler. She polished the brasses, sang in the choir, helped decorate the church at Christmas, Easter, and harvest time. She had found her own niche, her own place in the village scheme of things.

In the evenings she would either walk down the path leading to Grey Wethers to spend some time with Bridie McKenna, or relax in her own sitting room, knitting socks and sweaters for her grandson, or writing long descriptive letters to him saying how happy she was now that she had "come home."

Just after her arrival at the cottage, sorting through piles of old photographs and memorabilia, she had come across a snapshot of Rowan taken in the garden of the house in Eaton Square and had sent it to Berry, wondering if this would be the right time to tell him the truth. But no. Better not. Romilly would be furious with her if she did.

Emily remembered, ruefully, that Romilly had been furious with her, anyway, for going to live there at Charlotte Oakleigh's suggestion. They'd had a quarrel about that when her daughter drove down from Scotland to cast a contemptuous eye over Emily's new home.

"My God, Mother," she'd said angrily. "So you've come to this, have you? Why? That's what David and I want to know! Oh, I simply can't bear it!"

"Can't bear *what*, darling?"

"You know perfectly well! Choosing to live in a— dump—like this, when you might have made your home with us! Putting yourself in the hands of that—that *woman!* Mother, have you *no* sense of shame? Not *one* shred of family loyalty left? And what about Berry? How dared you come between my son and his grandfather? Everything was going so smoothly! Berry would have taken his rightful place in the Tanquillan Company one day! Now what is he? *Nothing!* Nothing at all! Just a struggling musician, living, if his letters are anything to go by, in near poverty! But then," her lips curled contemptuously, "like father, like son!"

"If you have quite finished saying what you obviously came here to say," Emily said quietly, "I think that you should leave now, since my new way of life is so obviously repugnant to you." She added, "I shall understand if you decide not to come back."

"Mother! How could you? I am your daughter!"

"Thank you for reminding me." Emily sighed deeply. "I must be an unnatural mother, then, because I do not feel affection for you now. Truth to tell, Romilly, you were always a silly girl, totally selfish and lacking in compassion and understanding. I think that I might have forgiven your silliness—what I cannot forgive is your snobbishness, your utter disregard of your son's happiness. But then you never understood Rowan, either, and he and Berry are very much alike."

"That is Berry's misfortune, not mine," Romilly said bitterly. "But to think that you have allowed that woman who ruined my marriage to come between us is too much to stomach. It's as well I came, if only to set things straight between us, once and for all! You need not worry, Mother, I shall not trouble you again!"

But because she was Romilly's mother, and because she still remembered her as the child she had once loved, Emily's heart was torn as her daughter drove away next morning.

And then, because Emily had so much to do in the house and garden the suffering and hurt her daughter's presence had caused her were soon thrust into the background. She turned with keen delight to hoeing her lettuce-bed, tidying up the greenhouse, and finishing off the pullover she was knitting for her grandson who was doing so well in Paris.

Unfortunately, when it came to his debut at the Acadèmie Municipale's annual dinner, she came down with a heavy bout of influenza.

It was then she rang up Charlotte, and asked if she would go in her place.

Chapter Twenty-Eight

Charlotte had returned to Paris with a sense of relief, of homecoming. She had been absent far too long. The past two summers she had worked in New York with Howard and Virginia, launching the American branch of "Carlotta." She had stayed with Helen and Bill Fortescue, co-directors of Forts Department Store on Fifth Avenue, at their sprawling Colonial house on Long Island.

New York had not appealed to her. The city had overwhelmed her. The buildings were too tall, the traffic too noisy, Americans too hospitable, assuming that any evening not filled with cocktail and dinner parties was an evening wasted.

And yet she had found small oases of peace, in Central Park, for instance, with its breathtaking view of Manhattan's West Side seen from the Sheep Meadow.

She had liked the Hudson River, too, with its hooting tugs and great ocean liners gliding past the statue of Miss Liberty; had loved the horse-drawn carriages gliding along beneath the trees in Central Park.

But New York could not compare with Paris in the spring. How strange that she had once thought she would be out of place here, when Howard had first debated the idea of a fashion show in the spring of 1922. She had been so young and gauche then, trying her wings for the first time in an alien, bewildering atmosphere.

Now, seeing the trees in new leaf along the Champs

Elysées, the pavement cafes with their gaily striped awnings and bustling waiters, happiness dappled her mind as the sunlight of a perfect May day dappled the grass beneath the budding horse chestnuts in the Tuileries gardens.

Tired of obsequious maîtres d'hotels, Charlotte had chosen to stay at a small hotel in the Rue Lafayette, wanting to come closer to the heart of Paris, to forget about clothes and business deals for a few days, to live as a tourist would. To this end she had brought very little luggage: two lightweight skirts, blouses and cardigans, low-heeled shoes, and one evening dress for Berry's concert, a simple emerald silk gown with a matching jacket.

The Hotel Gautier was typically pre-war French, with a creaking birdcage of an elevator and heavy ornate furniture. The facade, seamed with wrought-iron balconies, overlooked the busy Rue Lafayette; the dining-room smelt of garlic, wine, and cigars, richly blended fragrances which Charlotte always associated with France, and with Paris in particular.

She had slept well in a deep featherbed with brass headboard, and woke early, refreshed, to bathe, dress, and breakfast on croissants, honey, and coffee, on the balcony of her room, surveying the busy street scene below. Traders were setting out their stalls with fruit, flowers and vegetables.

Suddenly two black-cassocked priests appeared, eyes downcast beneath their birettas. They strode purposefully along, the hems of their robes swishing about their ankles, rosaries bouncing briskly about the waists, reminding Charlotte that this was Peggy's wedding day.

She had carefully considered her wedding invitation, and decided that it might be more diplomatic if she did not attend, knowing that Maggie's hostility towards her had not lessened over the years.

Instead, she had made Peggy a gift of a cream slipper

satin wedding dress, veil, and matching accessories, along with a cheque, to provide a small nest egg.

Half-closing her eyes, she imagined how lovely Peggy would look, tall and slim, with her dark hair fluffed out in a cloud about her piquant face. Maggie, she knew, would have made a great fuss about Peggy accepting the dress and the money. But Charlotte loved the girl, and wanted her to be happy. She hoped—prayed that she would be.

After breakfast, Charlotte wandered out into the street, pausing to look at the stalls, whistling softly at the caged birds hopping madly from perch to perch. She would have liked to buy all of them, and opened their cages to set them free. But how would they fare, even if she did? Birds, as well as humans, became conditioned to their own limited environment. Those bright, lovely scraps of brown and yellow feathers would not survive for very long among the sooty roofs of Paris.

Glancing at her watch, Charlotte saw that it was almost time to meet Berry, who would be at the Hotel Gautier at ten o'clock. Berry, whom she still thought of as the boy she had last seen as a shy, gangling youth of eighteen.

The foyer seemed especially dim after the bright sunshine. Charlotte had bought an armful of pink carnations from one of the market stalls. Thinking to put them in water before Berry arrived, she smiled at the concierge and hurried towards the elevator, not noticing, in particular, the tall broad-shouldered man to whom the woman was chatting in quick explosive dialect French.

Charlotte simply assumed that the man must also be French, since he answered her fluently in the same easy colloquial fashion.

Berry thought afterward that if he lived to be a hundred he would never forget the way Charlotte suddenly entered the hotel foyer, and stood there, momentarily framed in the doorway, silhouetted against the light, her arms full of flowers, hair glinting like a halo. She was dressed in a pale blue skirt and matching blouse, a cashmere cardigan about her shoulders, a pink scarf knotted loosely at her throat. She hurried past the reception desk on her way to the elevators and turned in surprise when he softly called her name, looking up at him, head a little to one side as if she could not believe her eyes. She spoke his name, breathlessly, then turned, smiling, to the concierge, and handed her the flowers, saying, "For you, Madame."

"Now, let me look at you properly," she'd said, taking hold of his hands. "Why, Berry, how tall you've grown! How you've changed!"

"For the better, I hope."

He would always remember that she had lowered her eyes at that moment, and a warm tide of color had suffused her cheeks. He had asked her, later, when they were walking together by the Seine, why she had suddenly fallen silent when they left the hotel. He had to know the truth: was she disappointed in him?

"No, of course not. I simply felt embarrassed when I realized that you were a man whom I was treating as a child. But then, you see, I still remembered you as—not a child exactly, but certainly not the way I see you now. It must have been galling for you, being sized up that way by a kind of elderly aunt."

"I—I have never quite seen you in that light, Charlotte," he said quietly.

She slipped her hand into the crook of his elbow. "Well, no matter what we thought, we are here now! Oh, isn't this a simply glorious day? I feel like a girl again, as if Paris had cast a magic spell over me." She smiled up at him. "You have no idea how wonderful it is, this feeling of absolute freedom."

"Yes, I think I have. It's a feeling I've grown used to myself since I came to Paris." His face became suddenly serious. "I have you to thank for making that possible,

353

for looking after Madre." His fingers tightened suddenly on Charlotte's arm. "Please tell me, is she very ill?"

"No, not really. Don't worry, she's simply suffering an attack of influenza. She asked me to give you her love, to say she'll be thinking of you tonight."

Berry pulled a wry face. "Tonight! God, I'm dreading it!"

"Yes, I understand how you feel. It isn't easy, putting one's talent on the firing line. That's the way I felt at my first dress show. I was terrified of failure, yet thinking all the time how hard I had worked to achieve success— knowing that nothing really mattered except the pleasure I derived from my work, and that no one, however critical, could take that away from me."

They stopped walking to look down at the river, leaning their arms on the parapet to gaze at the boats, barges, and bateaux-mouches cutting cleanly through the water, creating ripples which fanned out, glinting in the sunlight.

Watching the play of light on Charlotte's face, Berry knew that his schoolboy infatuation for a beautiful older woman had deepened into a man's all-absorbing love for her.

"Tonight," he said huskily, "will you sit in the front row, where I can see you?"

"Yes, of course." She looked up at him, and smiled. "Now, what about lunch? I'm terribly hungry."

"So am I! What would you like to eat?"

"An omelette, I think."

Looking across the table at him, she thought how proud Rowan would be of his son, how much Berry reminded her of his father. And yet there were subtle differences between them. She studied him carefully as he ordered their meal. Berry's hair was longer, curlier than Rowan's, his eyes more widely spaced, upper lip slightly longer. At that moment she realized how wrong it was to draw comparisons between Rowan and his son. She had not fully understood that Berry was not a mere facsimile of his father, but a person in his own right. That thought faintly disturbed her, but she could not have said why. Not then. Not at that precise moment.

She took her place early in the concert hall, choosing an end seat, close to the platform. Glancing at the programme, she saw that he would play first Rachmaninov's Third Piano Concerto. She watched him, heart in mouth, as he took his place at the keyboard, knowing that never again would she confuse the son with his father. For this man was not Rowan. He looked like Rowan, smiled like Rowan, spoke like Rowan, but he was not Rowan.

Her heart beat faster. Berry Tanquillan had emerged, at last, from his father's shadow.

Much later she would ask herself if her love for Berry was born in that crowded concert hall, if the warm tide of joy, of utter happiness that flooded through her as she listened to him play, was the start of the affair. If so, she had not realized it. And what if she had? What would she have done? Walked away before it was too late? Left him a brief formal note saying that she had been called back to London on urgent business?

Tossing restlessly in bed, she would ask herself, over and over, if her love for Berry was born then, or much earlier than that: the minute she saw him in the drawing-room at High Tor? But who could say for certain when love happened?

A crumb of comfort lay in that she had not known the danger of that weekend alone with him. She had simply believed that her sudden, singing happiness had to do with Paris in Maytime, the scents and sounds of the most romantic city in the world: the lights of the city seen from the balcony of Berry's apartment in the Rue des Quatre Saisons, the heady scent of herbs, lavender, and night-scented stock from the Provencal pots on his tiny roof garden. The joy she experienced in his success accentuated her delight in the supper he prepared for them after the concert: a simple meal of crusty French bread, paté, salad, and strawberries, which they ate together at a wrought-iron table under the stars.

Time would never dim the memory of that night: the sound of music drifting up from the street below, where someone was singing a plaintive French love song to a piano-accordion; the sudden bursts of laughter, the distant hum of traffic, the lighted windows of other apartments shining out into the velvety darkness; a woman in a white dress standing on the balcony opposite, leaning her arms on the railings, throwing a coin to the street musician.

She had asked Berry what would happen to him now that the concert was over.

"Oh, you know," he'd shrugged his shoulders dismissively, "Maître Robillard will send for me the first thing Monday morning and berate me soundly for playing so badly, then he'll go on to say that he has arranged a concert tour for me, a very minor one, of course, and warn me not to get a swelled head about it, since the world is full of second-rate musicians struggling to earn a living."

"And where will this concert tour take you?"

"To Italy, most probably."

"But isn't that what you want?" Charlotte frowned, disturbed by the sudden, guarded expression in Berry's eyes.

"Yes, I suppose so . . ."

"But you are not sure?"

He stirred restlessly. "It's hard to explain. The truth is, I love Paris so much, I shall feel homesick away from her."

Berry had wanted to tell Charlotte then that he was in love with her. The thought of going to Italy, or anywhere else without her, was unbearable.

Instead, when they had finished supper, he played Debussy's "Clair de Lune" for her, hoping that, somehow, she would understand what he was trying wordlessly to tell her he loved her.

It was long past midnight when she picked up her gloves and handbag, and said that it was time she went back to her hotel.

"But I will see you again tomorrow?"

"Yes, of course."

"Where shall we go?"

"I leave that to you." She walked quickly down the curving staircase to the hall below, her hand resting lightly on the iron banister. "After all, Paris is your oyster now."

He went with her to find a taxi. When she had gone he thought bleakly that even Paris, in Maytime, would prove of little value without its pearl of great price.

He went to meet her, next day, but the weather had changed. They had lunch together, then hurried into a cinema near the Place Vendôme, to see Garbo as Camille in *La Dame aux Caméllias*, an American film with French subtitles.

When they came out, the sun was shining again. Berry stopped at a flower-seller's barrow near the cinema, to buy her a bunch of roses.

It was then she knew that she had fallen in love with him. Even so, she pushed the thought to the back of her mind as being too ridiculous for words, trying hard to convince herself that any woman might imagine herself to be in love, in Paris, in springtime, with the May trees in blossom. Especially vulnerable was a woman of forty, savoring a kind of springtime madness of the heart in the company of a man almost half her age, who had reminded her how it felt to be young again.

She realized, too late, that she should not have gone back to his apartment with him, but despite, or possibly because of her weariness, she made no demur. Still not aware of what was happening, she was content to rest awhile on the shabby sofa near the piano, while Berry put the kettle on for a cup of tea.

"I feel exactly like La Dame aux Camélias," she said contentedly, stretching her arms, laughing as Berry covered her feet with a rug, "and you are Armand Duval . . ."

Suddenly she wished that she had not said that, remembering that Armand Duval had been in love with Marguerite Gautier, his Dame aux Camélias; that their love affair was destined to end disastrously, if, indeed, it had ever existed beyond the imagination of Alexandre Dumas fils.

"Charlotte, my darling," Berry said quietly, taking her in his arms, "don't you know—can't you guess how I feel? I loved you the first moment I saw you. And I've gone on loving you! No, please don't turn away! Oh, Charlotte, my love, my love . . ." He kissed her gently again and again, holding her tightly, whispering her name.

For one passionate, uncaring moment she gave herself completely to his embrace; thrilling to the touch of his mouth on hers, knowing how much she loved him; forgetting everything except the feel of his hair beneath her gentle, exploratory fingers, the swift, uneven beating of his heart so close to hers. Then the shame of what she was doing rose up like bile in her throat, nearly choking her.

"No!" she cried desperately. "No, Berry, please let me go! You don't know, you don't understand! What are you saying is quite impossible!" She struggled away from his arms. "Oh, God! I wish I had never come! This is madness! Berry, I'm old enough to be your mother!"

"Do you really think I care a damn about age?"

"You don't understand. That isn't the only thing that stands between us. I should have told you the truth from the beginning." She was speaking quickly, urgently. "Oh

God, I've been living in a fool's paradise! I was too happy to face reality . . ."

"What truth?" he asked, puzzled.

She couldn't bear to hurt him, to watch the eager look of love in his eyes replaced by contempt perhaps, or disgust.

"I loved your father," she said at last. "I knew he was married. It made no difference. We loved each other so much." Tears welled up in her eyes. "Your father did not die in an Army sanatorium as you have been led to believe. He died on a beach in Cornwall, saving a child's dog."

Berry frowned, then uttered a short laugh, sounding almost relieved. "But surely . . ."

"No, please let me finish. The child was ours. Our daughter Kathy. Now do you see how impossible it is that we should love each other?"

She stumbled to the door, blinded with tears. "I'm sorry. So very sorry. Believe me, I never meant to hurt you!"

"Charlotte! Wait!"

"No! Don't try to stop me. There's nothing more to say."

Turning, she ran swiftly down the curving staircase and out into the street below.

Chapter Twenty-Nine

She returned to London with the feeling that her shining bubble of happiness had burst suddenly. A mountain of work awaited her.

As much as she disliked the idea of using the skins of dead animals to embellish her designs, Charlotte knew that fur was gaining in popularity both in England and America: mink, Persian and Indian lamb, American broadtail, and squirrel.

She began work in a fury of concentration, designing tailored mink coats with flaring skirts and neatly fitting waistlines; tweed coats with massive fur collars; chunky tweed jackets with fur sleeves; elegant fur evening capes with matching muffs. She worked until her eyes ached, and she dreamed about fur. Dreamed until she awoke, at the crack of dawn, to begin worrying about Berry.

How could she have let it happen? That wild, singing moment of utter, absolute joy, when she had clung to him uncaring of the past, not thinking about tomorrow. She had felt sick and cheap when she hurried down those stairs to find a taxi; filled with disgust, not for Berry, but herself. A woman of her age behaving like a lovesick girl.

Tired of fur, she had made up her mind to leave her drawing board early when Howard Ryder came into her office, bubbling over with ideas for promoting a new perfume to be called simply "Carla."

Ryder, who never embarked on any venture less than

360

wholeheartedly, had been in constant touch, since the new year, with a master French perfumer to create the subtle, lingering fragrance he had in mind to enhance Charlotte's creations. After all, Coco Chanel had made a fortune from Chanel No. 5.

"Everything's proceeding full speed ahead," he said jauntily, perching on a stool and lighting a cigar. "The glass designers have come up with some marvelous ideas. By the way, I've chosen gold and white packaging, subject to your approval. Why, what's the matter? You don't look exactly overjoyed. What's the matter, love? Tired after your trip to Paris?"

There were times when she disliked Howard Ryder.

"Of course," he went on blithely, ignoring her silence, "we'll have the official launch here in London, invite the press to take photographs. Then we'll do a similar launch in Paris, in September . . ."

She turned on him fiercely. "I have no intention of going to Paris! Damn you, Howard, and your perfume! Now, would you mind clearing out of my office, and smoking that revolting cigar of yours somewhere else? Can't you see I'm busy?"

"My God, Carla, what's come over you all of a sudden?" Ryder eased himself from his stool, puzzled by her attitude. "I thought you'd be delighted at the way things are going for us! I know you're tired, with the Americans pressing for the winter designs, but this new perfume is important, at least I think so, and if you don't pull your weight to promote it both here and in Paris, we might as well forget the whole venture."

"I'm sorry, Howard. But I don't intend going to Paris!" The thought of going back there so soon filled her with dread. She pictured a city shorn of springtime, with the sad leaves of autumn drifting down from the trees in the Tuileries gardens.

Ryder regarded her clinically, wondering what was wrong with Paris all of a sudden. He thought she liked the place. Ah well, women, who could begin to understand them? "Sorry, darling," he said lightly, "I can see I've caught you at a bad moment. Sleep on the idea, you'll feel better in the morning." He hoped to God she *would* feel better in the morning. "By the way, Ginny and I are about to be saddled with my mother, and Julian. Mother hasn't been too well lately—something to do with her asthma, She's seeing a Harley Street specialist next week. Will you come to dinner tomorrow evening?"

Laurie bounded into the house.

"It's happened at last, Aunt Charlotte," she gasped breathlessly. "I'm to have a screen test at the Boreham Wood film studio on Sunday afternoon! You will come with me, won't you?"

"Yes, of course, darling."

"Oh lord, what if I don't make good?" Laurie said, fearfully. "What if I'm still too fat?"

Charlotte laughed as she ruffled Laurie's spun-gold hair. "Fat? Why you're as thin as a herring. Your mother would have a fit if she saw you!"

"Just as well she can't, then." Laurie sighed deeply. "Film stars need to be as thin as herrings or they look like plum puddings on the screen, according to Madame Kowlinska. It's a funny thing, though, my legs never seem to get any thinner. Oh well, they'll have to photograph me from the waist up, that's all."

"Laurie, dear, are you really happy about—all this?" Charlotte asked softly. "Are you quite, quite sure that this is what you want from life?"

"Yes, of course. At least, I *think* it is. The only thing that worries me—I feel that I am somehow losing touch with myself. I scarcely recognize myself any longer. I thought that acting was something that one did quite naturally, like—breathing, but it isn't like that at all. It's darned hard work!"

Virginia and Howard Ryder's home reflected Howard's taste for the Regency period linked to his wife's color sense and flair for floral decoration, so that the house seemed more like a showplace than a home. Indeed, it had often appeared in those glossy magazines which specialized in photographing well-known socialites against the impeccable perfection of their drawing-room background.

Virginia drifted downstairs to greet Charlotte, wearing a dazzling black and white creation she had bought during a recent visit to New York.

"Darling, how lovely to see you! Howard and Julian are in the drawing room, fixing the drinks. I've just been up to say goodnight to William. By the way, Mrs. Ryder is having dinner in her room, but she wants you to go up later. The poor old girl's a bit tired and short of breath."

Virginia never stopped acting, Charlotte thought. She walked as though in some permanent invisible spotlight, so sure of her charm and poise, her ability to dazzle, as she led the way into the drawing room.

Julian turned. Charlotte noticed that he was walking now without the aid of a cane, as he came toward her, smiling. "How nice you look," he said lightly. "That dress reminds me of the one you wore the first time we we—bumped into each other. Do you remember?"

Charlotte laughed. "That is one incident I am scarcely likely to forget."

Howard thought, as he offered them dry martinis, that now Julian had found his feet again he was obviously not going to let the grass grow under them. The good-looking bastard was out for the kill. He could read all the signs. Julian had been as restless as a caged tiger, awaiting Charlotte's arrival. After dinner, she and Julian went up to see Mrs. Ryder.

"Oh dear," Amelia said breathlessly, "I feel so awful being waited on hand and foot. It's this chest of mine, though how I came by it, I can't imagine. Still, I suppose the man in Harley Street will be able to cure it."

She was just as pink and pretty as ever, Charlotte thought, bending down to kiss her.

"I do hope we'll be able to see something of you while we're in London," Mrs. Ryder went on, "though we're only staying till Tuesday. That's right, isn't it, Julian?"

"I see no particular reason why we should not stay longer, if you want to," Julian replied in that offhand manner he had adopted during his illness, "except that Howard and Virginia are leaving for Paris on Wednesday."

"Oh," Mrs. Ryder's face fell, "but we could go to a hotel."

"Why don't you stay with me?" Charlotte suggested. "I'd love to have you, and there's plenty of room."

There had always been plenty of room, she thought, since Kathy had never looked on the Glamorgan Square house as home: one of the reasons why she had been glad of Laurie's bubbling presence to fill the emptiness.

"There now," Amelia said blissfully, "wouldn't that be nice? I feel better already." Secretly, she detested this house with its feeling of being stage-managed by her self-possessed daughter-in-law.

When they had said their goodnights and closed the door on the smiling Amelia, Julian laid his hand purposefully on Charlotte's arm. "Before we go downstairs," he said, "there's something I want to say to you."

She turned to face him, thinking she knew what that "something" was; uncertain if she wanted to hear it.

"I want you to marry me." He paused. "Don't tell me you are going to tremble and say, 'This is so sudden.' You must know how I feel about you. I'd like to know exactly how you feel about me."

"I'm not—in love—with you, if that's what you mean."

"No, well, to be honest, I did not think for one moment that you were. But love is for the very young."

"Is it?" she asked, remembering Berry, wondering where he was, if he hated her now.

"I was speaking of romantic love—starry eyes—that kind of nonsense. Scarcely applicable in our case." He smiled sardonically. "Not that I don't love you. I do. Enough to spend the rest of my life with you. I want you to be the mistress of my home. My wife, in every sense of the word."

"But what about my work? My—career?"

"Is that really so important?" He put his arms about her.

"I don't know. I'm not sure. But it is a part of me. You must give me time to think . . ."

"Yes, I can see that you would need time," he said with a touch of his old bitterness, "to choose between me and your drawing board."

"It isn't like that at all, Julian, and you know it. There are others, lots of others, who depend on me for their livelihood . . ."

He kissed her suddenly, passionately. "I'll do everything in my power to make you happy. I think you realize that, if we did marry, I would want you in every way possible."

Drawing away from his arms, she said slowly, "But there is a side of my life of which you know nothing. I—I have a child—a daughter—family commitments . . ."

"While my life is an open book, is that it?"

"No, of course not. No person's life is like that," she said gently.

"I was right when I said that you were an enigma. But I care nothing about your past life. I'm in love with you, Charlotte, and despite what I said just now about romantic love, there is nothing in the least bit staid or middle-aged about my feelings for you. We might even have a child!" He buried his face in her hair. "Above all, I could make you feel safe and secure, and I think that would be important to you."

"Please, Julian . . ." But Charlotte wondered if there was not a grain of truth in what he said.

She did not love him—but perhaps there came a time when a woman needed peace of mind far more than the passion and pain of love.

"I think we had better be going down now," she said. "Virginia and Howard will be wondering what has happened to us."

"What *has* happened?" he asked.

"I'm not quite sure."

"Don't cling to the past too hard, my darling," he said. "It is too heavy a burden to carry alone."

They had never been in a film studio before. Laurie said it reminded her of an aircraft hangar, while Charlotte thought that this was scarcely the "magic factory" of her imagination, a queer echoing barn of a place in which to produce romantic dreams for the love-starved masses. Apart from that, no one appeared to have heard of Miss Laurie Grayler, due to be tested for the title role in *Slave Girl of the Orient*. Not, that is, until Madame Kowlinska appeared, wearing a mink coat in the middle of a heat wave, her forehead beaded with perspiration, and the chunky bracelets on her wrists jingling like temple bells.

"I vill zoon set ze vheels in motion," she said, with a ferocious scowl. "Zis ees ze vay zey vork here, never lettinck ze right hand know vot ze left hand ees doinck. Ze vonder ees zey ever make ze movinck pictures at all, zince all zey do ees zit around on zeir bumpfs doinck nozzing!" So saying, off she teetered on her three-inch heels to "zet ze vheels in motion."

"Now, darlinck, zey are ready for you in makeup," Madame said triumphantly. "All you hev to do ees zit steel, and relax."

Laurie cast an imploring glance at Charlotte. "I feel more like Lady Jane Grey on her way to the scaffold than the Slave Girl of the Orient," she muttered as the makeup man took charge of her. And what a pity, Charlotte thought, that Laurie, with her elfin face and fair silky hair, had not been chosen to test for a more suitable role. Lady Jane Grey would have been perfect for her. Watching the makeup procedure, Charlotte bit her lip anxiously as the man in charge began to apply a layer of heavy dark Leichner cream to her niece's soft rose-petal skin. She could not help it. "Isn't that a bit too dark?" she said sharply.

The man, Fred his name was, obviously born within the sound of Bow bells, gave Charlotte a long lingering glance of contempt. "Look, lady," he growled, "she's supposed to be an oriental, not Mimi in the last throes of galloping consumption."

She sat quietly after that, not wishing to add to Laurie's distress as Fred began to work on her eyes. My God, she thought, she'll end up looking like Theda Bara if he isn't careful, as Fred conscientiously applied two circles of kohl and false eyelashes. But the horror was not yet ended. Charlotte tightly clenched her hands into fists as Fred taped back Laurie's blond hair and slid on a black wig: coarse, straight, shoulder-length, and not even very clean.

Unable to contain her anger any longer, she said in a low clear voice, "I'm very sorry, but if you imagine that I shall allow Miss Grayler to make a screen test looking like that, you are very much mistaken. I shall complain, personally, to Mr. Chandos!"

Madame Kowlinska, who had also been watching the proceedings, smoking a Russian cigarette in a long holder, said surprisingly, "I could not agree wiz you more. Zees child should not be made ze—how you zay—ze laughing-stock? No, eet eez not good enough!"

"I'm sorry, Laurie darling," Charlotte said gently. "Perhaps I have no right to interfere. After all, this is your life—your first real chance of success—the thing you have been waiting for. You may never get the chance of another screen test if you turn this one down."

Tears gathered on Laurie's false eyelashes and ran slowly down her cheeks, making little runnels in her makeup. "You are absolutely right, Aunt Charlotte," she said with a sob. "I look—grotesque! Will you—will you please take me home now?"

"Laurie, my dear, may I come in?"

"Yes, Aunt Charlotte." She smiled as her aunt came into her bedroom. "You know, I've been thinking," she said, "I'm not really cut out for—for well, you know, the bright lights. I thought I was, but I'm not."

She turned her head away, and Charlotte knew that she was crying. Strangely, not hot tears of despair, but gentle tears of relief. "It's funny, isn't it? One gets a dream in one's head, but it isn't necessarily the right dream. There is always just that possibility . . . It's like seeing the sky at night, wanting to reach out to touch the stars. I think I got so blinded with stars that I couldn't see reality any longer, but it's a vastly different thing sitting in the one-and-nine's in the cinema, and being up there on the screen. Gran was right, I'm a dreamer, not a doer. I'm going home where I belong."

"Laurie, darling, I feel this is all my fault. I shouldn't have interfered the way I did."

"You didn't, not really. You only said what I knew in my heart to be true." Laurie smiled. "I'm going home!"

She said mistily, "Funny, I thought I wanted to feel the sands of Malibu under my feet. I don't now, not any longer. The sand of Scarborough's good enough for me."

Chapter Thirty

Berry had been walking for hours, aimlessly, scarcely aware of where he had been or where he was going, until he realized that he had come by instinct to the Place des Vosges, where he had walked with Charlotte, what seemed a lifetime ago.

He had not been silent and withdrawn then, or impervious to the colors of stone, flowers, and the bright blue arch of the sky above the trees. He remembered clearly the children playing in the Place gardens, the sound of their laughter. He and Charlotte had explored the enchanted city as tourists would: sitting down to rest their feet when they grew tired; pausing to leaf through the books for sale on the Quai des Grands Augustins; stopping to admire the fragrant, colorful masses of blooms in the flower market. They had drunk café au lait at one of the pavement cafes, where yellow leaves fluttered down onto the tablecloth.

Watching the play of light and shadow on Charlotte's vivid, laughing face as he held out her hand to catch the leaves, Berry could not help thinking how young she looked: as ageless as Helen of Troy, or the Venus de Milo. But here was no legend or piece of sculpture, but a warm, vital, living woman with the sun on her face: mignon, as the French would say: delicate, pretty. No, not pretty—beautiful, possessing the artlessness of a child: unaware of her loveliness, of the way people turned to look at her, smiling, as if drawing pleasure from her happiness; as if her warmth had touched their lives for a fleeting moment.

Turning into the Rue de Birague, he could see her clearly in his mind's eye, smiling at him across a table under the stars. The love he had felt for her at that moment had been akin to pain, the longing to hold her in his arms an overwhelming urge which, later, he had been unable to resist.

And then, miraculously, he had discovered that she loved him too. He had known it from the first touch of her lips on his, the feel of her fingers in his hair. Then, suddenly, the delicately poised moment was ended. He had not grasped, immediately, the reason for the change of mood, the full implication of what she had said about herself and his father. And then she had gone, running away from him, her feet tap-tapping on the twisting stone steps leading from his apartment.

Night after night since then he had lain in torment, getting up in the early hours to pace his room or to stand on the balcony staring over the rooftops of Paris, facing the truth. Charlotte had borne his father's child. Somewhere that child, the sister he never knew existed, drew breath, because Rowan and Charlotte had loved each other. He remembered the snapshot of his father his grandmother had sent him. He stared at it; stared at that picture of the tall handsome man whose seed had also given him life. He buried his head in his hands, crazed with jealousy of his father.

Then, when his bitter anger and jealousy had subsided, he remembered that all this had happened a long time ago, and began to understand what it must have meant to them to face censure for the crime of loving. He understood many other things which had never made sense to him before: his mother's hatred of Charlotte; why his grandparents had lied to him; their strange reluctance to mention their son's name, as if Rowan had done something reprehensible, in loving Charlotte.

The more Berry thought about it, the more clearly the picture emerged of those bloody, brutal years of the First World War. He began to understand the need for men and women to seize a life and love while it lasted, uncertain of what tomorrow would bring. He remembered, too, that Madre, who knew the whole story, had never censured his father, or Charlotte, and nothing would ever persuade him that Emily's judgment could be lacking in wisdom.

Finally, he came to the realization that nothing could ever change his love for Charlotte.

His tutor and mentor, Maître Robillard, had arranged a concert tour for him, beginning in Florence in ten days' time.

Ten days! Quickening his footsteps, imbued with fresh hope and purpose, he made up his mind to go to England to see Charlotte.

The specialist had advised Mrs. Ryder that from now on she should never drink milk, eat chocolate, sleep on a feather mattress, or allow her cat, Pinky, access to her bedroom.

"Well I never," Amelia said plaintively, "of all the nonsense! Pinky has always slept on my eiderdown! Seems to me that, if I'm to live longer, I must give up everything that makes living worthwhile."

"You'll have to give up your eiderdown, too, Mother," Julian told her, "since that is also filled with feathers."

"Oh, pooh!" she cried. "Go away! Whose side are you on, anyway?"

Julian laughed. Watching him closely, Charlotte thought how much kinder he had become since quitting his wheelchair, this man who had proposed marriage to her.

Never once, since he and his mother came to stay with her, had he mentioned their conversation on the stairs that night. She had seen Julian in an entirely different light during these past few days, and regretted that he and his mother would be leaving Glamorgan Square tomorrow. The house would feel empty when the Ryders, and Laurie, had gone away.

She lay awake for a long time that night, listening to her wireless: the tunes of the thirties: "Ramona," "Chiquita," "What'll I Do?"

What'll I do when you are far away,
And I am blue,
What'll I do?

She would never stop loving either Rowan or Berry, but there came a time when the heart cried out for peace and security, an end to all the longing, seeking, yearning.

She switched off the wireless suddenly in the middle of a Nelson Eddy and Jeanette MacDonald duet, "Ah, Sweet Mystery of Life," remembering other tunes, other songs which had filled her life during the soul-shattering years of the Great War: "Mademoiselle from Armentières;" "It's a Long Way to Tipperary," "Keep the Home Fires Burning."

She had never believed that the kind of love she had felt for Rowan could happen twice in a lifetime: that tremendous force of loving which had swept her heart like a flame, paralyzing almost in its intensity. But she must not think of Berry; must shut all thoughts of him out of her life completely if she was ever to know true peace of mind.

Annie walked slowly to the attic, and looked out the wide dormer window at the slate roofs and chimneypots gilded with early morning sunlight.

Laurie would be coming home today. The letter she and Joe had received had set their minds at rest that this was what she really wanted.

But what would Laurie do with her life now? How would she face all the golden summertimes without Peggy and Kathy? Especially here, in this room, where the three of them had crowded round the old swing mirror on the dressing table to see their summer faces in the glass.

Peggy had always been the ringleader, of course. Poor Peggy, forever getting into scrapes. That teatime, for instance, when she had caught her heel in the carpet and dropped the tray she was carrying. And what had she done but stand there, laughing fit to kill herself at all those pineapple chunks and cherries floating on a tide of syrup.

"If I've told you once about wearing those high heels when you're serving the visitors' teas," Annie had cried in exasperation, "I've told you a hundred times!" But the unrepentant Peggy had simply run through to the kitchen to find a dustpan and brush to clear up the mess; had laughed even harder as the juice oozed through the bristles. Dear, funny, maddening Peggy, who sailed through life on a tide of laughter. How strange to think of her married and settled down. Annie hoped Gee Jones would be good to her.

Now Kathy had started mentioning, in her frequent letters to Annie, a man with a strange-sounding foreign name: Bergmann.

"He's Jewish," Kathy explained, "a refugee from his own country, one of the thousands forced to leave Germany under the Hitler regime. It seems unbelievable that such a thing could happen in this so-called 'enlightened' age. The Jews are a proud race; Adam is a charming, cultured man, a writer, obliged to earn a living as a sub-editor in a foreign country simply because he happened to have been born Jewish, and had the courage to speak the truth about the persecution of his own people.

"I should very much like you, and Uncle Joe, to meet him. May I bring him to Scarborough one day in the near future? I imagine you have already guessed that I'm in love with him." She had added a postscript to the letter. "By the way, I haven't told Mother."

Annie sighed, glancing around the room with its sloping ceiling and faded rose-patterned wallpaper, remembering the old days when the family had first moved into this house. There had been no misunderstanding between Kathy and Charlotte then. What had happened to cause the rift? Perhaps the seeds had been sown during Kathy's formative years, when Charlotte had gone to London to set up her business there, leaving Kathy in Scarborough with herself and Joe. Poor Charlotte, Annie thought loyally, it was not her fault that she had not been here to kiss Kathy better whenever she fell down and bumped her head; to read to her at bedtime, or run along the sands with her, playing games with Dog.

Things might have been different, Annie thought, closing the attic door behind her, if Kathy had been allowed to take Dog to London with her, but, perhaps subconsciously, Charlotte had not wanted to be reminded of the tragedy which cost Rowan Tanquillan his life.

Hurrying down to the kitchen, Annie had no premonition of what this day would bring. She simply knew that Laurie was coming home, that it was high time she set about cooking the visitors' breakfasts.

Saturday was always a busy day at the house in Abbey Crescent, the day when the "old" visitors departed after paying their bills, when all the beds had to be changed before the new guests arrived, the rooms cleaned and dusted, the laundryman paid. There was the silver to polish, the doorstep to wash, and the weekend shopping to do. But Joe would see to that. It was Joe she now relied on to "bring home the bacon" in a manner of speaking, her darling Joe, who made out the bills and received payment, who knew, to the last ha'penny, how much they could afford to spend on meat for the visitors' Sunday dinners.

* * *

'Are you sure it will be all right to arrive without any warning?" Adam asked, anxiously trying to concentrate on the road ahead, to avoid knocking down the summer visitors streaming across the road towards the stalls near the harbor.

"Of course it will!" Kathy hunched up her knees to avoid getting her legs tangled in the gears of Adam's battered two-seater. "I told Aunt Annie we would be coming as soon as possible. Oh, darling, I can't wait to tell them our news."

"But your uncle, he fought in the war, and I am a German," Adam said, frowning.

"You mustn't feel too sensitive about that," Kathy replied, "after all, there are Germans and Germans! I'm sure my Uncle Joe realizes that as well as I do!" She added, seriously, because she had always believed herself to be a serious-minded person, with no room for sentiment in her makeup, "I don't imagine, for one moment that the Germans wanted to fight that bloody, stupid war any more than the English did. The man in the street had no more idea what it was all about than the man in the moon. The politicians were to blame; the generals; the Kaiser. It was all a farce, from start to finish!"

"Even so, your uncle, he must feel a certain bitterness . . ."

"He never speaks of it now. In any case, no one could harbor bitterness with Aunt Annie around."

"You speak so lovingly of your aunt," Adam said thoughtfully, "never the same way of your mother. This worries me."

"You know the reason for that." Kathy stared moodily at the encampment of green bathing tents below the promenade.

"You mean that there can be no forgiveness for her?

375

And yet you suppose that your Uncle Joe will forgive my being German?"

"I don't really want to talk about my miserable past," Kathy retorted. "It came as quite a shock when I found out that the man I had always believed to be my father had no part in my creation."

"And the man who had everything to do with it? What of him?"

"I told you before, I don't want to know about him. My Aunt Bridie once went into a long monologue about how wonderful he was, but I simply walked out of the room. Now, shall we drop the subject?"

Charlotte's decision to travel with Julian and Mrs. Ryder as far as York, then on to Scarborough with Laurie was made on the spur of the moment. The thought of staying alone in London over the weekend had seemed suddenly unbearable.

When she told Julian her plan, in the garden after breakfast, he said quietly, "Have you thought anymore about the question I asked you?"

"Yes, I've thought a great deal . . ."

"And?"

It was such a lovely morning, with dew still on the roses, and a bird singing. A time of peace. A time for peace.

"Yes, I will marry you," she said.

"My dear girl." He seemed lightly stunned, then drew her into his arms and kissed her. "I still can't believe my good fortune. To be quite frank, I thought you'd say no." He laughed suddenly. "We must tell Mother at once. She'll be delighted."

"No," she said, "please don't let us do that. Not yet!"

"Why not?" He held her at arm's length, searching her face intently with his eyes. "You mean you are still not sure?"

She smiled tremulously. "I'd like to get used to the idea first. Please don't rush things. Give me time."

I've come, my name is Sybil,
My fingernails I nibble,
I'm quite incorrigible.

Kathy recited impishly when Annie came to the door.

"Kathy! What a lovely surprise! I thought you were the laundryman."

"Auntie, this is Adam. We're engaged." She proudly extended her left hand.

"Oh dear," Annie felt the world was spinning too fast. "I don't know what to say first. It's a lovely ring. Come in, Adam, I'm pleased to meet you. You must be famished. I'll cook you something directly."

"You'll do no such thing," Kathy said firmly. "We'll wait until the proper time. Where's Gran?"

"In the kitchen, shelling peas." Annie's heart lurched. Filly was in one of her critical moods today. Nothing had been right for her since she had come down grumbling that she'd been kept awake half the night by next door's visitors.

"Now, Mother," Annie said soothingly, "you know visitors like to have a get-together on their last evening."

"Ha," Filly snapped, "having a get-together's one thing, singing 'Nellie Dean' at the top of their voices quite another! They sounded crazy to me."

Annie could not help wondering what Filly would think of Adam, with his rumpled appearance, his untidy gray hair, and horn-rimmed spectacles. She knew that whatever Filly thought, she would say out loud.

Her fears were well grounded. "You're *what?*" Filly bridled when Kathy showed her the ring. *"Engaged?* I didn't even know you were courting! But then, nobody tells me anything in this house. Who is he, anyway?" She glared at Adam.

"He is Adam Bergmann," Kathy said, nettled by her grandmother's rudeness, aware that she had never meant as much to Filly as Laurie and Peggy did. Knowing the reason for her grandmother's coolness toward her did not help matters.

"Bergmann? You mean to tell me you're going to marry a *foreigner?* What is he, a Russian?"

Adam said courteously, "No, madam, I am not Russian. I am a German by birth. Of Jewish extraction."

Kathy closed her eyes. She could guess what was coming. *"German!* Good God! To think of it. A German in this house! My eldest son, my Frank, was killed by the Germans! A fine boy he was too! Slaughtered . . ."

Joe had entered the kitchen unnoticed by anyone save Annie, who threw him a despairing glance, uncertain of even his reaction. But she might have known.

"That will do, Mother," he said, speaking haltingly, as he had done ever since the war. "The past is dead."

"Yes, and so is my poor Frank!" Filly bumped down the colander of peas on the draining board, not caring tuppence that they bounced up and rolled into the washing-up water in the sink as she stalked out of the room.

"Oh God, Adam. I'm sorry . . ." Kathy's face crumpled. She had handled the situation badly in not foreseeing her grandmother's reaction to Adam. It was Uncle Joe's reaction she had worried about.

Annie's nervous tension had been steadily mounting all day. Now she scarcely knew if she was on her head or her heels, what with Kathy and Adam arriving so unexpectedly, the scene with Filly, the house in the throes of the Saturday changeover, and Laurie's train due to arrive at four o'clock.

Pinning on her hat to go to the station, Annie asked Kathy if she had told her mother about Adam yet.

378

"No, not yet," Kathy replied dismissively. "I don't suppose she'll care one way or the other."

"Not care? Your own mother," Annie said crossly, "of course she'll care. You *are* her daughter!"

"Her—bastard, you mean!"

"Kathy!" Annie's eyes flashed fire.

"Well, it's the truth." Kathy's cheeks reddened. The business with her grandmother had upset her, and Kathy, upset, became truculent, acerbic, unreasonable.

Knowing that she had deeply shocked Aunt Annie, she said, "I'm sorry. Isn't it about time we set off for the station, or Laurie will be there before us. Come on, Adam. Might as well meet another member of the family." But she knew that Annie had not forgiven her by the way she walked a little ahead of them, not speaking, unlike her usual smiling self.

"Oh, lord," Kathy sighed, holding Adam's arm, "now I've put my foot in it again."

"Some things are better left unsaid, *liebchen*," he said quietly.

"Oh, don't you start criticizing me!"

Adam thought, as they walked past a line of waiting taxis at the station, and Kathy pumped three pennies into the platform-ticket machine, that they should not have come to Scarborough without warning, but Kathy, recklessly impulsive as usual, would not wait. Now it disturbed him deeply to realize the depth and bitterness of her anger against her mother. The Jewish race held family unity in high regard.

The last person Kathy expected to see as the train drew to a halt was Charlotte.

Annie's day dragged on, enlivened by Laurie's presence, but worrying nonetheless, since Filly had still not put in an appearance, Kathy had greeted Charlotte less than warmly, and the atmosphere at the tea table was slightly charged, to say the least.

"Who is *he?*" Laurie had asked under her breath at the station, looking covertly at Adam, who seemed to be hovering about like a lost soul.

"Kathy's fiancé," poor Annie said, worrying about Charlotte, Filly, and the new lot of visitors wanting their teas.

"Her—*what?*" Laurie's eyebrows disappeared into her hair.

"I'll tell you later," Annie mouthed. "Oh dear," she said, "I wish I'd known Aunt Charlotte was coming with you."

"It was a last-minute thing," Laurie explained, "something she and Julian cooked up."

"*Julian?*" Annie's head began to throb.

"Hmmm. I have a funny feeling they're going to get married, or something . . ."

"*Married?*" Annie was beginning to feel like Alice in Wonderland.

"I expect she'll be telling you all about it," Laurie said matter-of-factly, thinking what a strange homecoming this was.

"Anyway, it's about time you got here," Annie said irritably. "Look at you! There isn't a picking on you!"

Poor Charlotte, she thought, to be handed a strange foreigner as a prospective son-in-law. No wonder she looked so pale and strained, as if she had received a blow in the face. And yet she was smiling at Adam, trying hard to conceal from him how hurt she was that Kathy had not felt it important to break the news of her engagement by letter or a telephone call.

The normally mild, good-natured Annie felt that she would dearly like to shake Kathy until her teeth rattled.

As they moved towards the ticket-stand, Annie caught Charlotte's hand. "I know how you must be feeling," she said, struggling hard not to cry.

Charlotte smiled. Squeezing Annie's fingers, she whispered, "I know. Thank you."

***

Looking at Kathy across the teatable, Charlotte remembered her running in circles on the grass of a Cornish garden long ago, red curls in disorder about her piquant heart-shaped face, underlip jutting at the merest suggestion of authority, and wondered if she had been too lenient, too soft with her.

Poor Annie, she thought, how hard it must be for her, trying to keep body and soul together: passing the plates, making conversation, pressing everyone to second helpings of tinned peaches, and chocolate cake. And how tired Joe looked, yet how radiant, sitting next to Laurie, gazing at her as if he couldn't quite believe that she was home again to stay. Then, moving like a slow, quiet current of happiness beneath her present distress came the thought of lilacs in the Tuileries gardens, the knowledge that nothing could ever destroy the memory of such happiness, however fleeting it might have been.

"Oh lord," Annie said wearily, as the doorbell rang, "who can that be?"

"I'll go," Kathy said briskly, glad of an excuse to leave the table.

"If it's someone wanting accommodation, tell them we're full up," Annie called after her.

The man standing on the doorstep seemed vaguely familiar to Kathy. She sized him up briefly. "If it's a room you're wanting, you're too late."

"I'm not looking for a room," Berry said. "I'd like to speak to—Mrs. Oakleigh, if that is possible."

"Mother?" Kathy raised her eyebrows a fraction, and Berry knew that the girl he was looking at was his half-sister.

"You'd better come in, then." Kathy frowned slightly. "What name shall I say?"

"Tanquillan. Berry Tanquillan."

"Tanquillan!" Suddenly she knew that this stranger

381

who bore more than a passing resemblance to herself must be her real father's legitimate son. Fury rose up in her, almost choking her.

Filly had brooded in her room, isolated by her anger, until sheer hunger forced her to go downstairs.

Now, avid for crab salad, tinned peaches, and chocolate cake, she paused, her slippered feet planted firmly on the bottom stair leading to the passage, to listen to the conversation.

At the name of Tanquillan, her head jerked up suddenly. She shuffled towards the front door to glare at Berry. Hunger plus anger made a deadly combination. The grievances of this day, and all her past days, boiled up suddenly inside her. First a bloody German, now an even bloodier Tanquillan!

Pointing a shaking finger at Berry, she cried in a shrill, high-pitched voice, "Get away from here! As long as I have breath left in my body, I'll not let a Tanquillan cross my doorstep!"

Kathy wondered briefly if her grandmother was suffering from senility. The signs were all there: trembling limbs, knotted hands screwed into fists, an inability to control her false teeth. *"Gran,"* she said sharply.

"Don't you 'Gran' me," Filly flung at her. "I suppose you think I'm dumb and daft—an old woman ready for a nursing home! But while I have a tongue in my head, I'm going to speak my mind! You!" she screeched, confronting Berry, "I suppose you are his son, his legitimate child, the one he fathered by his wife. But one woman wasn't enough for *him!* Oh no, he wasn't satisfied until he'd fathered a brat by my daughter, and ruined her life too!"

"Mother!"

Filly turned suddenly at the sound of Charlotte's voice. Adam stood behind her. "Mother! How could you be so—*cruel!"*

"Cruel, now, am I?" Filly cried hysterically, "because I spoke my mind! Because I said what needed to be said!"

"Kathy," Charlotte said bleakly, holding out her hand.

"No, don't try to touch me, Mother," Kathy replied icily. "You were eager enough to tell me I'm a bastard. You didn't think it necessary to tell me I had a half-brother in the bargain!"

"You wouldn't listen . . ."

"Please take me away from here, Adam," Kathy said stonily. "Now! This minute!"

Stumbling past Berry, she ran headlong down the path to the car.

Now that Filly had vented her wrath, the enormity of what she had done suddenly struck her. She began to cry, great racking sobs which shook her frail body.

It was then that Laurie took charge of her grandmother, whom she led, quietly, to the tea table. "Now, sit down, Gran, and have a cup of tea," she said firmly. But Filly shook her head. Shoulders heaving, she whimpered, "I've done a terrible thing. They'll never forgive me."

"Oh yes they will," Laurie said tenderly. "Tell you what, let's go to the first house at the Capitol, shall we? It's Ginger Rogers and Fred Astaire."

"You're a good girl, Laurie." Filly's lips closed greedily on the rim of a teacup. Looking up, she asked in a fierce whisper, "Is *he* still there?" She meant Berry.

"No, he and Aunt Charlotte have gone out," Laurie reassured her, thinking that the poor man, whoever he was, must be wondering what had hit him—ringing a doorbell and upsetting a hornet's nest. This beat the London School of Dramatic Art any day of the week. Turgenev just wasn't in it.

She wondered, as she fed her grandmother a piece of chocolate cake, if the play she had started writing would be any good.

* * *

The bright summer sky had paled suddenly, and rain clouds were massed on the horizon. They stopped walking and sat down on one of the seats near the entrance to the Spa bridge. "I don't understand why you came, what you hoped to gain by it," Charlotte said, but this was tiredness speaking, interlaced with emotion, Kathy's offhandedness had shocked her. She had liked Adam, but news of the engagement, handed to her as a fait accompli, had deeply wounded her. All this culminating in the scene with Filly and the hard, closed expression on Kathy's face, the bitterness of her words as she ran from the house, had drained Charlotte emotionally. She knew why Berry had come, but her immediate joy at seeing him again had been dissipated by this sudden weariness of spirit, a deep sadness that the shining moments of Paris, the happiness they had known there, no matter how illusory, had been tarnished. She knew why he had come, but wished that he had not.

Berry rubbed his forehead bemusedly, trying to find the right words. "What you told me about my father has made no difference to the way I feel about you," he said quietly. "The past is over and done with, as far as I'm concerned."

"Is it? Do you really believe that, in view of what happened just now?"

"I would give ten years of my life for it not to have happened," he said.

Charlotte stared at the clouds darkening on the horizon. "Have you thought what it would be like for us ten years from now? I would be a comparatively old woman, you still young with your whole future ahead of you."

Berry said very softly, "If another war comes—and I believe that it will—I might have no future at all."

Annie thought that she had never lived through so traumatic a day before. But it was not over yet.

384

When the doorbell rang violently at midnight, and kept on ringing, she climbed wearily out of bed and went downstairs.

Peggy was on the doorstep, weeping, surrounded by luggage.

"Oh, Aunt Annie!"

"What on earth . . . ?" Annie tightened the cord of her dressing-gown. "Whatever's the matter?"

"I had to come. I had nowhere to go," Peggy sobbed.

"But what about—Gee?" Annie held the trembling girl in her arms.

"I've left him! I never want to set eyes on him again as long as I live!'

Chapter Thirty-One

A family meeting took place in the early hours of the morning. Annie took Peggy up to the attic where Charlotte and Laurie were sleeping, since there wasn't another room vacant. Not that anyone seemed inclined to sleep. Charlotte and Laurie were awake and in their dressing gowns, then Joe came in to see what was happening.

Peggy's story emerged in a series of convulsive sobs. "We went to Blackpool for our honeymoon," she said, "to a proper hotel, with a dance floor, and a bar." The latter had proved Gee's undoing. He had got what Peggy termed "sauced" on their wedding night, and ripped the dance dress she was wearing.

Delicacy prevented her saying exactly what else Gee had done to her in that "proper" hotel bedroom, though she might have been more forthcoming if her Uncle Joe hadn't been listening. Curiously, her reticence was far more compelling than words. Annie could have cried when Peggy said, "I thought he respected me. All we'd ever done before was dance together, and cuddle a bit in the back row of the pictures."

Tears rolled down her cheeks. "Then, after the honeymoon when we got home, I went to draw some money from our bank account. You know the money I mean, Aunt Charlotte? Well, it had gone! He'd taken every penny. When I asked him what he'd done with it, he hit me, and told me to mind my own bloody business."

The whole pathetic story came out between sobs. Annie thought that most of the money Gee had taken must have been squandered on drink, since he appeared to have come home drunk every night to knock Peggy about.

"You should have told your dad," said the indignant Laurie. "He'd have settled his hash for him!"

"No, I daren't do that. Dad might have killed him. And me mother would have started moaning and saying 'I told you so.' So I came here. But Gee's sure to come after me. Oh God, Aunt Annie, what shall I do?"

"Don't worry," Annie said stalwartly, "he won't get past your Uncle Joe and me!"

Charlotte glanced anxiously at Joe, who would certainly come off worse in a physical encounter with Peggy's bullying husband—especially if Gee had downed a few pints of beer on his way from the station. The only safe plan was to remove Peggy from harm. "How would you like to stay with me, in London?" she suggested.

An expression of pure relief swept Peggy's tearstained face. "Oh, that would be lovely." Her relief was short-lived. "But I couldn't. What would Ma say?"

Maggie's belligerent shadow seemed to invade the room. Maggie, whose uncompromisingly harsh attitudes had robbed Peggy of so many chances in life—a good education, holidays at Grey Wethers, freedom, her place in the sun, Charlotte thought. And while Kathy had never shown the slightest interest in the world of fashion, Peggy, with her innate flair and style, was born for it.

"You are a grown woman with your future to think of now," Charlotte reminded her. "If you decide to stay with me, I'll arrange for your admission to a top modelling school."

She said nothing against Maggie, nor would she ever do so, but she knew the time had come to liberate Peggy; to liberate herself also.

Peggy's eyes were shining now. "Oh, Aunt Charlotte," she said breathlessly, "I can't believe it! *Me*, a model!"

Charlotte and Annie had had little time together so far. When everyone else had drifted off to bed, they sat for a short while in the visitor's dining-room, drinking tea.

There were so many questions Annie wanted to ask: why Berry Tanquillan had turned up out of the blue; what had Laurie meant about Julian Ryder; what did Charlotte think of Adam Bergmann? In any event, she did not need to ask, nor, she thought afterward, would she have asked any of those questions. Her relationship with Charlotte was so deep, so long standing that she knew, instinctively, what was going on in her mind.

"I'm in love with Berry," Charlotte said quietly.

"Yes, I guessed that you were."

"You're not—shocked?"

"Who? Me?" Annie fiddled with a napkin ring. "I'm unshockable."

"I sent him away. Told him to forget about me."

"Did you?"

"What else could I have done?"

"You're asking me?"

"I told him I'm going to marry Julian Ryder."

"And are you—going to marry Julian Ryder, I mean?"

"No." Their eyes met. Annie smiled.

"Because it would go against the grain to marry someone you are not in love with?"

"I shall have to tell him, of course. Break it to him gently."

"Better that than a lifetime of regret."

"Yes." Charlotte sighed. "I liked Adam, by the way."

"Hmm. He's just what Kathy needs. He'll be a steadying influence in her life." Annie paused. "I'm sorry about what happened. I wish she hadn't taken things so badly."

"It was inevitable, I suppose. At least she knows the whole truth now." Charlotte closed her eyes wearily. "Do

388

you know something, Annie? I don't really care any more. I'm tired of caring."

"I know what you mean. I've often felt the same way myself." Annie laid down the napkin ring which she had buffed to a high polish with a sleeve of her dressing gown. "It's time we were going to bed. It's been quite a day, hasn't it?"

Paris, in September, was just as Charlotte imagined it would be, with leaves fluttering down from the trees in the Tuileries gardens, and a pale autumn mist shrouding the river.

Every newspaperman in Paris appeared to be packed into the foyer of the Ritz Hotel in the Champs Elysées. The cloying scent of perfume hung in the air like a cloud as a bevy of salesgirls liberally sprayed "Carla" onto the wrists of the eager crowd of women anxious to try the new fragrance.

Charlotte remembered, as cameras flashed and champagne corks popped, a recent visit to the flower fields of Grasse, where the overpowering smell of lavender had made her feel physically ill.

Excusing herself as quickly as possible from the throng of autograph hunters and publicity seekers, Charlotte left the hotel by the kitchen exit, to the delight of the chefs in their tall hats. They blew her kisses, making her laugh. She began walking, breathing in deep gulps of fresh, unperfumed air; walked and walked until her feet ached, scarcely aware of where she was going. And yet, subconsciously, she did know—to Berry's apartment in the Rue des Quatres Saisons.

"I regret, madame, Monsieur Berry no longer lives here," Mme. Hotier told her in broken English. "First he went to Florence. Now he has gone to Canada and the United States of America. A whole year he will be gone, more's the pity. A fine young man. I shall never find another lodger like that one. His apartment is empty now. Even his piano is gone." She sighed deeply, regretfully.

"And the apartment?" Charlotte asked faintly. "What do you intend doing with it?"

"Why, relet it, à toute vitesse," Mme. Hotier said reprovingly, "what else? I am a poor woman, I cannot afford that such a fine apartment should stand idle for long."

"Would you consider letting it to me?" Charlotte spoke impulsively. "I should not come here very often, but I could pay you a year's rent in advance."

"Mon Dieu!" The old woman regarded her suspiciously. "A year's rent, in advance, you say? Ah well, who am I to look a gift horse in the mouth?" She shrugged her shoulders fatalistically. "You had better take the key."

Slowly Charlotte walked up the twisting stone steps to the top floor, inserted the key in the lock, and stood, trembling, on the threshold. Then, slowly, she began to walk round the room, smoothing each item of furniture lightly with her fingers, noticing the empty space where Berry's piano had stood, hearing, in her memory, the soft strains of Debussy's "Clair de Lune."

At last she opened the French windows leading onto the roof garden. Stepping out, she leaned her hands on the railing, looking over the rooftops of Paris misted with a clinging film of rain; feeling Berry's presence strongly; almost imagining he was standing there beside her.

The sky was slightly overcast, threatening rain. The summer of 1938 had been late in starting, Kathy thought as she drove steadily towards Grey Wethers. Now autumn was almost here.

The past year had lain as unproductive as a fallow field on her heart, a year in which she had scarcely existed at all. Drained of happiness, she felt she had no real identity.

She had given the forbearing Adam a hard time of it recently, refusing to set a date for their wedding, treating him almost casually at times, hiding the hurt she had suffered beneath an assumed mantle of indifference; filled with self-loathing. "After all, I *am* a bastard," she had snapped at him in the heat of a recent quarrel, "so you can scarcely blame me for behaving like one!"

It seemed to Bergmann that her personality had metamorphosed since that eventful day in Scarborough. He had tried his best to persuade his wayward Kathy that she should at least go home for Christmas, to no avail. Nothing, he said, could be gained, or healed, without discussion and forgiveness, but she had patently disagreed with his point of view, and said so with a bitterness which made him realize how deeply she had been wounded.

"My mother might at least have told me I had a half-brother," she cried angrily. "It's all very well for you to preach forgiveness, Adam, but how would you have felt?"

He said slowly, compassionately, "It is not right that you should torment yourself like this, or condemn others without a fair trial."

"By others, I suppose you mean my mother?" she asked contemptuously.

"No, I did not simply mean your mother but your grandmother too. One cannot live, as you are doing, with so much bitterness. Sooner or later it will eat, like a cancer, into the soul. I love you too much to watch you destroy yourself."

She had rounded on him fiercely. "Well, since you appear to have appointed yourself my spiritual guide, what would you like me to do—hurry to the nearest nunnery?"

His anger had been fully aroused then. "Stop it, Kathy," he said, grasping her by the shoulders, "you are behaving like a spoiled child! Call yourself names if you want to, but until you discover the truth about your real father, until you start behaving like a reasonable adult, there can be no future for me either. I do not want a child-wife, but a flesh-and-blood woman!"

"Are you telling me that our engagement is off?" Kathy

retorted, "because, if you are, you'd better take your ring back."

And then, because she loved Adam, could not really bear the thought of losing him, she had borrowed his car to drive down to Wiltshire to talk to her Aunt Bridie. She remembered as she switched on the windshield wipers, that she had simply got up and walked out of the room when Bridie had tried to discuss her real father—not poor Will Oakleigh, whose grave she had tended so assiduously, but Rowan Tanquillan, who had ruined her happiness and peace of mind.

Now, because she dreaded the thought of losing Adam, Kathy was prepared at least to listen to an account, albeit biased, of her mother's sickening underhanded love affair.

It surprised Kathy somewhat when her Aunt Bridie refused, point blank, to discuss the subject.

"No," Bridie said, after dinner, "I tried once before, and you wouldn't listen to me. The best thing you can do is ask Emily Beresford, whose daughter was married to your father. You could scarcely accuse her of lying, could you?"

"No, I suppose not."

And so Kathy went to see Emily.

Cornwall. She had never been to Cornwall before, or had she? Emily Beresford said that she had, so it must be true. If only she could remember. But how old had she been at the time? Three? How could a child of that age possibly retain memories of a past life shrouded by the mist of time?

A cottage called Stella Maris, Emily said, with steps leading down to the beach. Of course the previous occupant, a Mrs. Tregaran, was dead now, and so was her brother, old Thomas Rivers, who had spent most of his life in service with Kitty Tanquillan.

Emily had been kindness itself, explaining things quietly to Kathy, who knew that this woman, above all people, had no ax to grind. "I watched your father grow up," she had said. "He married my daughter for reasons that I shall not divulge, but it was always Charlotte he loved."

Kathy drove to the lane end and parked the car there, realizing that the lane was far too narrow to drive down. A queer lane, with deep ditches and towering hedges. When she came to the cottage she lingered for a minute, thinking there might be something about it to remind her of the time she had lived there, but there was nothing.

She walked on, down the crooked steps to the beach, wondering if she was trespassing. Puckering her forehead into a frown of concentration, she looked at the sloping breakwater with its covering of slimy green moss—and something stirred deep within her, an unaccountable feeling of danger, of sadness and loss underlaid with terror. She had not asked Emily how her father had died, and Emily had merely told her that Rowan came back from the war a dying man. And yet, here on this tiny slice of curving sand with the sea running in on the shore, Kathy sensed some half-remembered tragedy which had taken place there a long time ago; she seemed to hear a woman's voice shrill with anguish.

Retracing her steps, she walked back along the lane to the car, and saw across the fields the chimneys of a gray farmhouse near the cliff edge. Thrusting her hands deep in the pockets of her raincoat, she began walking along the rough path beyond the farm gate, thinking to call at the farm to buy a glass of milk.

Milk! A boy called Johnny Cilgerran used to bring milk to the cottage. And there was a little girl she used to play with who had a doll.

Skirting the field, she noticed a path—a tucked-away path half hidden by overhanging trees—and a strange feeling of excitement came over her. Someone, a tall man, had let Dog off his lead, and he had run away, wagging his tail, nosing after rabbits.

Yes, that was it. A tall man whose hand had drawn her back, a man for whom she had a secret, special name, only she could not for the life of her remember what it was. But perhaps this was all in her imagination or part of a childhood dream, and yet she could not resist the temptation to push past the trees. How narrow and dark it was, like a tunnel—but it opens out further on, she thought, where the lake is. Or perhaps it wasn't a lake at all, just a pond which seemed the size of a lake to a little girl. But it could not have been all that small because there had been swans building a nest there.

Trembling with excitement, she hurried on. If there were no lake, she would know that it had been just a dream. Pushing through the final barrier of branches, she stood stock still, and clenched her hands to her face. And then she knew that it had not been a dream after all. The lake was still there.

She walked slowly, in the rain, along the twisting paths of the Highgate cemetery where Emily told her her father was buried.

Turning up the collar of her coat, feeling the rain running like tears down her cheeks, she came across Rowan's grave so suddenly that the shock of seeing it caused her to tremble and feel sick.

Bending down, she read more closely the inscription on the stone cross, and wished that she had brought some flowers to place on the mound of grass-covered earth. And beneath that mound of earth lay her real father, the man she had rejected, who had given his life to save a small black dog. She knew that now, because she had telephoned Emily.

Suddenly her heart flowed out to him. "Dadda," she whispered.

She rang Adam later that day. In a voice breathless with excitement, she asked him if they could possibly be married next week, or the week after.

"I'll consult my diary," Adam said quietly.

"I wouldn't blame you if you didn't want to marry me after all," she said more seriously. "Oh darling, I've been wrong about so many things."

She rang next her mother's Bond Street salon, and asked to speak to Madam Carlotta.

"I'm afraid Madam is not here," the receptionist said.

"Oh? Then where is she?"

"She's in Paris at the moment."

"I see. In that case, I had better ring her there. Have you her number? This is her daughter, by the way."

"Oh, I'm very sorry, Miss Oakleigh, but Madam's apartment is not on the telephone. She left word that urgent messages should be sent to her care of a certain address. Shall I give you that address?"

"Yes, I think you'd better. This is rather urgent."

How strange, Kathy thought, when she had written down the address, that her mother had never mentioned an apartment in Paris. She felt slightly piqued until she remembered that there was a great deal about Charlotte she did not know, because she had never taken the trouble to find out. But all that was about to change now.

Above all things, she wanted her mother to come to her wedding, to make up for their past misunderstandings.

She realized, as she sat down, later, to write to Charlotte, how much she loved her mother.

Chapter Thirty-Two

Filly declared, adamantly, that she had no intention of going to Kathy's wedding. She angled her shoulders like wire coathangers as she spoke, her belligerent attitude induced by the fact that she had not set eyes on her granddaughter, or Charlotte, since that mix-up over a year ago, and had managed to persuade herself that she had done nothing to merit such wanton neglect.

At first she had been subdued and tearful when the affair was over, thinking that she had gone too far. Now she had succeeded in convincing herself that she had only told the truth and shamed the devil, as might be permitted a woman of her age and experience. Charlotte had done her an injury in not saying good-bye to her the day she left for London, taking Peggy with her, condoning the girl's silliness in running away from her husband when they had not been married for more than two minutes put together.

As for Kathy and that—*German!* He had been the cause of the upset in the first place, and Kathy deserved to be taken down a peg or two. No, she would not go to the wedding, and that was final.

"I really think you should go," Annie said anxiously at breakfast, after the wedding invitation had been received.

"Yes, well you would, wouldn't you?" Filly snapped contemptuously. "You're as soft as butter, Annie Grayler, and always will be!"

Joe, sitting quietly, spreading a slice of toast with marmalade, looked up suddenly. "I'd like to r-remind you, Mother," he said in that slow, careful way of his, "that you are speaking of my w-wife."

Filly stared at him, nonplussed. Joe, who seldom said anything at all, had laid down his knife and was looking at her with an expression approaching dislike. "Eh?" she mumbled in astonishment. "Oh, get on with your breakfast!"

But Joe had no intention of getting on with his breakfast. "It's all right, Annie," he said, brushing away his wife's restraining hand, "there are things that need to be said, and I—I intend saying them. I've kept quiet too long."

Joe faced his mother squarely. "A long time ago, when Frank and I were about to sail for France, I had a letter from Charlotte, saying she'd married Will Oakleigh." He paused. "I couldn't understand why she had done that, until Annie told me about her affair with Tanquillan. *You* never said a word. You wouldn't even talk about Charlotte. When I found out the truth, I remember saying to Annie that I thought you mere being c-cruel. It seemed to me a very cruel thing to turn away from your own flesh and blood, especially at a time when Charlotte needed l-love and understanding. But Annie stood up for you. She said it wasn't altogether your fault, that you had been hurt. That, without love, there could be no hurt, no pain or disappointment."

He uttered a brief laugh. "My 'soft as butter' wife was prepared to g-give you the benefit of the doubt, and she has gone on doing so. How many years is it since you came to live with us? Well, that doesn't matter. What matters is that every day we have had to put up with your damned intolerance and interference!"

"Joe!" Filly's mouth sagged open. "I am your *mother!*"

"You are also Charlotte's mother," Joe said levelly, "but no one would think so, the way you've treated her—

and K-Kathy. What crime did Charlotte commit that you could not forgive her? No, sit down, Mother. I-I haven't finished yet. As for Kathy, you've never really forgiven her either, have you, for being Tanquillan's daughter? That is why you felt impelled to blurt out the truth to her—believing in your right to say the first thing that entered your head—not giving a damn for other people's feelings! Well, I'm sick and tired of your hidebound, self-righteous attitudes. But you went too far when you insulted Annie, who has put up with you, all these years, without one word of complaint."

He got up from the table. "If it hadn't been for Annie, I'd have said all this a long time ago. From now on, Mother, if you wish to remain under this roof, you'll treat her with more respect. That's all I have to say."

Charlotte had often blessed the day she leased Berry's apartment from Mme. Hotier. The place had become her spiritual sanctuary, where she could live, not as a famous fashion designer, but an ordinary woman, shopping for bread and vegetables in the open-air markets; cooking for herself, eating her supper at a table under the stars.

Sometimes she would wake early and stand on the balcony, hands resting on the railings, to look out at the rooftops of Paris. On fine mornings, the city, widespread and beautiful, seemed to glisten like silver, and she would listen to the sound of churchbells ringing the angelus. Or, if it happened to be raining, the rooftops would gleam the color of wet mussel-shells, and the air would seem even fresher, the sound of the bells much sharper.

Yet often she was conscious of a deep loneliness, and wondered what she was doing here in Berry's apartment, attempting to relive her springtime of the heart without him.

One day, standing on the balcony, gazing over the city which seemed to radiate so much unquenchable gaiety and charm, she wondered why Kathy had answered none of her letters, and experienced a sudden yearning to be home in England.

She longed to see Berry again, but to what end, what purpose? Nothing had altered; nothing changed. Magic could not be conjured up like a dove from a magician's hat. It was time to lock away the past and face reality.

She motored leisurely across northern France to Calais. Usually she made the journey by train to save time. Now, she chose to squander the last few precious hours of her holiday, haunted by the feeling that she might not see the fields of France again for a very long time.

She broke her journey at Amiens, choosing to stay overnight in a small pension with a cobbled courtyard hung with late-flowering bougainvillea.

The dining room, with its rich scents of French cooking, was practically deserted when she went down to dinner. A breath of autumn, the lingering scent of a dying bonfire drifted in through the open door; the panelled walls were hung with indifferent paintings, etchings, old playbills, prints. Above Charlotte's table hung a relief map of the area.

Glancing up at it, the word "Somme" caught her eye. Suddenly Charlotte remembered the awful significance of that name, the scene of the bloodiest, most wasteful battles of the war. And then she leaned forward to study the map, and her eyes lingered over other place-names, Cambrai, Lille, Armentières, Albert, Arras. They rose up before her then, rank upon rank, the eager, smiling faces of the young and brave who had laid down their lives in a fruitless cause. They had been cut down, like wheat, before their rightful time of harvesting; buried far from home; laid to rest in the deep rich earth of a foreign land:

There, awaiting patiently,
Some never-granted amnesty

One saw them everywhere, in this region of France,
those cemeteries filled with the white stones of the fallen
British soldiers of that Götterdämmerung: that terrible
twilight of the gods which robbed a generation of its fathers, sons, and brothers.

Charlotte had sensed keenly, in Paris, the tension of the
present crisis: its effect on the women in particular. One felt
that tension as a tangible thing; could almost scent fear; saw
fear in the eyes of the old who had lived through the last
Armageddon and seen their homes destroyed, their land
usurped, their towns and cities reduced to ruins. And now,
unless a miracle happened, the heartbreak, the human misery and suffering was about to begin all over again.

When the waitress, a young girl Charlotte had seen earlier in the courtyard, brought the soup, she shook her
head. She was no longer hungry. Murmuring an apology,
she hurried upstairs to her room.

Kathy felt nervously excited as she and Adam waited, at
Manchester station, for the guests to arrive.

" 'The wedding guest he beat his breast, for he heard
the loud bassoon,' " she laughed, hugging Adam's arm.
Then, frowning, she said, "Strange I haven't heard from
Mother, but I expect that she and Peggy will arrive together. You won't feel stranded, will you darling, when
I'm surrounded by my loving family? I only wish yours
could have been here, too."

First to arrive were Annie, Joe, Laurie, and Grandma
Grayler. Remembering Adam's appeasement policy,
Kathy had resolved to greet Filly as if nothing untoward
had happened. It had taken some doing, bringing herself
to forgive and forget. She was somewhat taken aback when
Filly showed little inclination to be forgiven, as if *she* were

the injured party, which she felt herself to be, having been told to behave herself, by Joe of all people. Ah well, thought Mrs. Grayler, allowing herself to be pecked on the cheek by her granddaughter—one may lead a horse to water, twenty cannot make it drink, and nothing on earth would induce her to shake hands with that—*German*.

Annie stared anxiously at her mother-in-law's set face as they all trooped into the refreshment buffet to await the arrival of the London train which would bring the rest of the contingent; Harry, Bridie, and Peggy. Filly had that look about her Annie knew so well, that 'you wait and see' look. And then the train was signalled. Here was Harry to make a fuss of her. But Charlotte had not come, and Peggy had no idea where she was. "Ha!" muttered Filly, catching the tail end of the conversation, her shoulders making that curious hitching motion to accentuate her sagacity. "That's typical of Charlotte. Never there when you need her!"

Annie pressed Kathy's hand as they got into the taxi which would take them to the Carlton Hotel where Kathy had also booked a room overnight. "Charlotte can't have got your letter," she said, "or she would have come. Wild horses wouldn't have kept her away."

"I know." Kathy smiled to cover her disappointment.

Later, when Annie went to her room to say goodnight, Kathy was in her dressing-gown, hanging her wedding dress in the wardrobe. "Well, what do you think of it?" she asked.

"It's lovely, darling." Annie turned the blond silk dress on its hanger to admire the detail.

"Not a Carlotta model. I bought it off the rack at Sydenhams," Kathy said with a touch of bitterness. She paused. "Aunt Annie, did you know Mother had some kind of—pied á terre—in Paris?"

"Yes. What's on your mind?"

Kathy shrugged. "I just wondered if there's some man

or other she doesn't want us to know about. It seems so odd—no telephone . . ."

Annie said carefully, "Would you mind very much if there were someone?"

"It's true, then?"

"I know there's someone she cares for. But don't run away with the idea she's having an affair."

"You know who he is, don't you? Why won't you tell me?"

"It might shock you to know."

"I doubt it," Kathy said. "If Mother has found someone she cares for, what's stopping her?"

"You, mainly," Annie said forthrightly, "and that's all I'm going to say on the subject."

"I don't think Mother need worry about me any more," Kathy said seriously. "Adam and I are going to be happy together, and what Mother chooses to do with her own life is her own business. I want her to be happy, too." Her lips trembled slightly. "By the way, what's wrong with Gran? Does she feel slighted because I didn't ask Aunt Maggie to my wedding? If so, I'm sorry, but I really couldn't have borne it, and neither could Peggy."

"I don't know," Annie confessed. "I just think it must be very difficult for old people, especially at a time like this. Weddings can be very emotional—bring back so many memories. Perhaps, like children, they find the world a bewildering place to live in."

"Please, can't you go any faster?" Charlotte urged the taxi driver.

"What, in this traffic?" the man grumbled. "In any case, it isn't far now. Just round the next corner." He changed gear then braked abruptly. "Here we are."

Charlotte glanced up at the red brick building with its preponderance of cream-colored ornamentations, got out of the taxi, paid the man, added a generous tip, and

402

walked into the vestibule where a receptionist was seated in a glass-fronted office, knitting a sock.

"Please, could you direct me to the wedding room?" Charlotte asked urgently.

"Round the corner, first door on the left. Oh, *damnation!*" She had dropped a stitch.

This was no kind of place to get married in, Filly thought, glancing around the wedding room. There was no—*atmosphere*. She liked proper weddings in proper churches, with candles and music and a parson to say the important words. She sniffed. Might as well be sitting in the cheaper seats at the Odeon cinema. She almost wished she was.

Then a memory assailed her of her own wedding to Albert Grayler. How many years ago was that? She counted up on her fingers. Forty-six. No, it couldn't be. She remembered that day as clearly as if it were yesterday: the joy she had experienced when the organist began playing the wedding march, and she saw Albert standing there waiting for her, the light from the stained-glass windows shining on his penny-gold hair. *Albert!*

If only she had her time to come all over again, but there was so little time left to her now. The best years of her life had been frittered away living in other people's houses, not having a place, a soul to call her own. She belched slightly with nervousness, staring through tear-blurred eyes at the artificial flowers on the registrar's desk, longing for the old days, wishing Charlotte were here. Why wasn't she here? After all, this was her daughter's wedding day.

Well, perhaps it was all her fault, and Maggie's, the way they'd carried on about Charlotte's affair with that—Tanquillan. Funny, it didn't seem all that important anymore, just a storm in a teacup, really.

Filly clicked her false teeth in frustration. A fine kettle

403

of fish if a mother couldn't even be bothered to come to her daughter's wedding! She'd have something to say about that afterward, blessed if she wouldn't. Charlotte ought to have come.

The registrar looked up suddenly from the book he was holding.

Charlotte thought after the ceremony was over, when they all walked out together like the folk of Shields, that she would never forget Kathy's smile as she had glanced over her shoulder, or the way Filly had edged along to make room for her, saying in a fierce whisper, "About time, too, our Charlotte." But Filly was Filly, and could not change in a minute.

As Laurie and Peggy showered the bridal couple with confetti, a newspaper boy on the corner began shouting his wares in a hoarse voice.

Suddenly, Adam gripped his wife's elbow. "Look, darling," he said.

The placard was propped againt a lamp-post:

TENSION EASES
CHAMBERLAIN TO MEET HITLER

Chapter Thirty-Three

Charlotte discovered, in the spring of 1939, that Berry had completed his tour of the States and Canada and gone from there to Australia.

This information came her way by chance, when she bumped into M. Robillard at an exhibition of Gauguin paintings in the Louvre.

Henri Robillard remembered well the striking woman who had attended Berry's debut at l'Académie Municipale, reintroduced himself, and invited her to have coffee with him.

"Ah, madame," he said, with a widespread gesture of his expressive hands, "Monsieur Berry has a great talent for music, apart from technical brilliance. Not that technique is to be scoffed at, you understand, but that in itself is of little value without the heart, the feeling, the— *compassion.*" The maestro sighed. "I have often marvelled at such sensibility in one so young; such isolation of spirit. But perhaps that sounds too fanciful. I wonder if you understand my meaning, madame? I think that music is, for him, a means of escape, a sublimation . . ."

"Do you think he will ever return to Paris?"

"If that is possible. If the gods permit." M. Robillard's eyes reflected his concern for the future of his country if war came. "These are difficult, worrying times, Madame Oakleigh. Who can say for certain what will happen? Berry is an Englishman, and musicians of his stature hold, in my experience, a great feeling for their own soil, their own nationality. Take Chopin, for example . . ."

Charlotte left Paris, the apartment, in that blossoming springtime of 1939, with a heavy feeling of finality, as if she might never see again the lilacs in bloom in the Tuileries gardens, or the view from her balcony. She remembered, as she strapped her cases and waited for the taxi that would take her to the Gare du Nord, that fateful springtime of 1914, and Jenny's prophetic words: "In years to come, we will remember this Maytime with regret for a way of life that will never come again."

Change was already in the air: a kind of tension and fear, a sense of fatality masked by a desperate, almost frenetic gaiety and patriotism—a bright determination, by the people of Paris, to live life to the full for as long as it lasted.

She went with Howard and Virginia to New York in July, to discuss plans for enlarging the downtown factory and setting up a chain of boutiques in every major city all across America. "Carla" had become the nation's top-selling perfume. Now Howard wanted to add Carla soap, body lotion, bath-oil, and dusting powder to the line.

Success was like a runaway train at times, Charlotte thought. Once it got started, there was no stopping it.

London, in August, was hot and sultry: the trees motionless, the grass in the parks patched brown here and there from lack of rain; the last of the summer flowers, the crimson dahlias, salvias, and the multi-colored snapdragons flaring bravely against the shrivelled grass. The gray stone buildings in Whitehall were the scene of constant comings and goings as the crisis deepened over Hitler's uncompromising attitude regarding the Polish Corridor.

Driving home from Bond street, she asked Allanson to take her by Kensington Gardens, wanting to catch a breath of fresh air after a long, stultifying day at her drawing board planning the winter collection, mulling over the tweed swatches Howard had brought into the office with him, choosing the colors she wanted. She thought, as the car bowled smoothly along Prince Consort Road, that she had always liked this part of London for its links with Albert and Victoria; what bitter disappointment Prince Albert must have suffered to have been so underrated, even disliked, in the country of his adoption. And yet he had reigned supreme in the heart of one woman. She saluted him silently as the car passed the Albert Memorial, then turned her glance towards the gray bulk of the Albert Hall.

Suddenly, "Stop the car!" she cried. "Anywhere here will do! I want to get out for a minute!"

She knew she had not been mistaken, but she had not been able to take in the details at a glance. With fast-beating heart she hurried along the pavement, filled with a strange, singing joy, like music. *Music!* Slowing her pace, standing stock still, she looked up at the placard: "Beresford Tanquillan. Renowned International Pianist. 24 August. One Performance Only."

Hands trembling with excitement, Charlotte bought a ticket for that performance.

The years had changed him, she thought. He looked older, far more serious than she remembered, and yet his new air of maturity became him, adding a new dimension to his handsomeness. But how lonely, how vulnerable he seemed to her as he walked onto the platform, every inch the distinguished musician: gravely immaculate in his black evening clothes, a white carnation in his buttonhole;

hair swept back from his forehead, as if he had deliberately taken a wet comb to subdue the dark curls which she remembered falling onto his forehead in Paris; skin warmly tanned by his months under the Australian sun. He flexed his long sensitive fingers as he walked slowly toward the open Bechstein grand piano.

Leaning forward in her seat, Charlotte watched his every movement; heard every note as someone in a dream of delight; glorying in the perfection of his playing, the sheer artistry of his technique, remembering that day in the Louvre. What M. Robillard had said was true: Berry played compassionately, and his compassion transmitted itself to the audience. One might have heard a pin drop as the slow, crystal clear notes of Beethoven's Moonlight Sonata scattered, like a handful of brilliant jewels, into the vast, silent hall.

Then came Peter Warlock's "Capriole Suite," and Berry's lips curved into a smile as he played "Pieds en l'air"—the tune of an old French dancing master.

During the interval Charlotte scribbled a note which she handed to an usher. She had not meant to contact Berry. Now she knew she must see him again. God alone knew where he might be tomorrow. Bound for the other side of the world, most probably.

She found herself in a crowd of eager well-wishers awaiting admission to Berry's dressing room after the concert. Elderly women were fanning themselves with their programmes. There were men in evening dress, slender girls and their escorts—the "bright young things"—dressed for dining and dancing, chattering together in high-pitched voices, making her head spin.

"They say he always ends his concerts with 'Clair de Lune,'" one of the girls remarked, staring into her compact mirror. "I wonder why? I really must ask him . . ."

"He won't tell you, darling," drawled another. "He's

the strong silent type, you know, like Gary Cooper." She sighed deeply. "I could have *melted* when he walked onto the platform. I wonder if he's married!"

Charlotte hung back; turned away. She had not dreamt it would all be like this. All these people. Poor Berry, trapped in his dressing room. She hoped he would understand that she could not have borne to be among them, saying in a bright unnatural voice how much she had enjoyed the concert.

She was halfway down the long dark corridor leading to the stage entrance when she heard the sound of hurrying footsteps, his voice calling her name: "Charlotte! *Charlotte!* Wait!"

Turning, she saw him coming towards her, smiling, his face transfigured with love: the Berry she knew and remembered so well.

"Christ, Charlotte," he said, "I thought you'd gone. I thought I'd lost you!"

"What about all those people?" she asked.

"To hell with—people! Let's get out of here, the sooner the better!" Once outside, they walked to the main road. Berry hailed a taxi. "The Embankment," he told the driver.

Dusk had settled coolly on the river. The dolphined lamps had sprung into bloom. The Thames flowed silently between its banks, light trapped in its secret depths, swimming down, splintering and dissolving in the undertow.

They walked for a little while, not speaking, then Berry drew her to the parapet and they rested their arms on the cool stone, staring down into the light-starred water.

"What are we going to do, Charlotte?" he asked, despairingly.

"You mean now? Tonight?"

He smiled, his eyes fixed on the river. "Not just tonight, but for the rest of our lives."

"I don't know. I don't honestly know."

"I want us to be together always," he said.

"Are—are you going away again soon?" she asked bleakly

"Yes."

She glanced up at him, thinking that she had never loved him as much as she did at this minute. "Another—concert tour?"

"No," he said quietly, "I'm going to join up. The Air Force. I—I have my pilot's license. When I was in Canada, my friends there had a private airfield. Their passion was flying. They infected me . . ."

"But you *can't!* You *mustn't!* What about your music? Your career? Giving up all you've worked so hard to achieve?"

"I'm an Englishman," he said simply, making no attempt to hold or touch her not wanting to cloud her judgment in any way. He paused. "Charlotte, I want you to marry me."

But the old shibboleths were still far too strong. "No," she said hoarsely, "I—*can't* . . ."

"Because of my father?"

"No. Because of myself. Because I'm—too old!" She felt drained, suddenly, of energy, bereft of happiness. Turning away from him she said, "Please, I must go now. I'm so sorry. What else can I possibly say?" Stumbling forward, she hailed a taxi.

He seized her hands then. "Just one thing, before you go," Berry said urgently, "do you love me?"

It would have been so easy, much simpler to tell a lie. But Berry did not deserve to be lied to. Looking up into his strong, compassionate face, she traced every detail of his features with her eyes, wanting to remember forever the dark eyes beneath finely shaped brows, the slight hollows beneath his cheekbones; the firm jaw, straight nose, the way his brushed-back hair had suddenly begun to curl again onto his forehead; but far more than that, the joy

410

of loving which pierced her heart when ever she looked at him.

"Yes, Berry," she said, "I do love you, more than you will ever know. Far too much to cause you a moment's unnecessary pain or distress."

And then she was gone. Sitting in the back seat of the taxi, eyes blinded with tears she thought that the wheel had turned full circle. First the father, now the son, caught up in the terrible machinery of war. She had lived through all this before, during those days of crisis in the August of 1914: the feeling of time running out, of being hopelessly in love. And now the whole thing was about to happen again; the appalling waste of human life; the doubt and uncertainty; the fruitless longing and regret. She was just as powerless now as she had been then. "The Moving Finger writes . . ."

Annie wrote to her, on 30 August, to say that tomorrow 18,000 refugee children from Hull would arrive at Scarborough's Londesborough Road station. She and Joe had talked it over and decided to take in at least six of them.

"Poor little mites," she wrote in the letter, "I feel so sorry for them being taken away from their mothers. And just think how their mothers must be feeling."

But the refugees from Hull were a mere drop in the ocean compared to the three million other children being evacuated from the congested areas to places of safety. The London Underground was chock-a-block with them: little scraps of humanity wearing labels, carrying their gasmasks in cardboard boxes.

Charlotte read in the *Times:* "Compared with this great evacuation, the flight of the Israelites from Egypt pales to insignificance."

Paling to an even greater insignificance were her plans for the winter collection. Not that Charlotte cared tup-

411

pence about that. Ringing Harry at Grey Wethers, she asked him to make arrangements to house as many refugees as possible; to offer the house itself as a hospital or convalescent home. If—*when* war came, she would close the Bond Street salon; go to Grey Wethers to help look after the refugee children.

And in the midst of all this turmoil, where was Berry? Would she ever see him again? And if she did, what would she say to him?

Standing near the window, looking out at the square with its gleaming necklace of lights and the trees swaying softly in the cool autumnal air, she remembered the bombardment of Scarborough. She had run on that December morning across the Valley bridge to the station, braving flying shell splinters and great shards of glowing hot metal, the suffocating smell of cordite blowing in on the wind, to be with Rowan before his battalion sailed for France. She had been urged on by a desperate need to see him for what might have been the last time, uncaring of right or wrong, knowing that she risked censure, misunderstanding, her mother's condemnation, because she loved him.

If she had turned her back on love then, not risked the bombardment and the long, cold, nightmare journey to London, Kathy would not have been conceived and her whole life would have been different: less harsh, less complex, perhaps. But if she had not followed her heart that day, she would never have known the full glory of love, never have come to fruition as a woman.

The war had made all the difference: the knowledge that only today mattered, that tomorrow might never come. And how could she have lived the rest of her life with the regret that she had not dared everything for so great a love as theirs? Hers and Rowan's.

And now it was happening all over again, and the risks involved were every bit as great. If Berry went away, if he were swallowed up and lost in this new war that was coming, how could she bear the thought that she had sent him away not knowing how much she loved him?

Filly would never understand. Perhaps Kathy would not understand either, but Annie and Joe would, because theirs was the kind of love which exacted no price, expected no payment, made no demands.

Standing quietly near the window, watching the branches of the trees catching, holding momentarily, then relinquishing the lights of the square, Charlotte knew that there was something in the air tonight, a feeling of destiny, of finale.

Soon all those lights would be extinguished, the world would be plunged into darkness again. Men would move about the face of the earth blindly once more, singing their brave songs, reaching out for some remote star to guide them, clinging fast to the memory of love. And the women at home would wait, as she was waiting now, and bear children, and light torches of hope and love against the darkness.

The wireless was playing softly. Hutch was singing "These Foolish Things."

The smile of Garbo and the scent of roses . . .

The song conjured up poignant memories of Paris on a wet afternoon, a crowded cinema, and roses from a flowervendor's basket; Berry smiling down at her as he handed her the blooms.

What if she had lost him? What if he did not come to her?

And still the ghost of you clings . . .

Leaning her head against the glass, she looked at the silent square. Waiting.

These foolish things remind me of you. . . .

Blossoms drifted down from the trees. "You must feel half frozen standing out there without a coat." "Yes, but it was worth it, just to look at the stars." "I loved you from the first moment I saw you, and I've gone on loving you." "What are we going to do, Charlotte? Not just tonight but for the rest of our lives?"

Oh, Berry.

Suddenly she noticed the tall figure of a man walking slowly, head bent, beneath the trees. Someone deep in thought. The lamplight caught the gleam of his hair, the curve of his cheekbones. He stopped walking and stood still. She could sense his hesitation, this man uncertain of his future, reluctant to cross the road to her house, afraid of what her final answer might be.

Turning swiftly, she hurried from the room and ran downstairs, flung open the door, and stood there beneath the porch, silhouetted against the light, hands outstretched.

She called his name softly, opening her arms wide to embrace him, feeling the sudden warmth of his body against hers, the tight clasp of his arms about her, hearing his voice, hoarse with emotion.

"Oh Charlotte, I had to come, I had to!"

"I've been waiting for you," she said tenderly.

Together they walked into the house, and closed the door behind them.